Also by Alice James

1. *Grave Secrets*
2. *Grave Danger*

Grave SUSPICIONS

Published 2023 by Solaris
an imprint of Rebellion Publishing Ltd,
Riverside House, Osney Mead,
Oxford, OX2 0ES, UK

www.solarisbooks.com

ISBN: 978-1-78618-843-4

10 9 8 7 6 5 4 3 2 1

A CIP catalogue record for this book is available from the
British Library.

Designed & typeset by Rebellion Publishing
Cover and internal artwork by Gemma Sheldrake

Printed in Denmark

THE
LAVINGTON WINDSOR
MYSTERIES

Grave
SUSPICIONS

An adventure with zombies. And vampires.
And passion. And snogging.

Alice James

SOLARIS

To my beloved Mitzi and my precious Eileen.
You are always with me.

Previously in

~ THE ~
LAVINGTON WINDSOR
~ MYSTERIES ~

"I am sure my life would be a lot longer if it contained fewer members of the undead community but maybe, just maybe, it would also be less interesting. I mean, vampires and zombies tend to be great at ripping people apart and devouring them, which isn't exactly ideal, but they are rarely boring... Really, what's a girl meant to do?"

SINCE VAMPIRES CAME out of their coffins just a few short years ago, nothing in our world has been quite the same...

Lavington Windsor is a Staffordshire estate agent by day, but at night she raises the dead. She often finds herself called to the local morgue by her brother William, a police detective, so that she can interrogate recent murder victims about their deaths. She does the hard work and... he takes the credit.

Siblings. Seriously, who'd have one?

In Book One, *Grave Secrets*, she meets the charming vampire Oscar Guillaume, who hires her to find him a luxurious undead-friendly dwelling. The two fall in love and before long are making plans for happily ever after, even though their relationship is complicated because vampires have no interest in monogamy and Oscar already has a boyfriend. The adorable young doctor Peter has followed him to England from their Assemblage in Germany, but he is miserable and misses his home. Much less agreeable is Oscar's boss, the local vampire leader, Benedict Akil, whom she finds both terrifying and intriguing.

Oscar is pursuing a rogue vampire clan, the Gambarinis, who bring death and mayhem to the county, including killing Amelia Scott Martin, a gentle old lady who Toni helped to look after.

In Book Two, *Grave Danger*, Toni discovers that—rather than embodying love's young dream—Oscar is a psychopathic jerk who has a habit of accidentally killing his love interests by drinking too much of their blood. He nearly kills Toni, too, when she won't let him drink hers. She is only saved by Benedict, who, it turns out, is a powerful healer. Oscar is sent away indefinitely, leaving Toni alone to nurse her broken heart.

She distracts herself by attempting to solve a local murder case. A girl from Toni's old school has been strangled in the dead of night. Was it the creepy janitor Mikey, or the enigmatic teenager Paul who hangs out at the school after hours?

Just days later, Paul saves Toni's life when she is attacked by a member of a rival vampire Assemblage. It turns out that his homelife is awful so, in an impulsive moment, she offers him a place to stay. He also helps out a friend of hers, Mr Suki, who runs an appliance store in Stafford. Mr Suki is constantly trying to set Toni up with his son, the town's most eligible widower and handsome self-made millionaire Jay Singh.

Despite the eye-candy, Toni knows deep in her heart that her true love is not scrumptious Jay, dirtbag Oscar, or even arrogant Benedict, but the sweet and kind Peter. She discovers that he is going back to Germany, and they meet to say goodbye. However, instead of shaking hands and promising to stay in touch, they spend a wild and passionate night together. He won't change his mind, though, and departs back to his home in Germany the next day, leaving Toni with yet another broken heart and a sense of déjà vu.

Determined now to clear Paul's name, she lures the real culprit, the janitor Mikey Spectre, into revealing himself. Mikey is then throttled by an undead nun when he attacks Toni, and she raises him from the dead to write a suicide note to fake his own death. Benedict walks in at this point, and says she has more powers than she realises: if she can make the dead speak and remember their past, she must also be a witch.

And just when Toni thought her past couldn't hold any more secrets...

Chapter One

THE BUZZING OF my phone disturbed me from my awkward, sleepless rest. I scrabbled at it, taking the call before the sound of the ringtone could wake the man slumbering next to me. I'd realised earlier in the evening that our relationship was over, so the last thing I wanted was for him to open his eyes and opt for another round of eiderdown action.

I grabbed a crumpled pile of clothes off the floor, crept to the en suite bathroom and closed the door quietly before I put on the light. The call was from my brother, and when he rang in the middle of the night, it wasn't going to be a conversation that I wanted overheard.

"Hey, bro," I whispered. "Don't tell me—there's a really happening party on down at the morgue and I should put on a dress and join you there with all the cool cadavers?"

He laughed.

"Spot on, sis, but don't worry about bringing a bottle," he said. "The snack machine has as much warm lemonade as you want. Why are you whispering?"

I sighed.

"It's complicated," I said. "I'll tell you later. Actually, I'll tell you now because I don't have my car with me. I'm at Jay's—can you come and get me? Otherwise, I'm stuck here until morning unless I start hitchhiking."

There was a pause.

"Please don't tell me you two are splitting up," he said. "You only just introduced me to him and he's a really great guy."

"Wills, I can't talk about this now. Please come and get me and I'll play raise the dead body with you at the slabs."

I rattled off the address and ended the call before he could argue. Then I dressed as quietly as I could in the teensy cocktail dress and strappy heels I'd been wearing earlier. It was a swelteringly hot July night, and I hadn't even bothered with a jacket when I'd left my house.

I'd held housewarmings in smaller rooms than Jay's bathroom. Like every inch of his house, it had been decorated by a professional, which meant stark, minimal fittings, shades of magnolia, ecru, champagne and taupe, and far too many mirrors to suit a girl who'd just dragged herself out of the bed post-shag and needed to make a swift exit. Extensive titivation wasn't on the agenda. Basic hygiene was going to have to do.

I settled for cleaning my teeth and stuffing my hair into the collar of my marabou shrug. I wasn't poised to win any modelling contracts, but I wouldn't be mistaken for a vagrant and offered change. It was the middle ground I usually pitched for.

I crept through the bedroom, planning to sneak out without a word to Jay, but my conscience stopped me. I sat down by him and leant over to kiss his forehead. He had springy dark hair that I swept back before pressing my lips to his warm brow.

"Toni?" he murmured, still half asleep. "Alright?"

"Yes, it's OK, sweetie," I whispered. "Listen, I have to go. My brother's lost his keys and I have a set."

It was only a little lie, but I didn't like it. Lies have a way of coming back to haunt you, and I had enough things haunting me already. Still, 'I'm a necromancer and I have to raise the dead so that the living don't go unpunished' was an uneasy truth... I just crossed my fingers and told myself it was for the best.

Jay rubbed his face and sat up. He had a tousled, rumpled and rather adorable look to him. He was a good-looking man, and he looked just fine on my arm. Actually, he was a very good-looking man, and he looked just fine in my bed. If only... I shook my head briskly. If wishes were horses, we'd need a lot more stables. They might be the one thing Jay's house was lacking; it wasn't short of a home cinema, a gym, indoor and outdoor pools, or a tennis court.

"If you wait, I can take you," he said sleepily. "You don't have your car."

I felt a flood of affection for him and hugged him briefly.

"You go back to sleep," I said. "Wills is on his way."

What do you do when you know someone deserves to be loved but you just haven't fallen in love with them? I hadn't a clue and the passage of time wasn't giving me any either. Jay was maybe the best thing that had ever happened to me. I just didn't seem able to appreciate him.

I left him snuggling back into the bedding and went to wait for my brother in the large, taupe-coloured hall with its Venetian mirrors, ugly light fittings and cold, hard designer-tiled floor. Maybe it wasn't taupe—maybe it was called pebble or plaster or dune or something. Who cared? I would have painted the room in something a damn sight warmer, thrown away half the mirrors and put down some rugs.

I didn't have long to wait and, when I saw the lights of Wills' car through the many glass panels of the front doors, I slipped out to intercept him before he could get lost in the confusing turning circles at the top of the manicured driveway. I slid into the passenger seat and leaned across to hug him.

"Hey," I said sleepily.

"Hey, you," he said back. "Should I stop for coffee?"

"Yup. Need to raise the living before she can raise the dead. Four sugars please."

"Ugh."

He stopped at the all-night garage and bought us coffee. I sipped slowly as he drove us the rest of the way to the morgue. I wondered what unfortunate victim had died in such circumstances that my brother felt only I could reveal the truth of their demise. The fact was that we didn't get a lot of murders in my little county; any coroner's inquests tended to involve wayward cows or tractors. But my brother had a strong sense of justice, and we were both too soft-hearted for our own good... so when something really bad happened, we always seemed to end up here again.

He had the sense to realise that I was too sleepy for conversation and just drove while I got my head in working order. I was used to working nights, so to speak—you can't raise the dead in the day— but waking up in a hurry had never been one of my skills. It took all the coffee and most of the drive to get me to full consciousness. But they worked—by the time Wills had tucked the car away in an alley a couple of minutes from the morgue, my brain had reluctantly switched itself on and I was wakeful enough to check my handbag for salt and perfume.

"I hope tonight's rotting remains are feeling chatty, because I only have my nice atomiser on me," I said as we set off through the warm July evening. "And I've had a pretty crappy Friday night as it is."

Wills quietly unlocked the back entrance and let us into the building. The long, dark corridors lined with doors that concealed very uncanny contents were always going to be creepy. I wouldn't have liked being here on my own—with my big brother at my elbow, it was bearable. A pub would have been better.

"He's pretty fresh, rather than decomposing," he said. "Why was your evening crap?"

I shook my head and began to feed coins into the vending machine. The choice wasn't great. I hoped our cadaver liked cheese crisps.

"I'll tell you after we're done here," I said. "If you've got time, that is. Who are we interrogating tonight?"

"I always have time for my baby sister," he said, taking my hand and giving it a squeeze. "And it's a guy called Derowen Polkerris. Ring a bell?"

"The Cornish cheese millionaire!" I exclaimed. "It certainly does."

My brother laughed.

"He's about as Cornish as a Bakewell tart, as it happens," he said. "But yes, that's the guy. He was christened Darren Parker, if you are interested, and he was born three miles up the road in Doxey. But about forty years ago, he noticed the trend for artisan food that was growing and jumped on the bandwagon at exactly the right time. Some of his cows have even visited Cornwall, I hear, but only at the end of their active lives. He also owns a brand of Cornish pasties."

I'd certainly heard of Derowen. He lived in a Jacobean mansion close to Great Bridgeford where he spent his retirement drinking vintage champagne and batting off paternity suits. I'd even met him and his long-suffering third wife a couple of times at fundraising dinners that Jay had dragged me along to. On the last occasion, the fake Cornishman had put a hand on my bum as I was leaving. I hadn't lamped him for his behaviour, but only because the wretched man was eighty-four!

Wills led me to a room full of silver-coloured drawers. It was my least favourite place ever, but I kept ending up there. When he started messing with a trolley, I averted my eyes. He knew me well enough to cover whatever he unearthed with a sheet before I caught sight of it. Raising the dead had given me a lot of grief over the years, but not a strong stomach.

"So why don't you think you'll be able to find who killed him?" I asked, carefully looking at the exit sign over the door. "Is there no one who hated him? He seemed a completely dislikeable wanker to me."

My brother laughed out loud.

"The total opposite, sis," he said. "Do you remember in January when Bella was killed? The problem was that it looked like anyone in the county could have killed her, but no one would have wanted to... Well, this is just about the opposite. Pretty much everyone who ever met Derowen would have been happy to bump him off, but I don't see how anyone could have done it."

"Sounds intriguing..."

"It is. Two evenings ago, he was working very late in his office. He had several interviews, the last couple being with his housekeeper and then his wife. The last one didn't go well. He let her out of his office and closed the door behind her while she was still yelling. When it got to way past bedtime, his long-suffering secretary eventually banged on the door to ask if he could go home. When the boss didn't answer, he went in and found the man in a pool of his own blood. He'd been dead for a while. But the secretary and an electrician swear no one went in during all that time. It's like whoever murdered him must have teleported into the room. And out again."

He wheeled a sheet-smothered trolley out and I began to set up, pouring a neat circle of salt around the wheels resting on the bright white tiles, and then moistening it with the perfume from my bag.

It was a silly little bag, stiff green leather and about big enough to hold my keys and a tissue at a pinch. Jay had given it to me, one of the far too many gifts he had bought me for my birthday. A designer had made it. I was pretty sure they had charged more for it than I'd paid for my car. Some determined cramming had persuaded it to hold a salt cellar and a perfume atomiser; I like to be prepared. I would have liked a bigger bag, though—one capacious enough to hold some of those items that you shouldn't need at short notice, but that I too often seemed to: lock picks, a rape alarm, an industrial power torch, hair serum, lipstick, condoms. And thinking about the handbag and its giver, my mind wandered...

If I didn't want Jay, what did I want? Did I still think The One was waiting for me out there, somewhere, and that one day I would just round the corner and walk slap-bang into him and we would both just know and go off to live happily ever after with two point four cats? I winced. Deep in my heart, yes—that was exactly what I thought.

"What name will you call him by?" my brother asked suddenly.

"What?" I asked, confused. "Who: Jay? Paul? The cat?"

He laughed.

"I meant our fine deceased here," he said. "Is he Derowen or Darren?"

"Oh, him," I said vaguely. "I don't think it matters. Either will probably work."

I realised I'd been kneeling in silence at the foot of a stiff trolley holding the body of a murdered millionaire—while trying to work out how to dump one of the nicest men I'd ever met. I held out a hand and Wills helped me to my feet.

"Are you OK, sis?" he asked.

"Yup," I said with sudden determination. "Absolutely. Ready to cross-examine the chief witness?"

"Roger."

I opened six packets of crisps. Then I reached out and drew the power of the day into the corpse of a lecherous, recently deceased octogenarian.

"Derowen Polkerris, I summon you," I said. "Come to me."

He came like the wind. Here was a man who'd shuffled off this mortal coil before his time and hadn't been ready to leave. He could hardly wait to come back. He sat up with a little jerk, and the sheet covering his remains fell to his waist with a little swishing noise.

He was as wrinkled as a nylon sock that'd been tumbled dried too hot, and he was spray-tanned as orange as Irn-Bru. I noticed those things only peripherally, however, as they were no longer his defining characteristics. Those honours went to the seven bloody holes in his chest. They were still oozing slightly, and a piece of rib was visible through the largest. I'd rarely seen a man so thoroughly killed.

My legs wobbled and Wills caught my arm.

"Hang in there," he said in a jocular tone. "You've seen worse. OK?"

"Yup," I said, trying to sound convincing and failing. "What the hell happened to him?"

"Pretty much everything," he replied. "Someone clubbed him unconscious while he sat at his desk and then stabbed him seven times with his own letter opener. Four of the blows penetrated his heart. Nothing was left to chance."

I hastily opened the first packet of cheese crisps and handed it to my zombie. He wolfed them down in seconds and I handed him a second and then a third.

"Annatto," he said unexpectedly in a thin, whiny voice. "Sorbic acid. Monosodium glutamate. Partially hydrogenated soybean oil."

Wills and I stared at him.

"Well now," I said after a moment. "At least we know how he got his cheese to taste authentic. Shall I ask him how he died?"

Wills nodded.

"Please," he said. "Because his unpaid architect, his sacked housekeeper, his pregnant ex-mistress, his humiliated wife and his entire staff would have loved to have killed the old fart, but as far as I can work out, he must have been nobbled by magic fairies who could fit through keyholes."

I shrugged.

"Do my best," I said. "Derowen, tell me about your death."

He blinked at me and held out a hand imperiously for more crisps. I sighed and handed him two more packets. I hadn't liked the man when he was alive. Death hadn't improved him. He scooped the contents of the packets inelegantly into his mouth.

"I fell asleep," he said, spraying me with crisp fragments. "I fell asleep at my desk."

Will and I stared at him, flabbergasted and robbed of the power of speech.

"You have to be joking," I said eventually. "That's even worse than Bella's 'I heard a noise and someone hit me' tale. He's the world's most unhelpful zombie ever. Derowen, do you have any idea who killed you?"

He looked at me vaguely.

"No," he said without interest. "They should have used more salt in those crisps. And added E210 and E235."

I blinked.

"Hello? Earth to Derowen. Someone murdered you…"

But he wasn't listening. He held a crisp up to the white bright morgue lights.

"Too thin," he said. "Saves on ingredients of course but not enough crunch. Tell them to sprinkle on soy flour before the final fry."

I sent him back, shaking my head in disgust.

"Sorry, bro," I said. "That was the most complete fail. Want me to raise anyone else while I am here?"

He shook his head.

"We have another body here, but no name for her yet," he said. "She was found two days ago. We're working like Stakhanovite to identify her—she had a lot of dental work and some tattoos so we should get a match. I might drag you back when we have a name. Apart from that, there are those three poor Czech lads from that awful M6 crash last week. Their friend is still in intensive care; one of the dead kids is his brother."

I could see their names on the drawers: Olek Cernik, Pavel Nemecek and Radek Tabor. I'd read about the incident in the local newspaper. Four guys on a stag weekend who'd clipped the central reservation with their bumper. The car had rolled fourteen times. Three of them died instantly. The fourth was in a coma. Life could be depressing. If you hung around a morgue too much, you'd find a lot more to be depressed about.

He locked up and we set off back to the car together.

"I'm sorry I couldn't help with Derowen," I said. "Is it possible that the secretary and the electrician aren't telling you everything? Did any of them have a grudge?"

"Everyone had a grudge against Derowen, so I'm sure they did, but equally I can't see why either of them would lie when it makes them look more guilty than innocent," he said dubiously, "and the electrician is someone I know personally. He did the wiring at the new police station up at Rugeley. It doesn't look like he'd even worked for the man before. And their story might be backed up by CCTV—it turns out there were some security cameras in the office. We're waiting for the videos from the security company. I'd love to pin it on the housekeeper because he sacked her just an hour before he was murdered, but the secretary and electrician both swear she never came back afterwards."

"Well, keep me posted," I said. "I thought the man was an arse, but I doubt that makes it OK to kill him."

Wills let me back into his car. It was still far too warm, even for July, no need for brollies or coats. The streets were deserted and on the whole of our walk, the only living creature we had seen was a skinny urban fox rooting through a bin.

"Can do," he said. "Did you want to talk to me about Jay, or is it too personal?"

I sighed again. I was doing a lot of sighing that evening.

"Wills, you're right, he's a lovely guy, but he's un-datable," I said. "He's totally in love with his dead wife, and I can't imagine a bigger turn off than that without adding handcuffs and a rubber mask into the bed."

"Oh dear," he said limply, pulling the car onto the Rugeley road. "Are you sure? I mean, you could have misinterpreted the signs. And hell, you always exaggerate things."

"Oh, I'm sure," I said with feeling. "Wills, Evanka's photo is by his bed. It's on his desk. It's the screensaver on his phone. And his laptop."

"That's nothing," he interjected. "Maybe he just hasn't got round to spring cleaning his settings."

"Wills, her voice is still on his answerphone," I said. "He can't bear to delete it. And I found out last night that he still keeps her nightdress under his pillow."

There was an awkward silence.

"Are you sure, sis?" my brother said. "I mean, is it not possible it belongs to another lover? Just a suggestion."

"I wish," I said. "But we got a bit frolicsome this evening, and Jay's pillow went flying. Oh, don't laugh! And there was this nightie packed in tissue with sprigs of heather—her favourite flower—and it went flying, too. The tissue ripped, I rolled on the heather, and it got crushed... Oh, stop it!"

My brother was sniggering into the steering wheel.

"Sorry, Toni," he said, wiping his eyes. "I know it's sad but I'm just picturing you mid-bonk and..."

I punched his arm.

"Shut up, it was awful," I said. "Jay started to cry and everything. I had to fake two orgasms just to cheer him up. I'm fond of him, Wills, but this is the outside of enough. His family can't wait for us to announce our engagement and his daughters adore me but he's pining for a lady who died two years ago and turning to me for comfort. I'm done."

We drove in silence for a while.

"You know, sis," he said, after a couple of miles, "he'll get over Evanka eventually, and he'll be ready to fall in love. If you're there next to him, he'll fall in love with you."

I fiddled with the clip of my seatbelt.

"I don't think so," I said. "I think if it was going to be me, it would be me. I think he's looking for someone different. He just doesn't know it yet. And Wills…"

I fiddled with the seatbelt a little more. I looked out of the window. The sky was clear and full of stars. Tomorrow would probably be a beautiful summer's day.

"…Wills, I'm not a great catch for him either," I said quietly. "You know I'm still hopelessly in love with Peter."

He reached across to squeeze my hand again.

"I had worked that out," he said. "Is it hopeless? Do you hear from him at all?"

"That's almost the worst thing," I confessed. "I hear from him every day. He texts me, he emails me. I know the names of all his patients and how every single one of them is doing. You wouldn't believe what I've learned about oncology drugs. I am a sodding almanac. But I can't get him to come and visit me or agree to let me come to Germany. It's a bloody nightmare. I don't know if Lenz has him under his thumb again or—worse! if he's just fallen out of love with me."

There was another pause. Wills pulled up outside my house.

"I'm sorry," he said. "I think he's a daft prawn to let someone like you slip through his fingers."

He gave me a warm, big brother hug.

"Thanks," I said, a little sniffly with emotion. "You're the best. I'll call you tomorrow."

"Where's Paul, by the way?" he asked. "I can't see his scooter."

My eighteen-year-old lodger had moved in back in January. If all went well, he would move out in the autumn when his first term of university started. I would miss him horribly, but I was proud of him. He'd come from a home that wasn't so much broken as pureed, and he'd clawed his way out without a lot of help. He was alright.

He was also in an on-off relationship with Bethany, the receptionist at Bean and Heron where I worked. I didn't think it had been working out well recently. He'd been staying in and playing the drums a lot on his free evenings. When the relationship barometer was in an on phase, he spent them round at hers getting laid.

"He's gone to Amsterdam with some classmates, so I moved it round the back," I confessed. "He's taken all his exams and I'm carefully not thinking about what he's indulging in out there. He's back at the end of the week."

Wills whistled.

"Lucky him," he said. "I wouldn't mind a week in Amsterdam with the boys. What happened to Oscar's sports car, sis?"

I leaned in through the window and gave my brother a kiss.

"Ah, that," I said. "I sold it to pay Paul's university tuition fees. It was a pile of wank anyway."

Wills laughed.

"You're a soft touch," he said. "Hang in there."

I watched his taillights receding down the hill. I was tired through and through. There were still maybe a couple of hours until sunrise and I hoped to spend them unconscious. Under my eiderdown. I walked up the path to my porch. My heart sank. There was someone waiting in it. And there was no way it was a casual visitor. It was a vampire.

Chapter Two

To SAY I'D been avoiding vampires would be wrong, but I'd certainly been avoiding most of them. And I'd not seen the man standing alertly under the shelter of my porch since January. His name was Aidan, and I rather liked him, but he was head of security for one Benedict Akil, someone who terrified the life out of me... And someone I was very heavily indebted to.

I marshalled my resources and stomped up the steps.

"If you're selling pilfered goods door to door, I'm up for perfume, jewellery and a new phone," I said. "If you're... oh."

Aidan was holding my plump, elderly cat Winchester in his arms. The cat seemed fast asleep, one whiskery head resting in the crook of Aidan's elbow.

"Cats like the undead," Aidan said in his quiet voice. "Dogs hate us. How are you?"

I moved round him to unlock the door. I let him into the house and led him through to the kitchen. It was stuffy and cluttered, but I found it welcoming. The cat slithered out of Aidan's arms and twined around my ankles as I slumped down at the table.

"I'm fine," I said cautiously. "Solvent, healthy, happy. You?"

I could tell Aidan was relieved that I'd made him welcome. I was fairly certain he'd come with a summons for me that I didn't want to hear, but I didn't think he had a lot of choice about delivering it.

I would shoot the messenger another time.

"Me? Still dead," he said, rather charmingly. "You know why I'm here, Toni."

I looked up at him. He wasn't someone I knew well. He had pale English skin and soft, straight, black hair cut just above jaw-length. He would have been casually good looking as a man, but his vivid blue vampire eyes gave his features an unearthly, eye-catching quality. Vampires tend to be beautiful, and Aidan's death had endowed him with a beauty that I doubted he'd possessed in life.

There was also an aura of gentle sweetness that I knew had to be deceiving. Aidan came across as someone who wouldn't swat a fly, but he was the law enforcer for the most powerful vampire Assemblage in England. He swatted a lot of flies.

"Yes," I said. "You've come to drag me over to the Assemblage so that Benedict can give me a hard time about something."

He nodded. I looked around me at my cosy kitchen. The flagstones were original old terracotta. They'd sat on the floor for several generations. The dark green Aga was belting out a little too much heat for a July evening, but I liked the warmth. The cat had started to purr. There was vodka in the freezer… I really didn't want to go with Aidan.

"Tonight?" I asked reluctantly.

He nodded again.

"Yes," he said. "And now, please. It's nearly half past three, and the sun rises just before five. I've been waiting for you for a while. Where were you?"

I'd developed something like a social life in the previous six months. Before that, Aidan would have struggled to find an evening when I wasn't either at home or raising the dead just to have someone to talk to.

"Out," I said evasively. "Doing stuff. Give me five minutes. Benedict always looks like he's spent the whole day getting ready for a photoshoot and I can't face him like this."

Aidan laughed; he'd always seemed a very genuine person to me, not as arrogant as most vampires. Was it an act? It seemed unlikely.

No one else seemed to think so, and why bother putting on an act with little me?

"Just five minutes," he said. "If you hit six, I have a sack in the boot of my car. And Toni, you look just fine."

Sure, I did. I headed to the bedroom where I dragged a comb through my hair, wiped off the previous day's makeup and added a new layer. There wasn't time to change my crumpled cocktail dress for anything more suitable, but I put on flat sandals. If I had to run for my life, kitten heels weren't going to tilt the odds in my favour. Finally, I swapped the silly little green handbag for one that held a few more useful items and returned to Aidan in the kitchen.

"Just so we're clear, I'd rather go to bed," I said.

He grinned suddenly, and I saw the flash of his fangs.

"Me, too," he said. "It's a shame you weren't in when I called round at dusk."

Oops. Flirting with vampires was a very bad idea. I needed to remember that. Sometimes you could forget they were the undead—and that wasn't wise.

I rolled my eyes, mostly to cover up the fact that I was blushing.

"I'll follow you in my car," I said. "If that's OK?"

He shrugged.

"Sure," he said with his customary good nature. "But if you make a break for it, I know where your cat lives."

The drive to the Stone House takes you along the river where it runs past the foot of Cannock Chase. It's a pretty drive in the day. On a warm July evening, an hour or so before dawn, it's still agreeable. There's enough ambient light to see how the trees creep down the hill to the flood plain. There are a lot of sheep. Sometimes cows. Deer cross the road quite fearlessly in front of you. Knowing what was at the end, that night I totally failed to appreciate the journey.

I parked my car behind Aidan's in the courtyard. I'd not visited for six months, but nothing seemed to have changed. Torches lit our way as we entered and made our way down to the basement levels.

"Do you know what he wants?" I asked Aidan as I followed him. "Am I going to get slaughtered, ravished or just glared at tonight?"

Aidan looked a little perturbed by my shortlist.

"Just the latter, then, I think," he said. "He said he has a favour to ask you."

I shook my head decisively.

"Not possible, Aidan," I said. "That man doesn't ask favours. He doesn't ask for anything. He issues commands. Or diktats, maybe."

Aidan laughed.

"I suppose you're right," he said. "All I know is he said he wanted to speak to you privately, so I'll take you to his room. He can't give you too much of a hard time, you know; there's only an hour until dawn."

"Another lie-in ruined," I said. "Damn, I forgot to feed Winchester."

Aiden rolled his eyes.

"Give me your house keys," he said. "I'll go back and do it."

I passed them over. I was darkly amused to discover that Benedict's head of security had a heart as soft as butter too.

Benedict's room was at the end of a winding corridor, lit by more of the burning torches that hung in brackets from the walls. Aidan led me to the end and knocked at the double doors.

"Yes," said a familiar deep voice.

Aidan opened the left door and ushered me through. I cast a look of slight panic back at him, but he just gave me an encouraging smile and closed it behind me.

The room seemed unchanged, the elegant interior as always illuminated by hundreds of small candles and a blazing fire. Heavy sheepskin rugs softened a black slate floor, and the dark walls were ornamented with vintage mirrors and beautifully draped green curtaining.

Other things were also unchanged: the room's owner was sprawled in a chair by the fire and as per usual, he appeared to be squabbling with someone.

"Not at all," he said. "But if you wanted to procrastinate and put yourself in danger, you should have stayed in St-Bertrand-de-Comminges. I have enough enemies already. Deal with this. I won't tell you again."

He was speaking to a woman in a shimmering silver evening dress. She sat on a sofa with her back to me, immaculate dark hair coiled into a knot at the nape of her neck. She turned briefly to look in my direction, and I recognised Sophy, the vampire who liked dancing and who had been banished to France a century ago for violent revenge on a fellow nightwalker. She looked distraught, her pretty face pinched and drawn.

"I don't want to hurt anyone," she said in anguished tones. "I don't do that anymore."

He glared at her. I thought he was probably practicing for when it was my turn.

"Fine," he said shortly. "Then make it painless. I've said my piece and I hope you listened because I won't say it twice. If you'd faced up to this before then we wouldn't be here now. Find him and kill him or I'll do it for you. And I might take my time because I'm not as nice as you. Now go away. I have to deal with the lovely Toni Windsor. At least she is never boring."

He turned to me and gave me a smile that wasn't even skin deep. He showed his fangs slightly. I knew he meant to. They were long and very white. He was as elegantly dressed as ever in an understated but heavyweight dark linen shirt and faded black jeans. There was a wink of cufflinks when he moved his hands. He had pulled back his long black hair, which threw his sharp cheekbones and rather hawkish nose into prominence. His looks had grown on me over time—I rather wished they hadn't.

"I wouldn't dare bore you," I said, sitting down next to Sophy. "You kill people when you're bored."

Sophy gave my hand a brief touch and then fled. I heard the door open and close. Benedict ignored her. He stretched his legs out in front of the fire.

"A manifest falsehood," he said with deceptive sweetness. "I'm never bored when I kill people. Have you been avoiding me, my dear?"

The question threw me. I had, of course, but I hadn't expected he would notice. Didn't he have plenty of other people to make miserable when I wasn't around?

"I've been working on it," I said cautiously. "You're always telling me what to do. And you make me nervous."

He gave me an appraising look, and I was suddenly conscious of how short my cocktail dress was and the fact that my neck and shoulders were bare, exposing the veins in my throat... I swallowed slightly and futilely tried to tug the skirt of my dress further down my thighs.

"I can suggest several ways we might calm your nerves, little tiger," my host said. His voice had dropped to a purr. "But I doubt you'd acquiesce to any of them. And yes, I do have the tiniest of requests for you. I would have spent longer working up to it, but I hoped you'd be here earlier."

I looked at him warily. Every time I got tangled up with vampires, I ended up fighting for my life. No one had tried to kill me for six months, and I'd liked the down time. But I'd sworn fealty to Benedict. He'd saved Peter's life. He'd saved mine. I owed him... I raised my hands in surrender.

"I'm here now," I said. "Hit me with it."

He nodded without surprise. Of course, he'd never doubted I would do what he said.

"Thank you. Aidan will give you the name and address of a protégé of mine. I doubt he will make you nervous. He has asked for your help. Please give it to him."

"Why me?" I asked in confusion. "If I don't know him, why does he want my help?"

"Why do you think?" he said gently. "He wants you to raise the dead."

I felt the bottom drop out of my stomach. Benedict knew my secret, Aidan had weaselled it out, but this... this wasn't fair. Vampires and necromancers were ancient enemies. Benedict might have made some local wiggle room by offering some protection to Staffordshire's necromancers, but most members of the fanged would slay me on sight if they knew. I didn't want my living and breathing friends knowing about my powers—I really, really didn't want my dead acquaintances to find out.

"How could you do that?" I said, without thinking. "How could you betray me like this?"

"What?"

"I've spent my life keeping that a secret," I said, my voice rising. "I was an outcast. I lost friends hiding the truth. Pretty much all of them. This isn't fair. And you know full well that any vampire outside of Staffordshire would rip my lungs out if they knew what I was. Now you expect to be able to pimp me out to your friends like your pet necromancer!"

There was a long uncomfortable silence when I stopped shouting. At least, I was uncomfortable. Benedict looked unmoved. He got to his feet and stood in front of me. I looked up at him, suddenly fearful.

"I see," he said, his voice clipped. "And I am bored now, after all. I will tell you what I expect, Miss Windsor. I expect no arguments, no tantrums and no procrastination. Ring any bells? Good. I make few demands of you. I expect them to happen."

He reached down a hand, which I took without thinking, and tugged me to my feet, pulling me towards him so that we were pressed together. He lowered his head so that our lips almost touched.

"It was so sweet of you to visit," he whispered. "I'm sorry you couldn't stay longer."

And before I could even protest, he moved his mouth into mine. It wasn't a kiss—far from it. I felt his teeth slide into the soft moistness of my lower lip. There was a little jerk, a sudden metallic tang and then he deliberately sucked the blood out of my mouth. I made a little sound of protest, and I felt his lips curl up against mine into a smile I couldn't see.

"Neither caramel nor asses' milk," he murmured. "You taste of sunshine and unsated desire. Come see me when you're in a better mood. I don't like you in this one."

And he let me go. He stepped back to watch and for a moment I stood paralysed—his vampire powers had lit the wax taper of my libido and it flamed into a rush of unwelcome heat, starting in the little punctures in my lip and spreading into every single cell of my body. I caught his eye. He knew exactly what he'd done, exactly what I was feeling. For a moment I looked back at him like a bunny in the headlights... and then the spell broke.

I vamoosed. No other word for it. I fled the room and slammed the door behind me. In the corridor I tried to regain some composure, but it wasn't happening. I walked unsteadily back to the main passageway. Aidan wasn't around—he had probably thought my conversation with Benedict would take longer—and I put a hand to the wall to steady myself.

I heard female laughter and looked up. It was Grace and Camilla, vampire and consort. They were drifting towards me, hand in hand. They made a fine couple, Camilla—taller than both of us by far— with straight, milk-coloured hair that hung below her shoulders, and dark-haired Grace, willow slim and nearly as short as me but faking at least another five inches with terrifying stiletto heels.

When Camilla saw me, she smiled.

"Dearest, why didn't you come earlier?" she said in her soft voice. "We've had such a dull night. Benedict is in a temper with everyone, particularly poor Sophy. I thought it would pick up when Aidan said he was going to find you, but he never came back."

"Well, now Benedict is in a temper with me, too," I said mournfully.

Camilla hugged me. I hugged her back. She had a kind heart and a generous nature. She'd become a good friend. We went shopping together and did each other's nails.

Grace didn't hug me. She stroked a cool hand down my cheek. From her, that was pretty demonstrative. She was old and powerful and enigmatic, but she liked me. She was the only vampire I hadn't been avoiding the past six months. She and Camilla had taken to dragging me out with them in the evenings. I didn't mind. They were excellent company and went to cool parties.

"He'll get over it," she said. "Unlike Sophy, who's crying in her room. Come down to mine. I'm getting ready for my rest."

I hadn't been to Grace's rooms before. It was six months since I'd visited the Assemblage and I'd barely known her the last time I'd been in its confusing labyrinth of underground corridors. She led me down a mess of passages and two flights of stairs until we came to a Gothic door with a pointed arch. The room behind it was glamorous and dramatic. There was a lot of polished cast iron, expanses of black, crushed-velvet curtaining, and clusters of pillar candles in sconces and forged metal brackets.

It was certainly beautiful. Scratch that—it was breathtaking. But I didn't find it cosy.

"Camilla hates my rooms," Grace said, noticing my surprise. "But if she'd grown up in the squalor I did, she'd appreciate a little luxury."

I looked at her curiously as we arrayed ourselves on some outrageously elegant chairs. Grace was always exquisitely dressed. There was never anything casual about her. Her hair was always perfect and her clothes a coordinated dream.

"Did you have a hard life?" I asked. "I don't even know how old you are."

She laughed, but there was a touch of bitterness in her voice.

"Me and every other woman from my era," she said sharply. "I was a whore, Toni. And not a courtesan—just a poor girl who didn't have any family or enough money to eat. You would think the passage of six hundred years would mean I didn't care any longer, but I can't forget. I surround myself with all the opulence I never had when I was alive. Now, enough of me—Camilla and I want to drag you out on Sunday night."

I hesitated, but only because I was still digesting what she had just told me, not because I was in any danger of refusing her invitation. Staying up all night on Sunday would mean I'd be exhausted on Monday morning, but Mondays always sucked. In fairness, mornings sucked. No point in fighting it…

"I'm in," I said. "Where are we going?"

"Just to the bar. But Sophy has finally agreed to come with us."

'The bar' was a misnomer. It was an elegant lounge, in a disused wine cellar two storeys underground, which catered exclusively to the undead and their hangers on. The décor leant heavily to candlelit Gothic. No one ever seemed to pay any bills. Someone called Emir lounged behind the bar making cocktails and choosing the mood music. It wasn't possible to overdress.

I'd visited half a dozen times. So far no one had tried to kill me, shag me or drink my blood there, putting it very high up in the ranks of vampire haunts that I'd visited. It was in fact the only vaguely pleasant vampire haunt I'd encountered, and if I hadn't liked Camilla and Grace and free drinks more than I should, I would have steered clear of this one too.

And it was unlikely that drunk sports fans would accidentally wander in after a match; the place was situated two miles into the woods near Fradswell. It was in the ruins of an old baronial hall that had burnt to the ground half a century before. You had to drive over two cattle grids and through a ford. Gate crashers seemed an unlikely prospect.

"I think I like Sophy," I said carefully. "What happened to her that Benedict is making such a fuss about?"

"Ah," said Grace, "yes, that. She has picked up a stalker. Or rather, an unwanted admirer has followed her here from St-Bertrand-de-Comminges. We wouldn't usually care, but he was a member of their leader's coterie there, and far too well informed about our communities. If he hooked up with the English Defenders League, or another anti-nightwalker brood, he could make trouble."

"Does he plan to?" I asked warily.

I had reason to be cautious. The last time I'd encountered a mortal harbouring murderous thoughts towards the undead, he'd nearly taken me out to cover his tracks.

"I fear so," said Grace. "He's decided that she's been brainwashed into leaving him. We are all evil impediments to their union…"

Ah. A batshit freaky deaky person. Not good…

"Benedict said she should have dealt with him before," I ventured.

Grace nodded.

"She knew he was obsessed with her before she left France," she said, "but she didn't tell anyone because he was in another vampire's coterie. She thought he would just get over her when she was gone."

But he hadn't. And now he was somewhere out there planning to wreak revenge, and no one knew how to find him. Yes, I could see why Benedict was antsy about things. I could also see Sophy's point of view. Especially if the default solution would have been to remove her unwanted admirer from the gene pool. Vampires were a lot about stick and not a lot about carrot.

"Poor Sophy," I said. "She hasn't been lucky."

"Toni, she meant well, but she should have been more resolute," Camilla interjected. "She tried for a softer approach, but she's put us all in danger. I've seen the letters he's been sending, not just to Sophie but some of us at the Assemblage. Some of them were addressed to me." She dropped her eyes. "They aren't nice."

I reached over and squeezed her hand.

"You're probably right," I said with reluctance. "I haven't seen them. What do I know?"

There was a knock at the door and almost before Grace had called out a casual welcome, Aidan bustled in.

"There you are," he said. "I couldn't find you. I have to give you Nicky's details before I turn in for the day."

Both Camilla and Grace looked at me in surprise.

"Why does she have to see Nicky?" asked Grace. "Can't he sort out his own mess?"

There was a slightly supercilious tone to her voice, as though Aidan had suggested I adopt a particularly festering pet. He shrugged with convincing nonchalance and handed me a piece of paper.

"Toni's brother is a policeman," he said. "Maybe he can help. Toni, the girls are hunkering down; I'll walk you to your car."

He gave me a clap on the arm and inclined his chin to the door. Grace shrugged.

"Whatever," she said. "He's harmless enough. We'll pick you up on Sunday night, Toni."

I bid them goodbye, and Aidan and I wandered back to my car.

"What's up?" I asked. "I get the impression you have something to tell me."

"I do," he said. "I wasn't sure whether you would want anyone else to know. Toni, when I went back to your house this evening to feed your orange monster, someone else was there."

"What, in my house?" I asked.

"No, camped out watching it. Two men in a car. I took down the number plate—it's on that piece of paper I gave you with Nicky's details. I didn't notice them when I was there before, but I think they were there all night. They left when they saw me approach your house."

I shook my head, distressed.

"Aidan, I don't have a clue who they might be," I said. "But thank you. I'll tell William and ask him to look into the number plate."

He clapped me on the shoulder again.

"Sorry to bring bad news," he said. "And twice in one evening at that. Listen, it's nearly dawn—I have to go."

I watched him head back into the house and close the door behind him. My almost vampire-free six months had clearly come to an end. If I'd wanted a life free of nightwalkers, I'd gone about it all wrong... I should have used a stake.

Chapter Three

I DIDN'T BOTHER with a lot of Saturday morning. I had no work, no Paul to worry about and no pressing social engagements until the sun went down. I lay in until Winchester's mews became loud enough to penetrate my fog of sleep. Then I hauled my sleepy arse into the bathroom and showered until my eyes would both open and shut on command, rather than randomly when they felt like it.

I finally blundered into the kitchen to discover the message light was flashing on my landline. It could have been left pretty much any time on the previous day, I realised, and pressed play, hoping it was nothing urgent.

"Hi, Ms Windsor," trilled a chirpy and unfamiliar voice. "It's Karen here, John Jones's secretary. Can you pop in and see John on Monday? Any time after lunch will be good. He'll have finished any outstanding inquests in the morning. Give me a bell and let me know when suits you. If I don't speak to you this afternoon, have a great weekend!"

Her buoyant voice rattled off a number and bid me goodbye. I stared at the phone in simple bewilderment. Why on earth did the county coroner want to see me?

I could think of a number of reasons he ought to. There was the small matter of the dead English Defenders League thug that Bredon had decapitated the previous summer, but Benedict had 'dealt' with that corpse and I was happy to remain in ignorance about how. There was the janitor whose suicide I'd faked back in January after another of my zombies had crushed his throat, but I was pretty sure no one had noticed that he'd had his neck broken twice. There was… there was actually a very, very long list, now that I came to think about it. I just hadn't thought the forces of British justice knew anything about any of them.

I poured myself more coffee and glowered at the phone. I made myself some toast out of slightly stale bread. Now I would be wondering what the coroner wanted with me until I could call them back on Monday.

Had Paul been in residence, I would probably have made us an omelette or pancakes, but he wasn't. I missed him horribly. We were a perfect match as housemates. He introduced me to cool new bands, I introduced him to three-hundred-year-old dead people. I cooked simple meals with no more than four ingredients, he washed up. We both watched Hammer House of Horror re-runs and nineteen-eighties science fiction.

He'd been gone for just a week, and I wondered how I would cope when he went to university. Badly, all the signs suggested. I ate my toast morosely and added an extra two spoons of sugar to my coffee on top of the usual four. I needed rather more energy than usual to face the day.

First things first. I had to ring my brother and tell him that someone was watching my house. At night. I couldn't think who it might be— I'd stayed out of trouble for months. But that meant whoever was behaving like my own personal stalker… Well, they were unlikely to be vampires. So just for a change, I could turn to the police for help.

Wills answered sleepily after many, many rings. I was hard-hearted—unless he'd got lucky with Henry after dropping me off the previous evening, he'd had more sleep than me.

"Hey, sis," he said. "Was enjoying a lie in."

"Hey, bro. You're welcome. Want me to come over and cook you pancakes?"

He gave a sleepy chuckle.

"Damn, no, I still remember the last time. The ceiling still has fragments of batter stuck to it. You OK?"

"Yes, but Wills, this is important. A friend told me that two guys in a car staked out my house for three hours last night."

There was a pause. Then:

"Christ all-bloody mighty. Your friend sure?"

"Yup. And Wills, he works in security, so I think he's pretty clued up."

"He get the number?"

"He did. Got a pen?"

There was another pause followed by the sound of several things falling from a bedside table to the floor.

"Bugger," I heard a muffled voice say. "OK, got one."

I read out the number.

"He told me there were two men in the car," I added. "I didn't ask him what they looked like, but I can if you think it would help."

"If you…"

He broke off. There was the sound of an eiderdown being squabbled over and Henry's voice protesting in the background.

"Um, sis, have to go now," Wills said, sounding a touch more awake. "But yes, get a description as soon as you can, or your friend will probably forget what they looked like. Tell him to come in and talk to us if he likes."

Sure, that was going to happen. If the police station wanted to take a statement in the middle of the night…

"Will do, Wills. Will do," I said.

But he'd ended the call. Someone's morning was turning out a lot more fun than mine. Par for the course, Toni… I needed to change my life.

Not this weekend, though. I had to help out Benedict's mysterious protégé. I looked back at the piece of paper that Aidan had given me. Above the registration number that I had given Wills was a name and address: Nicky Carlyon, St Ambrose Rectory, Stoneydelph Waters. I looked at it through narrowed eyes. I'd seen that address before… but when?

I wandered into the drawing room and, plumping myself down on the sofa, I pulled up Stoneydelph on my phone. Inevitably, the wretched village was right on the other side of the county, Tamworth way, past that vile roundabout and a five-way junction... Then it came back to me. The rectory was one of the houses that Peter and I had driven to the night he had been kidnapped. We'd been trying to track down the Gambarinis, and the coterie hadn't responded to Benedict's summons because their music had been too loud. I'd forgotten because it was nearly a year ago and so much had happened since.

Well, I could get there for sunset with no problem. In the interim, I had enough energy to go shopping and that was about it. I assessed the house: in Paul's absence, I'd allowed it to run low on food as well as descend into chaos. I would try tackling the chaos tomorrow.

I wasn't exactly flush with cash, however. My career as an estate agent was never going to buy me a yacht. Benedict had given me some money the previous autumn. It had gone on paying for a gravestone for Jane Allardyce and the funeral bill for Amelia Scott Martin. I'd had a terrific run of commission payments in the New Year. They'd paid for a new boiler. And yes, I'd sold Oscar's car—it wasn't strictly mine, but I had all the paperwork. But I'd put that money into an account in Paul's name, earmarked for student expenses. He had five years of university to get through; just the tuition fees would be crippling, and I insisted he save all the money he made running the office at Mr Suki's store.

So wonga was thin on the ground and my lodger ate a lot. The only things hungrier than a teenager are the undead. My kitchen cupboard wasn't going to contain caviar anytime soon. We ate a lot of toast; fortunately, I was very fond of toast. My cat Winchester was on the cheap tinned cat food, bulked out with a lot of crunchies; that was less fortunate because he considered his natural prey to be the lightly grilled tuna steak. I stopped feeling sorry for myself and got myself dressed and into the car.

The supermarket on a Saturday lunchtime was a circle of hell that even Dante hadn't condemned the sinful to suffer. There were cross people. There were screaming babies. There were cross people with screaming babies. And there were lots and lots of queues. I escaped with a trolley full of essentials and a shortened fuse and leaned against my car in relief.

"Lav, how perfect," I heard a voice say. "Just when I desperately needed a shopping partner."

"Claire!" I spun round and hugged her. "This is so lucky. How are you? I haven't seen you for ages."

Claire was my absolute best friend. We'd been through college and a boyfriend together. She was generous and excellent company. I'd not met up with her for a couple of weeks and, with Claire, that meant that anything could have happened. She was a leggy blonde with plenty of chutzpah and an eye for the fine things in life.

"Yah, really good," she replied easily. "I acquired the most delicious new boyfriend, but he turned out to be a faulty model."

I laughed. Claire was a great friend, but I had a feeling she was tough to date. I would have laid money that her standards were high. A lot higher than mine. I didn't even require my men to be alive and breathing.

"Ate with his mouth open?" I asked. "Wore socks with his sandals?"

She shuddered.

"No, thank the Lord rejoicing. But when we went out for coffee the next morning, he pronounced it 'lar tay' and then picked up the cup with his little finger curled out. I faked an emergency phone call and fled into the shoe shop next door. Fortunately, I have an account with them, so they called me a taxi and I left through the back door."

I shook my head. And she thought I was picky about my men.

"Hideous," I agreed. "I can't believe they let them walk the street without warning labels. Will you take me out to lunch? I'm broke and now that you've talked about shoes, I want some."

Lunch was spent catching up on gossip. Claire was as amused as my brother about my poor boyfriend Jay.

"Darling, I'm not in favour of sex tapes," she said, posting anchovies between her perfect teeth, "but it would have been nice to capture that moment to laugh over when we're all old and wrinkly and can't get a shag for love or money. And talking of love, how's the adorable Peter?"

I gave an exasperated sigh.

"He is just fine," I said. "He wrote me a long and wondrously witty email this morning. He has a new MRI scanner on order, and it has made him very happy. If he were here in front of me right now, I'm not sure whether I would snog the man or strangle him with his own stethoscope. He's driving me up the wall."

Claire idly twirled a frond of rocket around with her fork.

"Not exactly spending your nights pining away for him in solitude and sadness, Lav…" she said. "I mean, you aren't coming across as the most lovelorn of ladies."

"Well, I very much doubt he's living like a frigging monk out there in Heidelberg," I snapped back. "He didn't get that good in bed by practising on his own. And I don't care, Claire. I actually don't care who he's sleeping with as long as we end up together. I've learnt that much from vampires. Love matters more than physical fidelity. But it's looking increasingly unlikely that I'm ever going to get anything more passionate from the man than an emoji so, yes, I'm window shopping and if I see something I like, I am damn well going to take it to the till."

There was a silence.

"Lav, I get it," she said, reaching across the table to pat my hand. "You love him, but you're worried that you've made a mistake. We've all been there. Just chill. We'll enjoy some retail therapy."

It seemed like good advice. We paid our bill and wandered over to a lingerie boutique not far from the Catholic church and compared scraps of underwired chintz and ruched crepe de Chine.

"There's a trade-off," Claire said, shaking a wisp of organza that seemed to be composed entirely of straps. "You wouldn't mind wearing this briefly. But after about eight minutes, chafing would set in. This is an item you put on to take off. It's not clothing, just recreational activity with laces."

"Don't knock it," said the lady standing next to her, a tall woman in her fifties with a very convincing blonde bob and hefty pearl earrings. "If they're watching the chiffon, they might forget you have a brain. Or pores. Or a heart to break. You're on safer ground then."

Her voice was raw. I stared at her for a moment. I'd met her before, twice in fact. It was Irene Polkerris, the long-suffering wife of the Cornish cheese millionaire and the very last person to see him before he'd been murdered. I could understand using retail therapy to power myself through grief, though a lingerie boutique seemed an odd choice.

"Hi, Irene," I said hesitantly. "I was very sorry to hear about your husband. I hope you're bearing up."

She glanced at me in surprise.

"You're Jay's girlfriend," she said after a moment. "You're lucky. He'll never leave you for a student nurse. Or his fucking accountant."

She raised her hands and clenched them for a moment. I was taken aback to find that she was wearing pretty cotton gloves even in the hot July weather. It seemed an odd fashion choice but given her choice in men, she was clearly given to making poor decisions. Before I could respond, she had rushed in again.

"'We should have children', he used to say to me. Why the hell did he want more children? He has four by his various mistresses. One of them is older than I am. Another is still in nappies."

Claire and I exchanged panicked looks. The torrent of sheer unadulterated misery pouring out of Irene was heartbreaking, but there seemed to be no way to close the floodgates. I held out a hand, but she didn't even see me.

"You know why he was finally divorcing me?" she wailed. "Now that gay marriage is legal, he'd decided to marry Maurice Posset. It turns out they've been lovers since boarding school. Eighty-four, and divorcing me for his lover boy."

I opened my mouth and then shut it again. Words deserted me. I knew Maurice well—he was Bernie's accountant, too, and came in every couple of months to mess around with figures for the agency. He was always beautifully dressed, with gorgeous silver hair and a taste for expensive shoes. He carried an old-fashioned Malacca cane he didn't need and flirted very politely with me and with Bethany. He had more charm than almost anyone I'd ever met—but the man was an octogenarian.

"Um," I said lamely. "Well, at least that won't happen now—?"

"You know the best joke?" she continued, clearly forgetting she was orating to a near stranger in a lingerie boutique. "He hadn't even told Maurice... The poor old dear came round to comfort me last night with a bottle of gin and some lemons and couldn't understand why I shouted at him through the door. When I finally explained, he was horrified. He said he wouldn't have married Derowen for love nor money, and there was plenty of both. We ended up drinking nearly the whole bottle together and we didn't bother with the bloody lemons."

The boutique owner threw in the towel and came out with a bottle of wine and four glasses. Mindful that I was driving, I had just the one glass—I thought Irene was going to need another bottle.

In a spirit of camaraderie, I bought a flimsy silk fragment I didn't need and couldn't afford. By the time we left, Irene was onto her fourth glass—clutched in her still-gloved hands—and had bought two negligees and a corset. The boutique owner had promised to send her home in a taxi.

"And that was exciting," said Claire as we walked back to the car park. "Poor dear. I'm amazed no one bumped Derowen off long before."

"I hear you—I only met him once for about five minutes and I was considering it myself," I said. "Fancy that about Maurice, though. Talk about hidden depths. Listen, Claire, thanks for lunch and for listening."

"Always here for you, darling," she said, kissing me on both cheeks. "You know what you need? You need a nasty, no-strings-attached self-indulgent one-night stand with someone hot and immoral."

I drove home in a thoughtful mood. It seemed like good advice if I'd known a candidate who fitted the bill. As it was, I would make do with a long nap, followed by a chocolate éclair and a glass of wine with the cat.

I SET OFF to find the mysterious Nicky Carlyon at around eight. The sun would set just after nine, and while neither Aidan nor Grace had stated that Nicky was a vampire, it seemed a safe bet. I wasn't happy about what had transpired between myself and Benedict—I rarely was—but he had a valid point. I had to reluctantly concede that I owed him and that I'd promised to help him out when he asked. As for the rest... I assured myself that I would stake him if I could when the opportunity arose. The world would be better off without him, me in particular.

The rectory was a way off the main road, set back up a hundred foot of driveway. I'd seen it only the once, and at night, and retained the vaguest of impressions. In the evening sun I had to laugh at the décor—two people's tastes were clearly at war.

Designer number one wanted Victorian noir, ornamental iron and looming glamour. Designer number two wanted to live in a giant doily. Overhanging yew trees warred with resin statuettes of bunnies. A tumbledown stone summerhouse with old stained-glass windows had to share a lawn with pink garden furniture and a gazebo curtained with shiny fabric covered in violet and yellow flowers. I was with designer number one, but it didn't take a lot to spoil the effect they were going for. One four-foot plastic unicorn painted like my-little-coming-out-party was doing the trick almost single-handedly. Not even black gates topped by hand-forged dragons could face down the unicorn. It had a jaunty little bow round its neck.

I parked my car by the front door next to something sleek and silver with four wide tyres, two leather seats and twin exhausts. Some things become antiques with time. My car was just old. I'd heard a vintage car in good condition could acquire a rarity value.

Mine had merely acquired rust spots, mildew, a dislike of steep hills and a smell of dog when it rained even though I'd never owned a dog. The silver beast was clearly pining for the open road. Mine didn't care for the open road—it wanted to be on location at the local garage, running up repair bills.

For politeness' sake, I sat in my car until the sun set. I let it get nice and dark before I walked up the short run of stairs to the front door and rang the bell. Someone took their time answering it. I was considering going back to wait in the car—a sundress and sandals were proving a little cool once the sun had gone for the night—when I heard footsteps inside followed by the sound of locks being drawn back and a key turning. Finally, the door opened.

Several things struck me about the blonde who stood there. One was that she was absolutely the prettiest woman I had ever seen, on camera or in real life. A second was that she was wearing a negligee about the size of a postage stamp and shoes even taller and less practical than Grace's. But these paled into insignificance next to the fact that she was pointing a twelve-bore shotgun at my face.

"Get away," she said. "I don't care who you are or why you're here. I don't want you and he doesn't need you. Piss off before I kill you, and don't come back."

I didn't have a death wish, but she wasn't very scary. Claire had taken me shooting often enough for me to know that my angry gun-toter needed to work out how to cock her weapon before I was in any serious danger. And, if she didn't hold it better, when she pulled the trigger, she would break her own nose with the recoil. I had serious doubts that she'd managed to load the thing at all.

"Hi," I said peaceably. "I'm after Nicky."

She raised the gun in what she probably hoped was a menacing manner. All I could think of was that if she managed to fire it now, she would probably lose an eyeball. And she didn't want to do that— she had sparkling hazel eyes thickly fringed with dark eyelashes and set under arching brows that looked both perfect and natural. She was tall and curvaceous with a chest that put even mine to shame. I didn't think the cross expression on her face was attractive though.

"I said I'll kill you," she said. "Didn't you hear me?"

I sighed and gestured to the gun.

"You know it won't fire like that," I said helpfully.

"Oh, rats," she said. "Have I left the safety catch on?"

"Nope," I said. "That's handguns." A thought occurred to me, and I added conscientiously, "And nail guns."

We glared at each other over the barrel. I was just wondering whether to have a go at clubbing her over the head with it when a lazy and rather sexy voice interrupted us.

"Kitten, can you get this in for me?" it said in plaintive tones. "My buttonhole is too small."

She whirled round and dropped the gun. It fell with a clunk onto the doormat, but I doubted that she'd even noticed. All her attention was on the willowy, white-haired vampire standing in the hallway, his shirt open and cuffs awry. He was clutching a pair of cufflinks in one hand.

"Oh, Nicky," she said, her voice overflowing with adoration. "Darling, of course. I'd do anything for you."

Chapter Four

It's rude to stare, but I couldn't help it. Nicky had straight white hair, swept back over his shoulders. And it wasn't Nordic white. It was the white of snowflakes under bright light. It made polar bears look beige. Not even Hollywood teeth were that shade of pale. The hair was eye catching enough, but it was only part of a disconcerting whole. He was tall and slim, his physique accentuated by skin-tight black leather trousers and a complicated silk shirt that looked as though it had been embroidered by nuns in the Tyrol. Bored nuns with a lot of thread to use up and no other hobbies... And it didn't button up, it laced. Or it was meant to. He'd clearly got as far as putting his arms through the sleeves and stalled.

He'd completed the eighties Goth pop star look with enough eyeliner to black out my car windows and a gold ring through one eyebrow. The effect was eerily attractive—beautiful rather than handsome, but certainly pleasing to look at.

And I'd seen him before, I realised. He'd opened the door to me all those months ago when I'd been helping to look for the Gambarinis... But Peter had been with me back then, so, murders and mayhem aside, they had been happier times. Nicky noticed me staring and did a double-take himself.

"Oh, it's you," he said, echoing my thoughts. "I remember you. You came with Peter Hilliard."

His voice was gentle, utterly without the arrogance I'd got used to from the nightwalkers. I reached out to sense him and there was almost nothing there. With Grace or Benedict, I would have felt the thrum of age and power, but not with Nicky. He barely registered on my vampiric radar.

"That was me," I said uncertainly. "Do you know Peter?"

He shrugged.

"I was at Heidelberg for a year," he said. "I doubt he remembers me. He was still a student."

The blonde looked peeved. She would clearly have preferred it if he'd thrust me down the stairs and slammed the door behind me, not gossiped about mutual acquaintances. She pushed between the two of us and began to put his cufflinks in.

"I've told her to leave," she snapped. "Make her go."

"It's OK," he said. His voice was gentle, a touch at odds with his outlandish appearance. "This is Lavington Windsor. She's here to help us."

Her back straightened and she jerked a shoulder at me. Even cross and bad tempered, she was lovely, but I was starting to dislike her immensely. Scratch that, I'd disliked her immensely straight off the bat considering the gun to my face. Now our friendship was really going into a decline. She finished the cufflinks and began to lace up Nicky's shirt. I could tell she'd done it before.

"We don't need help," she said. "What use would she be anyway? You're a super powerful vampire!"

He looked embarrassed, as well he might, and patted her arm soothingly.

"I asked the boss, Kirsty," he said. "I'm worried they'll come after you next. I couldn't bear that."

She didn't look appeased, far from it, but she didn't argue. Instead, she narrowed her beautiful hazel eyes at me, giving me to understand that I was to keep my greedy, needy hands off her undead boyfriend or face her fury. I didn't want a row, so I just met her seething gaze as yieldingly as I could.

"Whatever," she said. "I'll get dressed then."

It was provocatively said. I knew where she was going with it. She batted her lashes at Nicky in a suitably come-hither way, and then shot me an appropriately go-thither glare. Neither got the effect she wanted.

"Good idea, kitten," said Nicky. "I'll go over to the Stone House with Lavington here. I'll see you later."

It was clearly the wrong thing to say. Kirsty stamped her foot.

"Why do you have to leave me?" she hissed. "I've been waiting for you to wake. Don't you dare leave me and go with her!"

Nicky didn't immediately say anything. He had a resigned look on his face. If he hadn't been dead, I got the impression he would be taking a deep breath and counting to ten. As it was, I thought he was counting to ten.

"Kirsty," he said very softly. "Love, I need to feed."

She flung herself into his arms and pressed herself against him. I had bikinis with more square inches of fabric than she was wearing, and I could tell Nicky wasn't immune to her charms. He closed his eyes and buried his face in her shimmering gold hair. She looked victorious.

"Feed on me," she whispered, tilting her head to one side. "My blood's warm, Nicky. Bite. Drink…"

He raised his head. I thought it was a struggle for him to push her away, but he did it.

"I can't, you know that. I've taken a full pint from you this month. I checked my chart this morning. You can't give me blood for another week."

She drew her hand back and belted him across the face. He made no attempt to defend himself and she took the opportunity to whack him across the other side.

"I hate your stupid charts!" she yelled. "I hate your stupid Stone House and your stupid boss! I hate you and you've ruined my life!"

And she pulled back her arm for another shot.

"Hey," I said, disturbed. I felt that I'd wandered into a TV reality show, but way into the closing episodes, leaving me clueless as to why tempers were so frayed, half the cast were naked, and the buildings were all on fire. "There's no need for that."

She turned on me like a snake, but this time Nicky stepped in. He moved with the insanely fast blur of a vampire and gently caught both her hands in his before she could slap me, too.

"Kirsty," he said. "I have to go now. You have a nice bath. I'll be back as soon as I can."

"I won't be here," she yelled. "I'll be gone. You'll be sorry."

Nicky clenched his fists. Then he pushed her gently down into a chair and put his face in his hands for a moment.

"I hate doing this," he said, half to himself. Then: "Kirsty—I woke up, we kissed, and you told me to go and feed. I said I'd hurry back to you. You're going to take a lovely long bubble bath and phone your mum. You'll watch your new box set."

His voice was resonant, insistent, controlling. I realised he was compelling her and I watched in interest. I'd rarely seen it done. I didn't like it on principle, but then vampires did a lot of things I didn't like. So did politicians. Hell, so did my cat. Still, it didn't seem right. I raised a hand but before I could speak Kirsty stood up and kissed him on the cheek.

"OK," she said a little forlornly. "Hurry home."

And Nicky caught my hand and dragged me out of the house into the warm July night, scooping up a dressy leather coat en route. His fingers were cold in mine, narrow and fine boned. I looked down. His nails were perfectly polished and caught the light of the porch.

"Sorry about that," he said. "She's been under a lot of stress. Is that your car? Can you drive us to the Stone House? I go there most nights."

"I can," I said hesitantly, "but I don't like it. And Nicky, I just drove all the way here. And isn't that your car?"

I gestured to the silver, wide-wheeled beastie that was parked next to my heap of rust. But Nicky shook his head.

"It's Kirsty's," he said. "I don't drive anymore. Do you mind?"

I sighed.

"I do a bit, Nicky. I hate going to the Stone House. Benedict is terrifying and I'm always in his bad books."

"Oh," he said. "He's nice to me. But listen, angel, he won't be in tonight. He's going to meet with Isembard Blackwood Bordel. They're squabbling over some border incursion crap. And I'll find someone to give me a lift back."

I reluctantly got into my car and let Nicky into the passenger side. At least we could chat without Kirsty screaming at us. I pulled out of the driveway and headed back the way I'd come.

I took a sideways glance at my passenger. He was playing with the cuffs of his shirt. I thought of Oscar, sublimely confident in everything he did, or Grace, with her six hundred years of poise. Nicky was so unlike the other vampires I'd met. He seemed... young. That was it.

"How old are you?" I said, without really thinking. "Sorry, I shouldn't have asked."

"Does it show?" he asked bitterly. "I'm six years old. I'm the youngest vampire in the bloody county."

We drove in silence for a while. The roads were quiet, with few other cars or people about. A lone businessman was weaving along the pavement with a briefcase. He gave the impression of having been celebrating something...

"Stop the car," said Nicky suddenly.

I braked in surprise. The businessman was drawing closer. I could hear his voice raised in song... Nicky cracked open the passenger door.

"I hate the Stone House, too," he said, with a smile that was suddenly more alive. "Let's break some rules."

And he slipped elegantly out of the car.

"Wait," I said, but he'd closed the door behind him.

I watched in consternation as he approached the man, pointing at his wrist in the universal gesture of enquiry. The man responded, then they were talking, a moment of shared laughter. Nicky was gazing into the man's eyes... A touch on the shoulder, a sudden embrace. I saw the vampire's head jerk and then his victim's body was spasming in delight.

Moments passed. I wondered what to do—should I intervene? But it was over before I could even make up my mind, and as suddenly as it had begun. Nicky opened the passenger door and eased back in. His movements were lithe and buoyant, with a spring in his step that hadn't been there before.

"That feels so good," he murmured. "I never get tired of that. Do you think after a hundred years, or even a thousand, you would get bored of it?"

I thought of Benedict holding me in his arms, winding his fingers in my hair, of Oscar splashing his own blood across the snow in frustration…

"I don't think so, Nicky," I said frankly. "I really don't think the pleasure diminishes with time. And I really don't think you should have done that."

"Oh, lighten up," he said, curling up in the seat. "He had a nice time. And I healed him. No one will ever know. And now we don't need to go to the Stone House. Where do you want to go?"

I looked over at him. He looked well fed and well satisfied with himself. And he was ruining my Saturday night for nothing. I drew the car to a halt.

"Nicky, I want to go home and watch crap television and drink the bottle of vodka in my freezer, OK? I'm here because Benedict told me you need me to raise the dead. I didn't come to play chauffeur and watch you score blood off some unsuspecting drunken sot. So can we please go raise the dead so that I can go home, and you can go away and squabble with your horrible girlfriend?"

"She was on form, wasn't she?" he said. "You should have seen her when Camilla dropped round once. After she'd gone, Kirsty stabbed me with her own manicure scissors. Listen, angel, let's go to your house. You can at least drink your own vodka and I will tell you what's been going on and then take a taxi home. Sound better?"

It did. I'd rather have dropped him off by the pavement, run him over a few times and then gone home to drink on my own, but I would take the upgrade on offer.

"Fine," I said. "So, tell me: why do you need me to raise the dead?"

"I didn't know what else we could do. I think someone's been killing my coterie."

"You think? How can you not be sure? Either they've been killed or not."

Nicky slumped in his seat a little.

"I'm young, I need to feed every night. I had a coterie of four, and that just about worked. But three months ago, Lily left in the middle of the afternoon. She just left a note. A month later, Caroline went, too. Last week, it was Lorraine. But we heard on the police radio that Lorraine's body was found in a disused mineshaft up on Cannock Chase. Now I'm worried that the other two might have died as well."

It seemed highly likely to me. Getting caught up with vampires seemed to be a common cause of death from what I could tell.

"What do you know about how Lorraine died? How do you even know it was her?"

"She had all these tattoos of hummingbirds on her arms," he said. "A lot of ink. And they only found her because some guy walking his dog saw her wandering through the trees singing. He thought she was on drugs because it was cold, and she had bare feet. So, he followed her but lost her and then called the police. They were too late—she'd jumped down the shaft."

"Are they sure she jumped?"

"Completely. That particular shaft has been fenced off. She must have climbed the fence—which wouldn't have been easy—and flung herself off with quite a lot of force. They saw a shred of her dress on the fence or they'd never have found her at all."

"Could a vampire have compelled her to jump, and to write that note?"

Nicky looked thoughtful.

"Maybe, it kind of depends," he said. "Even I could have compelled her to write the note. But to make someone kill themselves? That takes a lot of power. You'd need a vampire like Oscar or maybe Sophy."

Peter had told me that Oscar's powers of compulsion were

extraordinary, though I knew from bitter experience that they didn't work on me, which meant I'd never seen them in action. But Sophy?

"Is she good?" I asked.

"Yeah, amazing—or so I've heard. Well, she used to be. Since the incident with Xan Hewitt all those years ago, she won't use her powers anymore."

"Why would a vampire want to take out your coterie, though?" I asked.

"That's the stupid thing, Lavington, they wouldn't need to," he said. "There isn't a vampire in this county who couldn't take me out singlehandedly before breakfast. And while they don't rate me, I don't think I'm on their radar enough for any of them to hate me. I really hope I'm wrong here."

I pulled up outside my house. Nicky looked at it appreciatively as we walked to the porch. We were greeted by a chorus of starving and pathetic mews as I opened the door.

"Cosy," Nicky said, picking up Winchester and draping the cat over his shoulder. "I get sick of Victorian grandeur now and then."

"I assumed the décor at the rectory was yours."

"Kind of sort of," he said. "And Kirsty has very definite ideas about how a vampire should live, but then she's also a bit of an impulse buyer. Did you see Rainbow on the lawn?"

"The unicorn? Could hardly miss him, Nicky…"

"Yeah, well, he was one of her drunken, late-night online whims. Got to love old Rainbow." He deposited his rather leggy form into one of my chairs and bundled the cat on to his knee where it sank into unconscious pleasure. He'd draped his black leather coat over a chair, and—in the light of my home—it proved to be frogged down the front, with gold clasps and lots of additional straps and buckles. It had a custom-made look. Vampires are vain.

"I like your kitchen, Lavington."

"Everyone likes my kitchen," I admitted. "And please call me Toni. Only teachers about to give me a bollocking ever called me Lavington. How did you meet Lorraine?"

"I didn't. Kirsty found her. She chose all my coterie. They were like sisters—I never got a word in edgeways."

I opened the freezer and looked at the vodka. Tempting, but I was feeling low and needy. If I drank it, I would probably take off all my clothes and do a little dance for Nicky by the sink unit. I sighed and made myself some tea and took out a couple of chocolate biscuits.

"OK, well, how did you meet Kirsty, then?"

"I'm from Brighton," he said vaguely. "But Kirsty was born here. When her parents split up, her dad got custody and he moved down south to the coast. But she always wanted to come home. When Benedict took me on, it made her very happy."

Benedict had called Nicky his protégé…

"When you say he took you on, what does that even mean?"

Nicky gave me a rather hunted look.

"I thought you'd know all this. I'm a hacker, Lavington, and I'm the best. By the time I was eighteen, I was breaking into investment bank trading systems and sucking out dollars like a bloody hoover. They still don't know it's gone. And it was child's play to me. Aged twenty-five, I was arsing round Brighton with a wallet full of cash, a cool flat over the pier and a wardrobe full of designer gear. I had a five-figure stereo and a six-figure watch. I'd even persuaded Kirsty to date me. I thought I was the boss. Then I bought a newer, even flashier sports car than the one I was being a twat in and wrapped it round a lamppost. I was paralysed from the neck down."

"Christ, Nicky, I had no idea."

"Angel, I'm not proud of it," he said. "My family was affiliated with a vampire, and they persuaded her to transition me. She has no status, and goodness knows I don't, so I was left looking for an Assemblage to take me on. Benedict agreed, and I wasn't going to say no. I don't have any powers to trade, but he wanted someone to hack into neighbouring Assemblages, government security sites, planning offices… I tell you, I'm busy."

Was that a background that was likely to build up enemies? Who knew? I sipped at my tea. And why would another vampire lure Nicky's coterie to their death, if that was even what had happened…?

"So, where's Lorraine?" I asked. "Can we raise her now?"

"No," he said. "I thought you knew. She's in the morgue."

I couldn't speak for a minute.

"You have to be joking," I said. "She's the girl with the tattoos and the dental work! If I'd known, I could have raised her last night. I was in the morgue with my brother."

"Your brother's the cop, right? Then no, we don't want the police involved. Her parents have claimed her body now. They don't know about me—they thought she just lived with girlfriends."

It's easy to forget that the dead weren't alone when they were alive. They used to be people, with all the love and loss that entailed. Lorraine was an unsolved mystery to me—to Nicky, she'd been a friend, and presumably a lover. To her parents, she'd been a beloved daughter. I presumed she'd been beloved—not everyone had suffered parents like mine. I realised with a jolt that Tuesday would be the anniversary of their death. The thought filled me with sudden and overwhelming tiredness. I hadn't had nearly enough sleep over the weekend.

"Nicky, next week, there'll be a post-mortem. If you don't want the police involved, I won't be able to raise Lorraine until they release her body. Go away and let me have some sleep, and if I think of anything, I will ask you."

He stood up with a look of confusion.

"What did I say, Toni? I'm so sorry."

I didn't know how to answer him. 'My parents didn't love me,' sounded too pathetic. 'My mother was a witch and she never told me,' sounded too pretentious. 'I'm just tired,' would have been a lie…

"Do you know any witches?" I asked at random, without putting much thought into the question.

"What? Apart from Emir?"

"Emir the barman! He's a witch?"

"Sure. I thought everyone knew. He's an illusionist."

I shook my head. Emir was enigmatic and a little odd, but a witch? A witch running a mysterious cocktail bar in the middle of the woods frequented largely by the undead and their hangers on... It made a strange kind of sense.

"I'd no idea."

"Well, apart from him, there's Mrs Holloway, of course."

The name rang a vague and distant bell.

"Keira Holloway? She runs the hair salon near your house?"

"She does that, too. She makes potions."

Hmmm. She sounded easier to approach. I gave Nicky's cold hand a little squeeze.

"Thanks. And listen, it's nothing you said. I'm just a bit down right now. I'll try to help you find out what's happened."

We called a cab and hung around waiting for it for twenty minutes. Nicky obligingly moved a chest of drawers for me that I couldn't lift and then sat on my sofa with the cat, entertaining me with tales of the undead scene in Brighton. I thought he'd drawn rather a short straw as a vampire, with no discernible powers to help distinguish him and the word's nastiest girlfriend, but he didn't seem to feel sorry for himself. When the taxi arrived and beeped its horn, he got elegantly to his feet.

"You're nice," he said suddenly. "I didn't expect that."

"Why not?" I asked in confusion. "Why wouldn't I be nice?"

"Angel, you dated Oscar. He's a complete wanker."

I had to laugh. It was all too true.

I walked Nicky to the taxi and waved him off from the pavement. He seemed sweet for a vampire. As the rear lights disappeared off down the hill, I heard a noise behind me. I swung round to look and nearly jumped out of my skin. A car was parked just a few feet behind me, both front doors open. There were two men climbing out of it even as I turned.

I couldn't have made out the licence plate in the dim streetlight, but I didn't need to. I'd utterly forgotten Aidan's warning—that my house had been watched the previous night—and I'd walked out and delivered myself to them like a Christmas parcel.

I took to my heels and fled back to the house and up the steps to the porch. I nearly made it. Nearly—but not quite. I felt my arm grabbed just as I reached out for the handle. I was jerked off my feet and fell to my knees, smacking my face on my own front door. I rolled painfully onto my back and blinked up at my attackers in the porch light. I'd never seen them before in my life. Both men were total strangers.

"She's only little," said the one holding on to my arm in casual surprise.

"Yeah?" said the other. "Who gives a fuck? She's still going down."

Chapter Five

I WAS BEING held by a man not much older than me, but I didn't think we had anything else in common. He must have been more than six foot tall, and his head was shaven, revealing that the spider tattoos up his neck didn't in fact stop there. His nose had been broken more than once, and the chunky scars above his chin gave the impression that on one of those occasions, a fist had also pushed his lower teeth all the way through his bottom lip. He looked rather disconcerted—whatever kind of person he'd expected to be assaulting that night, it hadn't been me.

The second man was shorter, wider, and a lot older, well into his fifties, I thought. He also had a shaved head, revealing pimply skin that might have benefitted from a few doodles to break up the scenery. And he looked angry, the sort of sustained anger that has been bubbling under the surface for far, far too long. It seemed to be very determinedly directed at me.

"You thieving little bitch," he hissed. "I waited years and now it's all yours."

I wanted to tell him that he had the wrong person and that I couldn't possibly have anything that was his. I also wanted to tell him to bugger off with his friend and leave me alone with a bottle of vodka and some crap television, but I hadn't got my voice back yet.

Anyway, he didn't seem interested. He opened my front door,

which I hadn't bothered to lock when seeing Nicky off, and caught my other arm, yanking me out of the younger man's grip and shoving me into the little hall. I didn't quite manage to get to my feet and skidded along on my knees until I hit the kitchen door.

"Let's do it inside," he said. "Lock the door."

I heard the younger man flick the locks across and panicked.

"I don't even know who you are," I gasped. "I don't have anything of yours."

I'd said the wrong thing. His face reddened and his eyes bugged.

"Don't you even think about giving me that crap," he yelled.

And he reached down and punched me in the face.

I saw stars. I saw planets. I saw constellations. I think there may have been little tweeting birds. There was also a world of pain and a taste of blood as he dragged me into my own kitchen and threw me on my back on the wooden table. I could smell the varnish, the slight hint of the soap I'd cleaned it with. Something dug into my back—I thought it was the plate of chocolate biscuits. I wanted my mind to focus on the fact that I was about to die but it just flittered around delivering random thoughts. Perhaps it was broken?

"Right," he said, and unbuckled his belt.

What is it about men who are about to kill you that they always want to stop for a spot of light rape first? Do they think it doesn't count if she's dead right afterwards? Like some sick version of the three-second rule when you drop a piece of toast...? I wanted to scream, but my mouth wasn't working either; it had formed an alliance of uselessness with my brain.

"Hey, hang on," said the second man suddenly. "You didn't say anything about this."

"What?"

"I don't believe in rape. My sister was raped."

"Oh, shut up and find a knife."

"No—and she's only a girl. You said this Windsor woman would be an old creaker like your mum. Bumping off an old codger is one thing, but she's just a kid. You know what they do to kiddie killers in the slammer?"

I looked up warily. The cat was peering down from the top of the larder, wondering if any of the three people in the kitchen planned to feed him. The younger, taller man was squaring up to my would-be rapist, who was holding his trousers up and looking at a disadvantage. My mind was starting to form coherent thoughts but they were all of them terrified and none of them helpful.

"Well, I thought she'd be old, too, but she isn't," he said. "And who the fuck cares?"

But my unexpected defender stuck his ground. He shook his head, making the tattoos on his neck stretch and squash. I watched them in confusion; the blow to my head had made me woozy.

"My sister's a redhead," he said. "You shouldn't do this."

They glared at one another for a moment in silence. It was broken by a hard rap on my front door. Both my uninvited guests jumped in shock. I opened my mouth to scream, but the short, older man was too quick for me. He let go of his trousers to slap a hand over my mouth, and they fell around his ankles as we tussled.

"Don't answer," he said quietly to his accomplice.

The tableau was frozen for an instant, me akimbo on the table with blood running out of my nose, a half-dressed man holding me down by one arm and blocking my mouth with the other hand while the second man stood staring at the front door in momentary indecision.

Then Nicky's gentle voice broke the silence.

"Hey, Toni, angel, it's only me," he called.

"Stay quiet, and he'll bugger off," said the man holding me down to his friend.

I made a spirited attempt to bite his hand, but he knew what he was doing. And in response he moved his other hand up to my throat and choked me—just a little, but air wheezed awkwardly into my lungs. I stopped fighting and lay still.

"Don't try that again," he said.

Then to my surprise, I heard the sound of the front door opening and closing. Nicky's footsteps approached.

"Toni, I forgot my coat," he said, a little plaintively.

He stepped into the kitchen, and I saw him take in the scene.

For a vampire, he was slow on the uptake—he just stood there and blinked for a few heartbeats. Fortunately, my attackers were too floored by his appearance to react any quicker.

When Nicky spoke again, the softness had left his voice and it was almost someone else speaking, someone with a lot more self-confidence and some backbone to their makeup.

"Oh no," he said. "That's not going to happen."

The tableau broke and both my attackers launched themselves at him. The tall man was the closest—much to his misfortune. Nicky moved so fast that I didn't see it happen. I only realised that he had torn the man's throat out with his teeth when the wall of blood sprayed over me like sticky rain. And not just me—my other attacker, my kitchen units, the bread bin, and the cat all got a goodly showering of gore.

I raised my dizzy head and stared in silent disbelief. The remaining of my two attackers was rooted to the spot once more. The only person in the room who seemed even more shocked by the turn of events was Nicky himself. The vampire stood stock still, clutching a bleeding corpse in his hands. He looked absolutely startled.

Seconds passed, and the room was so full of stunned silence that I could hear the little cuckoo clock above the bread bin ticking. Nicky didn't even move when my would-be rapist and murderer came to his senses, hauled up his trousers and fled through the hall and into the night.

The clock ticked for a few moments more. Nicky looked at me. His white shirt was now the colour of a matador's cloak. His hair had been liberally re-tinted. It wasn't a makeover that suited him. He dropped the corpse on the floor with a gesture of slight distaste. I didn't blame him.

"I've never killed anyone before," he said softly. "What do we do?"

I made an effort to sit up. It took a couple of attempts as my head was still spinning. I was compulsively swallowing little mouthfuls of blood and I wondered if my nose was broken. Eventually I managed to perch on the edge of the table, supporting myself on the heels of my hands.

I felt a moment's sadness; the dead man had tried to protect me in his own way. He hadn't been a good person but he'd had some morals. Had there been some chance he would redeem his life? If there had been, it was gone forever now.

"We call Aidan," I said. "This is vampire business now. I'm not getting the police involved."

Nicky looked at me more closely.

"You're hurt," he said. "Let me help."

He took me awkwardly in his arms. His delicate hands were cool on my shoulders. The wash of healing energy was almost ethereal in its touch, but I felt the pain in my face slowly recede and the throbbing in my nose fade. Nicky stroked my face gently.

"Would you take a little blood?" he asked. "I think that would finish things."

I recoiled and he let me go in alarm.

"I don't think so, Nicky," I said. "I'm a necromancer. I have an aversion to sharing blood."

He tilted his head to one side and looked at my face. I wondered what he was seeing—black eyes, a crooked nose, swollen lips?

"Try a little," he said in a wheedling tone. "A few drops…"

And he ripped back one cuff of his ruined shirt and idly opened a vein for me with his teeth. I felt my stomach roil and churn, but I'd done this before. He was right that it would help… And the kitchen couldn't get much more blood-filled. I caught his wrist in my hands and screwed my eyes shut. His skin was cool silk under my lips. The blood itself was lukewarm, sweet and salty at the same time, with a burn to it like sherbet or maybe whisky. I forced myself to swallow a couple of mouthfuls before I began to gag.

But it was enough. I hadn't realised that my vision was blurry until it cleared, or quite how sore my throat had been where it had been squeezed.

"Nicky, you're the best," I said, with very real gratitude. "Ugh, that's so repulsive!"

He followed my gaze to where the cat had leapt from the top of the larder, paddled through the spreading pool of blood and was licking thoughtfully at the corpse's neck.

"Agreed," he said. "Toni, do you have something I could wear? I think I'm starting to set."

"You're congealing! I think I have some old clothes of Peter's that will fit you, though they'll be too short. But Nicky, I don't want to track blood all over the house. We need to call Aidan first—corpse clean-up is a speciality of his."

Nicky bit his lip. The sudden sense of purpose that had infused him when he'd seen my life in danger had deserted him along with his self-confidence.

"Would you call him?" he said.

I reminded myself that he'd just saved my life. It stopped me emitting a sigh or showing any exasperation. And I rang Aidan without procrastinating.

"Hey, Toni," he said, picking up after just a few rings. "What's up? You've never called me before."

He sounded genuinely pleased to hear from me. I cut short his greeting.

"I know, but it's urgent. You know those guys who were watching my house? Well, they came back, Aidan, and they nearly killed me."

"Christ, are you alright?"

"I am, but only because Nicky dropped round. Aidan, he saved my life. Listen, one of them is dead and bleeding all over my kitchen floor. Can you help?"

There was a pause. I heard voices, then a burst of laughter. Aidan came back on.

"Benedict said to ask you if he still has his head attached or if you've removed it yet," he said in some bemusement.

I choked back a giggle.

"Not yet," I said. "Are you coming?"

"Twenty minutes," he said. "Don't spread the blood around."

I perched on the kitchen table with Nicky. We'd barely met and now he'd saved my life and given me blood and we were just about to dispose of a dead body together... bonding experiences. I looked up at him a little shyly. On a whim I got a clean tea towel out of the drawer, moistened it at the sink and began to clean the blood from his face. When I'd finished, he returned the favour.

"How did you open the door?" I asked as he dabbed gently at my chin.

"Oh, that. It's one of my very few talents, locks. Not many vampires can do it, but Benedict can. Doors just open for us." He dabbed at a patch of something sticky on my chin. "I nearly didn't come in—I thought you wanted to be alone—but then I thought how cross Kirsty would be if I came back minus an item of clothing!"

I straightened my back. I hadn't wanted to help him, and I still thought he had terrible taste in women and needed to stop feeling so inferior. But on two hours' acquaintance, he'd also shown he could be brave and kind. When the chips were down, he'd come through for me. He was in my good books. I reached out and took his hand, as fine boned as a bird's under my grip.

"I'm going to find out what has happened to your coterie," I said to him. "I promise. You won't regret helping me. And I'll tell Aidan you had to kill that jerk. I'll tell him you had no choice."

He gripped my hand back, a little too hard for a moment, and I was reminded that however gentle and mild-mannered he might seem, he was still a vampire. He could tear out a man's throat with his teeth in a moment of distraction and then wonder how on earth it had happened so quickly... Then I heard the sound of car engines and our tête-à-tête was at an end.

The previous time something like this had happened, there had been Peter to calm me down and Oscar to make everything seem right. This time around, there was Aidan in super-efficient mode and a load of people I didn't know. I took a long shower and then sat on the lawn. I listened to voices squabbling about how best to wash the blood out of my kitchen floor, off my Aga and out of my cat's fur.

After a while Aidan came to find me.

"Still no idea who they were?" he asked.

I shook my head.

"The man who left, he said I'd stolen what was rightfully his," I said. "But they didn't seem to know anything about me. And they thought I would be an old woman. They certainly weren't expecting anyone my age."

Aidan looked around to see if we could be overheard. No one seemed close by, and he crouched down on the grass next to me and spoke quietly.

"I thought maybe you could raise the one who died," he said. "Not tonight—there isn't time before dawn for me to get the corpse safely away and out of sight of any of the others—but tomorrow or Monday night if I can arrange it. That way, even if your brother doesn't come up trumps with the license plate, we should be able to work out who's after you."

I squinted at him, silhouetted against the light of my kitchen window. I disliked the fact that an increasing number of people seemed to be sharing my secrets. But in fairness, Aidan seemed to have made a genuine effort not to share this one.

"Benedict told you I can make the dead tell their secrets," I hazarded.

He nodded.

"I understand that's what he wanted you to do to help Nicky," he said. "You might as well do it to help yourself. I'll set things up and let you know. Is there anything we need to do with the body to make sure that you can still raise him?"

I was already shaking my head. Benedict spilled my secrets with far too much abandon; I hoped Nicky had some discretion or before long the county's undead would all know there was a necromancer in their midst.

"I can't raise him until I find out his name," I said. "For now, just don't cremate him. Enough fire separates the soul from the body."

"Not a problem," he said. "And Toni, please take care. I'll take Nicky home shortly."

And he swirled off into the dark. I wanted to say goodbye to Nicky, so I hauled myself to my feet and followed him back to my cadaver-free home. Before I'd made it to the porch, Nicky himself came out on the same errand. He was wearing a black t-shirt of Peter's and cut-off jeans. They were hardly his signature style and were both too wide and too short.

"You made me sound a lot more heroic than I was," he said shyly. "So thank you."

"You saved my life, Nicky, and then you gave me your blood," I said. "I think that's pretty heroic actually, so thank you."

And on impulse I hugged him. After a moment he put his slim arms round me and hugged me back softly.

"You don't know me," he said.

And he left.

I WALKED UP the steps where light spilled out of the open door and wandered back inside. I was left alone in a kitchen that smelt of bleach, with a bottle of vodka I no longer fancied, and a cross, wet, soapy cat. None of these things seemed at all appealing. I wanted company, comfort and friendship, so I raided the kitchen for food, threw it into my rucksack, and headed up the hill to the graveyard. Bredon would give me all of these things. In addition, if the remaining thug came back for round two, Bredon would tear his head off for me and offer to eat the damn corpse. This time, I would jolly well let him.

Summoning Bredon didn't take very much power anymore. He came so easily at my call that I felt he was waiting for it. And I'd almost got used to his increasingly young and handsome appearance. He'd always been a dashing and good-looking man, tall and muscular with dark curling hair, very heart-melting brown eyes and an enchanting smile. But in the eleven months that had passed since I'd first called him, his appearance had changed. He certainly looked more youthful, but there was more to it than that. He was somehow more physically imposing. Perhaps it was merely in his stance or the way he moved, but he seemed taller to me, his shoulders broader, his chest deeper…

Anyway, he'd always looked good, and now he was even easier on the eye. And dead or not, he was one of my closest friends. When times were tough, I always felt I could lay my troubles on his ever-broadening shoulders.

That night proved no exception. Just his presence was a reassurance as we sat together in the little mausoleum that I had made into a midnight picnic venue. The heavy metal door had proven no match for my lock picks. Back then it had opened on to a dark, dusty space, around nine-foot square of almost solid spider webs set under a slightly domed ceiling. I'd sent the spiders off to get fresh air and exercise and replaced them with rugs, cushions and a selection of chunky church candles.

Paul and I had started taking Bredon further afield, but there weren't enough hours of darkness left on this occasion. Bredon ate four tins of tuna and an entire catering jar of olives while I related the events of the evening.

"Dear heart," he said, his brow furrowed. "Are you certain it was you they were after? Think: did they ever use your name?"

They had. The younger man, now extremely dead, had uttered an odd phrase.

"'You said this Windsor woman would be an old creaker like your mum,'" I repeated. "Those are the words he used. I've no idea what he meant by them."

"I would say this then: that for some reason, your remaining attacker associates you with his mother. And not having met you, he assumed you were of an age with her. How old would she be, do you imagine?"

I cast my mind back, picturing the shaved head, lined face, sloped shoulders. I'd thought he was in his late fifties, certainly no younger...

"Bredon, she would have to be in her eighties if she was even still alive," I said. "And I know what you are going to ask, but no. I just don't know anyone that age, not anyone who's more than a passing acquaintance."

Bredon didn't contradict me, but he seemed unconvinced.

"Think back," he said. "Think harder. A man is willing to kill you for the wrongs he thinks you've done him. Not trifles, dear heart, but matters great enough to warrant murder. And the link is this mysterious woman, whoever she may be. Identify this venerable lady and you will know who wishes you ill and why."

I knew he was right, but I didn't have a damn clue. We left it there and talked of easier things.

Chapter Six

I SENT BREDON back to his grave just before dawn. The sun rises pretty early in July, so I shut the mausoleum door and napped a few more hours of Sunday away. By the time I walked back to my house through the woods, the neighbours were stirring, and the birds were singing. There was no one loitering around the house sporting a murderous expression, so I let myself in and appreciated the very fine job that Aidan had made of removing all traces of the night's events. No corpse and no blood, but also no breadbin. I could appreciate why—gore probably didn't wash out of unglazed pine very well—but that also meant no bread, which threw me off kilter when it came to breakfast.

I drank coffee and was just trying to decide whether the tub of ice cream in the freezer needed to step in as an emergency meal when the doorbell rang and I opened it to find my brother standing there with a packet of crumpets, all ready to meet their maker in a blaze of butter and honey.

"Thank God," I said, hugging him. "I hate eating ice cream for breakfast. Come in and I'll make you coffee."

Wills and I had grown up together in the little cottage. My life had seemed normal until I turned seven. That was when I began to raise the dead—and my parents began to pretend that they didn't have a daughter. My memory was hazy before that time, but I remembered cuddles and birthdays. What had I done to change things? Wills didn't know and now that both my parents and grandfather were dead, it seemed unlikely that I would ever find out.

I led him into the kitchen and made busy with the toaster.

"So, any news for me?" I asked as I dug honey out of the larder and butter from the fridge.

"Well, the car that your stalkers were in was stolen."

"No surprise. A total dead end then?"

"Well, maybe not. The woman who reported it stolen thinks her ex took it. His name is Dylan Moss, and he was released from jail two months ago. He came round to try and borrow money from her—she gave him a flea in his ear. But when she went out later to go to the shops the car had vanished. Did you get a description out of your friend?"

I nodded.

"There was an older guy, late fifties, stocky, shaved head," I said. "The other guy was taller and younger, maybe my age. Also shaved, but tattoos of spiders up his neck and head."

"That's Dylan for sure," Wills said. "In prison he had the nickname Spider-Man."

I looked down at the floor. It was immaculate. Just hours before it had been covered with Dylan's blood. I tried to banish the image from my brain, but now that he had a name it was harder. I could picture him as he lolled there lifelessly, the edge of his spine shining through the viscera of his open throat... The cat licking at the blood... The smell of meat...

Wills was saying something, but I failed to hear.

"What was that?" I said. "Sorry, I blanked out."

"I said, he's not known for violence against women," he said. "He was holding up service stations to fund a drug habit. He punched a till boy who tried to dial 999. The boy cracked his head on the tiles when he fell and died of bleeding on the brain. Dylan was in for fourteen, out in eight. I'm trying to get a list of prison mates who came out at about the same time, but that's harder than running a registration number over the weekend."

I placed coffee and buttery goodness at his elbow.

"What about Derowen Polkerris?" I asked. "Anything there?"

"That just gets worse. The secretary and the electrician seem to be determined to incriminate themselves. The wretched pair swear blind that after the boss threw his wife out of the room, not a soul entered his hallowed office until they found him all highly perforated and extremely deceased. They both assured me with honesty in their eyes that neither Irene nor the housekeeper came back."

I thought back to his description of the events.

"So, he sacked his housekeeper and then had a row with his wife, but he was killed after they both left?" I said, thinking out loud. "What's the housekeeper's name?"

"He saw them one after the other, but pretty much, yeah. She's called Daphne; she's been at the place even longer than he has. She worked for the previous family."

"Why did he sack her?"

Wills shrugged.

"I gather she wasn't fawningly deferential enough and he got sick of it. But she was long gone when he died, packing her bags. I'm hoping for something different from the security cameras, but that will take another couple of days because the footage goes to an agency and there's no one there until Monday."

I didn't say anything. I thought of Nicky compelling his vile girlfriend to let him spend the evening with me. A vampire could easily have made the two witnesses forget what had really happened. Someone like Nicky could have opened the lock more easily than me with my picks… Another thing occurred to me—a housekeeper who'd been at the hall for generations would know if there were any hidden ways. And I had to bet that, with Derowen's death, she was still on the payroll. People have killed for less. Out of anger. Out of fear. Out of jealousy…

"You know, I met Irene," I said. "I was buying lingerie with Claire, and she was in the shop. She's a bitter woman."

"I think she loved him. You'd think she was in it for the money, but no one I've talked to got that impression."

"I meant to ask—she was wearing these long cotton gloves. What's going on there?"

Wills looked awkward.

"I probably shouldn't tell you," he said. "I'm not sure that's for sharing."

"You probably shouldn't have let me into the morgue at two in the morning to play rate-the-crisps with her dead husband," I pointed out helpfully.

"I guess," he conceded. "Well, she self-harms. Apparently to cope with stress. Since Derowen died, I think it's got worse."

"Oh."

I couldn't think of anything else to say. Married as a young girl to a philandering tosser, loving him through all that humiliation and then losing him in such a violent way. I could understand it would take its toll. But slicing into your own flesh for release? That made me wince just thinking about it.

"No way they were defence wounds, Wills?"

"Absolutely not. Listen, sis, why is the coroner after you? I saw him at an inquest last week and he asked me for your number."

I'd forgotten all about that. I'd meant to ask Wills, but more serious events had driven it from my mind...

"I haven't a clue," I confessed. "His secretary Karen rang me on Friday, but I didn't listen to the message until yesterday. I'm hoping to see him on Monday."

"I doubt that. I think Monday's inquests will go on all day. He'll want to give those three poor Czech lads some attention after the events at the hospital. And that hopeless secretary of his has probably lost all the paperwork by now. Is there more coffee?"

I'd had enough of talking about death. Time to change the subject.

"How's Henry?" I said, pouring him a fresh cup. "Still gorgeous?"

"Absolutely always," he said with a smile.

The smile said it all. Jealousy isn't a nice emotion, so I hoped I didn't show any. Self-pity's not nice either, so I tried to hide that, too. But after my brother had left, I did sit in my kitchen for a while, wishing I could be in love with someone amazing who loved me back. And who didn't want to live a thousand miles away in a different country. Or beat me senseless when I disagreed with them. Or dreamed of a dead woman when they held me in their arms. Honestly, I didn't think I was being that picky.

I only realised after he had left that I had failed to super casually ask Wills about poor Lorraine, Nicky's tattooed dead girlfriend. I was cross with myself. The vampire had been more than good to me, and I'd forgotten all about him. I was clearly a bad, selfish necromancer who didn't appreciate when people were kind. I thought of calling my brother back, but I didn't know how I could oh-so-spontaneously work Lorraine into the conversation.

To distract myself from any self-flagellation that was going on in my brain, I took advantage of the rather lovely summer weather to mow the lawn and weed the rose border. I'd never been much of a gardener but then the cottage didn't have much of a garden. After a couple of hours, I was sitting on the grass with a jug of homemade lemonade, clad in nothing but cut-off jeans and a bikini top, and feeling smug.

I heard a car door go at the kerb and turned to look. It was a rather lovely cream-coloured Bentley. I knew it well, because it belonged to my boyfriend, soon to be my ex-boyfriend, the lovely Suki Junior, known to all his friends as Jay. He strolled across the lawn in the sun, looking more than handsome in a sand-coloured linen suit and a white shirt open at the neck.

"Hello, you," he said warily, sitting down next to me and kissing my cheek.

"Hello, you, too," I said, leaning into his kiss.

Then I didn't know what to do next, so I went and found another glass from the kitchen and poured him some iced lemonade. We sat in the sun together. The lawn slopes down to a wooded area that follows a stream-cum-drainage ditch down to the main stream at the bottom of the village. Some dragonflies had come up to dance on the lawn and tease the cat. Jay eventually reached across to take my hand.

"Sorry about Friday night," he said.

I looked at him. He was a lovely man. He was good company. And he was sexy—his paternal grandparents, who'd come to England from the Punjab fifty years before, had gifted him with good looks as well as a kind heart. He had golden skin, jet-black eyelashes a million times thicker than mine, and a very sweet smile. He had springy hair I loved to run my fingers through. And he was a thoughtful lover...

"There's nothing to forgive," I said.

And I meant it. I knew about loss—my parents and my grandfather had died together when I was eighteen. But he'd lost the love of his life and the mother of his children. I might have lost my past, but he'd lost his future.

"I'll give you some space," he said, reminding me that he was perceptive and clever along with everything else. "Elena's finished her A-level exams and I'm taking her to New York for three weeks. She's worked like a trooper, and she deserves a break."

"OK," I said easily, because maybe a break was all we needed, and time spent with his endlessly energetic eldest daughter would certainly stop him from brooding. "When are you off?"

"Tomorrow," he said.

I nodded, and he leant forward to press his warm mouth to mine. We kissed on the lawn in the sunshine for a while. Sunshine and kisses make for a dangerous combination. I was punch-drunk in moments despite having put nothing in the lemonade bar lemons and a handful of sugar.

And Jay was one of those men who drowned you in kisses... deep, passionate, make-your-head-spin kisses. They were kisses that made me gasp until I was panting. He twined one hand in my hair and tugged my head softly back until I was blinded by the sun in the sky and bewitched by the man in my arms. I completely forgot to wonder about how nosey my neighbours might be feeling or whether I had any deliveries due.

He must have shaved just before driving over. His skin was smooth and velvety and stubble free and I inhaled the scent of clean soap and shaving foam. I reached up to stroke his face with one hand and then follow the path of my fingers with my lips.

"I'm out of lemonade," I whispered. "Is there anything else you'd like?"

He put down his glass awkwardly on the lawn and it was the work of moments for him to consign my bikini top to oblivion and replace it with fingertips chilled by the ice. It was excruciating. And it was delicious. I squeaked with protest and then encouragement. Desire is like tinder—once it ignites, the flames just burn higher.

"I'll show you what I'd like," he said.

He replaced cold hands with his warm mouth, and I melted into his embrace like a little pat of butter. I lay back on fresh cut grass in the sunlight. He stroked me until his chilled hands were hot and tracked kisses across my torso until my entire body had turned into a taut erogenous zone of I-can't-wait. My cut-off jeans went the same way as my bikini top, and he was kissing the rest of me and fondling all the places that his kisses couldn't quite reach. And it was high calibre fondling. He had me writhing like a serpent and the heat of the sunshine became confused with the heat of my passion.

"I'm naked, sweetie, and you're wearing a suit," I said when he paused for a moment, and I recovered the power of speech. "And it's a lovely suit. I'd hate it to get grass stained."

"I'll show you grass stains," he pledged generously, but he went with the spirit of my words and the suit joined my cut-off jeans in being agreeably elsewhere and out of the way. "I'll show you a few other things as well if you're not busy."

"Not busy," I assured him. "So not busy. What were you going to show me?"

The sun overhead was still bright, so I closed my eyes. I felt Jay's mouth on mine, and the weight of his chest pressed me down into the grass. One hand pulled my hips to his, bringing us oh-so-close to where we were going...

"I'm going to show you how much I want you," he said, his breath coming faster.

And he did. I got the impression it was a lot. He showed me just what happens when a man aroused to the point of no return impales himself in a girl who's moments away from heaven. Good things, as it happened, quite excellent things. When he was done, I gave him time to catch some sunbeams and his breath and then showed him a few things in return. I got grass stains on my knees. And my elbows. And my hip bones. And elsewhere. We got a little carried away sampling a position I never seemed to get the hang of, and I got a mouthful of grass for my troubles. Sometimes, though, getting things wrong is the right thing to do. It means you get to try again.

Later we decided to wander inside and upstairs to my room to explore the underside of my eiderdown. Then it got too hot for the eiderdown, so we threw it on the floor. A little later the pillows got in the way too, so they followed. Afterwards, he picked blades of grass out of my hair and told me how beautiful I was. As I said, a thoughtful lover.

I still wasn't sure we were going anywhere, but he'd given me three weeks to work it out. Three weeks to work out if I was just being picky. Claire was always telling me I was picky, but then she was still single, too.

And I could kid myself that we were still together because I couldn't bear to hurt a man who'd already been hurt so much. But things are never that simple… I liked orgasms as much as the next woman. We were still together because it was still just about working.

Chapter Seven

WHEN JAY HAD left, I napped for a few hours. Then I showered and ate random things from the fridge. Camilla and Grace wouldn't pick me up until well after the sun had set, so I didn't expect them until ten. I put on a tiny, strappy sheath dress that I'd found in a jumble sale. It was made of pale yellow vintage silk with a beaded hem. I wore a lot of diamonds and some yellow kitten heels. I couldn't run in them, but anyone in the county who didn't wish me well would have to get past Grace first. They wouldn't stand a chance.

I also put my hair up into a chignon. It had taken Grace and Camilla weeks to teach me, but now I could do it myself with just a dozen hairpins and a mirror. And it was impossible to dress up too much for Emir's bar—vampires tend to have a soft spot for the fine things in life and they don't get the option of caviar or cognac. Vintage silk, a king's ransom in diamonds and posh hair? I would fit right in.

Just after ten, I heard laughter at my door, and opened it to find Camilla and Grace. Both were beautifully dressed—I'd made the right guesses—and they appeared to be much amused at something.

"What did I miss?" I asked, grabbing my bag and joining them on the porch.

Camilla merely giggled. Grace rolled her eyes.

"Camilla ran over a sheep," she said. "She hit it so hard it stuck to the bars on the front of my car. There was blood everywhere. Camilla put on the windscreen wipers, and it was like the prom scene from Carrie. I can't remember laughing so much since I tried to drink from a haemophiliac and ruined my leather coat."

"Sophy burst into tears and went home again," Camilla said. "We had to phone Aidan to come and remove the sheep because it was still wriggling and neither of us wanted blood on our clothes. He laughed so hard he dropped the sheep, and it bit him. I got hiccups. Grace won't let me drive it now."

The bars at the front of Grace's four-by-four did indeed look dented and sticky. There were traces of wool adhering to them... Well, she had a car built for taking out sheep and more, with its bull-barred front and smoked, bullet-proof glass windows. I'd teased her more than once that I couldn't find the button for the rocket launcher.

"You're all mad," I said, climbing into the back. "Please don't hit another one, because I already owe Aidan a favour and there is no way I want blood on this dress. Also, sheep are quite cute."

WE DIDN'T RUN over so much as a beetle on the rest of the drive, as far as I could tell. We drove through the woods to the bar without anything more exciting happening than the return of Camilla's hiccups. Summer nights aren't particularly dark, but the trees were packed densely enough to cut out most of the moonlight. Emir had clearly taken the view that if no one could find the place, he wouldn't get any unwanted guests dropping in. He didn't bother with signs, lights, tacks... We drove over the second cattle grid with a tooth-jarring rattle.

A hundred yards short of our destination, someone else had clearly had a high-impact evening. A dead stag lay just off the side of the track, its eyes glassy in a shaft of moonlight, hooves flung out in a dying gesture of protest. I watched him as he receded behind us into the blackness of the night. The local foxes and crows could look forward to a few days of venison. I felt a touch of envy. My kitchen hadn't seen a haunch of venison since the previous Christmas; Bredon and I were on budget ham until I made another decent commission.

In deference to footwear like mine, there was a gravel area just off the main track. A dozen or so expensive vehicles had parked there ahead of us. On the far side of the parking area, the ruins of Hawkeswaine Hall caught the light of the summer moon. It must have been a glorious building before it burnt down. The stone arch that remained was carved into curlicues at its zenith, and two dragons still perched on either side.

We walked beneath their empty gaze and across what must have once been a great hall. Now it was open to the sky, and it was hard to work out where the doors and walls must have been. The entrance to the cellar was where Emir finally admitted his bar existed. Two smoky torches illuminated the shadowy stairs that led down to the vaulted chambers where the long-dead earls of Hawkeswaine had stored their wine, cheese, venison and—legend had it—the peasant maids earmarked for their evenings of debauchery.

These days, or rather nights, it played host to debauchery of a different kind. I wasn't sure how Emir's business model worked—I'd never had to get so much as a pound coin out of my bag—but there always seemed to be a crowd of rather beautiful people. I pegged about a third of them as vampires, but unlike the occupants of the Stone House, they weren't perpetually squabbling with each other. I'd assumed that the rest were mortals, but now that Nicky had told me Emir was a witch, I wondered if perhaps the clientele was even more diverse.

It was about my sixth visit. I'd only ever come with Grace and Camilla, and while I hadn't felt the urge to visit without them, it now occurred to me to wonder if I could… would my car be stopped as it tried to drive through the shallow ford? If I made it to the stone arch, would I be kindly told to take my custom to somewhere more suited to my status, maybe to the burger stand behind Rugeley bus station… I'd driven to the Stone House many times, but I always got the impression that there was a list of names kept somewhere, and that if I were to drop off it at any point, my car certainly wouldn't make it to the top of the driveway. Did Emir also have a little list somewhere? Without my girlfriends, would my name even feature on it?

Emir had a table ready for us before we even entered the front of the bar—a trick he always pulled. I'd assumed CCTV was at work, but after Nicky's disclosure I wondered if it was something else. The world was darker and more numinous than most people realised. I was belatedly finding out that—necromancer or not—I hadn't realised quite how dark it was either. True, monsters didn't lurk under beds, but mostly because they'd found better places to lurk. I was currently preparing to drink champagne in one of those places.

I drank vintage champagne. I'd never tasted it before I met Oscar, and I now couldn't get enough of the stuff. It wasn't in my price range, but then the bill never seemed to land on my plate. As I walked in, I could see—and hear—Emir opening a bottle, and I knew it was just for me. Camilla would drink something sweet and creamy. Grace's tastes leant to beverages heavy on the haemoglobin.

Vampires like their scenery to be illuminated by moonlight, starlight or the flicker of flame. They like the shimmer of silk and satin, and have a fondness for slabs of black slate, granite and marble. They appreciate expanses of polished oak and burr walnut, punctuated by elements of wrought iron or brushed steel. Dark, buttoned leather goes down well, along with crushed velvet, vintage lace and gossamer curtaining.

Emir's bar had the lot, along with secluded banquettes, intimate recesses, little curtained alcoves and a selection of dark corners for doing dark deeds. As it happened, Camilla, Grace and I had little need for such privacy, typically having less intimate plans for our evenings out. Our favoured table was set next to the bar, close enough that Emir could sit with us in between serving other patrons. It was unoccupied, with four chairs ready. A glass of champagne in an old cut-glass coupe seemed destined for me. Something the colour of lemon curd awaited Camilla, garnished with a sliver of fruit.

Grace snorted.

"Anything for me, dearest Emir?" she said sweetly.

He sat down with us, undaunted by Grace's banter. He was an interesting looking man, not much taller than me but striking in appearance. Dark, hooded eyes under beetle brows set off a slim, elegant brown face. He had very white teeth and a knowing smile. He was always beautifully dressed, favouring something on the edge of black tie but with a little too much colour and too many paisley prints to fit the original brief. I liked him. A lot of people would have thought him short. I liked not having to crane my neck for once.

'There's a brunette in the back booth," he said. "If you're peckish, that is."

Grace laughed and took Camilla's hand. Turning it over, she kissed Camilla's wrist where the veins showed through underneath.

"I don't need to snack on barflies," she said. "I notice you have a new barman."

I glanced over at the mirrored recesses of Emir's inner sanctum. A tall young man with light blond hair and dark brown eyes was polishing glassware with a look of intense concentration and lining them up in neat rows. He was dressed in black with a paisley waistcoat in gentle homage to his boss. A crisp white cloth was thrown over one shoulder.

"A nice boy," Emir said. "He's come over from Prague looking for a coterie. He might as well make himself useful."

"He's set his sights high," Grace said.

"In Staffordshire? I suppose so, but there's nothing wrong with ambition."

Grace frowned suddenly and opened her bag, a miniscule, snakeskin bag with gold trimmings. She tipped out a sleek little phone and held it to her ear.

"It's my night off," she said brusquely after listening for a few moments. "Ask someone else."

There was another pause, and whatever was said brought a frown.

"Well, I will, then," she said. "But we either need Oscar back or we need to trade for someone else. I'm sick of this. Meet me on the main road."

She put the phone back in her bag and stood up.

"Ladies, I have to go. Camilla, you get to drive Toni back. Try not to run over any more livestock."

And before we could think how to respond, she was gone, a blur of vanishing vampire leaving behind the scent of irises and a somewhat despondent Camilla.

"Amazing," I said. "Benedict's managed to ruin our evening and he isn't even here."

"I don't mind so much," said Camilla. "But if we'd known, we could have gone out for fish and chips and a film together. You stay there, Emir—I'll ask your intern for a different drink. Something non-alcoholic, as it turns out I have to drive."

She walked to the bar and engaged the young man in playful banter. I watched them for a while, Camilla's elegant gestures, the young man a little shy and embarrassed by her flirting... I turned to Emir on impulse.

"If I came here on my own, would you let me in?"

"Of course! You'll always be welcome here."

He seemed genuinely surprised at the question. I shrugged.

"I'm never sure how these things work. And whenever I ask a vampire a question, I rarely understand the answer."

He laughed and gestured to the young man behind the bar who came and topped up my glass.

"It's all about status, Toni," Emir said. "Vampires and their pecking order. You have a lot of status, so having you here gives the place cachet. And that's worth a bottle of champagne or two, in case you're wondering why I never charge you."

"Me? Even after Oscar's rather extreme termination of our relationship?"

"Sure. As well as being close to Grace, you seem to be Benedict's pet project. He didn't lift his protection off you, even after you and Oscar parted, and it's well known he gave you his blood to heal you—something I've never heard of him doing for anyone else."

"And I guess no one has more status than Benedict."

Emir shook his head.

"Not really. He's a first-generation vampire as well as head of the Assemblage. Also, well, he's Benedict."

"What's the generation thing?"

Emir shrugged elegantly.

"Vampires originated in Southern Persia about three and a half thousand years ago. There were seven of them, apparently. Three are still around, and Benedict Akil is one, though I doubt that's well known outside England. They refer to themselves as the Children of Diometes, but I've no idea why. The further down the generations you go, the weaker they tend to be. Typically, they develop fewer powers. I don't know much more than that. Anyway, Benedict is a first-generation vampire... so no, you don't get much more status than that."

"So, Grace is second generation, Oscar third... What about someone like Nicky?"

"You know Nicky? Well, in terms of generation, maybe a hundred and twenty, hundred and thirty. So he certainly doesn't get status from his ancestry, and of course he's very young which doesn't help either. He has some because Benedict protects him and a bit more because his girlfriend's so beautiful, that little bitch Kirsty. But not a lot, and not as much as when he had his full coterie of glamour girls. Pretty low in the pecking order, our little Nicky. He might come here with Kirsty—she's something special and fiercely loyal to him—but he'd get a lot of snotty looks if he came on his own."

"Poor old Nicky," I said.

I meant it, too. The boy had managed to snare eternal life and it was filled with people looking down on him and the world's nastiest-ever girlfriend. He'd drawn every short straw going on after another. I drained my glass and held it out hopefully. Emir refilled it without a moment's hesitation.

"I meant to ask you, why doesn't this place have a name?" I asked him.

He shrugged.

"Come on, what would I call it that wouldn't be a wince-worthy cliché? The Virgin's Neck? The Haemoglobe Inn?"

I snorted.

"I do see your point."

At that moment, Camilla sat back down. She appeared to have acquired a milkshake.

"Why were you two talking about Nicky?"

"You don't like him?" I asked.

"I do, actually, though Grace says he's a nobody and I shouldn't bother with him. But I can't stand Kirsty, and she doesn't let him out on his own a lot."

"She didn't take to me," I said. "And I certainly didn't take to her. But she is amazing looking. Camilla, you look down. Do you want to go home?"

"Do you mind?"

"We can come another time."

We bid goodbye to Emir and to his barman, whose name turned out to be Jiří. We almost made it to the stairs before Camilla was collared by a mournful-looking vampire with an endless string of grievances he felt the urge to share. They made absolutely no sense to me, but he clearly hoped Camilla would convey them to Grace. Without a spreadsheet, I didn't have a clue how he thought she would keep track of them all, but I hung around until Camilla's eyes began to glaze, at which point my patience, never my strong suit, gave way.

"Sorry to interrupt, but she doesn't care and neither do I," I said helpfully. "Goodnight."

And I tugged Camilla up the stairs, keen to get to the top before the vampire remembered that he could rip off both of our heads with one hand.

"Thank you for the rescue," she said as we walked back through the warm evening air to where Grace's car was parked. "I feel sorry for him, but he hasn't a hope."

"What's his problem?"

"That's Peregrine Wall. He petitioned to come to Staffordshire from an Assemblage in Yorkshire. He's been here just under a year, but he hasn't delivered on any of his promises. At the end of the month, he'll have to find somewhere else to take him on or move to one of the unrestricted counties. He's been unlucky, but he was pretty lazy for the first seven or eight months, according to Grace. He'll never get an extension."

I shrugged. The ways of vampires were a mystery to me. Most of the time I was happy for things to stay that way.

Camilla opened the car and we wound down all the windows and set off back down the dark, overhung route through the woods. We made it about two hundred yards before there was a series of bangs and the car jerked viciously under us, swerved left and then spun to the right. Camilla braked frantically but to little effect. The bonnet of the car whacked firmly into the trunk of a tree with a smashing of glass and a crumpling of the bars that just an hour or so before had totalled a sheep. If we'd not been creeping along the forest track at a snail's pace, it would have been a lot worse. As it was, we were shocked and breathless.

"Oh no," wailed Camilla. "What have I done now? Grace is never going to let me forget this."

I glanced around the car. Lying on the track I could see pale, sparkly things, maybe a few dozen of them. I opened the door and walked unsteadily to the closest. I bent to pick it up, but managed to drop it and it tumbled a few yards, coming to rest just off the path in the light of the car headlamps. I followed and knelt to pick it out of the undergrowth. I held it in my hand and turned it round. It was a spiny thing of rough steel, four spikes coming from a central rivet so that however it landed, one would be pointing straight up, ready to tear into the rubber of a wheel. A modern-day caltrop, perfectly engineered for modern-day cars...

I realised the implications a moment too late, just as the metal spines in my hand were thrown into shadow by someone stepping between me and the car. I spun round to face him. He was silhouetted against the light, but I could make out enough to see that he was carrying a serrated knife the size of a scythe and wearing a rubber mask over his face.

"Camilla," I screamed. "Lock the car. Call for help."

And I turned and fled into the trees.

Chapter Eight

I WISHED I'D worn sturdier shoes and more clothes. I wished thorns weren't so sharp or so plentiful. I dearly wished that English woods weren't so full of undergrowth. But most of all, I wished I could see where the hell I was going.

I'd drunk enough vampire blood that my night vision was damn good. But it wasn't good enough to see my way through the tangled woodland by the pathetic bit of moonlight that was filtering through the trees.

I'd gone about thirty yards before I realised that my attacker wouldn't have to worry about being able to see. He'd be able to find me just by listening for the sound of a woman in inappropriate footwear falling over with every second step she took. I stopped fighting briars and dropped to the ground. Maybe if he couldn't see me and couldn't hear me either, I could just lay low until help came.

But the moment I stopped running for my life, my luck ran out too, because my pursuer turned on a torch nearly as bright as Stephen Hawking and began casting it around in my direction.

I swore under my breath. If I'd become an international spy or a jewel thief, or even joined the police like my brother, the occasional attempt on my life would be understandable. But I was an estate agent, damn it, and an honest one at that. People tried far harder than I deserved to wipe me off the face of the earth. It wasn't fair.

I also didn't have a lot of time, certainly not long enough for someone to respond to any pleas for help that Camilla could make, even if she knew the number of a fierce vampire who was loitering at Emir's right that very second. Ferns felt damp under my cheek. There were pebbles pressing into my calf. With my fingertips, I could feel soil, fallen leaves, perhaps the bones of dead birds. A live one, an owl, gave a hoot overhead.

"Come on, Toni," I whispered to myself. "Play to your strengths."

The trouble was, I couldn't think of any. The man in the mask was bigger than me, better clad for the task at hand and he had a torch. Oh yes, and a knife that appeared to be designed for gutting Godzilla. I was just a small redhead, flailing around in the bracken, clad in a nice yellow dress that was bound to reflect torchlight just beautifully when it chanced in my direction. And my special powers were pricing up real estate and raising the dead.

The dead... I pressed into the ground with my fingers. Countless woodland creatures must have breathed their last under these trees. I hadn't deliberately raised animals for more than fifteen years. They come up hungry and angry. It never ended well. But right now, it couldn't get a lot worse. I reached my energies down into the earth. No need to shed more blood. The briars had done that one little favour for me.

"I summon you," I murmured. "Come to me."

The torch had found me. It blinded me for a moment, and all I could see was an aureole of blazing sodium yellow. Then I heard footsteps, the crunch of leaves and moss underfoot. Boots stopped inches from my face, and through the acid glare of the torchlight I saw the gleam of light on metal, the serrated edge of the blade.

"I will kill everyone who stands between us," a softly accented voice whispered. "One by one, you will fall. Sophy loves me. You can't keep us apart."

The knife shifted in his grip. The torch slipped for a moment and the light caught his hand, the gloved knuckles contracting as he hefted his weapon...

But then the dead came to life under my touch. Not an owl, but the next best thing. A buzzard, its hooked beak and massive wings not really fully formed by my desperate flailing attempts at necromancy. A half-rotting and fragile creature, it nonetheless took flight and surged into the night air, screaming with hungry rage, and flew into the rubber-clad face of my attacker.

Without the mask he would probably have lost at least an eyeball, but as it was, all that the bird tore off was a strip of rubber around the cheekbone. He leapt back with a yell, tripped over a mound of heather and fell back onto his arse with a grunt that warmed my heart. I had bought myself two, maybe three, seconds, but it was all I needed to surge to my feet and run past him towards the road. I didn't think I could beat him back to the car but that wasn't where I was heading. I had another destination in mind.

It was where I remembered it from our drive, perhaps thirty yards further on than where we had ploughed the car into a tree. Glassy eyes, the broken jaw, one leg mangled by whatever impact had killed it... I didn't care. I skidded to my knees by the dead stag and placed my hands on its rigor mortised flank.

"You're next, sweetie," I whispered. "Up you get."

It scrambled to its feet in a furious rush, drowning out the sound of pelting footsteps just behind me. I flung myself to one side and the stag went past me with the snorting shriek of the angry undead and hurled itself at my pursuer.

Stags have antlers, but a lot of people don't realise they also have bloody sharp teeth and hooves like sharpened flint rocks. And if you get too close, all three sets of weaponry come into play. A cornered deer fights like a cat in a bag. As it turned out, so do dead ones.

It bowled him over with its antlers and went in with its front hooves before he could even sit up. He rolled over, got to his knees and lashed out with his knife, stabbing hard at tough, pelted skin, aiming for the delicate bits—sinews, eyes, throat. The knife went through like butter a dozen times, once right to the hilt. The stag didn't give a toss. It seized his knife arm in its teeth and worried it like a dog.

Rubber mask was done. Dropping his torch and his knife, he fled like a gazelle into the dark of the trees. The stag leapt after him, full of undead rage and hunger. I heard an uneven flapping of wings and realised that the buzzard was also in hot pursuit. The responsible part of me knew I should track them down and banish them. The tired, briar-gouged rest of me decided they could have a night of undead sport and rot when the sun came up. I slumped down by the side of the track and closed my eyes. The sounds of fleeing and undead pursuit faded away.

They briefly gave way to the orchestra of the night forest: owls, rustling leaves, the scurry of a fox. Briefly. Then there was shouting, the sound of a dozen vampires all trying to prove they were the toughest and the bravest. Thankfully they focused their attentions on Camilla, and it was only some minutes later that Emir approached me, holding a bottle and a crystal glass. I had caught my breath by then, and managed to drag myself to my feet and stagger most of the way back to the bar and lean my back against a tree. I wanted to just collapse on the bare earth in a nice comfy coma, but my dress was a little too short for sprawling on the path with decency.

"Camilla said a man in a mask chased you into the woods with a sword," he said, handing me a full glass of champagne. "And then got chased away by a giant red deer. Is she exaggerating?"

"Not a lot." I gestured to the knife, lying where it had been flung along with the torch.

"Fingerprints?"

"Gloves."

"Damn."

I drained my glass. He refilled it. About eleven seconds later he had to fill it again.

"Emir, did he get away?"

"I'm afraid so. Not a sign. Aidan and Grace are on their way. Do you know what he wanted?"

"It was Sophy's stalker. He said he'd kill everyone who was keeping them apart."

"Damnation. He needs catching!"

I felt suddenly exhausted. I thought of having to tell some kind of version of my tale over and over again to clever vampires who would know that deer don't attack humans and that a little mortal redhead, five-foot-nothing tall and armed with a caltrop and a bangle, wouldn't have made it through the scenario Camilla was describing... I caught Emir's hand.

"Will you take me home?" I said urgently. "Please, right now? I can't face any more this evening."

He looked at me thoughtfully, and I wondered if he was pricing up goodwill from me against bad will from the likes of Aidan and Grace... I rather thought he was. Then:

"I'll bring my car round. Wait here."

I leant against the tree. There was more shouting in the background, arrogant voices engaged in vampire one-upmanship. I saw a car slowly making its way around the track where Grace's four-by-four was still smoking. It drew up next to me and I opened the passenger door.

"Thanks," I said. "I appreciate this."

"Good, because Aidan may kill me."

"If it's Aidan you are worried about, he'll understand," I assured him as we set off. "I'll send him a text now and call him tomorrow."

"Please do," he said. "I prefer not having my business shut down."

I laughed. Now that I was no longer in danger of being gutted, and having just mainlined half a bottle of champagne, I was feeling all the euphoria of relief. I looked across at Emir, his face in profile as he peered at the twisting track through the trees.

"Nicky says you're a witch," I said.

The wheel jerked in his hands a touch and the car jumped on the road. He cursed under his breath and changed down a gear.

"Nicky shouldn't gossip," he said. "He shouldn't even know. That Holloway woman told him, of course."

"I'm a witch, too."

This time, he stopped the car. Just stopped it in the middle of the track and took it out of gear. He left the engine running and turned to look full at me.

"You share secrets very easily."

"Why not? I know yours, and I need someone to teach me."

"Witches don't teach, and they don't share, Toni. Not secrets, and not anything else for that matter. Witches stab each other in the back and steal each other's knowledge. Then they throw each other to the lions and lie about what they've done like it's going out of fashion."

I stared at him. He seemed perfectly serious.

"Well, maybe we could be different," I said, "because I'm not like that at all."

He didn't reply, just turned back to the road and put the car into gear. He drove me the rest of the way home in near silence, just asking for directions twice. When we got to the house, I had the sense to look around for my shaven-pated attacker, but saw nothing.

"Will you watch me into the house?" I asked. "Just stay until I am inside. There was some trouble over the weekend."

He nodded, still silent. As I opened the door he said suddenly:

"Come and talk to me. I don't have a phone and I rarely leave the woods, so come one night later in the week. I'll think about what you asked."

"Thank you!"

I beamed at him, but he held up his hand.

"I said I'd think about it, that's all. And bring an escort if you don't want to be propositioned. Grace's presence keeps them off you, but if you come on your own, that will change."

"I will, of course," I said, without really thinking about what he'd said. "Not a problem. Oh, and Emir…"

"What?"

"You should call it The Twice Shy."

"Call what the what?"

"Your bar. You know, once bitten…"

He groaned theatrically.

"Don't give up the day job, will you? Or your night-time one! Goodnight, Toni."

I got out of the car and waved to him. He stayed until my front door shut behind me and then, through the kitchen window, I watched him drive off into the night.

The house seemed free of homicidal maniacs, which made a nice change from the rest of my weekend. It contained a hungry cat, which I fed, and what looked like a million messages on the phone, which I listened to with a cup of tea.

"Hi, Ms Windsor. So sorry to bother you at the weekend, but it turns out that John is going to be tied up with inquests all day tomorrow. How does Tuesday sound? Give me a ring."

"Hey, sis. Listen, I found a guy who fits the bill for your second stalker. He is seriously not a nice man. Give me a ring. Love you."

"Toni, my darling, we're off. Elena says to text her details of what you want from the Big Apple. I think she wants an excuse to go to Fifth Avenue. I'll miss you."

"Lav, darling. Totally bored—where are you? Run out of vodka and there is nothing on the box. Call me before I start on the liqueur cupboard. What is crème de menthe anyway?"

"You stay away from Nicky, do you hear me? He's mine. We don't need your help and I don't want you around. Don't you dare speak to him again. Ever."

"Hey, angel, it's me. Listen, Lorraine's body isn't due to be released until Friday. They want a second lot of tox reports. Keep you posted."

"You little thieving, murdering bitch. Don't think this ends things between us. It only makes them worse. I'm still watching you. Got it?"

I stared at the phone. I got it—my life had become way too complex again. Vampires will do that. They just complicate your existence to hell and back. I needed to de-vampire my life. I shrugged and finished my tea. I'd tried elbowing the children of the night out of my affairs before. They were harder to get rid of than gonorrhoea and way worse for your health. I was stuck with them. I rinsed out the mug, trudged up the stairs and crawled into bed.

Chapter Nine

MONDAY DAWNED, MUGGY and hot, sweltering enough that I wondered if we were due for a summer storm. I abandoned thoughts of wearing anything warmer than a sundress and scrabbled through the piles of clothing on my floor for something clean that didn't need ironing. As I did so, I glanced sadly at the mud-stained, briar-torn skanky wreck that a few hours ago had been my vintage silk cocktail dress. After its adventures, it could look forward to a new career as a duster or possibly a glass cloth. At best. Sighing, I chucked it in the bin. I didn't dust and I certainly didn't polish glass. Its uses to me were limited.

I shook a few leaves out of my hair and examined myself in the bathroom mirror. My legs and arms were covered in a patina of scratches that suggested I'd gone six rounds with a basket full of kittens and come in a poor second. A bruise the size of a fried egg adorned one knee. I picked out something full length and floaty to mask my legs and covered up my wrists by adding a little crocheted cardigan. It was too warm for either, let alone both, but at least I wouldn't scare off the clientele.

I drove to the office in a distracted mood, broken only by a disturbing and intermittent clanking noise from the engine. A week ago, my biggest worry had been getting a jacket that matched my new apricot suede mules and hoping Paul didn't hire a prostitute while he was in Amsterdam. Now I had at least two suicidal maniacs after me, a wistful vampire to look after, and a murdered millionaire to find justice for. I also realised, with a little sinking feeling, that I had zero commission payments banked from my job—not ideal if my car was going to throw an expensive hissy fit on me. It was time to set some priorities: I needed to sell some property and then I needed to buy some wine.

Bernie and Bethany were squabbling good-naturedly over the wording of our monthly advert. Bernie wanted us to sound upmarket. Bethany worried that would deter people who were selling or buying in the two-up two-down terrace in Doxey range… I thought Bethany would win this one as she was currently spilling out over one of lowest cut of her summer tops.

"What do you think, Toni?" Bernie broke off to say as I flung myself down in my chair.

"I agree with Bethany," I said, turning on my computer and leafing through the post.

"You haven't even looked at the wording yet!"

"Shocking, isn't it? Bernie, I need money."

"Don't you have a rich boyfriend?"

"Yes, and I do that for free."

"Then you're undercharging. Helen costs me a fortune. And you spend it all on clothes anyway."

Helen was a good friend of mine. She and Bernie had been engaged for more than a year. I wasn't sure she should be marrying Bernie, but I wasn't in a strong position to criticise other people's relationship choices. I didn't have a stellar history in that capacity myself.

"Nonetheless, I am once again impoverished. Partly due to a lingerie expedition with Claire, I admit, but still broke."

"Marvellous. Model it for me, and I'll give you a bonus."

I sighed. Bethany rolled her eyes in silent solidarity. Bernie had hidden depths, but they were jolly well hidden. I'd been tempted to use a JCB to find them more than once.

"In your dreams. And my nightmares. No, I'm going to make a list of everything that's been on the market for twelve months and call them all to drop the price. Then I'm going to do the same with all our landlords who've been looking for a tenant for more than six weeks."

It was an unenviable task, but it kept me busy. It kept me from brooding too much on the rather unwelcome turn that my life had taken, namely one where people were interested in putting a full stop to my life or opening up my jugulars.

Mid-morning, Wills rang, and we agreed to meet for lunch. It turned out that phoning up endless lists of disappointed clients built up an appetite. I drove out to The Fat Fox and was persuaded to try Freddy Omaha's special of the day, a grouse burger with fat chips. My brother stuck to the venison casserole—he'd always been the more traditional sibling.

"So," I said, after I'd eaten enough gamey goodness to be able to hold a conversation. "Who's the rapey stalker who's shadowing my house, then?"

"That's one thing he hasn't gone down for yet, as it happens, but don't think that makes him Mr Nice. His name is Grahame Martin, known as Gin Martin. The age and description fit, but more to the point he was cellmate to our tattooed Spider-Man two years ago. He's got some connection with Staffordshire, too. His parents lived near Lichfield. He left home and moved to Shirley when he was about sixteen."

"Tell me about him—you said he really wasn't a nice person..."

Gin Martin had come from a good family. That might be the only decent thing about him. He'd started sniffing glue at school, working up the ladder to become an unsuccessful coke dealer by the time he was fourteen. An awkward period of stealing from his family, friends, neighbours, and distant hangers-on had been terminated when he'd pawned his grandfather's war medals, and his long-suffering parents had finally thrown the little turd out on the street. Several stays at Her Majesty's pleasure had gradually increased in duration as casual thieving gave way to mugging, armed robbery and eventually manslaughter. A security guard had put up some resistance. Gin hadn't held back. His subsequent staycation had been for nine years. He'd got out about ten months previously.

"But Wills, what in heaven's name does this have to do with me? I've never met him, never heard of him. Damn it, I've only ever been to Shirley once, and that was on a traffic diversion."

My brother was chewing a big mouthful of casserole. He chomped, swallowed and shrugged.

"Sis, it was the weekend. It was thirty-six degrees. Everyone was down at Lickey Hills or up at Dovedale. Not a lot of people were answering their phones. The ones that did had drunk a litre of Pimms. Give me a couple more days. I'll turn something up."

We ate in silence for a little while. I liked spending time with Wills. We didn't have any other family that we knew well enough even to send a Christmas card to. To be sure, there was a cousin somewhere and the odd aunt and uncle I'd maybe met once as a child, but not people we were in contact with. I didn't mind too much—extended families always seemed to come with a lot of demands and expectations plus their own internal feuds and squabbles—but it meant that Wills and I were pretty special to each other.

The end result, though, was that I couldn't risk him getting involved with any vampires. I just couldn't. And that left me in the awkward position of having to deceive someone I was normally scrupulously honest with. I didn't dare to tell my brother that Dylan Moss had bled to death on my kitchen floor. And with that in mind, I really wanted Aidan to get to Gin Martin before the police did and compel him to forget what he'd seen that night. I swallowed a mouthful of delicious grouse burger, took a deep breath and changed the subject.

"So," I said, as casually as I could muster. "Any news on that girl who was in the morgue?"

"A little. Her name was Lorraine Keel. She lived with a girlfriend out Stoneydelph way. She left a note saying things weren't working out. The friend didn't keep it. Next thing we know, Lorraine flung herself into a mineshaft up on the Chase. We've asked for tox reports because she had no history of any mental problems or drug abuse."

"Poor thing."

"There's no accounting for people. She was barely dressed—on the only cold day we've had in weeks—with nothing on her feet. They were ripped to shreds on the gorse by the time she got to the mine. There was a man who followed her but lost her before she killed herself. He said she was singing crazy stuff about a golden bird leading her to heaven."

"Could he have done it?"

"I don't think so. He's an old chap, a retired marine. Invalided out because he only has one arm and a dodgy knee. He couldn't have carried her a single step, let alone over the fence that surrounds the mine, and no way could he have flung her right in. It does look like a case of someone just spontaneously going crazy, so no point in dragging you in. You've always said you can't raise suicides."

I squinted at him over my burger. No, I couldn't. But Nicky had lost three members of his coterie in three months. And he wasn't exactly scary. If they'd all killed themselves, I'd eat my hat.

"Nope, can't do that," I agreed. "Any update on poor old moneybags Polkerris?"

"That whole thing just gets stranger. The report on the body is insane. From the positioning of the bruises, we are now pretty sure he was struck on the head while he sat at his desk. The room has an old fireplace and whoever knocked him out used the poker. It has a heavy brass ball on the end. Then they stabbed him repeatedly with the letter opener. He would have bled to death in moments. Then finally—get this—they dressed him in the heavy winter coat that was hanging on the coat rack."

"What? After he was dead?"

"Definitely. There's very little blood on the coat. And it was buttoned up, but there are no knife holes in it. He wasn't wearing it when he died. And just in case we weren't confused enough, the secretary and the electrician swear the body was slumped against the door when they went in—they are adamant that they had to shove it out of the way with the door to get in."

"So someone came and went through the window? Or the chimney?"

"The chimney's blocked up with a metal board. The window is a possibility. But the office is on the second floor. We found no signs of a ladder or any marks in the grass where it would have stood. And the wall below the window is sheer, no creepers or features."

"We're right back to teleporting pixies then?"

"Or someone who can jump sixteen feet from standing and then back down again. Maybe he was killed by levitating badgers, sis. It's as likely as any other explanation we've come up with."

We chatted about less gruesome things over pudding. I knew that Wills was deeply unhappy about Gin Martin. But he also knew that I'd resist any attempts to put a watch on my house. I needed to raise the dead. Needed to, not wanted to. It was a compulsion. I could miss the odd night here and there, sure, but more than that and I'd start doing it accidentally. We were never ever going to be able to go back to the restaurant where I'd had the stuffed quail starter after a heavy cold had kept me indoors for a week. A waiter had been badly pecked. Customers had fled into the kitchen. The maître d' still thought it was a very tasteless practical joke gone wrong. I wasn't going to disillusion him.

Wills was still frowning as we walked back to our cars. He held me by my shoulders and looked at me in some concern.

"Could you stay at Jay's house?" he asked. "He has a lot of security. Or you could doss down with me and Henry for a while. He's filming a lot this month, so you could get away at night no questions asked."

The empty house of ecru and beige? I shuddered at the thought.

"I'll think about it," I lied. "Thanks for the offer."

And I hugged him very thoroughly. I didn't have a lot of family, true, but I had Wills, and he was worth a million uncles, cousins and aunts. Of course, it also meant neither of us got dragged out to too many funerals, christenings or destination weddings, a curiously underrated benefit of small families.

I DROVE BACK to the office with too much on my mind. I seemed to be barrelling towards being single again before I'd even got used to being half of a couple. Worse, it appeared I was being dragged back into the world I thought I'd left behind me, where the undead and the living seemed to be vying to see who could take me out first. I decided to put all thoughts of corpses, would-be murderers and scary stalkers from my mind and concentrate on phoning vendors and landlords for the rest of the afternoon.

I was working through what I called the granny flat list—people who rented out an annex of their own home for income—when I came across a name that jolted me out of work mode.

"Bernie, this Keira Holloway we manage the attic flat for: is she the lady who runs the salon out Stonydelph way?"

"That's the one. Why?"

I scanned the paperwork and searched for a reason.

"None of her tenants seem to stay very long. Look: six months, eight months, four months... this one didn't even stay out her notice period and had to pay for five weeks after she'd gone."

"Oh, that flat. I remember now. Keira converted it for her daughter but for whatever reason the girl never moved in. All the tenants say the woman is creepy as hell and they can't stand it there. We need to find her an old, retired army chap with a skin as thick as a rhino's, but the flat is so pretty that it always gets snapped up by twenty-something lasses who then get creeped out by Mrs H."

Creepy, was she? That seemed at odds with someone who ran a successful hair salon. I dialled the number in the file and a woman's voice answered.

"Stoneydelph Hair and Beauty, Keira speaking."

"Is that Mrs Holloway?"

"Yes, dear, it is."

"Mrs Holloway, it's Toni Windsor here..."

There was a gasp, and the phone went dead in my hand. I rang back, but no one answered. I rang four or five times over the course of the afternoon. Eventually a girl's voice answered. She turned out to be the manicurist and said that Keira had gone home with a headache. I could try tomorrow... I said I would.

"Bernie, what's this Keira Holloway like?"

Bernie looked up from where he was building a little castle with his business cards. It was three storeys high. The man had real talent.

"Older lady, late sixties, early seventies maybe, very handsome still. Flashy dresser. I got the impression from something she said that she had a troubled youth. Divorced, one kid, I think." Another card went down. "Makes a lot of money from the salon, more than you'd expect. She bought a five-bedroom house through us shortly before you joined. Georgian place, just off the dual carriageway. Cash buyer. Only met her twice."

Nothing rang a bell. I'd never met the woman at all, and it sounded as though she was my more my grandfather's generation than mine. Why had my name alarmed her so much that she'd hung up and fled? I pondered the question on and off for the rest of the afternoon. On my drive home, I was distracted by the noise of my car. The engine was no longer making an intermittent clanking noise. It had switched to making a more regular grating sound. It sounded serious. Scratch that: it sounded expensive. Ah well, it would have to wait – just like my gas bill and the leak in the roof by the downpipe…

I parked my car at the kerb, scouted for potential murderers, and—seeing none—I let myself into the house and double-locked the door. I could have gone to raise the dead with Aidan. I could have found myself an escort and gone to chat witchcraft with Emir. I could have texted Jay and told him to book me on the next available flight to join him in New York. Claire was probably free for cocktails if I wanted. Oh, I had plenty of options.

But I didn't have the energy for any of them. I took the phone off the hook, made a large plate of cheese toasties and finally took my nice little bottle of vodka out of the freezer. A year before, I would have whiled away despondent evenings like this by watching crap television or listening to miserable music. But not these days. These days I had an even more depressing way of filling the hours. I sat down at my laptop and re-read five months of correspondence from Peter.

There were letters telling me how happy he was that patient A was responding to treatment and his delight that patient B could now be discharged to their parents. There were paragraphs detailing the kind donation a millionaire parent had made, pages and pages on the marvellous new equipment the clinic had installed with the money... There was a whole letter talking about some great new painkiller that had just been licensed for use in Germany.

Oh, and there were reams about how completely he loved me, how much he adored every single atom of my being, how badly he missed me, how every time he closed his eyes he saw my face, my form, my features... There was enough of that to warm the cockles of the hardest heart. But not mine anymore.

Because there was not a single line saying that he was looking forward to seeing me, nor suggesting when we would meet, when we could finally be together, not for a night, for an hour, for even a single damn moment in time. There was no invitation. There was no calendar date. There were just words. I was getting very, very sick of words. Not even Peter could sustain my affections on persuasive handwriting alone. Oscar had killed my love for him with a single blow. Peter was slowly torturing it to death with his endless bloody words.

I always found myself bemoaning my terrible taste in men, but this time I didn't think I was the one at fault. Hadn't Peter and I been perfect together, made for one another? Just this once, I felt my taste had been spot on. How was it my fault that Peter was hung up on some crappy ex just because Oscar was simultaneously charming, hot as hell and a god in the sack? Oh, and also a psychopath who'd been dead for three hundred years. Seriously, Peter was way better off with me.

I didn't drink the whole bottle. Not quite.

Chapter Ten

TUESDAY DAWNED, I wished it wouldn't. It was hot and bright. I was hungover as hell.

I stood in the shower until it went cold, hating the water for being so noisy and jetting so firmly into my pounding temples. My scratches were starting to heal but I still looked like the victim of a crack elite squad of attack cacti, so I found another long summer dress. Most of the marks on my arms were below my elbows, so I added lace gloves. Then I drove slowly to work wearing sunglasses.

I hadn't expected to enjoy the day under any circumstances. It was exactly seven years to the day since my parents and grandfather had died. The anniversary always left me feeling despondent. The self-inflicted nausea and pounding headache were almost a pleasant distraction. Almost.

I was late, Bernie was grumpy, and Bethany was in floods of tears. It turned out that she hadn't known Paul was in Amsterdam until a mutual friend had mentioned it in the coffee shop that morning. She'd dumped him two weeks previously, but she'd intended him to stay in his room playing the drums and mourning the loss of her affections, not rollicking away until the small hours with his mates in one of Europe's top party destinations. I didn't think she would get him back. The trip to Amsterdam had been booked for weeks. Paul had seen this coming.

Bernie and I sent her out to buy stationery. We didn't need any, but the sound of breathless weeping didn't add to Bethany's limited phone technique.

Due to my tardy start, I'd already missed what could well turn out to be a seriously revenue-generating telephone call. Irene Polkerris had rung, and she had asked for me by name. She wanted me to find her a place to retire to in Dartmouth. Would I contact Crispin and schedule a time to visit her? There was a phone number...

"I seriously doubt she's actually thinking of a seniors' retirement flat by the coast," I said. "This isn't a woman who's after a granny annex with a stair lift."

"Two hundred foot of river frontage with parking for six cars and adjoining flat for staff."

"She never said that."

"No, but a tenner says she will."

I thought of Irene Polkerris, bitter, lonely and drunk in the lingerie boutique. Many women would have been vengeful, victorious. She just seemed bereaved.

"I'll find her somewhere lovely," I said. "Somewhere beautiful she can rebuild her life."

"Make sure you find her at least seven figures of lovely," said Bernie. "If you're going to go gallivanting all the way to the south coast at the woman's beck and call, we should at least get a decent commission. Go and find out what she wants, and I'll draw up a deliciously swingeing contract."

"You're in a beautiful mood."

"Bean and Heron has VAT payments due."

"You always have VAT payments due."

"I blame the government for its intransigent insistence on charging me VAT. Are you going to ring this woman?"

The Crispin in question turned out to be a secretary of some kind. Unlike Bethany, he had an exquisite telephone manner and a lovely English voice. He was so very pleased I'd called. Irene would be simply delighted. Could I come the following afternoon at four? That was just perfect. Everyone was so grateful. I felt soothed and appreciated.

It was like getting a massage through the earpiece. If I ever became a billionaire, I would track Crispin down and poach him. Just having him read the weather forecast to me over breakfast would set me up for the whole day.

I rang the coroner's office next. The phone was answered by Karen, not one iota less chirpy than her phone messages had suggested.

"Ms Windsor, how lovely to speak with you after all this time," she said when I'd introduced myself.

All this time—what on earth was she talking about? She'd only left her first phone message three days ago. I was more confused than ever.

"Um, yes, absolutely," I said vaguely. "So, I could come in tomorrow morning. Say eleven?"

"Super. If you and John can get all the paperwork sorted pronto, I'm sure he'll want to take you out to lunch."

Really? I'd met the man just twice, both times at my annual industry party. There weren't a lot of inquests in Staffordshire and the post of coroner was definitely part time. When not ruling on probable cause of death, Mr John Jones also worked as a solicitor, a little one-man practice. He drew up and executed the occasional will. I knew he also did a little light conveyance work, the legal finagling of buying and selling houses. I'd even recommended him to clients, all the old ladies who I thought would benefit from his old-world charm.

But we weren't friends and, while I thought I'd know him on sight, I wasn't one hundred per cent certain. I didn't think he'd been acquainted with anyone in my family, either, but the effusive Karen's words suggested a shared history of something, something I was completely clueless about.

I thanked her and entered both appointments into my diary. When the time came, I would wing it. I was used to that.

I worked my way a little further through my lists, but I was distracted. When Bethany came back, her eyes still red and swollen, I took a long look at her. She was pretty and flirtatious. I didn't know any bad of her. But she didn't have the serious streak that characterised Paul, or his innate sweetness. I rather thought my lodger's single status would hold. He had all my sympathy. No one knew how that felt better than me.

Maybe I had some inner sweetness, too, after all.

I drove home in the afternoon sun, stopping only to buy wine and chocolate and take a break from the heat of the car. The noises from the rust-mobile—which pre-dated air conditioning by many years—continued to escalate, ruining what would otherwise have been a pretty journey alongside the river. I arrived at the cottage in Colton to find something much prettier and utterly unruined in place, namely Henry Lake, my brother's beautiful boyfriend, topless in the sunshine and attacking my house with an electric drill.

I stood and watched for a while. Who wouldn't? Henry was one of the best-looking men I'd ever seen. He was as English as Henry or I were, but he'd got his divine good looks from his Jamaican forebears. And he was as kind as he was handsome. My brother had scored the jackpot. I hoped he knew it.

Wills had also told me that Henry was pretty busy—but for whatever reason, he'd decided to spend what little downtime he had on me. It was typical of the man. I would have been even more grateful if I had a clue what he was doing.

"Hey, call the rozzers," I said cheerfully. "There's a half-naked man drilling holes in my wall."

"I already called them," he said, putting down the electric drill and coming over to give me a dusty, sweaty hug that nearly made me swoon. "They said they'd be off work about six and would pop round for a beer. I should have this finished by then."

"That's great—I think. What exactly are you doing?"

"Wills told me about your stalker, petal. I'm fitting you a personal security system. It doesn't actually do anything yet, but the cameras will put most people off. They're just bits left over from the set I put in for my dad at the yard. Looks damn impressive though."

"Ah."

He was right. My attacker would probably stop short of assaulting me in my own home if he thought the images were being beamed worldwide in real time. Elsewhere I might need other deterrents, but I could probably sleep safely in my own bed at night. I didn't spend a lot of time in it these days, but it was a kind thought.

I made us each a tumbler of gin and tonic, garnished with ice and a slice and a slug of bitters, and took them out onto the porch. I watched while he ran wires and cables through a hole in the wall, which he then carefully backfilled with white paste.

"Was this Wills' idea?"

"It was mine, pet. I had most of the bits lying around and a day off. I won't finish it in one go, but it will look good."

"Thank you."

"Any time. Um, pet, I think Wills may drop past your parents' grave on the way back."

Ah. I made a mental note to put even more beer in the fridge... My feelings towards my parents were mixed at best, and certainly very confused. Wills just missed them bitterly.

"Oh, that. Henry, I don't go there anymore."

"I can't blame you. Everything Wills has told me... sounds like you had the pointy end of the pineapple."

"Does he say that?"

Henry screwed a final bracket into place and stood back to admire his handiwork. I stood back to admire Henry.

"He told me that when you were about seven, your parents stopped talking to you. Like, not a single word ever again. He said it was like they pretended you didn't exist. It must have been just incredibly hurtful. I mean, I can't imagine how that would feel."

Not good, was the simple answer. If my grandfather hadn't been there to bring me up, I might have starved to death. Neither my mother or father would ever have noticed...

"I was quite young, Hen, and after that Grandfather Robert just stepped in to look after me, but I do sort of remember when it happened."

"Wills says he remembers the actual hour."

"What?"

"That's what he said. He also told me that when he was about sixteen, he had a huge row with your parents about it. He was shouting at them, telling them how badly they treated you and that he wouldn't stand for it any longer. He said your mother just started crying and said over and over that she'd always wanted a daughter. He said it was so upsetting that he never tried again."

"Oh."

We talked easily, my brother and I. We talked about food, relationships, zombies, money... you name it, all without restraint. I hadn't thought there were any taboo topics. But in fairness, this was one I generally tried to introduce only after I was horribly drunk or once I'd already started crying. Sometimes both. I could understand why we hadn't made a lot of progress on it. Henry's words made me wonder if I shouldn't broach it one sunny afternoon when I was feeling cheerful. And stone cold sober.

I hugged Henry.

"Thanks," I said, and I meant it. "I never knew he did that for me. Are we done out here?"

"For today, pet. And my glass is empty."

When Wills joined us, he was quiet. I thought he didn't want to mention the date, so I just poured him a beer. We joked about less sensitive topics, like who might be staking out my house and trying to kill me and whether chimpanzees should be granted basic human rights.

Henry: "Of course."

Me: "Monkeys are creepy."

Wills: "Sis, I think they're apes, not monkeys."

I waved them off shortly afterwards. Wills pressed me again to come and stay but I turned him down. I had my scary cameras now, and my trusty guard cat. Way better than a monkey any day.

Then I had a second shower and put up my hair. I dug out the laser-cut suede dress that Camilla had given me in the New Year. I teamed it with all my diamonds and some black leather stilettos that would have given Grace a run for her money if anybody could have run in them. Then I teetered all the way to my car and drove out to Stoneydelph. I parked two minutes' walk from Nicky's house and waited for the sun to set.

I texted him as the sky went dark:

Will you come to the bar with me? I need an escort.

His reply came twenty minutes later:

Sure. Can you pick me up? PS: You're safe! Kirsty is at her mum's.

Nicky opened the door as I parked the car at the old rectory. He was dressed much the same as before, tight leather trousers—this time in dark navy—and a cream shirt with more lace on it than my underwear drawer. Somehow, he'd got his own cufflinks in this time. His eyeliner matched the leather trousers and his hair hung in an ice-white shimmer to his shoulder blades.

He bounded down the stairs with a long gait and smiled at me as he opened my door. He had the palest blue eyes of any vampire I'd ever seen. He courteously reached out a slim hand and helped me to my feet.

"I didn't think I'd see you so soon," he said in his gentle voice. "You're lucky Kirsty was out. If she'd answered the phone and heard your voice, she'd probably have staked me by now. Come in while I find a jacket."

His smile was very slightly lopsided, not quite symmetrical. I hadn't noticed before. Somehow it suited him.

"Nicky, she's a horrible person," I said, following up the steps into the hall. "Why are you even with her?"

"Come on, angel. Who cares about personality with looks like that? I haven't seen a continental shelf more impressive since *Life on Earth* went off the air."

"You don't mean that! That's despicably shallow."

"Believe me, there is nothing shallow about that continental shelf."

"Nicky!"

"Seriously, Toni, she wasn't this bad when I first met her. And she could have anyone, but she's stuck with me. Even when I transitioned, she didn't leave me. I couldn't desert her now."

"That's why you're still together?"

He didn't answer straight away. He dropped his gaze to the floor as he led me through the hallway. Then he shrugged one slim shoulder and swept the curtain of hair back from his face. I noticed belatedly that his eyebrows perfectly matched his hair.

"You don't bail on people," he said. "She's loyal to me. I owe her."

I searched for a change of subject.

"What's with the hair, Nicky? It can't be natural."

We'd reached the kitchen. It was the size of my house with acres of pale beech and stainless steel. A host of appliances gleamed at us. I didn't see Kirsty as a cook. Who of Nicky's lost coterie had wanted a sous-vide and an Italian ice cream maker?

"I bleached it when I was alive," he said, picking up a longish swede coat from the back of a chair. "After I transitioned, it stayed this way. You want a drink?"

I shook my head.

"Not really—we should get going," I said vaguely. "Though while I am here, maybe I could look round? Just for a few minutes... If I'm to work out what happened to your coterie, I should try to get a feel for them. You know, what they were like."

Lily's room was an explosion of white, broken up only by some beautiful watercolours, seascapes in brilliant hues. It was charming but unfussy. The bathroom was bare of cosmetics. Toothpaste and a bar of soap appeared to have been her sole beauty routine. In the wardrobe, jeans and casual t-shirts rubbed shoulders with a battered leather jacket. Lily wasn't a high maintenance girl.

"She was a painter," said Nicky, breaking into my thoughts. "She did these."

"They're lovely. Nicky, was she pretty?"

"Probably you wouldn't think so, but she was adorable. She was kind, thoughtful... She was so peaceful to be with. I remember thinking when Kirsty brought her home for the first time how lucky I was. She was my favourite. All the vampires in Heidelberg said to be careful when you have a favourite. Make sure the others don't get jealous. But she was just so sweet."

Caroline and Lorraine had shared a room. It was a riot of chaos and hair spray. Nail varnish jostled for space with shoes. Eye shadow elbowed flagons of perfume out of the way. A bed the size of a football pitch was piled with frilled pillows and fluffy toys. There were four kinds of curling tongs. I felt right at home.

"Were they lovers?" I asked.

He nodded, picking up a pillow and idly plumping it.

"They were lovely girls, heaps of fun," he said. "Always giggling, laughing. Caroline was forever plaiting my hair. They were both hairdressers. I suppose that's how they met Kirsty. This is my room."

I hadn't asked, but I followed him in. It wasn't unlike the previous bedroom, though slightly less disordered and with a gentle scent of excruciatingly expensive aftershave. There was also a shelf that drew my attention.

"You're a photographer. I didn't know," I said. "OMG, this is a Leica! You must be good."

"I was the total weirdo at school, angel," he said. "Can you imagine? Goth, computer geek, hand-developed film… I don't use the camera anymore though. Not since I died."

"Why not?"

There was a pause.

"I only ever took pictures in natural light."

"Oh. Nicky, I keep saying the wrong things. I'm so sorry. And you must miss them so, your girls."

"Lavington, this house is like a bloody mausoleum. I hate it. And I have to go over to the Stone House or the bar almost every night to feed and it drives Kirsty mad. I've been wondering for weeks what I'd been doing wrong to drive them away, but now it's worse. It looks like the three of them were killed when it was my job to protect them. And I loved them. I'd have done anything for them. I'm still praying I've jumped to conclusions here."

I looked at him in concern. His ice-blue eyes were glossy with tears. I didn't want to embarrass him, so I pretended I hadn't noticed and headed back down the stairs.

"Even Kirsty?" I asked in jocular tones.

He laughed a little forlornly.

"She's not very lovable, I know, but she had a hard life. I think I said that her mum went to prison when she was a teenager, and it broke up the whole family. The courts gave Kirsty over to her dad, and he took her to the south coast. It was to get her away from the shame of it, from people who knew the truth, but of course it meant leaving all her friends."

To prison? Nope, that was news…

"I didn't know. What for? I mean, what did she do?"

"She was importing exotic ingredients, the worst kind—rhino horn, tiger teeth, leopard pelt, turtle shells. She got six years. It was tough for Kirsty—she and her mum are close even today."

I looked at Nicky. He had lost his usual spark and his indolent energy had evaporated.

"Come on, Nicky, let's get out of here. You need cheering up and I need a drink."

I dragged him down to my car and we headed off. He was quiet for most of the drive, but as we turned into the woods he suddenly asked:

"Why do you need to visit the bar?"

"I need to see Emir, and he's pretty nocturnal. Also, he said I'd need an escort and you're one of the only vampires I actually like."

"He's right. You'd get hassled without one. Especially the way you keep everyone guessing."

"What do you mean by that?"

"You were with Oscar for a few months. Then you spent a week with Benedict. Now you turn up with Grace. All very high-status vampires… you certainly get tongues wagging. Suggests you're still window shopping, not decided yet on what you're taking to the till. You'd get a lot of attention if you turned up alone."

I hadn't thought of it that way. I didn't want to look like some fickle vampire groupie, playing eenie-meenie, available for overtures… I narrowed my eyes at Nicky. He had a big, fat vacancy in his coterie. I didn't want him thinking I might fill part of it.

"I'm done with all that," I said firmly. "Oscar cured me of any inclination to shack up with the fanged community. You nightwalkers can find someone else to snack on."

"Well, even if you weren't, I am not vain enough to think you'd choose me over Grace," Nicky said. "Or Oscar."

"I thought we'd agreed Oscar was an absolute wanker? And doesn't everyone know he tried to kill me?"

Nicky shook his head.

"He's short tempered and has no self-control; I doubt he meant anything, just lashed out, so he probably thinks it's all in the past to you, too. And he was fuming when Benedict sent him away. He still wants you back."

"What!"

"I've heard the gossip. He wants to be allowed back to Staffordshire so that the two of you can pick up where you left off."

"That's never going to happen," I said firmly as I turned the car with a jerk onto the gravel parking area by the bar. "I'm done with him. I'm done with vampire lovers, full stop. They're just a whole heap of trouble and I can get into enough of that on my own."

Chapter Eleven

THE SCENE SEEMED unchanged from my previous visit. The trees loomed, the moon provided insufficient light, and the gravel was unsteady under my shoes. Sophy's prowler would find me an easy target. However, this time I had a vampire at my back. He might not be the biggest, baddest nightwalker in the county, but I knew from personal experience that he could rip a mortal attacker's throat out for me.

He also had lovely manners. He opened the driver door, just as he had back at the rectory, and helped me out of the car. This time he kept hold of my hand in his own cool clasp.

"What's with the hand holding?" I asked.

"You said you wanted an escort," he said in mild surprise. "This sends a signal."

"Explain."

"You should know this. You were with Oscar for months."

"He never brought me anywhere like this. It would probably have cramped his style, the philandering twat. And he was hopeless at explaining anything. You're the only vampire I've ever met who speaks actual human, apart from maybe Aidan."

He laughed.

"They're pompous," he said. "Like to sound impressive. Firstly, holding hands with a mortal is always alluring for a vampire because of your warmth. We love heat of any kind. Secondly, it sends a signal that you aren't available. Emir's is a good place for the barflies looking to just give casual blood or mortals looking to join a coterie. This says you aren't either. Only someone very aggressive will approach you if we walk in like this."

"OK."

His hand was almost cold in mine, his touch very gentle. I let my fingers fold round his. We walked through the old stone arch and down the steps into the warm depths of the bar.

Emir had added dry ice-fog and some softly throbbing electric music to the ambience. He'd also taken delivery of some huge church candles, each standing about eighteen inches high and about a foot across. He liked to keep playing with the atmosphere. Tonight, he was going for Hammer House of Horror chic. I thought he'd got it spot on.

Once again, Jiří was behind the bar. I did a double-take and looked more closely. This evening he was wearing makeup, which he hadn't been the previous night. It was skilfully applied, the foundation and powder a perfect match for his pale skin, but I could tell. I shrugged. Perhaps the boy was exploring himself; I wished him luck. He was also assiduously polishing something. I couldn't imagine why—it all looked gleaming to me.

Emir raised his eyebrows at me when I walked in. Was he surprised that I'd accepted his invitation, or by my choice of partner? I wasn't sure, but I walked determinedly to my usual seat. Nicky let go of my hand to tuck the chair in under me with easy charm, but he didn't sit.

"I have to feed, angel," he said. "There'll be someone here. You can have your chat with Emir."

"There are two brothers at the table behind the mirrored pillars," said Emir from behind me, leaning over to place a coupe of champagne at my elbow. "In the red leather booth. I think you met them a couple of weeks ago."

Nicky gave him a nod and disappeared into the misty depths. The dry ice swallowed him up after only a few paces.

"I like tonight's décor," I said. "Especially the giant candles."

"We aim to please," he said. "But it turns out they drip. I'll be scraping up wax for months. Interesting choice of partner."

"I like him."

"He's not popular."

"Why on earth not?"

"Vampires tend to be luddites about technology. They don't see the value in what he does for the Assemblage, so they think Benedict shouldn't favour him. Also, there's Kirsty. She fills a lot of cold, undead hearts with jealousy. But you didn't come here to chat about little Nicky."

"Emir, I never realised I was a witch. I don't understand what I'm doing. I think I need someone to teach me."

"Witchcraft isn't popular, Toni. Anything powerful tends to come with uncomfortable strings attached."

He began his great lecture: witches drew on the power of the earth. They could change the nature of things in subtle or transient ways. To do anything much more than that would require what he called a cantamen or enchantment, something not dissimilar to a recipe for a complex dish or a formula for perfume. Fifteen separate ingredients, say, all mixed in the right order at the right time in the right way... Eye of newt and toe of frog. With a cantamen, witches could change things more profoundly.

My head was spinning. "Emir, if these cantamen things are so complicated, how does anyone work them out?"

"You can't, Toni. They only come from demons. You have to bargain for them. That's why they're so rare—and so often a bad idea."

"What might an a cantamen do?"

"Make you fall in love, make you kill your brother. Turn wine to water, lead to gold. Make a fire seem cold or a frozen lake hot..."

"Create a big mess, in other words..."

"Not something to be done lightly," he said. "But first things first—if you're a witch, you should be able to see through my illusions."

He took the little votive candle from the centre of the table and blew out the flame.

"What am I looking for?"

"You should be able to see the wick through the illusory flame that I make."

"OK."

I watched but nothing happened. I shook my head.

"I can't see it, Emir."

"You can't see the wick?"

"No, I can't see a flame."

"What?"

He was looking at me in absolute shock, his dark brows drawn together. He actually pushed his chair back a little from the table to put distance between us. I hadn't seen such a reaction since I asked Brian Baker out when I was eight. Brian didn't just say no, I think he left skid marks. I waved my hands in confusion.

"I said I can't see the flame at all," I said again. "What am I doing wrong?"

"Possibly nothing," he said a little grimly, taking out a pack of cards and throwing one down. "What's this?"

"King of spades."

"Damn it! Toni Windsor, I'm not the teacher you're looking for."

My heart sank in disappointment. Emir wouldn't help me. Keira Holloway wouldn't even speak to me.

"Why not?" I asked. "Are you sure?"

"Quite," he said in clipped tones. "Your witchcraft is so strong that I can't even make you see my illusions. I'm just a hedge witch compared with you and, two minutes ago, I thought I was something special. If I try to teach you, I'll probably get us both killed. Enjoy your drink and don't drive home alone. I've increased security, but I can't guarantee Sophy's swain isn't in those woods."

And he stood up and joined Jiří behind the bar.

I sat at the table and looked into my glass of champagne. My parents hadn't left me anything in their will. They'd bothered to make one, as it happened, leaving everything to my brother. Wills had offered me my mother's jewellery, but I hadn't wanted it. In any event, my grandfather must have seen the way the wind was blowing—he'd left all his possessions to me, including the house. He'd left Wills just the special bequest of a golden pocket watch. But it turned out I'd got something from each of my parents after all. From my father, I'd inherited the necromancy that ran in that side of the family. From my mother I had witchcraft, and it was quite an heirloom.

I wondered what might change Emir's mind, whether it was even worth trying. I thought his pride was wounded more than anything. He'd always seemed to like me. I decided to let some time pass before approaching him again. In the meantime, I could look to tackle the elusive Keira Holloway. My list of potential tutors wasn't very long, and she was the next and last entry.

I sipped at my glass and listened to Emir's soundtrack de jour for a while. My mind wandered as the candles burned a little lower and the dry ice ebbed and flowed. I hoped Nicky's evening was going better than mine. I hadn't worked out what I thought of him yet. His easy acceptance of lowly status seemed at odds with someone who'd looted his way to millionairehood and bagged the prettiest and least endearing trophy girlfriend in town. But then, people change. Maybe he was different now that he was dead. Or maybe he was playing a long game?

A figure sat down opposite me. I looked up, expecting Emir or Nicky, but to my consternation it was the mournful-looking Peregrine Wall, the ex-Yorkshire vampire who was apparently on the verge of being booted to the county line unless he got very, very lucky. He had close-cropped blond hair and rather Nordic features, a chiselled jaw and high cheekbones. I glared at him.

"I'm with someone," I said brusquely, "as you well know."

He reached across the table with the blur of a striking snake and seized my right hand in a hard, icy grip. I yanked back, but I could have saved myself the trouble. I hadn't a hope in hell of breaking the vice-like hold he'd taken. I jerked and made as though to stand up, but with vampire speed, his other hand was on my shoulder holding me down.

"Not anyone who matters," he said. "And if Grace doesn't want you after all, you don't need to downgrade that far."

Ah. He thought he'd hook himself a little redhead, favoured by Benedict, and thus raise his chances of being allowed to stay. Because naturally I'd take him in favour of poor Nicky, the little fledgling with nothing that gave him prestige... Of course, Peregrine would have to completely demean Nicky in the process, but the man clearly believed that he didn't have a lot of options left and a clock was ticking.

"I'm with who I want, and it's not you," I said. "None of this is what you think."

Peregrine planned to kill a lot of birds with one desperate stone. I could have told him it was the wrong stone and the wrong birds, but he'd boxed himself in.

The music stopped, throwing the room into silence. I looked up. Emir was now in front of the bar; he looked furious, his mouth a thin line. Nicky, emerging from the mist of dry ice, seemed frozen to the spot. I shook my head slightly at him. He'd told me he'd lose a fair fight against another vampire, but I didn't want him fighting my battles anyway. I certainly didn't want him hurt or humiliated because I'd asked him to be my escort. Vampires are like hyenas when they sense the slightest weakness. I didn't plan on showing any, and I didn't want him to either.

I reached out for Peregrine with my necromancy and could have laughed out loud. He was barely there, hardly stronger than Nicky. I'd banished zombies with more lead in their pencils. Associating with the likes of Grace, Oscar and Benedict had made it easy for me to forget what Hugh Bonner had told me a year ago, sitting at a pub table with my pint: vampires fear necromancers. There are reasons for that.

I wanted to get things right first time, so I drained my champagne glass with a single swig. Then, with a mental apology to Emir, I dashed the rim against the tabletop and watched shards of glass skitter across the wood. I pushed the palm of my left hand into them and watched a little red pool spread out around my fingers.

I spoke clearly. I knew everyone in the room would hear me. I hoped they wouldn't know what the hell I was really playing at.

"Let me tell you what you're going to do, Peregrine Wall, you undead pain in the arse," I said. "You're going to let me go. Then you're going to apologise to Nicky for taking his chair. Then you're going to say sorry to Emir for creating a scene in his house. And finally, you're going to sod right off and not come back. On your marks."

I made it a command. I drew the power out of the earth with my blood and I hurled it at him. Was it necromancy? Was it witchcraft? I no longer knew. Right then and there, I didn't care. I felt the energy course through me. It felt like the rush you get in your chest when you've just necked a schooner of whisky. It felt amazing. Utterly exhausting, but amazing. Next time I couldn't find a dead body to raise, I was just going to go out and find me a vampire to boss around. Then I would sleep for a week.

Seconds ticked past. He sat there and looked at me. He shook his head as though there was something crawling on it. A thousand fleeting expressions crossed his face and for a moment I thought he would challenge me, call my bluff. I pushed harder, like a hundred metres runner who just didn't care if they collapsed at the finish. And I felt his resistance buckle and then break.

Poor old Perry didn't seem to have the faintest idea of what I'd done to him, but he certainly did what he was told. He took his hands off me and stood up very meekly. He ducked his head humbly at Nicky.

"I'm really sorry," he said. "I think this is your seat. My mistake. And please forgive me, Emir, for any disturbance. I think I should be going now."

And he quietly walked out of the room towards the exit. The sound of his footsteps on the stone flags gradually faded away.

The silence was almost tangible. A quick glance around showed me a roomful of people with open mouths. Did they see how exhausted I was? Had they put two and two together? Had anyone realised I'd

broken the glass for more than artistic effect? I didn't think so...
Nicky sat down opposite me.

"Toni one, Peregrine total annihilation," he said. "What the hell
did you even do to him? He'd have to emigrate after that loss of
face even if Benedict did grant him an extension."

"Good," I said. "Loser. I don't like him. Did you manage to
feed?"

Nicky smiled. It was a smile of great contentment. It was the
smile of someone who hadn't thought they were getting their
heart's desire for Christmas but had just found it under the tree.
It was a smile that made mothers lock up their daughters. I could
have told those mothers they should lock up their sons, too, and
then their husbands.

"I won't tell you what I managed to do, angel," he said. "It
would make you blush."

I blushed anyway.

"Hush," I said.

I would have said more but Emir interrupted us.

"I don't know how you pulled that off, but I don't think I've ever
seen a vampire humiliated so effectively in public," he said. "You
also shouldn't have to keep order in my house."

I lifted my chin at him.

"In that case, I'm not paying for the glass," I said. "He just
needed someone to call his bluff and stand up to him. Now if you'll
forgive me, Nicky and I will be on our way. Goodnight."

I stood up and reached for Nicky's hand with my uninjured
right one. If I was going to have to hang around with the sodding
undead, I might as well learn the etiquette. Also, I'd used up almost
all my reserves forcing Peregrine to do my bidding. I could barely
walk. We made a dignified exit and I managed to make it out of
eyeshot before collapsing.

"Nicky..." I got out.

But he had sensed which way the wind was blowing and caught
me as I dropped. He lifted me with ridiculous ease and carried me
up the steps into the ruins. The moonlight was a little brighter than

when we'd arrived. I leant back against his shoulder and blinked at the sky through the curtain of his hair as we moved through the trees and back to the car.

"Was that necromancy?" he asked. "And can you drive?"

"Yes, and yes, if you give me a few minutes," I said. "And I think I can stand now. Do you think anyone else realised?"

He set me down and I leant against the car while I pulled myself together.

"I doubt it, but Emir was giving you strange looks," he said. "He and I were watching you the closest, of course. It wasn't obvious. To the casual observer, you just faced him down."

I opened the car and slumped in the driver seat.

"Nicky, I'm going to take you home," I said. "Then I'm going to sleep the sleep of the just, whether I deserve it or not."

Nicky climbed in the car next to me.

"Whatever you say, angel," he said peaceably. "I had more fun than you can imagine tonight, and watching you kick Peregrine off Emir's private table was definitely the best bit."

I turned my left palm upwards into the car's interior light. Four lovely punctures were still oozing blood. One sported a glittering splinter of glass. I had a feeling that there was an elderly box of tissues somewhere on the back seat, fighting for room between my winter coat, two boxes of land registry files and some shoes that needed mending. But before I could look for it, Nicky took my hand in a shaking grasp.

"Wait," he said, in a voice that made me wish we weren't shut in a car together.

He licked his lips. His teeth were white in the moonlight.

"Nicky, don't even think about it," I said. "I don't give blood, OK? I just don't."

"I'll heal you," he whispered. "Vampire saliva isn't much different from blood, you know."

"No! You are not drinking my blood. Not one sodding drop, OK? Not even a lick."

He jerked his head back but nodded. He seemed distracted, fervid…

"Give me a moment."

The car door opened, and he stepped out into the moonlight. I saw him pace up and down for a few minutes. He kicked a tree for a bit. I took advantage of the downtime to pull the last piece of glass out of my hand and chuck it through the window. When Nicky returned, he seemed calmer and more in control.

"OK, angel, good to go," he said, his voice back to normal. "Give."

I reached out my hand and let him take it. Once again, there was the light touch of slim, cool fingers wrapped round mine... I felt him pushing his healing power into me. There wasn't much of it, just as he'd said, but it was enough to stop the bleeding and close the wounds sufficiently to let me drive us home.

When he was done, he sat there for a few moments. Eventually I removed my hand from his.

"Sight of blood?" I asked.

"You wouldn't believe the effect it has," he said. "Think of the hottest, sexiest, most completely arousing image in the world ever, then multiply it by ten and you're halfway there."

I didn't answer him. I was completely taken aback by the image that had jumped into my mind at his words. Who'd have thought it? Well, well, well... I'd have to do something about that. Like a lobotomy maybe. I started the engine, and we headed off into the night.

"You were OK in the kitchen, when you healed me," I said after a few miles.

He shrugged.

"That was mostly bruising, to be honest. And I was stuck in a room with a dead man bleeding out on the floor, not shut in a warm car with a pretty girl spilling out of her cocktail dress."

"I am not!"

"Two speed humps and there'd be spillage."

"Nicky, shut up already."

He obediently changed the subject and kept me awake with idle gossip as I drove him back to the rectory. When we arrived,

I waved as I watched his slim figure lope past the rainbow-hued plastic unicorn and up the porch steps. He seemed genuine, a gentle soul, but then vampires can seem to be whatever they want. Oscar had seemed to be the man of my dreams, but he turned out to be the stuff of nightmares. Grace had seemed hard as nails, but I'd watched her cry her eyes out for someone she loved. Benedict seemed as heartless as a stone, but he'd held me in his arms once and stroked my hair. I usually trusted my instincts, but with vampires... that would just get you killed.

I HAD DRIVEN almost as far as Colton before I realised my mistake. I was exhausted and alone, and it was nearly two in the morning. I couldn't go home because in my current state I didn't dare walk the gauntlet to my own porch. And I couldn't even drive past and spend the night in the mausoleum; I lived on a dead-end road, and it was pretty certain that, if he'd staked out my house, Gin Martin knew my car. He'd see me go past—and not return. And I was too damn done in to raise a single zombie, even Bredon.

I pulled up and put my head in my hands. Why hadn't I driven back here with Nicky and called him a cab again? Or even camped out in one of his plethora of bedrooms and faced the wrath of Kirsty? I should have accepted Wills' invitation to stay over. I could have done a hundred things, but it felt too late for any of them.

I was tired to the bone and thinking wasn't easy. I wanted a few hours of safe, secure slumber. I put the car back into gear and did a clumsy U-turn, banging the back wheels into the curb. I wound down all the windows and inhaled as much oxygen as I could find. Then I drove sedately to the Stone House.

Grace's four-by-four was parked in the courtyard. All traces of mashed sheep had been removed. I blundered into the hall and—to my relief—walked almost bang into Aidan.

"Toni," he said with great cheer. "You look tired. Don't tell me you've come to raise your stalker?"

What was he even talking about? Oh, Dylan Moss, the man

Nicky had shunted off this mortal coil such a very short time ago...

"Not this evening," I said. "Though I do know his name now. I'm done with Tuesday, Aidan. I just need somewhere to crash for the night."

"Of course. Think you could cope with Oscar's old rooms? I guarantee they're one hundred per cent Oscar-free. Why are you laughing?"

"Irony, Aidan," I said, clapping him on the arm. "The irony of running for cover and ending up in Oscar's bed. Don't worry, I know my way from here."

Chapter Twelve

I DIDN'T OFTEN have vivid dreams, but this one felt uncannily real. Was it a memory, creeping to the surface as I slumbered?

I'm sitting in the kitchen, dangling my little legs off a chair. They don't reach the floor, not even close. I wonder why for a moment, before remembering that I'm only eight years old. I push the thought aside—I have more important things on my mind. Today is the day I'm going to make my mother talk to me.

Wills knows I love baking, and he's given me a set of letter-shaped biscuit cutters for my birthday. I've made the dough from scratch, and now I'm painstakingly cutting out the letters, one by one, and arranging them on the baking tray. There are a lot of slightly grubby fingerprints. I wonder if I should have washed my hands after swapping mud pies for real ones, but it's all rather too late to worry on that front. I carefully punch out another letter M.

I hear footsteps behind me, and I swivel round. My grandfather, clad in an outdoor coat, is standing just inside the room, his hair still moist from the rain. A marmalade spaniel, whose name I think is Tuba, is scampering around at his heels. Grandfather Robert is a tall man—I get my diminutive stature through the female line—his hair still mostly red with white wings at the side. A darkly bearded face that rarely smiles looks curiously down at me.

"What are you doing, little Lavington?" he asks in his gruff, low voice.

I stick out my bottom lip because I'm engaged in exactly the sort of enterprise that he definitely disapproves of. He's warned me against trying to attract my parents' attention. I haven't listened. I rarely listen to anyone.

"Baking," I say evasively. "Sugar biscuits."

The first few letters are laid out, my guilt writ large and in pastry: 'I Love Mu...'

He frowns.

"Let it go, little one," he says, patting my shoulder clumsily. "It won't work."

"Yes, it will."

"I'm sorry," he says, half talking to himself. "I meant it for the best. It's not your fault. Blood will out, they say, but I'll damn well stop it if I can. Let's make different words."

"No!" eight-year-old me screams. "No, no, no!"

And I hurl the baking tray across the kitchen, sending dough, plates, a spaniel, and a bottle of milk flying, and run out into the rain. I make it to the lawn before he catches me, snatching me up into his big arms and holding me close.

"Lavington," I hear him say into my hair. "Little love. It's not your fault, it's mine."

"Then I hate you," I scream, flailing in his arms. "I hate you, I hate you, I hate you!"

And I struggle so fiercely in his grip that he drops me, and I slam into the wet, muddy grass...

...and I woke up with a start.

I'd always refused to spend the night at the Stone House. Oscar aside, vampires had made me nervous even back then. The only time I stayed over, I'd been too badly injured to notice an alien invasion, let alone the décor or the thread count.

Now I could see that Oscar had good taste when it came to soft furnishings. The bed I was lying in was comfy enough that a spoilt princess would search in vain for her pea. Frankly, she could probably have lost a whole prince in a mattress that big and fluffy and had a lot of fun finding him again. It was a bed made for luxuriating in—well, it was made for many other things, too. Given its dimensions, Snow White and all seven dwarves would have had room to play bite-my-poison-apple. But I was on my own, so I just basked for a little while.

My lie-in came to a disappointing end when my awakening brain reminded me that it was Wednesday, it was past seven o'clock, and I was due at work. More to the point, I had come out for the evening sporting a black cocktail dress, stilettos and no coat... so I had quite a walk of shame ahead of me.

Or perhaps not. Someone had dusted and kept the shower supplied with shampoo in the five or six months since Oscar had departed. They hadn't, however, emptied any of the drawers. I found a t-shirt and jeans in one that I was shocked to recognise as Peter's. The outfit would be too wide for me and too long, so I ruthlessly cut the bottom off the t-shirt with my nail scissors and belted the jeans in until they stayed up. I didn't have to roll the hems more than twice—leaving them long hid my evening shoes.

But the clothes smelt uncannily of Peter. My eyes pricked. The wretched man had stolen my heart and then buggered off to Heidelberg with it. When I was through with this round of crazy people trying to kill me or drink my blood, I was damn well going to deal with him. He could either earn that heart—or I was having it back.

There was a fat, cream envelope sitting on the bedside table. The lettering on the front was copperplate, sloping and perfect: 'Lavington Windsor.' Inside it said simply:

My dear, you are always welcome in my home. I will arrange a room with fewer associations. Be careful with the enclosed—I can find you a better teacher than Emir.
Ever yours,
Benedict Akil

A bundle of documents sealed with ribbon and wax were presumably 'the enclosed.' Typical of him to throw me out and then tell me I was always welcome. I tucked the whole lot under my arm and walked out to the car park.

The Stone House looked rather lovely in the day, a very old building even for the county of Staffordshire, with formal gardens that I knew gave way to a more riotous tangle as you headed further in. My car sat incongruously amongst its high-ticket neighbours, its rust patches at odds with the gleaming chrome of the Bentley to its right or the polished yellow paintwork of the little Caterham perched on the left. The Morris—with duct tape accessories, three hub caps and a soft patina of rust—looked completely out of place, like a tramp who'd accidentally crashed a gallery opening and was hanging around for the free canapés. But it clearly liked its new surroundings because, when I turned the key in the engine, there was a brief unhappy grinding noise and then silence. My car had finally died.

I swore and banged my head on the dashboard a couple of times. I could have got exactly the same effect by kicking a hub cap, but I was wearing the wrong shoes. Eventually, I left the keys in the ignition and walked back to the house. I headed up the main staircase and into the attic. Camilla's room was a riot of pink set under the eaves. We were good enough friends that I thought she would forgive me disturbing her.

She was Grace's consort, and they seemed an affectionate couple, but the vampire also had a coterie of five sporty and energetic young women, which she casually referred to as her Amazons. As far as I could work out, they helped to provide security to the Assemblage in between running marathons, collecting black belts in martial arts and generally being fearsomely fit and healthy. All five seemed to consider Camilla as some kind of adorable but exotic bird that had accidentally landed in their nest. They flocked to her on the rare occasions when they wanted their hair plaited or their nails painted. Only when I got to Camilla's door to find one of them emerging wearing a dressing gown and a distinctly post-coital expression did it occur to me that they also flocked to her for other things.

I can be slow sometimes.

I should have guessed, of course. Peter had told me that within a coterie lines became blurred. Certainly, the pretty girl who gave me a sleepy 'good morning' was unabashed by our encounter. She was about a foot taller than me with curling black hair and features not a million miles away from Henry Lake's. I remembered that her name was Jenny Barlow and that she always seemed to be practicing something called ninjutsu or stripping down motorbikes.

"Hey, Toni," she said with an enormous yawn. "You're too late. I wore her out and she's fast asleep."

She gave me an affectionate hug, one that teetered on the brink of being more than affectionate and lasted long enough to make me wonder when a hug turned into a cuddle. Or even when a cuddle turned into an embrace... I looked up and she grinned down at me.

"I, on the other hand, still have some energy left," she said suggestively.

I laughed. I took the compliment in good spirit but kept my half of the hug platonic.

"Actually, my car is dead," I confessed when she let me go. "I came to see if I could borrow the four-by-four if it's back on the road."

"No one will mind," she said. "I'll tell Camilla when she wakes up. The keys are inside. What happened to that green heap of junk that you usually drive?"

"It's taking a nap in the courtyard. At least, I hope it's a nap! Could be a coma."

"I'll look at it, if you like," she said, as we walked down together to the hall. "Probably lifting up the bonnet and giving it a good talking-to will do the trick."

"Good luck with that. I strapped it shut with duct tape eleven months ago and now I can't open it at all."

She opened the door of Grace's car for me and watched me clamber up into the high driver seat.

"Who were you with last night, by the way?" she asked as I closed my seatbelt and started the engine.

She was aiming for offhand, but I could see how curious she was.

"Sorry to disappoint on the gossip front, but I was all alone in Oscar's rooms, me, myself and I."

"Boring, Toni, but better than with Oscar. Now don't hit any sheep. Camilla is never living that one down."

And she waved me on my way.

I MADE IT into the office by nine, cat fed, hair washed and sporting a miniscule sundress in celebration of the fact that Nicky's healing had also taken care of all the scratches on my arms and legs. I needn't have hurried. By ten, the chirpy Karen had rung to postpone my mystery meeting with the coroner for yet another day. The Czech inquest was dragging on, she explained. The family had found out about the incident at the hospital. Nothing was ever simple. She was sorry. John was sorry… I wanted to be sorry, too, just to join the club, but I was too sleep-deprived to care.

My strangest call came at noon, not on the landline but on my mobile, when a local number I didn't recognise came up.

"Hi, this is Toni."

"This is the vet at Hopton," a woman's voice said in lovely English vowels. "I think I have your cat?"

"What? Round, orange, drools, sounds like a rusty hinge?"

"That's the one."

"Is he alright? What's he doing up in Hopton? I live on the other side of Rugeley."

"He's sitting on our receptionist right now having a lovely head scratch," her voice said in amused tones. "But as for why he's here, I don't know. I found him about half an hour ago clawing his way out of a cardboard box on the practice doorstep. Your phone number is on his collar tag."

Oh, that. On the other side it said: "My name is Winchester. I am well fed and a shameless liar." It wasn't working. People still gave him treats and he was still getting rounder. I assured the unknown vet that I was on my way and headed up to Hopton in my borrowed car.

The directions she'd given me weren't hard to follow, but you wouldn't expect to find a vet in such a small village. I assumed she picked up a lot of equestrian business from the local stables, and maybe family pets from all the army accommodation nearby. The land is a little too hilly for cows, but as you head down towards Stafford or Sandon, or back down Weston Bank, there is some flatter pasture for cattle. Maybe she did a little agricultural work, too.

A single-storey brick unit was set back a little from the road, with the words 'Mary Hollands, Veterinary Practitioner' stencilled above the open door. Mary herself was standing in the doorway with a half-smoked cigarette in her hand that she dropped and ground under her heel as I walked up from the car. She was in her fifties, with dark grey hair that she clearly couldn't be bothered to colour. She was wearing scrubs with wellies, but I thought her civilian garb would be pretty similar.

"I gave him a check-up while he was wandering round the place trying to steal my lunch," she said. "He's fighting fit for his age. Needs his teeth cleaning though. Did you bring a cat box?"

She was an overpowering personality, hard to talk over, impossible to interrupt. She also appeared to have great concerns about Winchester's health and none at all about who had stolen him and dumped him on her doorstep.

"Um, no. I..."

"If you like, I'll do his teeth and drop him off on my way home. I live out in Abbots Bromley, and I have a spare carrier."

"Thank you, that would be—"

"Great. Write your address here. Lovely. If you're out, I'll just decant him into your garden."

I gave up and left her with the cat. Some people are a force of nature. Doubtless a fine bill would make its way onto my roster of impossible debts shortly.

I drove back down the hill in a thoughtful mood. What the hell was going on? Who would take my cat and drive him halfway across the country to a remote village, and why? I realised far too late, when the man lying on the back seat sat up and grinned at me in the rear-view mirror. His pimply shaven head was horribly familiar.

"No vampire to protect you now, is there?" he said, leaning forward. "Just you and me. Keep driving."

There was a flash of silver and I felt something sharp and cold at my neck. I'd been taken in by the oldest trick in the book.

I felt sick. How had I been stupid enough to fall for his ruse? Chasing a cat I'd never even wanted, that was how. The knife was pressed into my throat, just above the strap of my seat belt. I felt my heart racing. I closed my eyes for a moment and then opened them hastily to watch the country road ahead.

"Oh my God. You're Gin Martin."

"Decided you know who I am now, have you? Well, don't think it will change anything. And there's no Dylan to stick up for you either this time. Turn left here."

My mind was whirling. When I'd pleaded ignorance, it had just made him angrier, but I still didn't have a clue why he was mad with me in the first place.

"I don't care about the money," I said. "You can have it. I don't want it."

"Oh no, I already tried that," he said. "You and your fancy lawyers, saying I had no rights anymore. Like I said, if I can't have it, you're not getting it either. Turn right here."

The steep road led down into the woods on the far side of Weston Bank. I knew it gave way all too soon to a mud track and then petered out. I'd come for walks here on Boxing Day. You could get lost in the trees for weeks if you wanted to. The coverts went all the way up to David's Rock. No one would hear me scream.

"You don't have to do this."

"Listen, I want to do this. I can't fucking wait."

I glanced at him again in the rear-view mirror. I couldn't persuade him. I couldn't argue with him. And Nicky couldn't save me this time. I wondered how many air bags the car had—lots was my hope. Unlike Gin, I'd fastened my seatbelt.

"You should have done this in my car," I said. "I'd never have dared try this in the Morris."

And I stamped my foot down hard on the accelerator and then spun the steering wheel sharply to the left. The tree never even saw us coming.

Chapter Thirteen

TIME PASSED, I drifted into a half-asleep, half-awake blur. There was a smell of disinfectant, a beeping noise and a room that wasn't my own. The lights were too bright, and the bed was too hard. Why did I have this nasty blanket, and where was my eiderdown? But who cared because, oh God, that taste of heaven was in my mouth again. If I lived to be a hundred, I would never tire of it. Careful, Toni, not something to develop a penchant for...

"You should have told me before."

Benedict's voice, angry, impatient... no surprises there.

"I know, don't tell me. I was abroad, and when I got back it took me a while to work out how to get hold of you. I eventually contacted her stupid ex in Heidelberg."

Paul's voice? Wasn't he meant to be in Amsterdam?

"Hmmm. Dear Peter. At least he has a use. No, don't go—I will want to feed when I'm done here."

"You want to drink my blood?"

"Yes. Look at her, quiet and peaceful. It's a miracle. If she was awake, she'd be shouting at me by now. My little Toni, I've never known anyone so desperate to bring an end to their existence."

"Will she be alright?"

"Yes, until the next time she does something stupid. Undo your shirt."

But then I drifted away again.

When I eventually came to, Paul was sitting in a plastic bucket chair by my hospital bed. He was dozing but, as I pushed myself up to sitting, he opened his eyes and smiled. I couldn't believe how happy I was to see him again. How was I going to cope when he went to university?

"Hey, you're awake," he said. "Thank God. The food here is disgusting."

I laughed. I felt ridiculously well, like someone who'd spent six weeks at a health spa.

"You've missed my toast, I know," I said. "No one butters it like me. How long was I out?"

"A whole week."

I blinked. Seven days of my life just gone… No appeals process, no refunds. Also, another week of potential commission payments lost for ever.

"Well, I'm back now. How was Amsterdam? Is your liver still whimpering?"

"The highlight was getting stuck in customs for fourteen hours because Sean threw up on his passport."

"Good. I have a bone to pick with you."

"Benedict said you would."

"Damn it, Paul, I'm so indebted to Benedict already. I can't believe you sent for him."

"I had to! You wouldn't wake up. And then the bloody police accidentally lost your stalker."

"What?"

"The gamekeeper who looks after Brick Kiln Covert heard your car crash. You just had a massive bang on the head and a few broken bones, but there was this guy who'd been thrown through your windscreen. It was some jailbird, Grahame Martin, and apparently, you'd already reported him for watching your house at night. There was a knife found, with his prints on, so the police assumed he'd attacked you and you'd lost control. He was in hospital, too, but he surreptitiously discharged himself three nights ago while his police guard was chatting up a nurse. Christ knows how—the guy was a mess. He broke his left leg, his right arm and his nose."

"So to find Benedict, you contacted Peter."

Paul's eyes narrowed.

"I did."

"What's wrong?"

"We had a disagreement."

"With Peter! What on earth about?"

The eyes became slits.

"Nothing."

Really, there was no accounting for men and their moods.

"Well, I suppose you meant well," I conceded reluctantly.

"Would you rather still be in a coma?"

"No, but it's on the cusp. Did you bring me some clothes?"

He had, and I dressed in a rush. We sneaked out of the hospital and into a taxi before anyone could notice that my broken bones had mysteriously healed along with any contusion to my skull. In the cab, my delight at seeing him again somehow buried my annoyance that he'd embroiled us with vampires again. I hugged him impulsively.

"I missed you," I said. "I even missed you practicing your drums. Oh, and I need to tell you: Bethany found out you were in Amsterdam. Your name is mud in our office."

He returned the hug quietly. He looked serious, an expression that I didn't think that Bethany's histrionics had triggered.

"I thought you might die," he said suddenly. "I was so shocked that I didn't think of that vamp..." He broke off with an awkward glance at the back of the cabby's head. "I didn't think of Benedict for ages. And you just lay there. Your brother had to be held back from killing Grahame Martin. I've told him you're OK, by the way. The house is so full of flowers that I think even the cat has hay fever."

The damn cat. If it hadn't been for Winchester... I buried the thought. I'd been incredibly lucky. And I might be cursing Paul for asking Benedict to heal me, but I should probably just be grateful I wasn't still in hospital waiting for my bones to heal.

"You did the right thing," I said reluctantly. "Thank you."

I lay back in the car seat. It was a bright July afternoon. I watched the green hedges flash past and then the trees along the bottom of the village. It was Wednesday; I'd been out cold for a week. Again. I needed to stop doing that. I was getting into bad habits. Hanging out with vampires, nearly getting killed, being lovelorn...

We pulled up outside the house and I saw to my surprise that my little green Morris was at the kerb, last seen faking death at the Stone House. It looked cleaner than before. The duct tape had gone from the bonnet. One or two of the rust patches had also been vanquished. And hang on a minute, it had four hub caps. It had only sported three since I'd bought the damn thing.

"Just out of interest, my car..." I said curiously, paying off the fare.

"Yeah, some fabulous-looking late night fantasy called Jenny dropped it off," Paul said. "I made her tea, and she stripped down my moped. Can we keep her?"

I froze. I didn't want Paul associating with any more vampires. It might be hypocritical, but they hadn't brought a lot of joy into my life; near death experiences, yes, but joy... not a lot. I feigned a laugh and changed the subject.

"Yeah, I think she's out of our league. Oh yes, and she also prefers girls. Well, seeing as we have wheels, how about buying up the deli counter at the supermarket and packing some dinner for Bredon tonight?"

"How about we take him out?" he countered.

"We have no money."

"OK, picnic it is."

I told Paul about my travails while we made up our al fresco supper—being watched from a stolen car by Gin Martin and Dylan Moss, and their expectations that I would be old like Gin's mother. Paul frowned when I described the man's conviction that I'd taken something he'd waited for, something he'd already tried to get back, but which I and my 'fancy lawyers' had said he had no rights to anymore.

"An inheritance then," mused Paul. "His mum left you something he thought would come to him."

"I wish," I said, arranging pork pies in a row and beginning to slice strawberries. "A new car would be nice. Shall I whip this cream, or do you want it poured?"

We had plenty of time to kill before the sun set. There were a million answerphone messages to plough through, all telling me to get better. I read the good wishes on a dozen deliveries of flowers. Everyone from Irene Polkerris to John Jones the coroner had sent me a bunch.

I threw caution to the winds and told Paul about Derowen Polkerris, the rich philanderer who any number of disappointed creditors, sacked staff and disenchanted lovers might have wanted to kill. I told him about ethereal Nicky and his lost coterie. I told him about tragic Sophy and her stalker. And I told him how my quest for a witch to teach me about my powers had stalled. If I couldn't trust Paul, who could I trust?

Halfway through telling him the very last item on my list, I remembered the wad of documents Benedict had left for me in Oscar's room. I'd never got round to looking at them because just a few hours later I'd been lured out to Hopton by the obsessed Grahame Martin. They were still on the bed where I'd thrown them when I got changed out of Peter's clothes that morning a week ago. I brought them down, and we sat around the kitchen table and broke open the bundle of papers.

I knew what they were at a single glance, but Paul frowned.

"What the hell are these?" he asked, very reasonably.

"They are contracts with a demon," I said. "Azazel, to be specific. And they're in my grandfather's writing."

"What's the funny brown ink?"

"Paul, they're written in blood."

"That's extremely creepy but at the same time kind of cool."

"That's not the worst. The bloody things are written in Latin. I never studied Latin."

Paul laughed and leafed through the papers.

"Well, as it happens, I did study Latin. And I happen to know that Bredon did, too. So, if you like, I'll make a start on them, and we can take them up with us this evening. I never ever thought all those nights of learning Roman vocabulary would come in useful. You look upset."

I waved my hands vaguely. Yes, I sodding well was upset.

"My grandfather lied to me, Paul. He said to never bargain with demons. He made out it was something he'd never done, but that was a complete fabrication. Benedict told me as much back in January, but I didn't really listen. Now I have to wonder how many other lies Robert Windsor told me."

He'd been the one constant thing in my childhood. True, he'd been far too strict and rarely all that affectionate, but he'd always been there—unlike my parents. But given this great mess of lies he'd told me, I had to ask myself: had anything really been real?

Paul just shrugged and tugged the lid off a biro.

"Toni, I come from a family of professional liars. Half of them lie about their names, let alone what they've done and why. All of them lie about having actual driving licenses, let alone insurance. Most of them have lied under oath. Don't sweat the small stuff."

I still minded. I finished making up our picnic and stood by the sink watching him. He was gazing at the text with great concentration, chewing the end of the pen. Occasionally he would jot down a word and then go back to chewing. After a few minutes he looked up.

"What's the theory behind this kind of bargain?" he asked.

"Demons like Azazel, Paul, they know everything. They know the past and the present perfectly, though they can't see into our minds. And they can't interfere directly, so they interfere by telling us things: lies, half-truths, things we shouldn't know, things that should be forgotten. Or they persuade us to do things for them. They can't lie in a contract written in blood, but they'll stab you in the back if they can, so it has to be well written. I gather that necromancers like Latin because it's hard to have too many interpretations of a single phrase."

He nodded.

"Which would be the issue with English. But the problem here is that your grandfather's Latin isn't very good. He's lucky he didn't make more mistakes."

I thought for a moment. Grandfather Robert hadn't been a particularly educated man, not that I'd been aware of, anyway. It was news to me that he could read and write Latin at all, so hardly a surprise that he hadn't been the most proficient of students. I was starting to wonder how much he'd really taught me, and how much he'd been winging it all along while letting me feel my way. He'd been great at telling me to try harder and concentrate, but I'd rarely seen him raise the dead himself. Now that I cast my mind back, I certainly hadn't seen him animate them. But of course, if that was witchcraft, and I got that from my mother, then he wouldn't have been able to animate them at all. No wonder he'd been so fanatical about circles of protection... unlike me, he wouldn't be able to sense if the spirit had departed the body, leaving it nice and empty for a demon to take up residence.

"I'm starting to think he made some big mistakes," I said. "Any idea what all this nasty scribble is about?"

"Not yet. There are two separate contracts, though, one dated twenty-one years ago and the other fifty-six."

Such a long time ago... One from when I was a little girl, the other long before I was even born. But Paul was still speaking.

"...and there are four things that look like poems that Robert refers to as cantamen, two with each contract."

Four of them? My grandfather never told me witches existed, let alone that I was one—something that he must have known all along. But now it looked like he'd bargained with bloody Azazel for these damn things, which as far as I knew, he couldn't even have used himself. And what had he wanted so badly that he'd cut a deal with Azazel, twice, when he must have known his Latin wasn't up to the task?

I'd been telling myself off for being a hypocrite with Paul, but I shouldn't have been so hard on myself. Apparently, it was in the blood.

"How long would it take to translate the whole lot?"

"Toni, I haven't done this for two years, and the wretched stuff is handwritten and pretty faded. Even with Bredon's help, I won't finish them tonight. Though he'll probably be more used to translating handwritten text than me."

"Do you mind doing this?"

"No, I'm enjoying it. I like studying, remember? I'm the geeky one."

Later that evening, I curled up in the little mausoleum, vaguely listening to Paul and Bredon arguing over declensions, whatever they were, and whether my grandfather had actually meant to use the dative rather than the genitive. They eventually decided that he hadn't, but the debate took a while.

We'd taken care leaving the house, first turning off all the lights, then sneaking out of the back door and walking to the church through the woods. Even so, I was unhappy that Gin Martin was still on the prowl now that Paul was home. Last time I'd embroiled Paul in one of my schemes, he'd ended up with two broken legs. I didn't want him mixed up with any of this. I'd offered him a home free from criminals and late-night police calls. If I wasn't more careful, he'd have all that back on his plate again with a side dish of vampires and some witchcraft for dessert. And Azazel. I couldn't let that happen.

"Wake me well before dawn this time," I called, slumping on a pile of cushions. "We might as well stay here until then."

But sleep was slow in coming. I had too much to think about. What had happened fifty-six years ago? I was never good at pub quizzes. I thought Harold Macmillan had been prime minister, but that was about it. Then, as I finally drifted off, it hit me. Fifty-six years ago, my father had been born.

Chapter Fourteen

THERE'S NO POINT in trying to rouse a slumbering teenager with anything short of heavy weaponry, so I left Paul to have a lie-in and drove to work. I hadn't anticipated the welcome I would receive. Bethany gave a little squeak and clapped her hands when I walked in, but Bernie enveloped me in a huge, grope-free cuddle.

"Jesus, Toni," he said. "The hospital said you were in a coma and had broken enough limbs to play knuckle bones just by jumping up and down. I wasn't sure we'd see you again."

"Um," I said brightly when he finally let me go. "Do you think they confused my notes with someone else's?"

I didn't like lying, but it struck me that a bit of misdirection at this point wouldn't go amiss.

"I guess," he said. "Bless you, you look fine. Coffee, Bethany. Get us some coffee."

A week of unanswered messages had piled up, but the office had been quiet before my accident, and they didn't take me long to work through. I rescheduled my appointment with Irene Polkerris for just after lunch, while the coroner's chirpy secretary assured me that John could see me the following morning at eleven.

I rebooked a swathe of other viewings and agreed to retrospectively arrange electricity and gas certificates for a landlady whose granny flat had been snapped up by a tenant the previous week, just hours after I'd persuaded her to drop the rent. He'd wanted to move in the same day. I scrabbled through her files. She was a cat breeder from near Stone with an annex that had been empty for nearly four months.

"Mrs, um, Fletcher, we don't have references, a deposit... Are you sure?"

"He paid six months in advance. Cash," she said abruptly. "As long as he's not cooking crystal meth in the kitchen, or learning to play the saxophone, as far as I'm concerned, he's the perfect resident. For that, I'll waive the no pet clause all the way up to rhinoceros. I don't really care if he's running a brothel."

I could see her point.

"Do you think he is?" I asked out of curiosity.

"No," she said. "He cooks with a lot of garlic and plays a lot of Richard Clayderman."

Before driving over to the Polkerris mansion, I rang Wills to find out where he was on the CCTV he'd mentioned. In my mind, I hadn't ruled out the electrician or the secretary. My brother had, I knew—he'd met the electrician and trusted him—but their stories didn't hold water.

"Hey, sis," he said when he heard my voice. "I never thought I'd be pleased that you hang out with vampires. Is it all true what Paul said? You're completely OK?"

"Fit as a fiddle," I said. "Back at work, earning my keep. Listen, by coincidence, I am going over to meet with Irene Polkerris. Did anything happen on that front?"

"Sort of," he said. "We released the body this morning. And I finally got to see the security camera footage. Toni, it really doesn't help. It fits with all the witness statements. Daphne the housekeeper didn't sneak back and neither did Irene, and the secretary and the electrician are in the clear, too. All I can think is that someone got into Derowen's room without going through the door. I've even checked the roof, but there's nothing. The office is in one wing of that bloody mansion of his, and there's decent security for the whole grounds. Whoever got in there knew what they were doing to evade being seen."

"Well, when I go over, I'll ask whether they have a plague of ninjas or any secret hidden passages for concealing renegade priests. Where's the body now?"

"That mansion was built as an abbey. There's a little chapel at the far end of the grounds where the vicar holds services once a month. The graveyard is still licensed and Derowen's will arranges for him to be buried there. His coffin is in state in the chapel right now."

No wonder Irene wanted to move—she was stuck in the house her husband had been murdered in, and soon his corpse would be interred there, too. I understood her urge to flee to the south coast. She was putting as many miles between her and the murder as possible without actually emigrating. She had my sympathy.

I drove over to Great Bridgeford and then followed directions to the Polkerris house. A long, long Jacobean frontage, glittering with hand-poured glass, was set back up a curving drive. Lawns were manicured. Flowerbeds were weed-free. There were some expensive-looking statues. There was no plastic unicorn.

I parked the Morris next to a very modest original Mini of similarly venerable age. The radio aerial had long since been replaced with a wire coat hanger. I wondered whose it might be. Derowen had travelled by chauffeur. I didn't have Irene down as the sort to skimp on her car. On the occasions she was sober enough to drive, that was.

My musings were interrupted by the front door opening. A rather beautiful man in his forties with pale red hair came out to greet me. He was dressed with great neatness and no ostentation. An inoffensive tie was perfectly knotted.

"And you must be Toni Windsor," he said in lovely English vowels. "I'm Crispin. I've been looking out for you. And good gracious, you're a fellow ginger."

His voice was quite as lovely as I'd thought on the phone. He should have gone into radio. He shepherded me gently into the house and up a curving flight of stairs.

"Thanks for coming down to meet me," I said. "Is the Mini yours?"

"It is—like you, I love those vintage English cars."

I laughed.

"You're crediting me with too much taste," I said. "The Morris was cheap, and those engines go on for ever."

We walked past a small kitchenette, and he ushered me into a cosy sitting room. Sun streamed through the glass. From the windows, a view of curving lawn and a rose bed the size of Wales gave way to woodland. I caught sight of a deer. This was what money bought you. Who knew?

"Too true," Crispin was saying. "Can I bring you tea? Coffee? Biscuits?"

I sat where I could see the lawn and then looked up at Crispin. The calm of his voice wasn't matched by his face. Dark shadows under his eyes said he hadn't slept well in days. His hands shook slightly.

"Honestly, I am fine. I hope you don't mind me saying how sorry I am about everything. It must be frightful—for you, as well as Irene."

He sat down abruptly and put his face in his hands. He didn't speak for at least a minute and when he did, the lovely voice trembled.

"I'd never seen a body before," he said. "I don't even watch detective films. You could smell the blood. I'm never eating meat again. Irene and I—we just want to be somewhere else. And I feel like this house is cursed. He's going to be buried just beyond the damned gazebo, for Christ's sake."

"I'm so sorry, I shouldn't have said anything."

"It's alright. I think about it all the time. I can't sleep."

I went through to the kitchenette, found some china and the kettle, and put on a brew. I made two mugs of builders' tea and added plenty of sugar. There were some chocolate biscuits, which I shook onto a plate. Finally, I dug out a tray and ported my booty back through to where Crispin was hunched in his chair. He'd regained a little poise.

"Thank you, but you're the guest, you know," he said, taking a mug and gulping some of the contents down. "It's my job to make the tea."

I sat opposite him and mainlined four chocolate biscuits. They were the expensive Florentine types with little raisins in, and nuts. They were also completely out of my budget. I'd been on plain digestives for weeks.

"I like making tea," I said. "And I shouldn't have mentioned it. I'd no idea you were the person who found him. I didn't realise you were Derowen's personal secretary. I would have been more considerate if I'd known."

Crispin cupped his hands round the mug. He didn't look like he could stab anyone with a letter opener. He didn't look like he could stab a letter with one.

"It was the most awful evening. He was in a foul mood, and he wouldn't let me go home. He doesn't run the business from day to day anymore, so mostly I work on Irene's charity projects—fundraising dinners, race meets… I wouldn't have stayed otherwise. But that night, he wanted a whole load of redundancy letters doing—he loved penning those, I can tell you—and nothing I did was right for him. Then Irene came in, crying. The bastard had left divorce papers on her bed, can you believe it? After thirty-five years!"

I thought of the fake-tanned lizard who'd groped my arse in front of his wife. Yup, I could believe it. It didn't make it OK for someone to murder him, but I was softening towards his killer.

Crispin fumbled in a pocket for a handkerchief and blew his nose noisily.

"She was twenty when they met, you know," he continued. "He was forty-nine. People said she was a gold digger, but you've met her. She's not like that. God knows why, but she loved him. I'm glad he's dead. When I find out who killed him, I'll shake his hand."

I ate two more biscuits and drank some tea. I didn't have a lot to say in response to Crispin. I actually felt a little uncomfortable listening to him because I knew how he felt. If I thought too deeply about it, I wasn't pure as the driven snow when it came to revenge. I'd hunted down and taken out the vampires who'd kidnapped Peter. Crispin sounded quite loyal enough to have killed Derowen for breaking Irene's heart—he just could never have pulled it off.

I looked up to find him watching me anxiously. Did he think I would tell Irene what he'd said, that he'd broken down? Was he regretting his outburst?

"I'm not a gossip, you know," I said. "You're very loyal to her, and that's a good thing."

"Thank you," he said. "But not everyone feels the same. The police asked over and over again. Who went in after he shut the door on Irene? I told them no one, but they didn't believe me. And Mel, the fellow who was replacing the lights, he told them, too. But I still think if there hadn't been the security camera footage, we'd both be in jail."

"I'm glad you're not," I said on autopilot.

"Thanks," he said, equally distracted. "I'm better now. Shall I take you through to Irene?"

We walked through elegant corridors. They had a personal touch that Jay's endless expanses of ecru were missing. There were cut flowers, some pictures that had actual pictures in the frames rather than just clever splashes of paint, ornaments that weren't ugly... Irene hadn't left the décor to professionals.

"I think it's a good idea for her to move, you know," I said. "Even if he'd died naturally, there would be so many reminders. What does she need with this enormous place anyway? It must have twenty bedrooms. And who wants their own graveyard?"

Apart from me, of course. I would have loved my own graveyard. I pondered the possibilities as I followed Crispin. En suites were all very well, a croquet lawn made for lovely summer parties, but for me, a well-stocked cemetery was always going to come out top of the wish list. Lovely moss-covered headstones, the occasional well-embossed cenotaph, a mausoleum or two, the odd Gothic angel...

We turned into a corridor to find a woman idly dusting a mirror. She turned as we approached. She had softly-lined, oak-coloured skin and her fine-boned face was framed by tight, black ringlets that had been rather ruthlessly scraped back into a careless bun. We had come upon the elusive Daphne... Clearly, Derowen's unexpected demise had indeed put her dismissal on hold for the time being.

She nodded at us, dignified and elegant, and I could see instantly why Derowen must have hated her. She had all the assurance and poise that he'd never attained in life. The wonder of it was that he hadn't canned her when he bought the house.

"She's not having a great day," she said to Crispin in a soft Staffordshire accent before nodding in my direction. "I hope what you've brought her will cheer her up."

I regarded her thoughtfully. Here was the woman who'd lived in this labyrinthian rabbit hole for decades and knew all its secrets. Had she crept up on Derowen through a secret route that even the police had failed to discover and ended his life in a fit of cold-blooded vengeance? She didn't look the type to me, but then— as my brother was fond of saying—if all murderers looked like murderers, they'd be a bloody sight easier to catch.

"I hope so," I said. "I take it you're not exactly prostrate with grief at Derowen's demise either."

She raised her chin at me, a half-smile creeping across her face.

"I can see what you're thinking," she said. "But no, I didn't kill him. I would have done given half a chance, mind, but I wasn't prepared to go to jail for that sad sack. I'm with Crispin; I'm sad for Irene but the world's a better place without him."

She nodded again, this time in dismissal, and Crispin and I made our way past her and down the corridor.

I frowned at her words. Was she taunting me? Did she know my brother was investigating Derowen's murder, or was I just seeing potential killers on every corner?

Crispin distracted me from my daydream by knocking on a door panel, and I realised we had reached our destination. There was no answer, but then a sleepy voice said something I couldn't make out, and he pushed open the door. Irene was sitting on a sofa, a magazine hastily pulled onto her lap. It was upside down. There was a bottle of wine in a cooler on the little table at her elbow and a crystal glass. The glass was empty. The bottle wasn't far behind it. She looked like she hadn't slept either. I didn't think her dreams had been sweet ones when she did manage to nod off.

"Miss Windsor," she began.

She didn't get much further because all the wine she had drunk was getting in the way.

"Toni, please," I said, as I sat down and took out a folder full of maps and house particulars. "How well do you know Dartmouth? I think it's the most beautiful town on the south coast." I was chattering to cover up the fact that my hostess had temporarily lost the power of speech. "Except, of course, it's not on the coast but a few miles up the estuary, so you don't get the harsh coastal weather."

She blinked.

"I went once on holiday as a child," she said vaguely. "I always promised myself I would live there."

"Well, here's what I think," I said.

I told her what I thought. I showed her where the tourists went and how to avoid them. I pointed out where the sun shone and where the ferries docked. While I nattered on, Crispin removed the wine and brought coffee. After two cups, Irene's eyes started to focus. She picked up the top brochure I had placed in front of her.

"This one, again," she said.

"Five bedrooms, self-contained annex, water frontage, mooring rights, half acre of garden and a roof terrace with a sliding glass ceiling. Georgian frame, parking for six cars."

"It's the best of all these."

"That's why it's on top. It's also empty. I can have you in there in a week."

"Done. Make it happen."

"You don't want to view it?" I asked in alarm.

"I want to get out of here. Crispin will sign anything you need."

"Fine."

She finished a second cup of coffee. I noticed she was still wearing long cotton gloves. They looked brand new.

"How's that nice boyfriend of yours?" she asked unexpectedly.

"Jay? Nice, as always," I said evasively.

"Too nice? Don't tell me you're going to trade him in for a bastard. Pick a kind man, my dear. Save yourself the grief."

"Irene, if we only fell for the good ones, the world would be a better place. The last man I had a serious relationship with punched me in the face, and the one I'm currently in love with appears to have left me for his career. If I could fall in love with Jay, believe me, I would. I'm still trying."

She laughed then.

"Don't trust your heart, young lady. Take it from one who knows."

It wasn't the first time I'd been told that. I left her looking at her coffee cup. I thought she was contemplating upgrading it for vodka. I didn't blame her.

Daphne was still dusting when we emerged, though she'd moved a few yards down the corridor. She looked up and smiled somewhat enigmatically, as poised as before.

"Did you find her a new home?" she asked.

"I did," I said. "Will you go with her?"

She shook her head.

"Staffordshire's my home," she said. "With luck, whoever buys this place will keep me on, and Irene will want someone to stay here until a buyer is found."

I nodded and tried not to look too dubious. She'd kept her job. People have killed for a great deal less.

"Good luck," I said. "I'll put in a good word for you. Maybe just don't mention the murder when I show people around? It's been known to deter the keenest of buyers."

She laughed.

"I can imagine. Don't worry, I won't let them think the dead will be summoned from their graves before they've so much as exchanged contracts."

Something she said gave me pause but I couldn't place it, and before I could interrogate my subconscious any further, she turned back to her cleaning and Crispin ushered me away.

* * *

I TEXTED NICKY in the afternoon to find out if the police had released Lorraine's body. He would get the message when he woke and, if we could manage a Kirsty-free evening, I could question his girlfriend's corpse about how she'd died. I could have asked Wills about the body, but displaying interest in the case wasn't going to act in Nicky's favour. More to the point, if I threw police attention onto the Assemblage, it wouldn't act in my favour. Getting Nicky into trouble would make me feel bad. Getting on Benedict Akil's wrong side would get me killed. Slowly.

I drove home wondering how far Paul had made it through my documents. I'd poked a nose round the bedroom door before heading off to work, and the body on the bed looked deader than a lot of the ones I raised at night. The chances of Paul having woken at all weren't that good.

Turns out, I'd underestimated the recuperative powers of a teenager. The cottage was empty, and he'd left me a note.

Yes, I got up, he'd written, adding with a burst of honesty: *Eventually! But Bethany has rung every eleven minutes and I am throwing in the towel and fleeing the house. I've gone to try and persuade Jenny that it's OK to be bi. Well, actually, she has a new distributer for the moped. I'm taking it round so we can fit it together. I will be back tonight some time. Sorry I didn't finish translating your creepy contracts.*

The note made me frown, not because I needed Paul to tell me his plans, and not really because I wanted him to translate the contracts right then and there. They were decades old—one was older than me—so a day here or there could hardly make the difference. No. I was frowning because Paul's friendship with Jenny drew him into the circle of the Assemblage, something that I'd really hoped to avoid.

The more I thought about it, the more I'd totally failed on that front. I'd thrown him together with Benedict when I'd asked the vampire to heal him. It was only natural that Paul would think of Benedict when I was hurt. But, I recalled with sudden horror, if the conversation I'd vaguely overheard when I was half unconscious was real, then Paul had given his blood after I'd been healed, and that made my own run cold.

Because I remembered just how good that had felt. It was a feeling that time was never going to dull or make less alluring. Had it been the same for Paul? When he and Jenny had pulled apart his little bike and reassembled it, would he hang around for sunset and try for a repeat? I put my face in my hands for a moment. Paul wasn't a child. He would be nineteen in the autumn. I had to let him make his own decisions. I'd just never wanted him to know these ones were out there to be made.

I ate toast, sitting on the sofa with Winchester on my knee, and watched some rubbish until the sun finally dipped behind the trees. A while later, Nicky's text arrived.

It was a little convoluted:

Yes, but Kirsty and both families there until maybe midnight. Some Catholic thing? Vigil, I think. No idea. My mother is Jewish. It's St Fremund's. Meet you there say 1am?

I sent back my agreement and perched on the sofa, wondering how to fill the hours before it came to me. Sod it—why summon just one zombie on a warm summer night? What were cemeteries for? I would pack up some undead-friendly food and head over to St Fremund's without waiting. I knew the graveyard there—it was down the hill from the church, and no one would bother me. I could make some new friends while nasty Kirsty pretended she was sorry that Lorraine was dead. There was really no point in being a necromancer if you didn't raise the dead. I tipped the cat off my knee and headed towards the kitchen.

Chapter Fifteen

ST FREMUND'S WAS one of the older churches in the county, with a long narrow graveyard that wound down towards the river. I'd not tried rousing its occupants from their rest, but only because the place was such a long drive from Colton.

There was also a helpful schematic of the graves and their occupants pinned up in the porch. I appreciated the gesture. St Fremund's might not be as old as St Chad's in the centre of Stafford, but it wasn't far behind. With the best will in the world, it was tough going to make out sixteenth century names after the passage of time had smoothed them to dimples and laid down an inch of moss and lichen on top. I selected as my targets Jeremy Penny, 1520-1588, beloved husband, and Pearl Lester, 1505-1561, devoted wife. They would be the oldest corpses I'd ever raised.

The supermarket just outside Stoneydelph had piled the discount shelf with some rather nasty-looking fruit cakes. They'd been seventy-five per cent off. I hoped neither Jeremy nor Pearl were gourmands because I was pretty sure those cakes had been made with lard rather than butter and bulked out with soy. They were topped with 'chocolate flavour buttons.' I ate one as I wandered down the hill to the lower graves. It contained no chocolate—and no flavour either. It wasn't a night to raise picky zombies. Derowen would probably have thrown the damn cake back in my face.

Devoted wife Pearl didn't. Pearl ate four of them and told me what an arse her husband had been. I'd not heard the word 'feckless' used in casual conversation before, and I wasn't really sure what it meant. Pearl was though, and from what I could make out, the long-departed Mr Lester really hadn't had any fecks, not a single one, nor any other redeeming virtues. I let her rant for a bit before sending her back.

Beloved husband Jeremy Penny wasn't much better. He didn't feel very beloved. His wife was pretty but distant and all his children had red hair. Jeremy was a blonde. The head groomsman, though, he was ginger. And younger, thinner and cuter than Jeremy... Jeremy glared at my copper curls. Nope, we weren't going to be friends. I sent him back, too.

It was close to midnight by then and I only had five cakes left. I would probably need them all for Lorraine. I'd also cut four slices into each wrist to drag my reluctant revenants from their eternal sleep. If I drained myself of much more energy, Lorraine's rest would remain undisturbed. I slung everything back in the boot of my car and sat in it with the lights off.

I watched the beautiful Kirsty leave first, her gold hair catching the faceted light of the church windows. She didn't look very mournful. She looked as hard as nails, her perfect features lovely but unyielding. It struck me for the first time — why wasn't she grieving, too? I disliked her so much that I hadn't thought about it rationally. But Nicky said she'd chosen his coterie, that they were like sisters... I'd accepted what he'd said at face value, but now I had to wonder. Had he been economical with the truth? Because I didn't think I was looking at a girl who'd just bid the third of her sisters goodbye. Kirsty slung an expensive-looking coat onto the back seat of the sleek silver car that I'd previously seen parked outside the rectory and roared off with a screech of rubber.

Next came a man and woman, Lorraine's parents, I assumed. His arm clutched her to him, and her cheek was pressed into his chest. The light caught the studs on the collar of her jacket, the little crystals in her ears, and her tears as they poured down her face into her neck. You don't just kill a person when you murder them—you destroy a family, friendships, hopes and dreams. The man helped her into a small saloon, and it drove off into the night.

There was only one car left, an elderly black hatchback with nearly as many rust patches as my Morris. I rather thought I recognised it and when I saw the man locking up the church, the sandy hair bright above his near dog collar, I remembered where. It was Father Luke Emmanuel, last seen feeding me coffee in a little church up in the hills near Doveridge. I opened the car door.

"Father Luke," I called. "It's me, Toni. Toni Windsor."

"Well met, sister. I'm filling in for the parish priest down here for a few weeks. But you're a little late to pay your respects?"

He walked to my car and took both my hands in his. He looked pleased to see me but wary. I couldn't blame him—I was lurking outside a church in a car with my lights out at midnight. My motives had to be complex at best.

"I'm waiting for Lorraine's boyfriend, Father," I said hastily. "Her parents didn't know about him. We wanted to wait until everyone had gone."

There. All true. Not a single lie, just omissions. My conscience was nearly clear.

"I see," said Father Luke. "Well, perhaps that's for the best. I take it there's no point in me locking up then?"

I looked embarrassed. He knew full well that I'd picked the locks of the church up at Doveridge. To cover for my guilt, I walked over and shone my torch at the church door.

"Nope," I said. "Only three barrels. I could do that in about four minutes without the torch. But don't worry—I'll lock it again when we're done here."

"Come in, then, and wait for your friend," he said.

We walked into the church, and he put on a few lights for me. I'd never been inside the building before, and the red sandstone exterior that I'd occasionally driven past hadn't prepared me for such an architectural gem. The church was properly Gothic, with a bank of original lancet windows down each side. Some still sported their original tracery, though the majority had been shored up at some point. A couple dozen traditional, bottom-numbing dark pews ran down each side. Overhead paintings had been lovingly restored and the ceiling dotted with birdcage lights with soft, diffuse bulbs that illuminated the interior with an almost candle-like glow.

They shone down on wooden racks supporting an old-fashioned coffin, a wooden tomb of glossy pale wood with brass handles and curlicues. It stood just in front of the sanctuary, solitary and alone. I thought of walking through Nicky's house, the riot of colour, the bonds of friendship he'd described. All three young women had come to this, and only one would be given a decent burial. My fingers curled into claws for a moment.

I made my way to the coffin through a jungle of blooms. A hothouse of flowers filled the church until the scent of gardenias and lilies drowned out the incense. Thousands of pounds worth of flowers. Had Nicky stumped up for them?

Father Luke echoed my thoughts.

"Is this mystery boyfriend the one who sent the flowers?" he asked. "Lorraine's family certainly couldn't have afforded them, and I doubt that hard-eyed young lady with the blonde hair would have sent so much as a daisy."

"I think so. It would be like him."

"Well then, it was a kind gesture. I don't think the family realised. They were too overwhelmed to notice the flora. The coroner was very kind. His verdict allows her to be buried here, but the inquest was an ordeal I wouldn't wish on anyone. They will wonder all their lives if they should have known she wasn't well or was so unhappy that she killed herself."

Nicky's quiet voice interrupted us. I spun round to see his silhouette in the church door, sharp against the porch light. His white hair shimmered slightly in the light. He was wearing all black for once, including a long, flappy coat that I would have found meltingly hot on such a warm summer night, but that Nicky—being cold blooded—would probably have happily upgraded for a fur tepee.

"She didn't," he said, with his usual gentleness. "She was killed, and when I find out who did it, he'll die, too."

The words were spoken with such sweetness that neither Father Luke nor I processed them for a few heartbeats.

"Nicky," I said reprovingly, not because I expected anything less from vampire justice, but because I didn't think he should have said it in front of the priest.

He shrugged one slim shoulder.

"It's the truth," he said. "I should have looked after her better. At the very least, she'll have vengeance."

"Vengeance, my son, is God's work," said Father Luke in fierce tones.

Nicky tossed back his hair with a poise that I knew to be assumed. He carried it off well, though. The dim lighting helped.

"Then I'll be the hand of God."

I bit my lip. This was a conversation that shouldn't be happening. Nicky should have been more tactful, and I should have kept the two of them apart. But Father Luke raised his hands in a gesture of conciliation. Perhaps he thought Nicky's words just the ravings of the bereaved.

"I'll leave you to mourn, young man," he said softly. "Be careful."

And he left us in the half-lit, flower-scented bower of the church and headed out into the night. After a few moments, I heard his car start up and drive away. We were alone with just the dead for company.

"What do we do now?" asked Nicky tentatively.

His semblance of calm confidence had vanished with Father Luke's car. I glared at him. I should never have agreed to meet him here. I should have come on my own.

"You go and wait outside," I snapped. "I raise the dead and you stay out of the way. There's no 'we' in this."

"I want to see her!"

"Nicky, it's not like that," I pleaded. "The dead aren't like the living. They don't want to be here, and they don't have a lot of spirit or emotion left. You won't get back what you lost, you know.

Lorraine won't be the person you remember. There won't be a touching goodbye. Please believe me. I do this a lot."

"But..."

"No, no, and no way. Nicky, please just bugger off, or I won't do this at all."

He spun on his heel and vanished into the dark in a swish of black coat. The church door slammed behind him. I sat on a pew and put my head into my hands for a moment. I was being a complete cow, and poor Nicky got enough of that at home from Kirsty. I should have been kinder and, like Father Luke, remembered that Nicky's dead girlfriend was lying in the church, this holy place he'd filled full of flowers. Well, I'd done it now, and it couldn't be undone. I could apologise later. But for now? For now, I would do what I'd come for.

I opened my handbag and took out salt and perfume. I'd brought two screwdrivers, too, just in case, but thankfully, I wouldn't need them. The coffin was open, its occupant lying like Sleeping Beauty, waiting for the prince I'd sent out into the dark with a flea in his ear. Well, she would get me instead.

I'd never raised the dead in a church. It felt slightly sacrilegious. Surrounded by statues of saints, a hundred crucifixes and the stations of the cross, I felt I was breaking a million rules. But Lorraine didn't care. She came to my call as the scent of my perfume rose above the aroma of flowers and the cinnamon bite of incense.

Whatever injuries she'd sustained, the undertakers had done a good job of covering them up. A round, freckled face was set under a magnificent mane of black curls. Nicky had said she was a hairdresser. Well, she was a good advert for her profession. The eyes she opened were bloodshot and rheumy, but they'd been dark once, sparkling with life. What had Nicky said? That she'd been heaps of fun, always giggling and laughing, and that he'd never got a word in edgeways. Well, he could have got them all in tonight, because Lorraine was a modern-day Marie Antoinette. All she wanted to do was eat cake. I let her mainline two before I began my questions.

"Lorraine Keel, tell me about your death."

I was desperately hoping for something simple while knowing in my heart I wouldn't get it. A simple murderer didn't coax a sane young woman to throw herself into a mineshaft with bleeding bare feet. I couldn't have been more right. Her voice was sweet and low when she answered, but it didn't tell me anything useful.

"There was a golden bird," she said. "It was taking me to heaven. So I followed it."

I heaved a deep sigh. If anything, she was being less helpful than Derowen Polkerris. She might be less objectionable, but the results were just as useless.

"It sang the sweetest songs," she continued. "The whole world was filled with music. Bells and chimes and the sound of waterfalls. I sang, too."

"Let's go back, then, Lorraine," I said, with as much patience as I could muster. "What happened before that? Before the sodding golden bird?"

My goodness, Nicky had spoilt his household. She'd idled out of bed at nine, the housekeeper had cooked her pancakes and then she'd deep conditioned her hair. She'd gone to a spa for a massage and a facial and then wandered back for lunch. There was a delivery for her—some sexy lingerie, a silk slip—that she assumed was from Nicky, so she'd tried it on. And then her narrative slipped. It stopped making any sense...

"The golden bird was singing," she said mistily, showing more enthusiasm than your average dead person usually did. "It was so beautiful, so lovely. Have you ever heard it? It promised to teach me to fly."

Well, she'd gone flying. Briefly. I ground my teeth with frustration.

"Go back again, Lorraine. The parcel: was there any message on it? Are you sure Nicky sent it?"

"He gave us presents all the time," she said, flatly, the enthusiasm gone now that she wasn't talking about the damn bird. "I hadn't worked since Caroline left. He was always trying to cheer me up. Shoes, jewellery, perfume, clothes."

Out of the corner of my eye, I saw movement. Nicky had disobeyed me after all. He'd crept back into the church. He walked towards the coffin, his eyes fixed on Lorraine. They were filled with something in between hope and horror. I thrust another cake at her, and she crammed it into her mouth. She used both hands.

"Nicky, please just sod off," I growled at him. "This will only make things worse. The girl you loved isn't here."

He ignored me and came to stand at my elbow.

"Lorraine, it's me. It's Nicky," he said, urgently. "I'm here now."

I could have told him she wouldn't pay attention. I was the necromancer, not him; only I got to tell the dead what to do. She didn't even register the vampire's presence. She just held out her hand hopefully for the last cake.

"I'm hungry," she said to me.

"Lorraine, I miss you," he said. "It's so quiet without you all."

But she looked at me, her face covered in crumbs. She licked her lips and held out her other hand, too.

"Feed me," she said. "Please."

"Lorraine," Nicky whispered desperately, a break in his voice.

Why couldn't he have stayed in the bloody car park for ten bloody minutes? No one ever listened to me unless I'd dragged them out of a grave first.

"Lorraine Keel, I release you to your rest," I barked. "Go in peace."

She lay back obediently on the silk cushioning of the coffin and closed her eyes. Nicky stood, rooted to the spot, as I began to clear cake crumbs from her face and hands.

"She didn't know me," he said. "I thought at least she'd know me."

"She's dead, Nicky," I said. "I'm really, really sorry. I tried to stop you. I didn't want to make things worse. I can drag them back, but they rarely want to be here. Maybe half a dozen times in all the years I've been doing this, I've found someone who came back with some spirit in them."

I thought of Bredon, my one true success story, and the venerable and charming Sir Caspar de Beaumont, resident of St Chad's in Stafford. Maybe, now I put my mind to it, that lively and loathsome lizard with the wandering hands, Derowen Polkeriss. He'd risen from his trolley at the morgue with a little vim and vigour. But not little Lorraine Keel. She'd been perfectly happy being dead before I hauled her back to eat stale, cheap cake in a dark church...

The church door slammed again. Nicky Carlyon had left. I couldn't blame him. The girl he'd loved had been murdered, and he'd hoped to say goodbye to her that night. If I'd realised, I would have pretended I couldn't call her and come back another time. It was a lesson learned.

However, I'd also hoped he would escort me back to my little cottage. I was once again left to sleep elsewhere or walk the gauntlet from car to house and hope that Gin Martin wasn't lurking in the dark. I weighed up my options as I turned off the lights and shut up shop, and then remembered with a rush of relief that I wasn't alone anymore. I drove as far as the bridge at the bottom of Colton and dialled Paul's mobile. A sleepy voice answered after just a few rings.

"Mffff," it said. "S'mffff Toni?"

"Hey," I said. "Are you at the cottage?"

"Yeah. Um, why?"

"Can you put on the lights and open the front door? If Gin is lurking, he won't make a move if he thinks he's being watched."

"Sure. Two minutes, yeah?"

When I arrived, the house was a blaze of lights—he'd turned on every single bulb in the place. The door was ajar, and a half-awake teenager was leaning against the jamb. I blinked. Yup, he was wearing an eiderdown. Fair enough—I hadn't given him a lot of warning. I parked up at the kerb and bounded inside. It's good not to be alone in the world.

Chapter Sixteen

I SLEPT THROUGH my alarm and woke late enough that I arrived at work with wet hair and no breakfast inside me. The former, the passage of time would solve. For the latter, I bribed Bethany to walk across the square for coffee and bacon butties.

I was pleased to find some messages responding to my marketing offensive. My diary was still pretty sparse, but no longer blank enough to keep Bernie moaning about laying me off. I was congratulating myself on a job well done when my mobile rang.

"So, it's Mary," a bossy voice said. "I forgot to tell you—you need to re-register your chip."

Who? What? Where?

"Um," I managed. "This is Toni."

"Yes, yes, I know. It's Mary Hollands, the vet from Hopton. Your cat's chip needs re-registering."

"Mary, thank you for calling, but I don't have a clue what you're talking about."

There was a sigh. It was unpleasantly familiar. Teachers at school had used that sigh on me a lot.

"I finally recognised your cat while I was cleaning his teeth," she said. "He was Amelia's cat. He has a front incisor missing. I took it out two years ago when he broke it on a dog.

"Anyway, I micro-chipped him at the same time and the chip is still registered at her house in Salt. If you drop round, I'll give you the form."

She hung up before I could say anything else, but that was for the best because I didn't have anything to say. I stared at the phone in complete disbelief. It had been that simple all along, but I'd not made the connection.

I knew why Gin Martin hated me. I had a good idea why the coroner wanted to see me, too. And if I'd only had half a brain, I'd have realised both things the minute my brother had told me his name. I shook my head and called Wills. There was an easy way to be sure.

"Hey, bro. I think I know who Gin Martin is and why he wants to kill me."

"Good luck to him. He has four broken ribs, a fractured skull, a pin in his ankle and a cast on his left arm. But seriously, what have you found out?"

"Do you remember the old lady I used to look after? The one who cooked for me all the time, Amelia Scott Martin…"

"I never met her, but yes. You talked about her all the time. She died last year, yes?"

Indeed. She'd had a troubled death. Killed by vampires, raised as a zombie, and then killed by vampires again. They'd torn her limb from limb. Christ knows how Benedict had covered it up, or what was actually in her coffin. I'd paid for the funeral, and I didn't have a clue.

"Mmm," I said. "That's her. Well, I think Grahame is her son; it's more than just the name—she told me her son had turned out badly. And now that I cast my mind back, she even told me about the medals he stole. I didn't connect it until the vet reminded me that I'd accidentally inherited Winchester from her. Now I think she must have intentionally left me something in her will. I think Gin tried to claim it and lost, but for some reason I don't know anything about it. Can you look into it?"

"Yes, but are you sure?"

"I am, and here's why: John Jones works as a solicitor. He does wills. And I always recommend him to the old ladies who buy or rent through us because he's so courteous and charming. He's a complete gentleman. I can't remember doing it, but I would definitely have recommended him to Amelia. I think that's why he wants to see me. I don't think it's anything to do with his being the coroner. I think he did Amelia's will for her before she died, and I reckon he wants to talk to me about this mystery inheritance. And Gin wants to kill me for it."

There was a silence. Then:

"Yes, OK, that makes a lot of sense. Doesn't help us find the little wanker, but at least we know his agenda. I will call probation back and check it out. Please watch your back, sis, and if you see anyone limping towards you with a nasty look in his eye, remember to push him under a bus."

I laughed and went back to work. At quarter to eleven, I hoisted my handbag and walked across the town square. There are some old-school shops selling twelve-bore shotguns, cigars and riding leathers. I'd never made a purchase, but the window shopping was fun. The market was in full swing, with stalls selling hand-poured chocolates, hand-made soaps, hand-painted ties and Denby seconds. There was a busker playing a zither very badly. I bought a box of chocolates for the long-suffering Karen. She'd spent two weeks trying to arrange for me to meet up with her boss, and I wanted us to get off to a good start.

As I paid for them, I recognised the figure next to me. It was Jiří from the bar, fingering an ornate box of soap at the stall across from the gun shop.

"Hey," I said. "Not that one. Lavender irritates my skin."

He looked up with a start. Did he even recognise me? We'd never spoken, and he'd only glanced at me a couple of times across a dark bar. He was wearing makeup again, but this time I realised it wasn't because he was exploring his feminine side—he was covering up a massive black eye. In the dim light of the bar, it had worked but in sunlight I could see the tell-tale swelling and the sheen of powder.

"I didn't see you," he said very politely in his soft Prague accent.

"It's Jenny, isn't it?"

I laughed.

"I can tell you've never met Jenny," I said. "You really wouldn't get the two of us confused. She's twelve inches taller than me for a start."

He inclined his head civilly. I couldn't put my finger on it, but he seemed ill at ease with me.

"Forgive me," he said. "I recognised you as one of Grace's coterie, but we never spoke."

"Oh, goodness, no," I said, acutely embarrassed. "I'm not at all. I'm not in any kind of coterie anymore. I try to keep away from vampires, to be honest, but Grace is OK, and Camilla is adorable. I was just there with them as a friend."

For a moment he looked really shocked, and I couldn't think what I'd said that was so upsetting, but then he schooled his features back into a look of gentle interest.

"My mistake," he said, again in quite a formal way. "I will remember. What happened to your coterie?"

I sighed. I didn't know Jiří from Adam, but if I didn't answer his question, he could get a distorted version of the truth from anyone in Emir's bar that evening.

"I was in love with a vampire, Jiří, but he turned against me and nearly killed me," I said. "And the other member of our coterie, who I really love, left me to go back to Heidelberg, so now I'm all alone. It's not a great anecdote and it doesn't have a happy ending. If you wanted a better story, the new James Bond opens at the weekend."

"I'm sorry," he said. "To be parted from the one you love, that's life's cruellest blow. Why don't you follow him?"

"Jiří, he doesn't want me to, OK? I asked. He told me not to come."

Jiří picked up the soap again and turned it in his hands.

"You should go anyway," he said. "Make him change his mind."

I blinked. This was incel talk. I hardly knew the man, but he was already telling me how to rework my love life. In quite a creepy way.

"I'll think about it," I said, as I edged away. "And don't buy the lavender soap. Get a nice rose or jasmine. Lavender is for old ladies."

I left him fondling the soap. I couldn't put my finger on it, but I found him a little unnerving. There was something not right with the man. But who was I to throw stones? I raised the dead for a hobby. I made bungee jumpers look staid.

JOHN JONES' OFFICE was in a lane off St Chad's Place, on the ground floor of one of the lovely, old, red-brick buildings that make up the edge of town between the old courts and St Mary's Church. I pushed open the glass door to find a small reception desk. The extremely well-preserved woman behind it could only be Karen. Determinedly blonde curls framed a face so friendly and good-natured that not even working for the coroner appeared to have taken its toll. Huge brown eyes were set over an even huger smile. She had a few lines, but they were all laughter lines. No dents from frowning. This lady never frowned. No wonder John Jones was able to run such a successful little business on the side. With his charm, and Karen's smile, he would never run short of clients. They'd come here just for the company and never mind the bill.

"Hi, you must be Karen," I said. "I'm Toni Windsor."

"Oh, my goodness, aren't you like your father?" she said, completely throwing me off my stride. "I would have guessed just from the hair. We were in the same class at school, you know."

I stared at her with my mouth open. After a few moments I remembered to close it again. It would stop all the thousands of questions I wanted to ask but shouldn't from tumbling out unchecked. Then I drew in a breath.

"No, I didn't," I said. "I don't know that I've ever met any of my parents' friends. Have you come across my brother? He looks just like the photos of Dad when he was younger."

"I've met him a couple of times," she said, nodding so vigorously that the blonde curls bobbed up and down; she had a voice like chiming bells. "The police detective. Such a lovely boy. Now let me take you through to John. He was delighted when you rang yesterday."

"Thank you," I said, and dumped the chocolates on her desk. "I brought these for you."

She was effusive in her thanks. I got a hug. Some people's full-on enthusiasm is fake and repellent. There was nothing fake about Karen. Wills had told me she was hopeless as a secretary, but you'd hire her just for the smile when she brought you morning coffee. She was still chattering merrily if rather randomly to me as she knocked on a dark wooden door: how my father had always liked history, how she'd been hopeless at sports, how busy the coroner had been with that terrible accident on the motorway...

"...and now, of course, with the brother still unconscious, the police are appealing for more witnesses," she burbled. "John, Ms Windsor is here."

She pushed open the door and we stepped into another world. John Jones had studied law in the days before computers and mobile phones. I doubted he could type his name. His room was a giant bookcase broken up by a window and the door. His desk was awash with stacks of papers; there was an old-fashioned phone on it, a desk lamp, some brass bulldog clips – all the office accoutrements that a young upcoming lawyer about town would have no use for. The man getting up from behind it was immaculately dressed in a charcoal suit, crisp cotton shirt and a club tie. Light grey wisps of hair were neatly cropped. Slightly milky blue eyes twinkled over a wide face. Mr John Jones, coroner and part time solicitor, was as good-natured as his secretary, though entirely dignified.

"Dear Ms Windsor," he said. "How good of you to come. Who would have thought this would take so many months? Please take a seat. Karen, if you'd be so kind?"

He very chivalrously tugged out a chair and then tucked it in for me. Karen scurried out and returned moments later with a foiled bottle and three glasses. I watched in simple confusion as my host stripped off the lead, unwired the cork and then popped it out with nearly as much competence as Benedict Akil. He poured three foamy glasses, handed two around, and raised the third.

"To probate," he said.

We chinked decorously. It was like being with vampires. I didn't have a clue what was going on. I chugged down most of my glass.

"Thank you, Mr Jones, but you know, I am a little in the dark here."

"Dear me, I hoped my letters explained everything."

Ah. A tiny light bulb went on in my head.

"Yes, um, here's the thing," I said carefully. "I've never had a single letter from you."

Mr Jones looked quite shocked.

"Good gracious, but I must have sent you thirty over the last eleven months," he said. "Karen's fingers can type your name and address all on their own by now. Karen dear, what address have you been sending Toni's correspondence to?"

Her face was a picture. I hadn't seen such an expression of oh-what-have-I-done since I tried to clean my own teeth with hair removal cream.

"Oh, my goodness, how stupid of me. I've been sending them to the address in Salt. They've all gone to Amelia's house!"

Mr Jones looked quite horrified. He tugged out a handkerchief the size of a sail and mopped his face with it. I broke in hurriedly:

"Well, no harm done, is there? Perhaps you could just summarise the details for me?"

"Of course, of course," he said. "Thank you. As I am sure you know, Mrs Scott Martin left you her entire estate. She wasn't rich, her income being in the form of two annuities and a pension which expired with her death, but she owned the little house outright, and there are some savings and a little jewellery. The latter I have here in my safe."

She hadn't left me a little something. She'd left me a lot of everything, the whole damn kit and caboodle. My heart broke a little—my occasional visits must have meant a great deal to her, and I'd never realised. I should have gone more often. But no wonder Gin was pissed off at me. He'd thought a nice nest egg was coming his way; instead, it had all come to me. Well, it served the murderous little wanker right.

Mr Jones was still speaking.

"Her son Grahame contested the will, which delayed everything, but as I explained in my letters, he was ultimately unsuccessful. I am now finally able to give you the keys to the house and a cheque for the remainder of the moneys due to you. And I think after eleven months, that calls for a little celebration."

Maybe so, but I sat in stunned silence as he placed various official-looking documents in front of me. I managed to remember my name sufficiently well enough to scrawl some signatures. When I had signed enough paper to make my wrist ache, he handed me a small leather box, a set of keys and cheque for six thousand pounds and change. Then the three of us finished the bottle of champagne and went and ate a steak in the hotel across from the old court.

Karen and John must have found me a quiet companion. I was too gobsmacked by the turn of events to do much more than listen and contributed pretty much sod all to the dinner table conversation. Not that it mattered—the elderly coroner was an entertaining companion and regaled us with tales of the county's mysterious deaths and inquests past.

"My brother said you've been snowed under with this car crash on the motorway," I said eventually.

He shook his head.

"I don't know what to make of it, dear Ms Windsor," he said. "At first, we thought a tragic accident. But now a lady has come forward and claims she saw a second car deliberately force the first off the road. And the boys themselves are not what they seem. Their visas claimed they were in England for a stag party, but none of them are getting married, and all four, it transpires, bought one-way tickets. The only one left alive is still unconscious in the hospital but, two days after the crash, someone broke into his room and stole all his possessions. It's both tragic and mysterious, and I, for one, have no idea what's behind it all. Now, will you peruse the dessert menu?"

The answer to that question was never going to be no, and after a fat slice of lemon meringue pie and some coffee, I ambled back to the office. I left a message on Aidan's phone asking if I could raise the body of Gin Martin's accomplice that night. The corpse of Dylan Moss might well know where Gin was holed up, and it turned out that finding out why the man was on my case hadn't given me any ideas on how to get him off it.

And I certainly wasn't going to offer to recompense him for dear Amelia's decision to cut him out of her will. He'd been a little toad as a son, never visiting her, stealing her possessions, you name it. Amelia had wanted to leave things to me, and I was fine with that. This gift horse could have the skankiest teeth in Christendom, but I wouldn't be looking in its mouth.

I rang Wills from my desk.

"So," I said, by way of introduction, "Gin Martin has it in for me because his mother left me her house."

"It fits," he said. "I just got off the phone from his probation officer. Who, by the way, hasn't seen him since the day he left the care of the residential arm of the Ministry of Justice. His mother died a month before he was released. He has no siblings and was boasting he'd get everything."

"Yeah, well, I get everything, and he can't have it," I said. "Amelia wanted it to come to me, and I'm not letting that rapey gobshite have a single doily after the way he treated her—and me! I'll fight him down to the last damn china kitten."

My brother laughed down the phone.

"Right now, you might win," he said. "Short of clubbing you to death with his crutches, I can't see him taking you down."

Chapter Seventeen

I DROVE HOME in a thoughtful mood, stopping only to buy a dozen end-of-line panettones from the Italian deli that was closing down. Then I remembered I'd just inherited a house and a box of jewellery, so I added a chilled bottle of champagne. I knew who was after me and why. Grahame Martin had come with his friend on a little revenge spree, but it had all gone sour. He'd watched Dylan Moss' blood spray across my kitchen, and he'd ended up in hospital after a trip through a car window.

It struck me for the first time that I had probably written off Grace's car and not even apologised. Still, she'd thought it was hilarious when Camilla had whacked into a sheep with the thing. She was probably still snorting about the fact I'd used her windscreen to take out Grahame.

Except I hadn't taken him out, had I? He was still lurking out there somewhere, madder than ever. I shook my head. If the sorry cadaver of Dylan Moss couldn't help me, I would think of something else.

To my relief, Paul was in when I arrived back. More to the point, bless him, he was sprawled at the kitchen table with reams of nasty demon contracts spread out around him and was chewing on a new biro.

"Your grandfather was a loon," he said conversationally.

"He was a necromancer who hated necromancy."

I put the kettle on and fed the cat. Paul had probably fed him twice already, but the pair of us were weak-willed when it came to resisting feline wiles.

"I never wanted a cat," I said, as I chucked tea bags into mugs. "Trust Peter to give me a bloody cat and then bugger off to Heidelberg. I've always wanted a spaniel. Or one of those big German Leonbergers. You know, Paul, that's exactly what Grandfather Robert was like. He hated his necromancy. He was so angry when he found out I raised the dead. It was like a personal offense."

"And now I know why."

I stared at him and pulled a chair out so that we sat opposite each other.

"Really? It's in there?"

"Certainly is. In the first contract he agrees to do some completely random tasks for Azazel that I am still trying to get my head round. But in return he gets these two cantamen, or enchantments. The second one has a name—Glauce's Wedding Dress—and I haven't the faintest idea what it does. The contract doesn't say. But the first one, well, Azazel makes that just for your Grandfather Robert, and all the details are in there. And get this: it's designed to ensure that none of Robert Kendrick Windsor's descendants possess any paranormal powers."

"But it didn't work. Azazel stabbed him in the back?"

"He did, but not in the way you think. I told you—your grandfather's Latin wasn't good enough to pull this off. He used the word 'heredes.' It means male heirs or descendants. It's not gender neutral."

"You are joking. Azazel screwed him over with bad conjugation?"

"Bad declension, if you want to split hairs. Or heirs. But yes, that's exactly what he did."

I made tea for us both. The irony was painful. My grandfather had jumped through some dangerous hoops to eliminate necromancy and suchlike pandemonium from his family. His sons and grandsons would never have powers. Nothing at all. But the girls in the family?

We would slip through the net he'd cast. And when his son had married a witch, they'd produced me. Trouble squared.

"That's horribly hypocritical," I burst out. "Raising the dead and bargaining with demons to make sure that we couldn't raise the dead or bargain with demons."

"Worse."

"Worse?"

"I've had longer to think about this than you; I've had all day. Your grandfather wasn't a witch, right? So, as well as all this, he also had to persuade a witch to cast this enchantment for him because he wouldn't have been able to do it himself."

Paul was right. My grandfather was like a priest preaching prohibition in the pulpit and then mainlining two bottles of communion wine in the vestry after mass. Consorting with witches so that no one else could consort with witches. I wasn't impressed.

"OK, that's pretty bad," I admitted.

"That's not all. You told me your grandfather was ninety-one when he died, right?"

"Yup."

"Which was almost exactly seven years ago."

"Si, senor."

"But he didn't come into his powers until he turned forty, right?"

"Jawohl."

"So this little project, making sure his descendants wouldn't have any more powers after his generation, it must have been almost the very first thing he did."

Oh my God, he was right. I did the maths and shook my head in disbelief. My grandfather had been the world's biggest ever killjoy. He'd even…

"Paul, this is almost tragic," I said. "If he was honest about when he started raising the dead, then it happened just when he was about to become a dad. So he finds out he's a necromancer when my grandmother is about to give birth. And the next thing you know, he's desperately calling up demons to try to make sure his gifts don't make it to the next generation. And he was only just in time—the first contract is dated the year my dad was born, just before his birthday."

Paul chugged some tea.

"As I said, a necromancer who hated necromancy. That's quite an identity crisis. Do you want to hear any more?"

"I don't know. I haven't enjoyed your revelations so far."

"Well, there's not much more, as it happens. The second contract is much like the first—your granddad agrees to carry out some bizarre tasks for Azazel in return for two more of these bizarre cantamen. One he refers to as Tabula Rasa and the other as Helen of Troy. Mean anything at all?"

"Not a sausage. Paul, for goodness' sake, you're the one who studied Latin. Your Classics has to be better than mine."

"Toni, I listened in class. I even listened in home economics. Believe me, they never taught us any witchcraft. I'd have paid attention."

"I bet you would."

"For sure. Simple enchantments to attract girls and get out of cross-country? I'd have been top of the class. Listen, I'm going to type this up for you so you have a copy that you can actually read. I've been practicing for when I have to write out prescriptions and I can barely read my own handwriting anymore. No one else stands a chance. I'll do it tonight, unless you have more interesting plans."

I planned to go with Aidan to raise Dylan Moss from the dead and cross-examine him as to the whereabouts of his murderous arse of a cellmate, as it happened. I didn't think Paul needed to know that.

"I need to meet with a vampire," I said a little evasively, picking at a cuticle. "I will cook us something before I go."

He didn't say anything. I picked up one of the sheets of paper and pretended to scan it. Was I waiting for him to break some ice I didn't want broken? I was determined not to be the hypocrite my Grandfather Robert had been. Who was I to beg Paul not to associate with vampires? I'd moved in with one. And was I going to implore him not give blood to Benedict? Hardly—we both knew just how good that felt. I felt the moral high ground shift under my feet and collapse. Break the ice, would I? It had always been pretty thin.

"You can come if you want," I said. "I'd like the company."

I made cheese and ham toasties. I was feeling particularly weak-willed that evening, so Winchester got one, too.

"You're using the nice ham," said Paul curiously. "What are we celebrating?"

I thrust the cold bottle of fizz at him.

"My unexpected inheritance," I said. "Take the foil off that and pour."

We chinked glasses and sat down for our rather thrown-together celebratory meal. I explained about Amelia's house and how I'd come to be left in complete ignorance by Karen, the lovely but useless receptionist-cum-secretary.

"So you inherited a whole house eleven months ago and never knew until today?"

"I know, crazy, isn't it…"

"You have keys and everything?"

"I nearly went there straight from work, but I was worried I'd find Gin Martin ahead of me, pouring petrol through the letter box followed by a match."

"And the vampire called Aidan has been storing a corpse for you to raise ever since the vampire called Nicky ripped its head off for you just exactly where we are having supper right now?"

"He didn't rip the head off. He just tore out the throat. Believe you me, if he'd torn off the head, we would have needed new light fittings, too."

"It's really concerning that you know that."

We finished with ice cream eaten out of the tub. I put the carton down for the cat when we were done. I ran a classy establishment. Amazing that I never got any tips.

Aidan appeared around an hour after the sun had set, knocking very civilly on my door. I invited him in for a few moments while I assembled bits and pieces for the night's project, namely a bin bag full of stale panettone and an extra torch in case Aidan forgot that neither Paul nor I could see in the dark.

"I don't think you and Paul have met," I said carefully, watching them size each other up like a pair of wary cats. "Aidan, this is Paul; he lives with me and he's studying to become a doctor. Paul, this is Aidan. He's Benedict's head of security so don't piss him off, please."

They shook hands carefully.

"I know who you are," said Aidan unexpectedly. "Benedict put you under his protection."

"What?" I squeaked. "That isn't true. Paul, tell him that didn't happen."

Paul looked at me in mild concern.

"He mentioned it in the hospital, actually," he said apologetically. "I forgot to tell you. But that's a good thing, right?"

"No," I said. "It's a bad thing. A very bad thing."

Aidan interrupted me.

"Toni, I know that you and Benedict rarely see eye to eye, but his protection is no small gift. He pays his debts."

I looked down at the table. I'd accepted earlier that I couldn't run Paul's life for him, but things had slipped out of control so quickly.

"You live your lives at war, Aidan," I said. "Your relationships are majorly screwed up. You kill each other as though it's a sport. Death isn't a sport; I should know. I just hoped Paul would make better life choices than me."

Aidan looked a little sad.

"Do you hate us so much?"

I thought about the question. It deserved more than a flippant response.

"I don't hate you at all. I hate Oscar a little for breaking my heart, nearly killing me and for driving Peter and me apart. But no, apart from that I don't hate any of you. I'm fond of Grace, there's a lot about Nicky that I like, and I have a very, very grudging respect for Benedict. But I think I'd be a safer person, with a quieter life, if I'd never met any of you."

Aidan smiled then.

"That's fair," he said. "Paul, do you want a safe, quiet life?"

"Hell no."

"There you go, Toni, from the horse's mouth. He wants his fair share of peril and that's that."

I raised my hands in defeat.

"I know when I'm beaten," I said. "Let's go raise Dylan Moss from the dead and put the fear of Toni into him. Where did you put him, by the way?"

Aidan confessed that Dylan's body was sharing a coffin with that of Mr Philip Brick, the venerable dentist from Abbots Bromley who'd been buried very recently up at Baswich Cemetery. Mr Brick had been generous with his painkillers, selling them at a knock-down price through the back door of the dental clinic. He'd also been clumsy with his drill when it came to patients. In a masterstroke of timing, he'd managed to drop dead of a stroke just as the drug squad were squabbling with two separate litigation lawyers about whose case would be heard first. I'd never met the man, but once again congratulated myself on having very good teeth.

"Fair enough," I said. "It should be deserted up there by this time. Let's go. You lead, Aidan; Paul and I will follow in my car."

Baswich was one of the largest cemeteries in the county, with a crematorium at the centre for those who didn't fancy being eaten by worms or raised by necromancers. The gates, locked at night, yielded without much protest to my picks and we walked past a row of young hornbeams to the fresh graves, piled high with flowers and keepsakes.

"I've never been here before," said Paul. "It's bloody huge. You could raise a top-notch zombie army with this lot."

I thought back to the last time I'd tried that. It had worked pretty well. Still…

"Not tonight," I said, scrabbling in my handbag for salt and perfume. "I didn't bring nearly enough panettone."

Dylan Moss had been dead only a few days, so I thought he'd be trivial to bring back. But I couldn't have been more wrong. For a while I thought we'd come too late and that he wasn't there at all. I knelt by the circle of scented salt and searched futilely. For minutes there was nothing, not a trace of the essence of that tall, tattooed drug dealer who'd stood in my kitchen and unexpectedly defended me from being raped by his ex-cellmate. Then I felt a fleeting contact, like searching for a diamond ring in the sand, and suddenly feeling the touch of smooth shiny metal. Nearly too late, but not quite.

I unhooked the little golden knife that my great-grandfather Ignatius had used. These days, I wore it on a chain round my neck, the sycamore flanges closed around the razor-sharp blade. Just before I made the cuts in my wrist, I remembered Nicky's reaction in the car to fresh blood… I looked up at the dark-haired vampire, standing very close and watching me.

"Aidan, I don't think you want to watch this."

He tossed his head slightly. Had I offended him? Impugned his control?

"I'll be fine," he said, a little shortly.

I shrugged and went to work. It took three cuts across each wrist before I could drag Dylan back across the void. He fought me every step of the way, slipping through my grip like jelly half a dozen times before I could pin him back into his body and yank him up from the grave. When the tall form finally stepped out of the earth, I was shaking, and sweat was beading on my forehead.

You wouldn't have guessed it, though, from Dylan's appearance. He stood blankly in front of me, carelessly surveying the graves around him. Exhausted by the effort of getting him there at all, I hadn't made the best job of resurrecting the man. His body was somewhat mildewed, his neck still torn from Nicky's endeavours, and he was just a little… decomposed, the flesh livid and bruise-coloured, and a touch bloated. The spider tattoos walked across an ugly and discoloured landscape. And I could dress it up any way I liked, but the man smelled bad. This corpse, it festered. Damn, it festered a lot.

I thrust a panettone into Dylan's limp grasp. He might not be the best zombie I'd ever raised, but his appetite was as good as any. But the chewed cake was spilling out of the holes in his throat. I gagged.

I drew the little blade across my left wrist again, twice, and pressed my hand into the grass so that blood ran into the soil. I pushed power into Dylan Moss, trying to shore up the mess I'd made of raising him from the grave.

It was a partial success. His body straightened a little, and his features became more defined, the swelling and decomposition receding. But the wound in his throat simply became fresher and more well defined, the edges sharp where Nicky's teeth had shredded the flesh away...

"This is no good," I muttered to Paul. "What should I do?"

He was staring at Dylan in a mixture of revulsion and fascination.

"I'm getting an interesting anatomy lesson here, as it happens," he said distractedly. "Alright, what should you do? Toni, is it possible that he's like this because this is how you remember him? Could you maybe think about him before your friend removed his jugular, his oesophagus and one or two vertebrae?"

It was possible. I sighed and took another slice into my right wrist. I closed my eyes and pictured the man who'd stood in my kitchen and said that his sister had been a redhead, remembering how the spiders had wriggled when he'd turned his head...

"Better," Paul's voice said, and I opened my eyes.

My cadaver was perfect, his posture just as I remembered it. Every eyelash was distinct, and the wet smell of decay had vanished. I, on the other hand, was a sweaty, exhausted mess, sprawled on the grass clutching a small gold knife and a bag of cake. I shoved a second one in Dylan's direction and let him eat the whole thing before I began my interrogation.

"Dylan, do you know where Gin Martin is staying?"

He took his time answering, and when he did, his voice was thick and slurred. I'd managed to drag his spirit back, but it was still barely there. The moment I let it go, it would be off. I doubted I would be able to bring him back another time. We hadn't left things a moment too late.

"We saw a flat in the classifieds, five floors up in a skanky block just by St Patrick's. We guessed it would be empty and it was. We stayed there. No one took any notice."

"Give me the address."

He did, and I knew the block he'd described. It was not a million miles from the appliance shop that Jay's dad ran and where Paul worked on odd days. It had been scheduled for demolition to build modern flats, but then the development company had pulled out. Half the residents had gone by then, though, and it had become rundown enough that I wouldn't have taken any of the flats on to my books. I don't like lying, and ads that included phrases like 'more than sufficient rats, fleas and cockroaches to start a small amateur wildlife project' apparently deterred tenants. As did photos of interior décor where the delightful patination of black mould was artfully broken up by swathes of spray can graffiti. The view from the top floor windows was particularly fine, especially given that it wasn't obscured by the likes of curtains. Or any glass.

"Why does Gin want to kill me? Is it just the house thing?"

"He got some sleazy lawyer to try and get her will overturned. Didn't work, and then the guy landed him with a massive bill anyway. They had a row, and Gin took the shyster apart in his office. Didn't kill him, but not much short. That was parole broken, wasn't it…? After that there wasn't much else to lose. He said you must have brainwashed the old woman, that no one could do that to him. I just went along. He said there was jewellery, some medals we could pawn."

Again? Gin had stolen and sold those medals once already! He was a piece of work.

"How did he get my address?"

"How do you think? Beat it out of that lawyer."

There wasn't much else to be got out of Dylan. Neither he nor Grahame Martin had any another address. Their sole asset seemed to be a stolen car that I doubted Gin could drive with his leg in a cast. And they hadn't exactly put down roots since moving into their squat—I doubted they'd rushed out to get library cards, join a gym, or sign up to the local bingo hall. After all the trouble it had been to raise him, I hadn't got a lot out of poor old Dylan. I let him go and sat on the grass catching my breath. I would try the whole standing up thing in the fullness of time.

"Was that a total waste of time and panettone?" I asked Paul and Aidan.

"Maybe not," said Paul. "I can't see why he would move from his squat. He doesn't know you can cross-examine cadavers."

I looked to Aidan for corroboration and didn't like what I saw. He was gazing down at me with an expression of naked hunger, his blues eyes flickering from my dripping wrists to my neck and back again. His lips were parted. I could see a glimpse of fang. My heart sank.

"Aidan, think about something else, please," I said, as politely as I could manage. "Go for a little walk. Read some sodding gravestone inscriptions, maybe. Recite some Vogon poetry."

He didn't answer, just looked at me with that hungry flickering gaze. I racked my brains. I was bleeding on to the grass and I didn't have enough energy to crawl.

"Paul, there's some lemonade in my car, and a first aid kit in the boot," I said hurriedly. "Can you get them please? And really quickly!"

"Sure," he said, looking at Aidan and me in confusion. "Right now?"

"Yup," I said.

I watched Aidan through narrowed eyes as I heard Paul's footsteps recede. He had drawn his lips back a little to show more fang. His eyes were full of stars. My stomach roiled.

"Aidan, bloody hell, bugger off and get a grip," I snapped. "Even Nicky has better self-control. I trusted you."

He reached down for a moment, his hand millimetres from my face, the fingers stretched out in a yearning grasp of lust… and then in a blur of movement he vanished into the night.

Chapter Eighteen

Why had poor old Dylan Moss been so tough to summon? Why had his spirit so nearly vanished into the ether when others were still hanging around after centuries? As I slumped on the grass and waited for Paul, I pondered the question. My theory was that those who trod lightly on the earth departed it easily. Derowen Polkeriss had left a big, cheesy footprint across the land and a whole load of people who couldn't stop thinking about him because they bore such grudges. Was that why his spirit was still so firmly grounded? Dylan hadn't left much behind for people to remember him by. No family that I knew of—an ex-girlfriend who hadn't wanted him back, a jailbird mate who would probably have traded him in for two packets of fags and a litre of extra strength cider. Not much of a legacy for cellmate Spider-Man.

Paul's voice broke me out of my reverie.

"Put your hands above your head. It'll help. It will slow the blood flow quicker."

That was way too much effort. I just held them out and he knelt in front of me, lacing my fingers in his and raising them up so that we were poised like the contemplative scene in a bad contemporary dance.

"I feel daft," I said. "Is this necessary?"

"Trust me. There is no first aid course I haven't done.

Including the one for drunk people who climb up lamp posts and then fall off them."

"There is no way a course for that."

"Not exactly. But my eldest brother did it for real one night and it took a while for the ambulance to arrive, being as the fuckwit had pawned my phone the previous day and bartered his own for four ounces of Jamaican gold. Where's Aidan gone?"

"He's looking for his self-control."

"You reckon he'll find it behind the crematorium?"

"He certainly wasn't finding it here."

Paul held my arms up until we were both bored. Then he cleaned and bandaged the cuts with bits and pieces from the first aid kit. He knew what he was doing, no doubt about that. Before long, my wrists were bound up in neat white strips and there was no more blood to be seen.

"You never got this from a pharmacy," he said conversationally. "Half this stuff is prescription only and most of it's labelled in German."

"It was Peter's; it's been bouncing around in there for months," I said briefly. "Don't tell me you speak German, too?"

"Only to GCSE level. Drink the lemonade. You need sugar."

I drank the lemonade. I ate some panettone. It wasn't bad. After about twenty minutes, I felt well enough to wander back to where we'd parked the cars. We got there to find Aidan waiting. He looked calmer. Had he just taken the time to get his bloodlust under control or had he made like Nicky and sated it with some random passer-by? I glared at him. I neither knew nor cared.

"Everything alright now?"

"Toni, I apologise. I didn't expect that to happen. There was more blood than I anticipated, and…"

He paused.

And what? Hadn't I been wearing enough clothes? Wasn't I modest enough? Had I brazenly tempted him with tasty blood? I swore in my mind that if he tried to make this my fault, I would stake him.

He didn't.

"…and nothing. As I said, I'm sorry. It won't happen again."

I took the apology at face value.

"We're good then," I said carefully. "Want to help me find my murdering stalker?"

"Right now?"

"Yup."

"Are you well enough?"

I shrugged.

"No time like the present. If I wait until daylight, you won't have my back. And Aidan, the guy is a giant plaster cast. I don't think he can put up much of a fight."

He laughed, the tension between us dissipating.

"It's a deal then. You lead and I'll follow. I don't have a clue where this block of flats is."

We drove back into town, up Tixall Road and onto Corporation Street. It was well past midnight, and the streets were deserted. On a Friday or Saturday, we might have found the odd singing student or stumbling drunk. That evening, there was not a soul. I stopped at the entrance to the mouldering block of flats. Dylan said they had made their home on the fifth floor, in flat eleven. I could have turned the address over to Wills and gone to bed—but Gin had watched Nicky rip a man's throat out in my kitchen. That was information I didn't plan to share with Her Majesty's constabulary.

There was a main door, the kind that in a more salubrious establishment would have been operated by the tenants' master keys. I didn't need my picks. The door swung open at my touch, and the sodium yellow streetlamp illuminated a sorry vestibule area that had been charmingly accessorised with bags of rubbish and an old sofa. Something scuttled under the sofa at our approach. I hoped it was a rat because all the other alternatives were worse.

I cast my torch around. There was a lift, but the doors had been torn off a long time ago, and it now housed two dead shopping trollies and the remains of a bicycle. I squinted at it in the darkness.

"We're too late," I said. "He's not here anymore."

Aidan had been scoping out the room, his vampire vision revealing its rather unsavoury secrets to him without the need for torches. But he returned at my words. Even in the torchlight, his eyes were vividly blue.

"What makes you say that?" he said.

"He has one leg in a cast," I said, "and one arm, too. This flat's on the fifth floor. There's no way he could make it with the lift out of action."

Aidan nodded. He gestured to the stairs.

"Want to take a look anyway, now we're here?"

"Sure, but it's going to take me a while to get up those stairs in my state," I said. "You go on ahead and I'll follow."

"Aren't you going to tell me not to kill him until you get there?"

I shook my head.

"I'm done with playing fair. He may still have some friends out there, but I'm not one of them. If you find him, I don't care if you kill him. It will spare me any residual guilt I'd have to feel if you did it while I watched."

Aidan didn't reply. He just raised his eyebrows and then turned and disappeared into the darkness of the stairwell. I turned back to find out what Paul had been doing for the duration of our chat. Ah, of course. He'd been poking under the sofa with a bicycle spoke for the rat. Why hadn't I guessed?

"Coming?" I said.

He dropped the spoke.

"Guess so. You want a piggy-back, invalid?"

I laughed.

"Give it your best shot. I'm not sure I'm that light, you know."

He managed two flights, and we trudged up the final three hand in hand. We found Aidan wandering round a flat that wasn't as bad as the one I'd turned down. The glass in the windows was intact, the lights turned on, and the kitchen appeared to contain functioning white goods. I mentally priced the place up. It would do for someone who hated cold callers—and wanted to lose weight pounding up and down with their shopping.

Dylan and Grahame had travelled light, but they'd left enough behind to turn my stomach, namely a cheap digital camera filled with photographs of me taken through a car window. There was little else of note, and the milk in the fridge was dated the same day that Grahame and I had experienced our little car accident. We had indeed come too late to the party.

I sat on the kitchen counter, scrolling through the camera's memory card: me at home, me at work, Amelia's house, Amelia's garden, my garden, me snogging Jay in my garden, me and Jay playing our own version of naked twister… I deleted those last ones hastily and began to sincerely regret that Nicky had only ripped off one head in my kitchen.

"You get anything at all of use out of tonight's little escapades?" asked Aidan.

"Yes and no," I said. "Jealousy. Envy. Anger. He blames me for tricking him out of a lot of money. He blames me for trashing his parole. I bet he blames me for Dylan's death, too, and I am pretty sure that he thinks the car crash and his injuries are all my fault. Aidan, he's not going to give up and go away. This jerk has really got it in for me."

"So…"

"So we've been doing this all wrong. I don't need to track him down. He'll come to me. I just need to make sure I know when and where."

"That's all very well in theory, Toni, but pulling it off could be tricky."

"I'll work it out. Aidan, thank you for tonight, but I need to be asleep now."

The stairs were easier on the way down. I bid Aidan goodnight when we reached my car and, to show him that there were no hard feelings over the slightly icky bloodlust incident, I gave him a hug. He returned it hesitantly.

"I'll follow you home," he said, "just in case we meet Mr Martin off schedule."

We didn't, but it was a kind thought.

As I was dropping off to sleep my phone beeped. It was a text and I read it sleepily:

Angel, sorry I bailed last night. I was about to make a complete twat of myself. Again. You did warn me. Anyway, I know you're trying to help even if I don't show it well. Love, Nicky.

I thought of poor Nicky, living in that increasingly empty house that a few months before had been a little slice of heaven for him. What had he said? That the girls were like sisters, and he never got a word in edgeways, always giggling and laughing, insisting on plaiting his long white hair... All gone now: Caroline, Lorraine and his precious Lily. Lily, who had been kind, thoughtful, peaceful to be with and just so sweet.

I looked at the ceiling. I was changing. I used to be an estate agent by day, a necromancer at night, and pretty easy-going twenty-four-seven. When I thought of Nicky, I thought I might be becoming something else, too. I was turning into an avenging angel, and that would not be the best career choice I'd ever made.

I sat up and rubbed my eyes. I was brooding too much to sleep anyway. I turned on my bedside light and fiddled with the phone for a bit until I had a vaguely satisfactory reply.

Hey Nicky, not a problem. I am sorry too. But listen, I need to look around your house again. Let me know when works for you.

I pressed send and turned off the phone. Late night texting tended to end with me drinking too much vodka and sending begging messages to Peter. I was done with that. I turned out the light again. This time, I slept.

IT'S MY FAVOURITE dream. Is it real? Did it happen?

I am six years old, curled up in the kitchen on my mother's lap. She smells of the cinnamon buns we've been baking, spice and sugar and happiness. She is singing to me, stroking my hair. Her own hair is black, waist length and slightly wavy. She's tugged it back into a ponytail to keep it out of the flour, but tendrils have escaped and frame her face in dark, Medusa wiggles. The rope of South Sea pearls she always wears is dusty with icing sugar.

"You're my little angel," she says, stroking my own orange, corkscrew curls. "Tiny flame-haired angel. Such a little thing, my Lavington. My precious angel."

She kisses the top of my head. I hear the sound of raisins hissing and popping in the baking oven, butter sizzling against the sides of the cake tin. I snuggle into her arms, warm and happy and safe.

When did it end? What did I do?

Chapter Nineteen

I WOKE EARLY the next day. I would have thrown on another sundress and enjoyed the warm weather, but while my wrists were mending nicely—vampire blood has its benefits—they were still ugly enough to need long sleeves, so I found something lacy that hung down all the way to my fingertips. I then managed to surprise Bernie, Bethany and myself by getting into work early and completing a morning of stultifying, boring admin. With nothing left to do for the afternoon, I left shortly after lunch and drove over to Salt.

Amelia's cottage looked unchanged. I hoped that wasn't the case, because last time I'd been inside, there had been the remains of four corpses in the cellar arrayed in a most unappealing tableau of blood, estranged organs and broken glass.

I realised as I parked that John Jones must have arranged for the garden to be tended. It wasn't the immaculate picture-postcard that Amelia had maintained, but the grass was mown, and the beds vaguely weeded. Entering the house, I realised that the kind, old solicitor must also have organised some kind of housekeeping service. There was a smell of polish and room freshener, and no sign of dust or spiders.

I walked through the house and memories assailed me. Amelia making me lapsang souchong tea; Winchester begging for sponge cake; Peter so near to dying in my arms; Oscar kissing me with blood on his lips; Benedict close by me in the dark… I shook my head. I wasn't here to reminisce. I'd told Bernie I wouldn't come back after lunch and given myself an afternoon to start getting the house tenant-ready.

In my job, I'd done a lot of house clearances. I'd never done one for myself, but I knew the rules. Orange sticker for anything you want to keep, they take the rest, sell it and you split the proceeds. The firm we used was honest and I gave them a lot of business. I thought they would do their best.

There wasn't a lot. Amelia's taste had run to a lot of kitsch china, ideally perched on doilies. I found an elderly, fox-fur jacket that would keep me warm while raising the dead in winter, and a vintage barograph that I thought Paul might like. In the final drawer I found a neat leather presentation box—the war medals that had proven so contentious. I bit my lip; I would donate them to the local charity for ex-servicemen and women, and that would be an end to it.

When I couldn't put it off any longer, I opened the door to the cellar and turned on the light switch. The fact that lights went on at all suggested that Benedict's minions had been busy at some point. I walked down a little nervously, but I needn't have worried. No blood, no glass, not a sign of the terrifying battle that had taken place. The luggage containers that the vampires had slept in were gone, as was the wooden chest that Peter had been nailed to. The cellar was utterly empty and as clean as a whistle. I could remember it that way from now on. I walked back up the stairs. I'd laid a little demon to rest, and that was a good day's work.

I locked up carefully, feeling a little sick at the thought that Grahame Martin might be watching me at that moment. It was daylight and the village was busy, so I felt safe. But I also felt slightly violated. The man had watched me in secret, photographing moments that were intimate and private. I really needed to weed him out of my life and, as I'd said to Aidan, I was finally prepared to resort to any proven method of eradication. Weedkiller, flamethrower… I was no longer going to be choosy.

I drove home to find the house contained a definite absence of Paul. It did, however, contain a neat pile of typed up notes—bless him, he'd finished the translation of Grandfather Robert's contracts for me. I might not know why my poor old grandfather had risked his life dallying with demons, but I would have a better idea of what he'd been trying to accomplish with his meddling.

Or so I thought. The truth of the matter was that the contents were bewildering.

In the first contract, Azazel stated half a dozen utterly pointless tasks for my grandfather to carry out. He had to paint a sigil in oil on a particular step one night, leave a lit candle in a wood one morning, place a newspaper in a trunk, cut down a tree, mend a fence, lock a gate... They all seemed pretty much unconnected and none of them made the slightest sense to me.

In return, Azazel gave my grandfather two cantamen, or spells, or whatever you wanted to call them. The first was just as Paul had described: it would ensure that male descendants had no paranormal powers. End of. There was a recipe with sixteen ingredients, and Shakespeare would have loved every single one. Eye of tiger, hair of badger, a virgin's tears, a sprig of rosemary picked by moonlight, the juice of rowanberries picked by starlight... Almost too corny to be true. Only the sight of the battered pages, inscribed in brown, antique blood, convinced me the magic could be real.

The second spell was referred to as the ancient cantamen of Helen of Troy. I had a name, but there was no information at all on what it did. There was another Shakespearean recipe: tooth of bat, the wing of a hummingbird, the powdered horn of a rhino, the fingernail of a murderer and a dozen equally unalluring ingredients, all mixed in the shell of a turtle that you shattered as the new moon rose... Much more of this and I would need to buy a broomstick and spray Winchester black.

The second contract, the one from when I was a little girl, was exactly the same. A roster of inexplicable little tasks for Grandfather Robert and—in return—two more recipes. As

Paul had said, one was named as Tabula Rasa and the other as Glauce's Wedding Dress. Trawling through the internet suggested that Tabula Rasa referred to wiping a slate clean, and that Glauce had to have something to do with a cursed wedding dress, but once again I had no idea what the cantamens had actually done or why Robert had bargained for them.

I looked at Paul's neat printouts sitting next to the originals. This was stuff from my past. I could turn my back on it, or I could follow it through and find out where it led. Half of me wanted to bundle the whole lot up and give it back to Benedict. Thanks, but no thanks. But the rest of me knew I couldn't do that. Because someone I'd loved had told me a lot of lies. The grandfather who'd been both mother and father to me when I was growing up had grossly deceived me. I had a right to the truth.

THE SUN WOULDN'T set for a couple of hours. That suited me just fine. Emir had said he wasn't the teacher I was looking for. Well, tough, because he was the only one I had. I would beard the barman in his den before the undead woke up and beat me to it. And if he still wouldn't help me? Then I would chase down the elusive Keira Holloway.

I dressed to impress in case I ended up staying, and on a whim opened up Amelia's little jewellery box to see what it had to offer. It had seemed avaricious to examine the contents in front of John Jones and the lovely Karen. I also had the uncomfortable thought that they'd expected me to know exactly what it contained. Amelia had been high-handed in her own way, changing her will but never letting me know. I suspected she'd planned to tell me in her own good time but had been wiped out by vampires before she could get around to it. But the fact remained that—contrary to what the coroner and his secretary seemed to think—the dear old lady and I hadn't been that close. Not close enough for me to know what jewellery she owned. Certainly not close enough that she should leave me all her possessions. It seemed sad to me that apparently there hadn't been anyone else. I would just respect her wishes.

The box contained three or four pretty brooches (not particularly my kind of thing and a little old-fashioned), a string of moon-coloured pearls that would go out of fashion when hell froze over, and an exquisite diamond engagement ring. It was so tiny that it would only fit on the little finger of my left hand. It might be small, but the centre stone was at least a carat. I blinked. It was a ring that could hold its own with all the diamonds that Grace and Benedict had given to me. The long-dead Mr Martin had invested wisely. I left the pearls and the brooches for another day and loaded myself with diamonds and a tiny, gold sheath dress that Claire had decided clashed with her hair. I wore flat sandals. Over the past couple of weeks, my paranoia had been building and I just couldn't rule out having to flee for my life even on a casual evening's bar-hopping.

I drove to Fradswell Woods, the first time I had ever done so in daylight. They seemed slightly less creepy and daunting, but only slightly. For someone who didn't want casual visitors, Emir had chosen well. I passed the tree that Camilla had collided so dramatically with. It had come off a lot better than the sheep. I couldn't see a mark on it.

The ruins of Hawkswaine Hall, eerie and uncanny at night, were glorious in the evening light. A single, tumbledown turret loomed over the stone-flagged expanse that must once have been a great hall. The odd mouldering wall poked out between thick ivy and the leaves of young trees. The dragons that guarded the entrance were a theme that ran through the remaining stonework: hints of a carved tail, fang or wing were still evident in the weathered, cut stone. One wall in the trees still rose to two storeys high, and a single intact window framed an arch of darkening sky. The odd piece of timber was still evident, poking out of the stonework, still blackened and scorched from the fire that had razed the mansion to the ground so long ago.

The car park had two cars in it: the elderly and mud-splattered four-wheel drive that Emir had driven me home in, and a vast people carrier that I assumed must be Jiří's. I walked through the dragon-bracketed stone arch and found both men casually sweeping up dead leaves and the detritus of winter from the remains of the great stone hall. Instead of their usual immaculate eveningwear, they were both wearing grubby jeans and warm coats. Emir was laughing about something and Jiří was protesting quite shyly.

"No, not true," he said. "He drank a little blood, but I haven't seen him again. I'm not casting my sights that high."

I turned my heel slightly on a loose stone and they both turned my way. I didn't think either of them looked particularly pleased to see me. Jiří looked wary, and Emir gave me a hunted glance. I'd come without an invitation, so a rapturous welcome would have been a bit much to expect, but I still felt my heart sink a little.

"Hi," I said, as cheerfully as possible. "Emir, I need to speak with you."

"Right now?"

"Yup, can't wait."

"Not one minute?"

"Nope."

He looked unconvinced and I couldn't blame him. I'd clearly taken my time getting ready and ambled up without losing my breath. Then he broke into a reluctant grin.

"Fair enough," he said. "Jiří, finish off here, would you? I'll be downstairs with Toni here."

He gestured to the stairs that led down into the darkness, and I walked down ahead of him. I had to stop after half a spiral to let my daylight-blinded eyes accustom themselves to the candlelit dimness. He waited patiently, but it only took a moment.

"You're quick to adjust," he said conversationally. "You must have drunk a lot of blood."

"Less than you'd think."

"Powerful blood, then…"

He had a point. Nicky probably didn't count, but Benedict Akil and Aneurin Blackwood Bordel—you didn't get much more powerful than that.

"I guess."

We reached the bar. I was surprised to find it brightly lit. The ceiling bulbs were cunningly recessed. I hadn't realised they were even there.

"You have electricity," I said unnecessarily. "I didn't know."

He looked amused.

"I worked without it for two years, but it was tough to keep bringing the ice in. And have you tried getting blood out of velvet seating or silk curtains without a steam cleaner? I got a generator four years ago now and put in underfloor heating at the same time. The undead prefer the thermostat set to sauna, as you know."

I laughed.

"I don't envy you the bills in winter," I said. "Though I suppose underground spaces retain heat well."

He courteously tugged out my usual chair for me.

"Is your errand truly urgent, by the way? You don't look as though you've worked up a sweat to get to me…"

I shook my head.

"I just needed to talk to you before the clientele arrived," I said. "I don't have an escort. I rather thought Nicky might text me tonight, so I dressed up just in case, but it's probably not the best idea anyway. I'm sure he wouldn't mind, but I nearly got him into trouble last time. I didn't want to ask again."

"You probably did him some good, at the end of the day, you know; his reputation certainly didn't suffer. I'll set up the bar while we chat, if that suits you."

I didn't mind and I watched as he prepared egg whites and squeezed limes. I was no great scholar on the mythology of cocktails, but it seemed to involve a lot of glittering glassware and many bottles. There were spoons and straws, a rack of sharp, stainless steel tools, a lovely vintage chrome soda siphon, glass and steel shakers.

"You have quite the hobby here," I said. "You said you've run this place for six years. What did you do before?"

He gave me a hunted look, but then realised the question wasn't loaded.

"I made so many enemies that I'm hiding out in the woods in

Staffordshire running a bar for the undead," he said wryly. "It's not unusual to be paid to cast cantamen but have no idea what they do. It's not wise either. I plan to pick my own enemies from now on rather than letting other people pick them for me."

"I'm sorry, I didn't come here to pry."

"I realise that. But there are reasons I don't have a phone, rarely leave the woods, and don't read newspapers. Why are you here, though? I meant it when I said I couldn't teach you."

I took a deep breath.

"I need educating as much as teaching, Emir. Right now, I need to know something about these enchantments or cantamen, as you call them. Are there famous ones? Ones that are somehow defined by their names?"

He looked distinctly startled.

"There are. You read about them in myths. Back in the time of legends, angels and demons walked closer to the earth. They called them demigods, or nymphs or muses and suchlike, but that's just nomenclature. They would make these cantamen for themselves, so you can be sure they didn't tuck in a sting in the tail the way that a demon would try to do today. So it's always safer to ask for an old spell rather than trying to design one yourself. You can be sure all the bases are covered when you bargain for it. But Toni, why do you need to know this?"

I took a deep breath. I needed to minimise lying, partly because I disagreed with it, but mostly because I was rubbish at it. And when you lie, you create an alternate narrative that you have to keep going. I just wasn't organised enough to be a good liar.

"Someone in my family bargained for three of these damn things, these ancient named enchantments. And I don't have a clue what they do."

"Three! That's..." He broke off for a moment. "That's unprecedented."

"Why?"

"No one, but no one, gets three cantamen out of a demon without messing up, Toni. Not for a thousand years. Necromancers just don't have that kind of power anymore. But you have just the names?"

I crossed my fingers; I could pretend I'd misunderstood him later. Because while I didn't have a description of what they did, I had instructions on making them...

"Just the names."

"Go on then."

"They're referred to as Helen of Troy, Glauce's Wedding Dress and Tabula Rasa," I said in a rush.

He thought for a moment.

"I've never heard of the last two, but everyone knows what Helen of Troy does."

"I don't."

He looked amused.

"I thought all you English studied Classics? Helen is the daughter of Leda, the Queen of Sparta and a powerful witch. The day her daughter is born, Leda enchants an egg made of clay and makes it into a paste, which she paints on Helen's face every day. Each time, the mud makes her daughter a little more beautiful. Every time she runs out of clay, Leda has to cast the spell again, but it works. By the time Helen is sixteen she is so beautiful that a hundred men fall in love with her."

"That's not the version I heard."

"There are lots of versions. But that's the spell. A clay that makes you beautiful."

"All that trouble for a face mask?"

"One that works..."

He had a point.

"I suppose," I conceded. "The other two?"

"Not a clue, but I will look for you. Toni, whoever this person was in your family..."

"Yes?"

"Were you fond of them?"

I nodded.

"Very."

"Then don't look too closely at what they did in return for these things, because you won't like what you find—I guarantee it."

I bit my lip.

"I know what they did, Emir. I just don't understand it."

He touched my hand briefly.

"Take my advice—live in ignorance. Do you want to squeeze these lemons for me?"

I recognised the careful change of subject for what it was and juiced fruit for a while, but I couldn't get my mind off what he'd said.

"So, if you had this mud, you could make yourself—literally— the most beautiful person in the world?"

"That depends. Have you checked the ingredients, how long it takes to make, or the shelf life maybe? Leda was a queen, remember. If the recipe called for powdered rubies or the fresh eyelashes of a stillborn lamb, she could probably order them by the case. You or I might struggle. Sure you won't stay when I open up?"

Another change of subject. I let it go that time.

"Not without an escort for when the fanged brigade slip from their coffins and begin their nightly business of causing trouble for all and sundry," I said. "Unless you think my little performance the other night might act as a deterrent against the children of the night?"

"The nursery children of the night would like the challenge, I'm afraid."

"I'll go, then. I wasn't sure."

"It's probably for the best. I'll make you something to try before you go, if you like?"

It seemed a nice enough idea, and I watched as he blended spirits, bitters and a dash of egg white together and then shook them up with some ice.

"What's the egg white for?" I asked idly.

"It gives the drink a silky texture and a soft foam on the top," Emir said, handing me the finished masterpiece, a martini glass containing a tiny cone of red liquid.

As I sipped, Jiří wandered down the stairs, wiping his hands on his jeans.

"Your new recipe?" he said to Emir.

"I found a guinea pig," Emir answered. "Well, Toni?"

I wanted to like it, but... Nope.

"Too bitter for me, Emir," I confessed. "I like my champagne classic."

He laughed.

"I chose my guinea pig badly, then," he said. "I'll try to help you with those names, Toni, but I meant what I said. You need a better teacher."

I gave him my unfinished glass.

"Thank you," I said. "Please let me know if you work anything out. And Emir..."

He tilted his head to one side.

"Yes?"

"Are there other witches in Staffordshire? Apart from you and Keira, I mean. Well, and me."

He shook his head.

"I don't think so, Toni; we're a rare breed in England. The purges all but wiped our kind out. And not a lot's changed, so watch your back."

I DROVE HOME as the sky darkened, still all dressed up with nowhere to go. I hadn't heard from Nicky, which left me without any kind of plan for the rest of my evening. I scouted the distance between car and camera-clad porch—no Gin Martin. Unlocking the door, I heard the sound of Paul venting some spleen on his drum kit. No reconciliation with Bethany then. I waited for a pause in the crescendos and yelled up the stairs:

"Paul, have you eaten?"

The drumming stopped. He appeared at the top of the stairs. He did a double-take at my miniscule dress, perfect hair, and glittering array of diamonds.

"Wow," he said. "You look amazing. And no, I was going to make cheese on toast in a bit. Why?"

"Because I cashed a cheque for six thousand pounds this morning and spent an hour doing my hair," I said. "Let's take a cab both ways to Lichfield and eat dinner in the swanky bistro by the cathedral. I haven't properly celebrated inheriting a whole house yet. We should do that."

"Deal. You should have a housewarming, you know?"

I stared at him for a moment.

"Oh my God. You are a genius."

"Thank you. Always nice to have it confirmed, even if I haven't the slightest clue why. Why, by the way?"

I shook my head.

"I just worked out how to catch my stalker, and it's all thanks to you. Now we really need to celebrate. I hope that bistro has plenty of champagne on ice because we're going to order lots."

And if anyone offered me something sophisticated looking in a martini glass, now I knew to say no. Life was confusing enough. People kept changing the rules around me, not to mention the goal posts. But I knew what I liked: champagne and raising the dead. Everything else could just fall into line. And now, I knew just how to make it.

Chapter Twenty

THERE'S NOT A lot you can do with a hangover other than suffer through it. I applied tea and toast, and the panacea of aspirin. They had no noticeable effect, so I put on my best leave-me-the-fuck-alone expression and drove to work, squinting into the eyeball-searing sunlight of a warm Friday morning in July.

I added extra coffee at my desk, but it wasn't working. My liver was angry with me, and it wanted me to suffer. No good can come of arguing with one of your own major internal organs, so I distracted myself by filling in all the application forms to turn Amelia's little house into a cash-generating rental investment—certificates for electricity and gas and a myriad of their paperwork friends.

It still wasn't lunchtime, so I continued with the little sales push that I'd begun what seemed like a million years ago. One name still stood out on the granny flat list: the evasive Keira Holloway. Phoning the woman hadn't worked. I would beard her in her den.

If English witches were as rare as Emir said, then it was highly likely that it was Keira who'd cast spells for Grandfather Robert. And while the members of my family didn't look like the back ends of buses, we'd clearly none of us spent our time slathering the ointment of Helen of Troy on our skin.

But Bernie had said Keira was beautiful. More to the point, I had a feeling that Keira would have asked for serious payment for casting the first cantamen, the one that should have made sure none of my family had paranormal powers. The one that my grandfather had got so wrong… I needed to organise my thoughts.

I pulled a piece of paper towards me and jotted down my thoughts:

My grandfather never wanted to be a necromancer.

It was a start. Not a lot of use, but I ploughed on:

He found out he had necromantic powers when he was about to become a father and decided the next generation wouldn't get the same chance.

I had no hope of fathoming the why at this point. Perhaps I could just figure out what he had done and worry about motive later. The rest was speculation anyway. I wrote carefully:

Keira Holloway was the witch my grandfather knew.

It made a lot of sense. She was a witch, and witches were rare. And why else would a woman I'd never met want to avoid me so badly? Alright, next:

Keira demanded that Robert bargain for the recipe for Helen of Troy as her fee for casting the other spell.

And that was it, the missing link. I was certain that I was right. It explained why there were two spells in the contract, but only one that my grandfather had used. And if I was on the right track, then the second contract probably followed the same lines: one cantamen for my scheming grandparent, one for greedy Keira. I didn't know which was which, of course, or what either of them did, but I knew I was on the right path.

Glauce's Wedding Dress. Tabula Rasa. Glauce had something to do with a cursed wedding dress, but tabula rasa referred to the ancient wax slates the Romans used that could be erased to nothing again by heating them. Tabula rasa—a clean slate. Philosophers used it to talk about the clean, pure mind of a child, not yet defaced and scribbled on by the memories of life. A cantamen of forgetting, maybe? Did Keira even know? Was that her spell, the one she'd asked for, or was it the one that she had cast for my grandfather without ever knowing what it did?

Benedict had once mentioned Oedipus Rex to me. Emir had talked about the time of legend and myth, when angels and demons walked the earth. Helen of Troy came from that time. I might find the answers there. I'd studied a little Classics, one of the penalties you paid for getting into grammar school, and Paul would know more. We could seek out Glauce and Tabula Rasa there.

I put down my pen and crumpled up the piece of paper. I turned it over and over in my hand as though it might somehow reveal more secrets to me in its new form. Bernie's voice, right by my desk, jerked me out of my reverie and I stuffed the ball idly into a pocket.

"Jill Fletcher rang about her lodger, by the way. She wants to know if she needs to check his residency."

I stared in confusion, my mind blank for a moment. Then it came to me—the landlady who bred cats and who'd acquired a tenant who'd paid in advance but had no references.

"His what?"

"Whether he's allowed to stay in the UK."

I felt my brow furrow.

"Bernie, she didn't tell me he came from abroad. And I can't remember anyway. This is Staffordshire. The last time a foreigner visited our county, I think it was William the Conqueror on his way to Stamford Bridge."

"Well, check it out, would you? I think she's safe if he comes from within the EU, but I can't remember either."

I nodded, distracted. For some reason I thought her lodger might hail from France, maybe. That was what she had said. Or had she…? I would have to call her. Then I remembered something else.

"Bernie, I'm having a housewarming tomorrow—I do hope that both you and Helen will come."

"A housewarming! You've moved house?"

"Lord no. But Amelia Scott Martin left me her little cottage in Salt in her will. It's taken months to sort things out with the solicitors, but now that it's mine, I thought we could celebrate before I get tenants in. Bring a bottle and some nuts."

He agreed very readily. Bernie would turn up to the opening of a packet of crisps and then try to fondle the crisps. Claire often called me picky. Well, Bernie wasn't picky.

Before heading off to try and corner the elusive Keira, I texted everyone I knew who might possibly want to come to my impromptu housewarming on Saturday: my brother and Henry; my dear old school friend Lawrence and his boyfriend; Claire... On a whim I also left messages inviting the charming John Jones and his secretary Karen along with any significant others or random hangers-on they might want to bring. I felt obligated to invite Bethany and hoped Paul would be OK with it. I overcompensated by texting him and telling him to ask any of his friends that he wanted. Finally, I sent a text inviting one very special, secret, mystery guest. I felt a touch of guilt when I pressed send, but it passed, and probably more quickly than it should have done.

"Bernie, see you tomorrow night," I said, sliding from my desk. "I'm going over to Stoneydelph to see Keira Holloway, and then I'll probably go straight home from there."

I SWORE IN traffic for what felt like forever, but probably wasn't. Truth be told, I was nervous. I was about to impose myself on someone who had made it very clear they didn't want us to meet. But more worrisome was that Keira appeared to have played an instrumental role in the screwed-up mess that was my family history. Was I going to come back empty-handed, or find I'd opened a Pandora's box that should have stayed firmly nailed shut? Past experience suggested the latter.

I'd never visited the salon before. It had a good reputation, but it was a long drive for me. I also wasn't much of a treatment girl. There isn't a lot a hairdresser can do with two foot of orange corkscrew curls, and when it came to face packs or manicures, I wasn't the target audience. Not that I didn't like the idea, but it had always been out of my price range and the thought of sitting still for that long left me wincing.

I did a bit of a double-take when I parked. The salon exuded

Alice James

an air of luxury that I associated with high-end hotels or London spas—lots of Nordic-style wood and glass at the front, wide parking bays for just a few cars and a hand-dressed stretch leading up to the entrance. I'd checked the prices online, and they were high but not exorbitant—though there'd been a mention of 'bespoke client services' that didn't come with numbers attached. Was I missing something? How did she get enough clients to pay for this setup, buy a five-bedroom house and—now I saw what was sitting in the reserved parking bay—a very shiny sports car? The Delph wasn't Stafford. Or Birmingham. Or even Stoke. It certainly shouldn't have been millionaires' row.

A bell chimed sweetly as I walked in to find a very pleasing little hairdressers-cum-beauticians, with clean lines, many mirrors, fresh-cut flowers and air laden with lovely, expensive scent. Keira was standing by the reception desk looking at a stack of CVs. She couldn't have been anyone else. Bernie had described her as in her late sixties, but I put her a little older. I could see how he'd made his mistake, though—I'd rarely seen a more fabulous-looking woman. She had that exquisite white-gold hair that owes everything to the kind passage of time and nothing to a chemist's box, high cheekbones, a full sensuous mouth and the figure of an eighteen-year-old girl. Yes, someone had made good use of Leda's clay eggs.

She was standing next to a plump brunette with multi-coloured hair and green lipstick. Long, glossy talons made me suspect that this was the manicurist I'd spoken to.

"He isn't exactly what I had in mind either, dear," she said in clear Staffordshire vowels. "But we're two stylists down and this isn't Kensington. At Sloane Square, I could throw a café latté and hit six out-of-work colourists without aiming, but not here. We'll take him on probation."

Then the bell of the door jangled a second time, and she turned to look at me and smile in welcome. She had a smile that lit up the room. She wasn't aging gracefully; there wasn't a term for what she was doing, but it was damn impressive. I returned the smile quite involuntarily. I knew our rapport wouldn't last. I also couldn't shake the impression that I'd seen her before even though I knew we'd never met. I couldn't pinpoint it, but she looked familiar. Before I could wonder further, she walked over to me and held out a hand.

"Hello, dear, I'm Keira."

I looked at her hand as I took it. Perfect. Yes, it was starting to line slightly, but she had long, elegant fingers and the nails—unpainted— were smooth and finely shaped, the beds a perfect half-moon of white.

I looked at her for a moment before replying, but I didn't need to answer. She took in my signature Windsor tangerine ringlets and the green eyes that my brother always joked we must have stolen from a cat. Her mouth dropped open and she visibly swallowed. I'd read *The Lady of Shalott*. Keira thought something very bad was finally catching up with her.

"Please go," she whispered. "I never meant any harm."

"There are things I need to know."

She turned sharply towards the rainbow-haired manicurist.

"Why don't you take your lunch break now, dear?" she said shortly. "The sun's out."

The girl looked a little startled and then scurried out of a door behind the reception desk. Keira turned back to me.

"I can't help you," she said. "And if I could, I wouldn't. He should never have asked me. I was just a girl and after that, nothing was the same."

"Keira," I said carefully. "My whole family is dead. You're the only person I can ask."

She blinked.

"You don't know?" she said, relief flooding every line of her body. "You don't know what we did?"

"I know what the first contract was for," I said. "I worked that out. But not the second."

She laughed a little bitterly.

"How about that? There's irony because I never found out what the first cantamen did, the one I cast on your grandfather. Now, please leave."

"No, you have to tell me. I don't care about whatever he gave to you for payment, but I need to know about the second one you cast for him. I have to know what else he did to my family."

"Oh no, you bloody don't," she snapped. "It's all too late for that. Now get out or I'll call the police."

I narrowed my eyes at her.

"Tell me," I said. "Please. I'm not here to make trouble."

"Sure, you've come for a pedicure and a bikini wax. The door's that way. Feel free to close it behind you and don't come back."

Once again, I was sure that I had met her before. Her mannerisms were familiar. I looked at her, trying to place the face, the voice... She looked back at me and for a moment her tough façade dropped.

"I'm sorry," she said. "The bonds between a mother and her daughter are sacred. I would never have done it if I'd known."

And she turned and left through the same door as the manicurist, slamming it hard behind her.

Thoroughly disgruntled, I stomped back to the car. I'd made some progress—Keira had indeed been the witch my grandfather had known—but I had no leverage to make the wretched woman tell me more. I saw the manicurist perched on the wall by Keira's shiny car. She was basking in the sun and eating a sandwich. I waved and she waved back cheerfully enough. I sat next to her on the wall.

"I'm sorry she chucked you out," I said. "She didn't need to do that on my account. I'm Toni, by the way."

She swallowed a mouthful of sandwich.

"I'm Marge," she said, and I recognised her voice from when we'd spoken on the phone. "And don't worry. She always chucks me out when people call about the facial."

Suddenly things fell into place. Keira didn't just use the clay of Helen of Troy on her own face. She sold it. Bespoke client services, a product that did what it said and made you prettier... no wonder she could afford a sports car, a five-bedroom house with an annex and a salon that looked like it had been teleported from St John's Wood or Primrose Hill.

"Too pricy for me," I said, hoping for more. "I think."

She shook her head so fiercely that the multi-coloured strands waved around her like snakes.

"If you have the money, do it," she said. "If you can borrow it, you should. It's like a miracle. If I save up all year, I can get it at my staff discount, and I tell you: that's what I do. I know ten grand seems like a lot of money, but it's not. You get what you pay for."

Ten grand. Ten thousand pounds. Ten big ones… Keira pitched it high, but then the ingredients couldn't be easy to source, and you wouldn't want to be found dealing in them. Rhino horn, turtle shells—all things that would get you sent to prison. A little alarm bell went off in my brain. Someone else had wanted those ingredients. Someone else had indeed gone to jail for getting them…

"Thanks, Marge," I said. "I really will think about it."

I was about to leave when a random thought struck me.

"Has Kirsty been in today?" I asked with studied casualness. "I vaguely thought I might bump into her."

She gave me an odd look; I couldn't quite gauge her thoughts.

"You missed her," she said. "She came in earlier. She and Keira are still not getting on so well."

Huh? Where did that come from? I shrugged.

"Not to worry, Marge. You enjoy your lunch now."

I sat in the car with my mind whirling. I hadn't come here to find out about Nicky, but there was definitely a connection. Keira was missing two hairdressers—so was Nicky. And there was more: Keira needed some seriously dodgy ingredients for her special treatments—and Nicky had told me that Kirsty's mother had gone to jail for importing the exact same things. I wrinkled my brow. Now that I put my mind to it, it was Nicky who had told me about Keira in the first place. So there had been a connection from day one—but did it matter?

I took out my phone and texted Nicky:

I need to come round tonight. It's important.

Chapter Twenty-One

I WAS CROSS driving home, and the hot afternoon sun melting me through the windows didn't help. Neither did the fact that the driver side window chose that exact moment to stop opening. By the time I pulled up outside my little home, I was sweaty, sweary and grumpy, but every negative emotion melted away at the sight of Henry Lake, shirtless, standing on a stepladder and poking at a security camera with a screwdriver. He was clearly close to finishing installing my cameras, which was a shame. I'd hoped it would take a lot longer…

"Hola, amigo. Weren't we going to fit those above the bed?" I called, climbing out of the car and giving the nearest hub cap a kick for good measure.

"I'm fitting the hi-res ones there, petal," he called down to me. "You know, with the zoom lens."

I walked to the foot of the ladder, and he sprang down and gave me a hug. I rested my head against his chest for a moment. I didn't have a lot of family, not cousins by the dozens or sisters by the score, but I had Henry and Wills. I was blessed.

"What was that?" asked Henry, and I realised I'd spoken out loud.

"I said I'm glad I have you and Wills to look after me," I said, leaning into him. "I don't know what I did to deserve the pair of you, but I don't really care."

He laughed and gave me a great bear hug of a squeeze.

"Well, I should warn you then that Paul is in your lounge trying to wire in the video cables."

"Please tell me you are joking. Paul can't work out the loo roll holder, let alone refilling the salt mill. He'll electrocute the county."

"I heard that," said my lodger's voice behind me. "I heard that, and I'll have you know…" He trailed off.

"What?"

"Actually, Wills confiscated my screwdriver and took over the wiring and I've been relegated to pouring beer," he finished in some embarrassment.

I was relieved to find my brother and Paul getting on. I'd met Paul in unfortunate circumstances—he was a murder suspect in a killing my brother was investigating—and it was fair to say that he came from a bad family. Wills hadn't been pleased when I'd made him my house guest. He'd pictured drugs, stolen goods and unregistered cars passing through my address. I think he'd fast forwarded in his head to when I became a prostitute injecting heroin into my eyeballs. Now it seemed that geeky Paul had finally won him over.

"Yeah, well, I'll go and take over," I said. "You're rubbish at that, too. The glasses will be full of foam."

My men followed me into the kitchen where I found Paul had got as far as putting glasses on the table. There were three, and I added one more and started pulling bottles out of the fridge. The table, I belatedly realised, was rather laden. It was heaped with fat, dusty hardback books, some stacked on top of one another, others open, all marked with a myriad of sticky notes. Paul's laptop was open next to them. Before I could start to wonder what he'd been up to, my brother sauntered in looking smug.

"All done," he said. "He'd plugged the video cable into the phone. Oh, excellent—beer."

I took a couple of minutes to change out of work clothes and into a strappy little sundress, and we took our drinks outside. The July evening was too pretty to waste in a warm kitchen, so we sat on the lawn and chinked some glass.

"So, have you gone to view your inheritance?" Wills asked. "Wandered round your estate?"

I spluttered some beer.

"Hardly that, bro. Amelia's house is miniscule. It's smaller than this place. But it will make a perfect rental and that's one thing I know about. Are you two coming to my housewarming?"

"Wouldn't miss it. Did you ask Jay?"

"Christ, no. He's in New York, thank the Lord rejoicing. If he was here, he'd hire caterers. You wouldn't be able to get a word in edgeways over waiters asking you if you'd like another lark tongue mousse served in a banana leaf or some more scallops tartare with kumquat jus. I was just going to raid the deli counter at the supermarket and tell everyone to bring a bottle."

Henry and Paul were arguing good-naturedly over the controls for the CCTV system, a debate that led to the stepladders coming out again and some general fiddling around the roof of the porch. Wills took advantage to drop his voice.

"Talking of security footage, sis, I brought you a copy of the tape of Derowen's office. You still seemed interested, so I just thought... I don't think there's anything there, though. I've been through it and so have Agnes and Fiona. But take a look if you like. There's only about ten minutes—I cut out everything where nothing moves on screen."

He handed me a little data stick and I idly plugged it into my phone.

Derowen's office door. A tiny on-screen cheese millionaire enters after dinner. Time passes. Crispin moves in front of the camera carrying some files, then back again. Then to and fro a second and then a third time. He takes a pile of papers into the office and then comes out again without it. Finally, Irene comes in, captured briefly in the lens as she pounds on the door hysterically. Derowen opens it a crack, glaring at his crying wife. They disappear into the room, the door shuts. More time passes.

"No sound?" I asked Wills and he shook his head.

"No, quite an old system. Just the visuals."

I turned back to my phone.

The sands of time are still spilling. The door opens and a weeping Irene comes out. Briefly Derowen follows her and stands just inside the room before she turns on him, yelling, and he backs away, retreating into his office. He looks at her unemotionally through the doorway and then turns and closes the door behind him. Irene makes as though to walk away and then turns back. Placing her hands on the wooden surface, she speaks passionately for a moment. Nothing happens, and she turns and runs away out of sight.

Time passes once more. The room is darker, shadows have lengthened. Finally, Crispin—sleepy and keen to shut up shop for the night—knocks on the door. After thirty seconds of frantic knocking, he tries to push it open. He calls over his shoulder and the burly electrician comes to his aid. They force open the door a few inches and there is a hint of shoe, a stripy sock...

And the video ended.

"Anything?" asked Wills, his voice breaking into my reverie. "I can't see a damn thing that doesn't match what everyone said."

"There's something," I said. "I know it. Play it again."

We watched, chatting as the scene passed before us again. I could hear Henry and Paul laughing about something.

"Could someone have come in earlier, hidden themselves the whole time in the office and then left through the window?" I asked. "Is that possible?"

"Yes, if they have a bladder the size of Mars and live on pranic light. The tape lasts seven days and everyone who went in during that time came out again."

"Oh well, just a thought."

"A good one."

The video finished a second time. Then it struck me.

"The coat," I said. "He's wearing his coat. Look."

"Who? What?"

I rewound to where Derowen evicted the long-suffering Irene from his office.

"Look—he's wearing his coat. He wasn't when he went into the office—you said it was hanging in there on a rack. But then he is wearing it when he chucks Irene out."

And indeed he was. The spray-tanned octogenarian was wearing a dark duffle coat, buttoned up to the neck. The film only showed him for a few moments, but in that time—as he watched Irene depart—the coat was clearly on display.

"But that makes no sense," Wills said. "It was a hot day. There's no air conditioning in that building. Why on earth would he put on a coat?"

"This is the same coat that someone dressed him in when he was dead, right?"

"Yes, the same one, but Toni, like I said, he wasn't wearing it when he was killed. Someone put it on afterwards. He bled out on the floor a bit before they dressed him in it, and they buttoned it up. Even if the blood wasn't a giveaway, the coat isn't punctured."

I thought aloud.

"So, he was alive and wearing the coat when he let Irene out, but we have no idea why he would have put it on. But later, when he was killed, he wasn't wearing it, so for some reason, he must have unbuttoned it and taken it off. And then after he was bludgeoned unconscious and stabbed to death, he was dressed in it again—presumably by his murderer... Is that what you are saying?"

He just looked perplexed.

"I guess. But Toni, we are still missing something. It's not the Oscars. Why so many costume changes?"

"Was there any significance to the coat?"

He shook his head.

"It wasn't even his coat. It's Crispin's. The secretary left it in there when the weather was colder and forgot all about it."

"But that's even weirder. Why would he put on Crispin's coat? Scratch that: why would he put on Crispin's coat twice? I preferred it when we were speculating about teleporting pixies."

"You're a terrific help."

I laughed and clapped Wills on the arm.

"I know, I'm the best. Are you two staying for dinner?"

"Just for another tinny, sis."

After they had gone, I gathered glassware, empty bottles and cans and took them through to the kitchen. Paul's project was still occupying most of the table and I raised my eyebrows at him as he followed me in with the last bits and pieces.

"I know you doctors like to be open-minded about traditional medicine, but those books look old enough to recommend leeches and bloodletting," I said. "Not to mention mercury pills and sal volatile."

"Don't knock leeches, they're making a comeback," he said, sitting down and opening a volume at a marked page. "I borrowed these from Jenny. She nicked them for me from the Stone House library."

I bit my tongue because the first thing that sprang to it was a horrified, impassioned plea never to associate with vampires or their coteries. Coming from me, that would have been hypocrisy worthy of a politician. I was also going to have to get used to it, because Paul was an adult and would make his own choices. He'd already made a friend of Jenny, so I was way too late to this party. Instead, I asked with studied casualness:

"Find anything in them?"

He gave me the smug grin of a scholar who had just proved that black equalled white and planned to go and confuse some badgers.

"I found your Glauce, actually."

He pronounced it Glafkee; I'd had it in my mind as Glorker.

"You did? Tell me more."

I sat down opposite Paul, thoughts of his imperilled soul banished.

"There are always a million versions of these myths, and they all differ in odd ways, but I summarised the ones I found," he said cheerfully. "Ready?"

"Yup, fire away."

"OK, there is this witch called Medea who's married to Jason, as in Jason and the Argonauts. But he gaily announces that he is going to marry another woman, a princess called Glauce, and that Medea is going to be banished to another land. All very Greek tragedy so far and most of the versions agree. With me so far?"

Another ancient legend, another tale from the time of myths... I nodded and Paul carried on.

"Medea pretends she doesn't mind and sends Glauce a beautiful wedding dress as a peace offering. In some versions she also sends a crown, but that seems to be a later addition. Anyway, Glauce is getting ready for her wedding, and she puts on her pretty dress, but it's cursed. The versions differ here. In some, it catches fire, and she burns to death, and her father dies, too, when he tries to put it out. In others, she throws herself down a well and drowns. But here's the one you want: she follows a singing phoenix that promises to teach her to fly to Mount Olympus and flings herself off a cliff."

"What?"

"That's right. It's showing her how to get to paradise."

Oh my God, that was exactly what Lorraine had said, that a golden bird had sung the sweetest songs and filled the world with music as it took her to heaven. I was certain now. Nicky's coterie had been killed by witchcraft, by curses that my own grandfather had bribed out of the demon Azazel. I looked at the dusty tomes for a moment and then shook my head.

"Paul, thank you for doing this," I said slowly. "I kind of wish you hadn't, but it had to be done."

He gave me a searching look.

"You're upset."

"I am," I agreed sadly. "But not as upset as Nicky's going to be. All along he's been hoping I'll say that no one killed Lorraine. He's been crossing his fingers that Caroline and Lily are out there somewhere, still alive... But if Lorraine really was murdered then the others almost certainly were, too. And somehow Kirsty has to be involved. Her mother traded in cantamen ingredients—she went to jail for it—so there's no way this is a coincidence."

"That still doesn't explain why you're so upset..."

I clenched my hands into little fists.

"Because it's my grandfather's fault, all of it. There's no good use for this spell. It's wicked. It kills people, end of. But he gave it away just like that to get what he wanted. Lorraine's blood is on his hands, too, Paul. And probably Lily's and Caroline's as well. That's why I'm upset. I thought he was the one constant good thing in my past, but I'm starting to hate him for what he did. Him and Azazel, the pair of them."

I loathed agreeing with Benedict, but it was looking increasingly like the advice he'd given me half a year ago was spot on. You should never bargain with demons. It never ended well.

Chapter Twenty-Two

I SAT AT the table and mulled things over in my mind. Things were starting to click into place, but in a hazy and unformed way. Some made sense—Kirsty's unearthly beauty, Keira's avoidance of me—but others were still a complete confusion. Why had my grandfather been so desperate to end the line of necromancers that he'd been willing to brave Azazel? And what did Tabula Rasa do that made it worth going back a second time? Keira had obviously worked that much out, though she'd refused to tell me, but I doubted even she knew why.

And while there were a million better ways of spending a Friday night, I needed to talk with Nicky. I decided not to feel sorry for myself—I was going to more than ruin his evening, after all.

"I have to go and see Nicky," I said abruptly to Paul. "I assume you have plans, it being Friday and all that."

"Yeah, going to the pub with Sean and the guys," he said, gathering up the books and stacking them. "He owes us all some bevvies after leaving us stranded in customs for a whole day. What's Nicky like?"

The question came out of the blue. I considered it.

"Quirky," I said. "Funny. Very loyal, I think. Kind, but maybe a bit vain. Or even a lot vain, actually. Oh, and really clever. I don't know, Paul, he's not the sort of person I ever hung out with at university. The IT geeks were pretty nocturnal—they preferred to come out at night when the mainframes ran faster—but they didn't hang out in graveyards. And I don't know him very well. We've only met three times. Why?"

"No reason," Paul said. "Just looking out for you."

The sun was setting as I drove over to the Delph, turning the sky acid yellow and pink. The roads were full of tossers, cutting each other up, overtaking on the mini roundabouts and spurning the humble indicator to prove their general wankiness. I let them scoot past me as I ambled along in my daydream. If Nicky didn't have any enemies, who would take out his coterie? Was Kirsty in danger, too? How was her mother involved, the woman who had gone to prison for stockpiling eye of newt and toe of frog?

When the sun finally dipped behind the horizon, I was about fifteen minutes from the Old Rectory. I parked in the first layby I got to, intending to send another text to Nicky, but when I pulled out my phone, he had already replied to my previous one.

This is a bad time…

I sighed. I didn't blame him—Kirsty wouldn't be pleased at my calling round again—but I couldn't face putting things off. I'd had to steel myself to make the trip at all, knowing that nothing nice could come of it. I sent back:

Sorry, but it can't wait. I'm nearly at your house.

A few moments, then:

Like very bad time! Really can't wait?

Nope.

OK. See you soon.

I started the engine and was about to drive off when he sent a final text:

There was something I wanted to ask you anyway.

I sighed again. It was going to be one of those evenings. I drove through Nicky's wrought iron gates and past the unicorn of retina-singeing glory. As I parked, I realised that Nicky was sitting at the top of the steps in front of the half-open door, his chin cupped in his hands. With his customary chivalry, he came over to open the driver door for me, but he was missing the usual bound in his step.

"Hey, angel," he said. "Your timing's not actually that bad."

His voice was carefully neutral, but it didn't fool me. He was trying not to show it, but I could just feel the tension spilling out of him. I followed him up the steps to the door with a sinking feeling.

"How come?"

"Because this evening couldn't get much worse," he said.

And he pushed the door open to reveal the scene inside.

"Jesus on a bicycle," I said. "What the bloody hell?"

The hall was a sea of broken glass, the white tiles transformed into a shimmering crystal carpet of destruction, floating in a pool of red. Not blood, I realised after an initial jerk of horror, but wine, acres of spilt red wine. Little twinkling shards of pastel broke up the scene just in case you found it too Kandinsky for words.

"This is what you get when you throw the first bottle into the antique Venetian glass mirror and the second one straight through the chandelier," he said in a clipped voice. "And then hurl your entire collection of ceramic kittens into the mix because your boyfriend still isn't doing what he's told."

"Please tell me this isn't my fault," I said. "She didn't do this because you said I was coming round, did she?"

Nicky ushered me around the perimeter of the chaos, and we escaped into the kitchen. Kirsty's fury hadn't made it that far, and it was the same pleasing expanse of polished beech and stainless steel as before.

"Angel, I haven't even got around to telling her that," he said. "This one's all on me. You want a drink?"

I nodded without thinking, and he took a rather elegant champagne bottle out of the fridge and began to strip off the foil. There was coloured enamel across the glass. It probably cost more than my car.

"Don't open a bottle just for me," I said hastily. "I'm driving."

But he popped the cork off and filled a coupe.

"I wouldn't worry," he said. "There's still a fridge full of the stuff and Kirsty drinks alcopops. Or Liebfraumilch. Note she didn't waste any of her favoured tipples trashing the hall."

We sat across the kitchen table from one another, two people who didn't know each other very well forced to share a lot of confidences.

I gulped at my drink too quickly and looked at my host. To the casual observer, he looked himself. He was wearing navy leather trousers again, this time paired with a made-to-measure, cream silk shirt that hung perfectly on his slim frame. Gold eyeliner tonight, giving him a slightly fragile, fey beauty that would have disarmed me more if I hadn't spent the past year surrounded by vampires. But I was no casual observer; I was a necromancer, and I could feel him. More than that—I could read him like a book, and I knew I was looking at someone on the brink. There was a barely suppressed panic about Nicky. He gave me a slightly hunted look.

"This place used to be party central and now it's a bloody morgue," he said.

"Believe me, I spend a lot of time at the morgue, and they're very different," I said, trying to inject a note of frivolity into the proceedings. "There's a lot less broken glass and fewer unicorns, true, but the snack machine is crap, and the company leaves a lot to be desired. The last time they had a DJ there was when "Hopping" Harold Herring relieved himself in one of the high-voltage amps at Bingley Hall. It's amazing what 15,000 volts delivered straight through the todger will do to a man who's just drunk two litres of whisky."

He gave a wan smile.

"You're a breath of fresh air," he said. "I don't mean to be such dismal company."

"If it wasn't me, what set Kirsty off?"

"Ah, that. Yes, I said that if we were going to stay here, I would need a new coterie. Either that or I would need to move into the Stone House. But Kirsty, as you probably guessed from her little performance after she threatened to blow your head off, has a romantic notion that there will be just the two of us. Vampire and consort in domestic bliss."

"But is she even your consort?"

"Christ, no, Toni. I'm loyal but not a masochist. You make

someone your consort, it's a vow for life—eternal life in this case— not to mention a commitment to transition them to vampire kind. I don't have the rank to make that kind of promise, and even if I did, can you imagine an eternity with Kirsty?"

I laughed reluctantly.

"But is what she wants even possible? Could the blood of a single mortal ever be enough for a vampire?"

"I guess it's possible. Maybe a very old vampire who doesn't need a lot of blood. Some do, some don't, who knows why? Hugh Bonner had a coterie of just two, and he was young and not very powerful. And then you have Benedict, who has to drink blood every night even though he's as old as the hills... But I know I couldn't make do with a coterie of one, Toni. I need to feed every day. Four is a minimum for me. But Kirsty won't have it. What did you want to talk to me about?"

The sudden change of direction caught me off guard, but I didn't blame him. We weren't having a comfortable conversation. The trouble was, the one I had in mind wasn't going to be any better.

"I need to know how you came to take Kirsty into your coterie, and how she found the other three. Tell me from the beginning, because I am missing something—probably something you think you've told me, but you haven't."

He frowned, but nodded.

"OK, I was dating Kirsty already, before my accident. I met her in the boutique where she worked—luxury alternative clothing, handmade stuff that was a bit off-the-wall. She was a bit rudderless. She wanted to come home here to her mum, but I think she didn't want to crawl back with her tail between her legs, you know, like she'd not achieved anything with her life. She's a few years older than me, you know."

Was she? She didn't look any older than me, but then I had probably been blindsided by her beauty and forgotten to look any further. But Nicky was still talking.

"I had this cool flat—we moved in together. I was madly in love with her. Then there was my accident. When I was in hospital,

I knew it was over. I banned them from letting her see me so that I wouldn't have to wait forever for her not to show. I mean, I was crazy about her, but I wasn't stupid; I knew she'd never put up with a cripple."

"Did she ever try to come?"

He shook his head.

"Of course not. Anyway, after Ada Ferrars made me a vampire, things weren't much better. I had money but no status, and it turned out Ada had been warned not to try making any more fledglings. I was lucky—all her previous attempts died in the transition. But it meant that I was like an illegal immigrant in my own town—I shouldn't have existed. Then Benedict approached me; he'd wanted a hacker, and it turned out he'd planned to transition me himself, but Ada got in first. Christ, I wish she hadn't! Think how things would be different."

I didn't have to—I'd seen it. Nicky would be like Aidan or Grace—powerful, second-generation vampires who sat at Benedict's right hand. I tilted my head to one side... How different would he be? He dropped his voice.

"He sent me to Heidelberg for a year to train. When I got back, I went to Kirsty and asked her—I was really honest with her. She could come home to Staffordshire, we would live somewhere near her mum, and I would give her a life she'd never even dreamed of. In return, she would put up with all the crap of sharing me with a coterie and me being a vampire. She didn't hesitate. She picked this place out, and we were here within a week."

"Were you happy?"

He looked conflicted.

"Something had changed for me. I wasn't in love with her anymore. Human Nicky had adored her every sigh, but vampire Nicky... Toni, it didn't take long before I realised that I didn't even like her. But then she picked Lily—I think she'd decided Lily was homely and I wouldn't want to shag her. She was even less subtle with Caroline and Lorraine—committed lovers who she thought wouldn't even want to get frisky with her boyfriend. But

I didn't pull her up on it. I didn't care. The girls and I just fell for one another. I was in heaven. I got to code to my heart's content, and when I got downtime, I had three adorable women to fool around with and drink blood from. And Kirsty to hang on my arm whenever my status needed a bit of boosting. I thought I'd struck gold."

"Where did she find them?"

"She met Lily in Stafford town square, selling paintings in the market. Lorraine and Caroline were both stylists in Keira's salon—but I told you that, right?"

I sighed. This was exactly the kind of thing that I'd meant.

"Not quite, Nicky. You told me that she'd met them because they were hairdressers, which isn't quite the same. I think I know why you fell out of love with Kirsty, though."

He turned his gentle gaze on me. His eyes, that unexpected palest of blues, were laughing at me.

"I assumed that was because I'd realised that she was a complete cow?"

"I wish. Do you know what a cantamen is?"

"I don't know the word."

"It's a powerful enchantment that a witch can make. My grandfather gave Keira one called Helen of Troy. Did you study Classics?"

"Angel, if they didn't make a graphic novel out of it, I didn't read it."

"It makes a woman so beautiful that men fall in love with her. I am guessing that Keira made it for herself and for Kirsty... You fell for it, but when you died, the spell lost its power. I get the impression that both witches and vampires have some immunity to this kind of thing, so after your transition, her looks weren't enough."

Nicky didn't say anything for a while. Then he shrugged.

"They should never have been enough. It's kind of nice to know I wasn't that shallow. Toni, where are you going with this?"

I knew now. I didn't want to tell him, but there wasn't a lot of choice.

Kirsty was used to people falling in love with her left, right and centre, but at the end of the day she'd chosen Nicky. I doubted she'd been in love with him at the time, but she'd fallen hard at some point along the way, and definitely after his transition. But he'd fallen out of love with her, and no matter what he'd told me about trying to be even-handed with his four girls, I was sure she'd known. You can always tell. It wouldn't have mattered how carefully he'd allotted his time, his physical affections, or his gifts, she would have realised that she'd lost his adoration.

She'd chosen him a coterie of three people that she hoped he would never have any romantic leanings towards, but he'd defied her without even meaning to. He'd fallen for plain, homely Lily's sweet nature, while Lorraine and Caroline had fallen for him in turn. Vampires made the whole smorgasbord of sexuality very simple – pretty much everybody found them irresistible, and they were cool with that. When it came to their allure to us mere mortals, it wouldn't matter whether they were male or female or any combination—the desire would be there just the same. The two hairdressers that Kirsty had chosen wouldn't have been interested in a mortal man—but Nicky wasn't a man. He was one of the undead and they'd adored him. Kirsty had chosen the last people in the world that she thought would be competition for his affections—and he'd preferred all three of them to her.

In the end, I thought it all boiled down to jealousy—poisonous, simmering, toxic jealousy. And Kirsty must have realised that the same seam of loyalty that kept Nicky from deserting her would stop him from ever putting any of the other three aside. She must somehow have convinced herself—and her mum—that the three had to die, and that her own blood would be sufficient to sustain Nicky. And Keira had cast the cantamen that had killed them. It didn't fit with the Keira I'd met, but what else could have happened? I had no doubt that Caroline and Lily's bodies were languishing somewhere in Cannock Chase. There were a lot of old mine shafts.

And now I had to tell him.

"Nicky," I said reluctantly. "Nicky, listen."

But I didn't get any further. I was distracted by the crystal glass whizzing over my head, so close that I felt it brush my hair. When it hit the cabinet behind me, it exploded in a fountain of shards that reminded me of nothing so much as a Guy Fawkes Night rocket going off. I'd been looking at Nicky and hadn't noticed Kirsty's entrance. She stood in the kitchen doorway, her face white with fury, hand raised to let fly the wine bottle after the glass. I began to bring my hands up in self-defence, but Nicky was ahead of me.

He had sprung to his feet, moving with that vampire speed that I would never get used to. He folded her in a restraining embrace, her hands pinned against his chest and her head pulled in against his shoulder. The wine bottle clanked to the floor and rolled under the table, leaving a lake of golden German wine in its wake.

"You have to stop this, Kirsty," Nicky said softly. "Where the hell are we going with all this?"

"I told you not to see her," she hissed, struggling futilely in his grip. "I told her not to come here again."

I put my head in my hands. I should have gatecrashed Paul's pub trip and tormented Sean about throwing up on his passport. Even listening to drunk teenage boys make vomit jokes would have been better than this.

But Kirsty hadn't finished.

"You'll pay for this, you little slut," she said. "I told you—Nicky's mine and I won't share him. I'll use my mother's spells to curse you and you'll die, just like Lorraine and Caroline, and stupid ugly Lily, and no one will even find your bloody corpse."

Chapter Twenty-Three

I RAISED MY head slowly and looked up. Even drunk, with her hair all mussed and her face contorted with rage, Kirsty was still beautiful, still breathtakingly lovely. Nicky held her fast. He'd closed his eyes and I didn't think he wanted to hear what was being said.

"Nicky, please stop this," I said. "Please make it stop."

He looked up at me and nodded.

"Kirsty," he said, and his voice took on that familiar mesmeric quality, commanding, compelling… "Kitten, you're tired. Go upstairs and rest. Wait for me."

He let her go and she gave me a muddled look before turning away and trailing out of the room. She left behind a horrid silence. Nicky sat back down opposite me. He looked close to tears.

"Keira is Kirsty's mother," I said, trying not to sound too accusing.

"I told you that," he said in confusion.

I sighed.

"You didn't, you somehow omitted that trifling little detail, but I don't suppose it would have mattered. Nothing would have been any different in the end."

"What did they do?"

What hadn't they done? Everything had fallen into place. Keira had used the clay of Helen of Troy to make herself beautiful, and later her daughter. She'd also used it to build up her successful business.

And when my grandfather had approached her a second time, more than three decades later, she'd demanded Glauce's Wedding Dress as payment. Why she'd wanted it, I couldn't imagine. Was there an enemy who'd long since perished? Or many? It didn't bear thinking about.

But her plans hadn't all gone smoothly. She'd been caught stockpiling the ingredients for her spells and gone to jail. The late Mr Holloway had been given custody of their little daughter and taken her to the south coast. Kirsty had probably grown up like me—with no idea that she was a witch. I assumed she'd discovered it when she moved back up north and started working with Keira. When she'd found out, she hadn't confided in Nicky. Had she worried about his reaction if he discovered that all his love for her had only ever come from a spell?

Keira had a flat built for Kirsty, but her daughter never moved in. Instead, she came home with Nicky, the vampire who promised her a life of luxury and a home near her only remaining family. I'd assumed that Keira had somehow agreed to listen to Kirsty's pleas to help mend the rifts in their love life, but I'd been wrong. Kirsty had done it herself.

Kirsty had used Glauce's Wedding Dress, and I doubted she'd asked her mother for permission. Had Keira guessed? If so, what could she have done? The hated Lily was first, then Caroline, sent off to fling themselves into the unknown, with just a goodbye note. If I thought about it, there was no reason for the notes to have ever existed at all. All Kirsty had to do was say that she'd read them and thrown them away. No one would even wonder, and why risk forging them if she didn't have to...

Except she'd messed up with Lorraine. Someone had seen the girl in the woods, after she'd opened up her cursed box and put on that sexy silk slip that had arrived in a gift box and turned out to be her own shroud. And I'd come sticking my nose in just where Kirsty hadn't wanted anyone looking too closely.

If I'd left things much longer, would I have been next?

Nicky didn't say a word during my explanation, or for a while afterwards.

"Are you sure?" he asked. "Might you be wrong? I want you to be wrong so much."

"I might be, Nicky, but you can always ask her—I know you don't like it, but you can compel her to tell the truth."

He bit his lip and nodded.

"Will you stay?" he asked. "It won't take very long."

"Of course. Why wouldn't I?"

It was only after he'd gone that I realised what he meant; he was going to compel Kirsty to tell the truth and she was going to confirm what I'd said... and vampire justice didn't come with the chance of parole or an appeal. I sat in shock for a moment, and then I hauled myself to my feet and staggered through wine and glass fragments to the sink where I threw up a glass of vintage champagne. Vampire justice had an Old Testament consistency to it. That didn't mean I had to like it.

He was gone for about an hour, long enough for me to sip water from my champagne coupe until the acid burn left my throat, and time enough for me to clean up the glass fragments and the wine from the kitchen. I didn't attempt to tackle the hall, just walked around the chaos, and waited for Nicky just where he'd waited for me earlier, at the top of the porch steps. I heard his light step behind me, but I didn't even have the energy to turn around.

He sat down one step below me and looked out at the garden below us. It never gets that dark in the summer months, and I could still make out the silhouette of a unicorn against the iron gates. I could also see where the streaks of Nicky's eyeliner had run down his face as the light from the hallway caught the shards of glitter.

"And?" I said.

Nothing for a while, then:

"You were right. Apparently, there's a space behind the bathroom cabinet where she kept her stuff. She only discovered she was a witch after we moved here. She started helping Keira make her clay mask and found the other recipes. Keira only worked out what had happened when the local press reported details of Lorraine's suicide. That's when they fell out."

I didn't want to ask, I didn't want to know, but my traitorous mouth got the words out before I could stop it.

"How did you do it?"

"I was very gentle, Toni. I told her that she was right, that it would be just the two of us forever, me feeding on her and no one else. And then I drank her blood... All of it. She'd have felt nothing but pleasure."

The gentlest of deaths... He rushed in.

"I had to. I called Benedict, and he said that if I didn't do it, he would, or he'd send Aidan round. I couldn't be certain they would be as kind. And I couldn't have her knowing what was going to happen and be waiting for it. You know that."

Oh yes, I knew. I was proud of him, in an odd way, for doing it himself. He could easily have left someone else to carry the can. Poor Nicky—a month ago he'd never killed anyone. Now there was Dylan Moss on his conscience and poor, pretty Kirsty, eaten up with jealousy until it drove her almost mad.

I scooted down one step and took one of Nicky's hands in mine.

"I know," I said. "There wasn't a better choice. They all sucked."

He didn't respond, and I looked across to see that the shimmer on his cheek had become more than eyeliner. He raised a cuff self-consciously, and I looked away to pretend I hadn't noticed. Eventually I ran out of stiff upper lip and English reserve and opened my arms. Vampires don't sob when they cry, they don't have breath to catch, but there were enough tears to leave my shoulder damp. He pulled away after a few minutes.

"I need to be alone now," he said quietly, with all the dignity he could muster.

I watched as he walked into the darkness of the garden. Then I drove home.

SOMETHING WAS NIGGLING at the back of my mind, but it wasn't until I was cleaning my teeth and looked up at my sleepy reflection in the mirror, my shoulder shimmering with Nicky's gold eyeliner, that I realised what it was. I dropped the brush in the sink, and—cursing myself for my slow thinking and stupidity—ran back to the bedroom and rang Aidan.

"Toni," he said, sounding harassed.

"Keira Holloway," I burst out.

"I know. Nicky rang a couple of hours ago. I sent some people to her house, but she'd already gone. She left earlier today. She drove back from her salon in a rush, packed some bags and headed off as though the hounds of hell were after her, according to a neighbour. I'm trying to track her down, but it looks as though she crossed into Derbyshire before the sun set."

She'd fled just after I'd spoken to her. Maybe the manicurist had mentioned that I knew Kirsty. She may even have called Kirsty and found out that I was affiliated with Benedict. Keira had realised that a house of cards was about to fall down. Had she warned her daughter before fleeing? I was sure she'd find a way to blame me once she found out that Kirsty was dead. That seemed to be everyone's hobby these days.

I bid Aidan good night and then, because I'd had enough of Friday, I went to bed.

WHEN I WOKE the sun was high in the sky. I wasn't hungover, but Paul was. He winced around the house in a onesie, moaning about how bright it was. I made us both coffee and bacon sandwiches and the moans subsided a little. He improved enough to huddle in one of the kitchen chairs, only whimpering at intervals.

"You either had a really good evening that needed a lot of celebrating or a completely pants time with lots of sorrows to drown," I said, when he could bear noises as loud as my voice.

"Definitely the worst evening ever in the history of evenings," he said. "Setting aside war and famine, no one has ever had a crappier Friday night. Bethany turned up. I have no idea how she knew where we were, but she snogged Sean all night in front of me. She nearly ate the man's face off. He was muntered, so I can't really blame him, but Toni, she doesn't even like him. I tried drowning my sorrows, but they could swim really well."

"Oh Paul, I'm so sorry. What a bollocking mess."

"I don't get it. She dumped me very thoroughly. Now she says she didn't mean it. What the hell was last night meant to prove?"

I could have told him. I'd seen girlfriends do the same thing. Look what you're missing, you dumb male! Hey, don't you want me back? It rarely went anywhere good.

"She's confused, Paul. Not everyone is a logic freak like you. A lot of people think with their hearts and loins, not their brains. Including me at times."

He looked up at me. I thought it was the look of a man who needed another round of bacon butties.

"Me too, Toni, but I wouldn't do that. I left eventually because I knew I was going to behave badly if I stayed."

I got up and opened the fridge. I took out another dozen rashers. Paul's vigour might be temporarily dented by overindulgence, but a teenage boy can always find somewhere to tuck another fifteen hundred calories topped with brown sauce.

"I wish I'd left earlier last night, too," I admitted. "I don't want to play one-upmanship, but I honestly think my evening was worse than yours."

He looked a little shocked after I'd recounted the night's events.

"You've only met Nicky four times and he's killed two people," he said. "He sounds like a bit of a thug."

I laughed at that.

"He's almost the opposite; I think his nature is very mild. Being a vampire doesn't really suit him. Will you still come to my housewarming tonight? If you like, I'll call Bethany and un-invite her."

"I'll come. She may not show and anyway, you'll need some help. I won't wimp out on you."

He crawled off to the shower after two more cups of coffee and another round of sandwiches and then repaired to his eiderdown to recuperate. I looked out of the kitchen window. It was a beautiful day. The sun was as yellow as a yellow thing. The sky was free of clouds and as blue as a vampire's eyes. Little birds were barrelling across the lawn and Winchester was asleep in a sunbeam. It was a day for living, for getting out there and conquering the world. I went back to bed, too, and slept until lunchtime.

I dropped Paul at Amelia's little house and went to raid the off-licence. He was armed with balloons and streamers, while I was packing a piece of plastic for a bank account that was now six thousand pounds in the black. I thought we had all the ammunition we needed for a little light housewarming.

It struck me as I parked outside the shops that the previous housewarming I'd been to had also been my own—Peter, Camilla and I had run around Lichley Manor with party poppers while Oscar had rolled his eyes at us. We'd played parlour games by candlelight in the dirty cellar. Then Oscar and I had made love until the sun rose.

I didn't look back at my relationship with Oscar through rose-coloured glasses. I appreciated the good times—which had been brief—but I also knew that they hadn't made the bad times worthwhile. It was hard, though, not to miss the happiness of being in love with someone and being absolutely sure that they loved you back, truly, madly, deeply. I felt a little pang deep in my heart and went forth to vanquish it with retail therapy.

By the time my guests started to roll up, I was snazzily clad in a brand new outfit, right down to the lingerie. It was a denim-blue suede mini-dress that buttoned all the way up the front and left not a lot to the imagination. I paired it with cream kitten heels that I could sort of walk in. A bit. I'd decided that the fast-healing cuts on my arms no longer needed long sleeves; I could pass them off as gardening injuries.

The kitchen contained enough strawberries to host Wimbledon, and enough wine and beer to fill a bathtub. The latter became more than an analogy when Paul and I realised that Amelia's miniscule fridge wasn't cut out for house parties and filled her bath with ice.

I hugged Henry and Wills, shook hands with John Jones and his unexpectedly fabulous wife, and avoided Bernie's wandering hands. I poured beer and handed round canapés. Paul had set up a small music system and played a bewildering mix of tracks that seemed to span five continents and three centuries, but all somehow sounded slightly eighties. I suspected Paul Simon had been at the sherry.

The only damp squib was the weather. After weeks of golden beach days, a soft warm rain was falling, not enough to dampen my spirits but sufficient to stop my guests from spreading out into the garden. I didn't really care—I leaned contentedly against the kitchen sink and watched the pretty little house, all mine, filled with people I liked having a good time.

I noticed with some surprise that Bethany and Paul were talking to one another perfectly civilly. She was wearing a summer top and hot pants that—combined—contained less actual fabric than a sock. There was no sign of the feckless Sean. I forbore from poking my nose in. Women like Bethany—or indeed Kirsty—were completely beyond me. Maybe I just wasn't particularly vengeful, or fond of mind games.

The sun had long since set, and I wondered how my very special, secret, mystery guest's evening was going. I didn't think they would let me down. I let Paul turn the music up a little louder and opened the front door. The warm evening air swept through the cottage. It carried away all my stresses and strains. I looked out onto the drive and the village of Salt beyond. It was a lovely spot, and I could see why Amelia had chosen it. It was not unlike my home ground of Colton, a mixture of old and new houses, but mostly old, with the modern dwellings constructed in what would have been the extensive gardens of the old. Maybe when I was a white-haired old woman I could move here... Who was I kidding? When I was a white-haired old woman, I would need a retirement home within hobbling ground of a large cemetery.

I wandered back into the house. My party was in full swing. There was no dancing, but I could tell everyone was having a good time. The coroner and my brother were discussing the finer points of how hard bodies were to identify if wasps got to them first. Bethany sat patiently next to Paul on the stairs pretending to look interested while he attempted to explain the theory of relativity to her. Henry Lake was telling a riveted Bernie what had happened when he'd been on a film set with Christopher Lee.

I meandered through to the kitchen and collected a box of empty bottles, carrying them out through the front door. The recycling bin was at the side of the house, at the end of a long, narrow corridor formed by the wall and a high hedge. I chucked the bottles in one by one, listening to the glass explode over the sound of the music in the cottage. It's like jumping through puddles—irresistible.

The last one shattered with a particularly satisfying retort. Grahame Martin's voice behind me broke the silence.

"You should have stayed with your friends," he said.

I turned round and looked at him. He blocked my escape, filling the corridor as effectively as a fence. His face was a mess of cuts, bruises and hospital butterfly clips, and one eye was still swollen shut. He did indeed have one cast on his right leg and a second on his left wrist, but that still wasn't going to save me, because in his right hand he was carrying a knife with a twelve-inch serrated blade that looked like it could cut through concrete, let alone a few inches of Lavington. What is it with men and size? He could have slit my throat with a penknife. With what he'd brought, which I was close to classing as a polearm, he could have removed my head, limbs and major organs without breaking a sweat.

"Yup," I said. "More fool me."

"It ends here, you thieving bitch," he said. "I won't make it slow."

I couldn't contain myself any longer.

"You just don't get it!" I yelled. "It wasn't yours, it was Amelia's. All of it! And I'd rather see it burn than let you have so much as her bloody rolling pin. You were a rotten son and you're a horrible person. You know why it isn't yours? Because you don't sodding well deserve it. I hardly knew Amelia and I was a better daughter to her. None of this is my fault—it's all yours."

He yelled something back, but I wasn't listening. He raised the knife and stepped towards me, closing the gap between us: six feet, then five, four, three, two… and then Aidan caught him around the neck with one arm and sank his fangs into the man's throat. My special guest had arrived.

I tried to avert my eyes, but they had locked on the scene. I watched Amelia's son as he twitched and thrashed in his death throes. Aidan's eyes were closed in something near ecstasy. Even in the darkness of the corridor I caught glimpses of something dark, viscous and wet. The sound effects were worse. I'd heard them before, when Oscar killed one of the Gambarinis and when Benedict executed Diana. I'd forgotten how unpleasant they were, but if I was going to be squeamish, I should never have rung Aidan in the first place.

When he'd finished, he hung on with one hand to the pale, wrinkled carcass of Grahame 'Gin' Martin, holding the corpse up by its collar.

"You were certain he would come," he said, his voice replete, thick, content. "A good call."

"I was out and about all afternoon," I said. My voice shook a little. I wasn't really OK with what we'd just done. "The camera we found made me certain he'd be watching me. I thought the very idea of a housewarming to celebrate doing him out of his inheritance would be more than he could stand. And then I left my friends and wandered into a nice, dark dead end, in my silly shoes, at a time when he could be sure no one would hear us over the music. Yup, I was pretty certain."

Aidan looked at me—there was some respect in his gaze.

"You throw interesting parties," he said, drawing a reluctant smile from me. "Well, I'm glad you asked me along. I'll take this and be on my way. There's a tarpaulin in my boot."

"What on earth are you going to do with him?" I asked.

"Do you really want to know?"

I considered the question.

"Actually, no," I conceded. "I really don't. It can be your little secret, because I won't be raising him from the dead any time soon. It was quite enough trouble getting him there in the first place."

I watched Aidan heading off into the night and walked back through the damp evening air to the cottage kitchen.

I stayed there for a few minutes, trying to regain my composure. I would have handed Grahame over to the police, but he'd watched Nicky kill Dylan Moss in my kitchen. And it was hard to feel too guilty—the man had tried to kill me three times and kidnapped my cat. I'd told Benedict off for killing people when it was convenient for him. Was I any better? Had hanging round vampires changed me?

My attention was brought back to the moment by Claire wandering in carrying a bottle of champagne.

"Darling," she said. "Terrifically late, I know, but the dog show raged out of control. The blue rosette winner was in heat, and one of the runners-up got into her cage and you can guess what happened next. The two owners came to blows and we had to call the police. Was priceless—if you've never seen a Chihuahua shagging a Doberman, you've missed out. He hung on to her with his teeth."

I hugged her.

"I'm sorry I missed it."

"Don't worry—you can watch it later. The resident vet caught it on his phone. It had gone viral before the police arrived."

I laughed, but Claire was staring at my wrists in horror. The marks where I'd sliced them open to drag Dylan Moss back from the dead were horribly obvious in the vivid light of the kitchen, and I bit my lip. I should have worn gloves or longer sleeves after all—I wasn't as well healed as I thought. Better still, I should have taken advantage of Aidan's presence earlier to ask him to heal them, but between nearly being murdered and watching the vampire drain a man to death... Hell, it had gone clean out of my mind.

"Claire..." I began but she interrupted me.

"Please don't tell me you've started doing that again."

"Again? What?"

"You did it at university, off and on, I know. And after your parents died when I was living with you—sometimes I'd see the marks. You were always careful to hide them, but I caught sight. Lav, darling, I'm your best friend. What's wrong? What's made you start again? Is it Peter?"

I stared at my own wrists. Parallel cuts. Healing wounds.

"Oh my God," I breathed. "You think I self-harm."

She wrapped her arms around me, and I laid my head against her shoulder; from her voice, she was close to tears.

"It's nothing to be ashamed of, Lav. I won't judge you. I'll always be here for you."

I hugged her back and tried to say reassuring things, but my mind was elsewhere. Because she'd given me the final clue. It had been obvious all along, but I'd missed it. Now I knew exactly who had killed the obnoxious cheese millionaire Derowen Polkerris. And no one would ever be able to prove it.

Chapter Twenty-Four

I HADN'T DRUNK so much as a sip of wine with the prospect of Grahame Martin hanging over me, but even with him out of the way I didn't dare start. I was far too worried about what I might blurt out to Claire. The end result was that I was stone-cold sober at my own party. When the last of my guests had departed, I idly tidied up a bit and then drove back home with a slumbering teenager in the passenger seat next to me. Paul woke shortly before we reached home.

"Bethany was really sweet tonight," he confided in me. "She seems alright with things now. I think we can just be friends."

I cast a sideways look at him. I was no courtesan, but I'd been through the mill enough to know that he was living in cloud-cuckoo-land. Bethany had tried behaving like a complete cow and it hadn't got her what she wanted. She was now trying the sweetness and light approach as an alternative. We would see how long this new friendship lasted once she realised that her change of strategy wasn't working. I didn't try to warn Paul. Some mistakes you have to make for yourself. I'd made enough of them. Kit Maybury. Oscar Guillaume. Oh, and the rather beautiful Italian student who'd shagged me on Fridays and Claire on Saturdays and—as we eventually found out—some sweet theology major after choir on Sundays. I hadn't had the emotional energy to investigate weekdays, but I still harboured suspicions.

"That's great," I said wryly, hoping Paul had drunk enough to make me sound convincing. "I'm happy for you."

But he'd fallen asleep again and when we got back, I had to shake him for ten minutes to get him out of the car and into the house, after which he collapsed on the sofa.

I was too worked up to go to bed, though, so I tipped half of the contents of the fridge into my rucksack and walked up the hill to the cemetery. Some people relax by smoking or walking a dog. Not me. Forget golf clubs, art galleries and poetry readings. Keep your jigsaw puzzles and your knitting. All I want is a mossy tomb and a bit of moonlight. That night, there wasn't much moonlight, but the rain had eased off and I had an itch to scratch.

Half an hour later, I was sitting on the grass with Bredon, pouring out my heart. He had no hesitation in assuring me that Grahame 'Gin' Martin had got his just desserts. I got the distinct impression that the only improvement Bredon would have made to my plans would have been to transpose them to a location where he could have taken out the man himself. When I told him my conclusions about Derowen Polkerris, he nodded.

"Of course," he said. "Once you realise the sequence of events, the mystery ebbs, and the mundane fills the gap. Do you have a plan of action, Mistress Toni? You cannot take this knowledge to the forces of law and order."

"I don't know. I haven't worked it out. Maybe I need to ask the murderer why they did it. After that I'll make a decision."

I stayed with Bredon until the sun was ready to peep over the horizon, and then I walked home and slept the sleep of the just. Or the unjust. I was no longer quite sure, but I slept well all the same.

I had scheduled a leisurely Sunday brunch with Wills and Henry and drove over at about eleven. The rain of the previous evening had evaporated and, though the forecasters were warning of storms later in the week, it was another bikini-worthy day. I ambled into Wills and Henry's kitchen to find them arguing contentedly about how many eggs to poach and how long to toast the muffins for.

"Sis, he's going to burn them. They'll be black by the time he takes them off the grill. Talk some sense into the man."

Henry winked at me. All I could do was giggle. I thought his muffins looked perfect.

I sat and was fed coffee and tasty food. We chatted of this and then of that. I could tell that Wills was tactfully avoiding the subject of Jay. I knew he liked the man and thought I'd made a good boyfriend choice for a change. But no one knew better than my brother that you have to follow your heart even when the obstacles seem impossibly huge. Homophobia wasn't what it had been in the police force, but it would be a hopelessly naïve idealist who thought it had left the ranks entirely.

"Good party last night," he said after a while. "It was great that John Jones came along. He's a good guy."

"I really like him. I've been reading all the letters he sent to me over the last year—he fought very hard to make sure that I got my inheritance. What were you two talking about last night? Apart from the wasps eating corpses thing, which by the way I don't want to know any more about. I already heard too much."

He sniggered.

"Gruesome, I know. Nothing very exciting. Those four Czech boys in the motorway crash, actually. You remember that lady who said someone deliberately crashed into their car? Well, we tried to find out what they did just before they drove up that stretch of motorway. It turns out they filled up their car in the service station on the Toll Road. They also stopped for a bite to eat. The girl who served them remembers them particularly. And get this: they met someone there."

"An assignation?"

"Not at all. She said that in the queue someone began talking to them—he'd picked up on something they said and seemed quite excited. They ate lunch together, the five of them, and left together."

"In the same car?"

"She wouldn't have seen that, but no. There are cameras at the petrol station area. They left in one car; he followed them. And they waited at the exit to ensure he was right behind them."

And then later, he'd deliberately driven them off the road. Three had died. The fourth was in a coma. And then someone had stolen the survivor's belongings from the hospital. It made about as much sense as the wish list Azazel had given my Grandfather Robert.

"That's just confusing. Did the waitress say anything else? What the guy looked like, maybe, or what they said?"

He shook his head.

"She said he was wearing a beany hat, and she didn't notice his face much, but she did notice something interesting. From his voice when he ordered food from her, she said he wasn't English either."

"Another Czech?"

"Not at all. She's certain he was French."

I frowned. Staffordshire wasn't a key destination for foreign visitors. Most people travelling through on the M6 got on before junction eleven and left after sixteen.

"And the guy in the hospital?"

"Still in a coma. But I've put a round-the-clock guard on him. I don't need a fourth victim."

I nodded sympathetically. I didn't like to tell Wills that his clean-up rate this month wasn't going to look good. Gin and Spider-Man were never going to take the rap for breaking their parole and stalking his sister. And he was never, ever going to be able to call the killer of Derowen Polkeriss to book.

"Good luck," I said with feeling. "I hope you get the guy."

I drove home thinking about what he'd said. Could the man in the second car be the same person who'd attacked me in the woods? Sophy's obsessed fan had told me he'd kill everyone who stood between them. The odds of there being two French murderers in the county seemed low. But what was the connection between him and four Czech boys who'd claimed they were on a stag weekend but bought one-way tickets to England?

The house was quiet. Instead of Paul, it contained a scrap of paper.

"Sean got tickets to the rugby," it said. "Back Monday. Cross your fingers that we win."

I napped all afternoon. I hadn't been so sleep-deprived since I'd been dating Oscar. More to the point, I had plans for later that would mean another night with limited amounts of kip. I lay on the sofa and dozed with Winchester in the crook of my arm, occasionally waking when he turned over or chased a mouse in his dreams. When the sun set, we ate some tuna together and then I dressed myself in black jeans, black hiking boots and a black hoodie. I checked the batteries in my torch and then got in the little rusty Morris and drove over to the Jacobean mansion of a dead, Cornish cheese millionaire. I was going to beard a murderer in their den. I had a feeling it was going to be thoroughly depressing rather than dangerous.

I parked on the verge. I'd noticed where the cameras were on my previous visit, and I remembered their positions well enough to approach the house without passing through their line of sight. There weren't very many lights on, but on the ground floor, a section blazed out. I approached quietly, though I doubted that anyone would hear me through the glass. As I moved closer, I could see that the glazed French doors gave onto a cosy living room. I peered in through the glass. Yes, I'd been right in my guesses. There she was. And there he was. I raised my hand and rapped sharply on the glass.

Irene jumped to her feet in panic, bringing her hands up to her cheeks. She looked around frantically, as though seeking somewhere to hide or someone to help her. I tried the handle of the garden door and somewhat to my surprise it opened. Not a lot of use having television cameras and security alarms if you don't even lock the doors at night.

"It's OK, Irene," I said softly as I came in. "I know what happened. I know what you did."

And I turned to where the rotting zombie corpse of Derowen Polkerris sat opposite her, lolling in an armchair and stuffing his face with Cornish pasties. He was a right mess.

Even my grandfather had raised a better class of cadaver than this. Derowen had been buried in a smart suit. It was the only smart thing about him, and it was losing its attraction; the oozy bits of his body were beginning to soak through in patches. Any attempt at beautification by the undertakers had long since sloughed away, and Derowen's face was both bloated and saggy all at once, the eyes wet and glassy. And the smell. Ick. It wasn't good. It was every kind of bad. I gagged a bit and turned away.

Irene was staring at me. She had the look of a terrified rabbit that has been staring into the oncoming headlights for a while and knows something bad is going to happen but not what or how to avoid it. There were black marks under her eyes and her skin was waxy. When had she last slept? I shook my head. She didn't need to worry—she'd covered up her tracks so perfectly that not even I was going to be able to point a finger at her.

"I understand," I said as kindly as I could. "You went down to talk to him. You were really upset—you'd just found out that after all your love and forgiveness he was going to leave you for another man."

"I still love him," she said with a little sob, tears starting to track down her face.

"I can see that! You pleaded with him to change his mind, but he was so uninterested that he fell asleep. He dozed off. You were begging him to save your marriage—"

She gave a bark of hysterical laughter that had nothing to do with being amused and interrupted me, "And the next thing I heard was a great loud snore."

She sat down again in her chair and looked up at me. I felt sorry for her. A moment's rage and here she was. There was a glass on the little table next to her. I picked it up and sniffed it. A tumbler of neat gin without so much as an ice cube; a tramp's drink. Why didn't she just swig it out of the bottle in a brown paper bag and be done with it? I continued:

"You hit him with the poker. Then you attacked him with the letter opener. Irene, what were you thinking?"

She shook her head. Tears dripped off her chin.

"I don't know! I just wanted a reaction. I didn't get it—I never did from him."

Poor, impulsive Irene; thirty-five years and then this.

"Then when you realised what you'd done, you raised him from the dead and made him put on Crispin's coat to hide the stab wounds. The police knew he hadn't been killed in it, so they assumed the murderer had manhandled him into it. But you didn't need to—you made dead Derowen dress himself. Then you ordered him to open the door and let you out. When you dismissed him, his body fell against the door. You can never be found guilty of killing him because the camera shows he was standing up, clearly animated, when you left him. You committed the perfect murder."

"I never meant to kill him, you know," she said. "It was a moment of madness. I want him back. I've been raising him every night since he was brought here. But I'm not a very strong necromancer. I doubt he'll last much longer..." She trailed off. Then: "How did you know?"

"Your gloves." I held out my wrists so that she could see the lines tracking up them where I'd cut myself to raise Dylan Moss. "You told the police that you self-harm, and that was why you were wearing those long gloves. A friend thought the same of me last night, but I'm a necromancer, too. I'm always wearing gloves and long sleeves to hide the evidence. I realised you were doing the same."

We sat in silence, broken by the sound of Derowen Polkerris loudly masticating a pasty.

"Are you going to tell anyone?" she asked dully.

"Who'd believe me? Or you, for that matter. And I think you're being punished enough already. Though you could probably use some therapy."

We sat together and watched Derowen. I thought a piece of his nose had fallen off since I'd entered the room. The smell wasn't getting any better.

"Can't you light a candle or something?" I said. "Who taught you to raise the dead anyway?"

She got to her feet and pottered around before finding something expensive looking in a cut-glass jar. She lit the wick and the scent of jasmine and rose began to compete with the aroma of decaying Derowen.

"My grandmother," she said. "She died long before I started, but she left me some notes. Feed them well. Never give them your blood; it gives them free will. Banish them before dawn. So many rules... I began about four years ago. I didn't do it very often. I never saw the point before Des died."

I looked across at the putrefying octogenarian. I couldn't see the point even now, but I hadn't spent thirty-odd years in love with the man.

"Do you want to say goodbye?" I asked, desperate to lighten the dismal atmosphere.

She frowned but nodded.

"Can you do that?"

"Yup."

I drew Ignatius' little knife out from under the neck of my t-shirt. I had a lot of repair work to do, and I thought a little blood would be needed. I drew the knife across my left wrist. Maybe just one cut would be enough. We would see.

"Derown Polkerris, I summon you," I began.

But that was all it took. He'd not been ready to quit the world when he died, and he was more than ready to come back again. I felt his spirit, dormant in his body, rise to my call. I closed my eyes, remembering having to remake the damaged body of Dylan Moss. I thought of the lecherous lizard king that Derowen had been when I'd met him in evening dress, his creepy, veiny hand on my thigh, smiling through his slightly fleshy lips. I opened my eyes and felt a flush of pride.

There wasn't a mark on him. He looked seventy-five, no more. His hair was thicker than I remembered, and the wet, mouldering eyes had become bright and shiny. He blinked at me and then at Irene. Then he nodded vaguely and picked up another pasty from the bucket that she'd placed at his elbow. He sucked it in like a chocolate button and swallowed.

"The new gourmet range," he said in a familiar thin, whiny voice.

"The paprika masks the taste of the soya granules. Tell Crispin they need to use less onion salt. And the gravy is still a little thin. More E509 might do it."

"I'm sorry I killed you, darling," Irene said softly. "I preferred you alive."

"The crust is a little dry still," he continued. "Perhaps a lighter glaze."

"I miss you."

He looked at her with the uncaring gaze of the dead. I thought he was a touch nicer dead than alive, and that was a first. But I could do better. Remembering Nicky's miserable last moment with Lorraine, I decided I could learn from my mistakes. I closed my eyes and gave him my commands silently. It took another little swipe with the knife, but I didn't think Irene had noticed.

"You look very pretty," he said flatly. "You always did. I was lucky to have you. Make sure you have a nice life. I left you everything, you know. It's an irony. You were the only one who never cared for my money and now you have it all."

She closed her eyes. I stood up and led Derowen through the French doors and out into the dark. We walked together under the trees until we came to his fresh grave. I dismissed him and then stood for a while, regaining my poise and giving Irene some time to regain hers. When I returned, she had dried her face and cleared away the bucket of pasties.

"Thank you," she said. "I didn't know that was possible."

"You have to get away from here, Irene," I said in a rush. "Away from this house with all its memories and away from that bloody grave. Go down to Dartmouth with Crispin. Don't wait. There are more nice hotels than you can shake a stick at. Go and stay in one of them while your house is made ready. You can't stay here. Promise me."

"I promise. I'll go tomorrow. As soon as I can pack a bag. Send me a large bill—I'll pay it."

I shook my head. I didn't do things that way. There wasn't much else to say, and I didn't know her well enough to give her a hug. I walked through the French doors and across the lawn back to my car. I drove home without even putting the radio on. There were any number of people who'd wanted Derowen dead, but it was the one person who desperately wanted him alive who'd killed him. Sometimes I thought my life sucked, but at least I wasn't in love with a dead man. At least, not anymore.

Chapter Twenty-Five

THE OFFICE HAD a little more life to it that Monday morning. Bethany seemed cheerful and Bernie was clearly pleased with the month's takings. More to the point, the sunshine must have finally got to that segment of the population who'd been saving up for a deposit. I spent all morning and the early afternoon showing three separate pairs of first-time buyers round potential purchases.

I was a little sick of pebble-dashed semis by then and planned to spend the rest of the afternoon trawling through paperwork. I was settling down to it when Bernie wandered through from the kitchen with a mug of tea.

"Jill Fletcher rang again. She said she didn't know whether the Czech Republic was in the EU or not."

I looked up from my keyboard.

"What on earth are you talking about?"

"Jill thought you'd know."

I thought about it.

"Oh, that. You remember, she asked if it was a landlady's duty to check if her lodger was in the country legally. I think she has to if they are from outside European Union borders or something, but post-Brexit I might be wrong. I was going to look the regulations up when she got back to me about where he came from. I take it he hails from the Czech Republic then?"

"Prague."

"I'll find out," I said vaguely, because I had a feeling that Bernie had said something that mattered, and I'd somehow missed the point. "I think it's one of that bunch of Eastern European countries that came in just before the Lisbon Treaty or something."

I made sure to sound unbothered, but something wasn't right. I couldn't put my finger on it, but it niggled away in the back of my mind. Eventually, I rang Jill and suggested going round with a pro-forma contract—a box-ticking exercise, seeing as the man was already ensconced in his new home—and doing a new inventory for her. She seemed broadly unbothered, too, and couldn't fit me in until the next afternoon anyway, but I felt a little happier after entering the appointment in my diary. I'd learned to listen to the little voice in the back of my head. Sometimes it talked sense.

My phone buzzed in my handbag, and I realised that the whole undead husband grimness of the previous night had left me so distracted that I'd not checked it since leaving Irene's house. I discovered some dull requests from clients, a few thank you texts following my little housewarming-cum-assassination evening and a message from Nicky that was nearly as depressing as seeing Irene watch the foetid body of her spouse eat Cornish pasties on the sofa.

Hey, Angel. I'm going back to Brighton on Tuesday night. I came round to say goodbye, but you were out. You might as well sell that damn house for me. I will throw in Rainbow for free. Love, Nicky.

After that, the rest of the afternoon dragged and when I got home to an empty house, Paul having not yet returned from a weekend of watching hunky men wrestle in the mud leaving me stuck in on my own. It was all very unfair, and I ate toast in front of the television with a mutinous expression. I was cross, bored, lonely and frustrated. Nothing that I'd done had turned out the way I wanted. I hadn't helped Wills resolve anything, and both Dylan Moss and Grahame 'Gin' Martin had been killed by vampires, an extreme solution that didn't gel well with me. Added to that, poor gentle Nicky was even more miserable than before I'd stuck my nose into his business.

I looked out at the late evening sun. It would set in half an hour or so. On a whim, I changed into the pretty suede sundress that I'd bought for my housewarming. This time I paired it with flat sandals that would be good for carrying boxes up and down stairs rather than giving stalkers the impression that you couldn't run very fast. Then I drove up the familiar route to the Delph and parked in Nicky's driveway.

The sun had set, but the security lights showed me that Kirsty's car was still in residence and the garden, too, was still littered with the detritus of someone prone to late-night, online, impulse purchases. I approached the front door hesitantly, unsure of my welcome, and rang the bell. I didn't think I'd be greeted by the barrel of a shotgun this time, but I hadn't brought a lot of joy into Nicky's life. He might have preferred me not to come at all. The door opened and I bit my lip a little nervously.

But I'd misjudged him—he looked delighted to see me.

"Hey," he said. "It's great you came. I didn't want to leave without saying goodbye."

He was wearing very dark leather trousers, somewhere in between aubergine and black, and another crisp, white shirt with more embroidery on it than the average wedding dress. It laced up with narrow leather cord. He'd managed to get his own cufflinks in again. He had his own uniform... Spontaneously I stepped forward and gave him a hug.

"I've come to help you pack," I said.

He laughed out loud.

"You've set yourself a tough task, then. Come see."

He caught my hand and tugged me after him into the house. The hall, a disaster of biblical proportions the last time I'd stood in it, was immaculate. It was dimly lit, true, missing a central light fitting and mirroring that had served as the main illumination, but the floor tiles were shiny and there was no trace of wine or glass.

I took things in only vaguely because Nicky was dragging me up the stairs.

"Slow down," I said, protesting only mildly because his mood was uplifting, and I'd been worried that I'd set myself up for another depressing night.

"Sorry," he said with his trademark, slightly lopsided grin. "I'm just pleased you came. There you go."

He pushed open the bedroom. It seemed unchanged to the casual observer, a pleasing chaos of stuff—male grooming products, discarded shirts, a pair of heavily embossed cowboy boots lying by the bed—with a familiar scent of expensive aftershave and ironed linen. The sole difference that I could make out was that a closed suitcase and a bulky leather holdall were sitting by the door to the walk-in wardrobe.

"Behold my packing," he said. "But if you're determined to help, you can carry one of them down to the car."

"That's all you're taking?"

"If you think I want to remember this place, you have another thing coming," he said. "But more to the point, there isn't a lot of space in my uncle's wine cellar, which is where I'll be living until I sort something better out. I have a van coming tomorrow night for the IT kit."

He didn't sound self-pitying; it struck me that he never did. He just took what life—or death—threw at him and carried on. There was an indomitable quality about him that I liked. I couldn't think of a damn thing we had in common apart from a fondness for eighties gothic music, but there was a lot to admire in his gentle determination.

"What then?" I asked.

"Benedict won't spare me for long," he said. "I'll build up a new coterie and come back to Staffordshire. But not to this place."

I thought he was sensible. It wasn't a million miles away from the advice I'd given Irene. Nicky's ghosts were less solid and stinky than Irene's, but I had no doubt they wandered the house with just as much determination.

"You and I don't have the best luck with relationships," I said. "I chose Oscar, and you chose Kirsty. I hope we both learned something."

"You lost Peter, too."

I blinked.

"Does everyone know about that?"

"Probably. You should never have let him go back to Germany. You won't get him out of the clinic a second time. Lens does good work, but it's a cult. He doesn't really think that people are entitled to their own lives. There's a training facility for young vampires there, which is where I was, but I could see what was going on."

"You think I should have tried to persuade Peter to stay?"

Nicky shrugged and sat on the edge of the bed.

"Yes and no. I've heard the gossip. He and Oscar shared blood for a decade. That's one hell of a bond. It wouldn't have been reasonable to expect him to stay in England with Oscar here. You know that Benedict sent Oscar to Cornwall?"

I shook my head. It was my fault that bloody Oscar was still alive in the first place...

"Is that why Benedict insisted I should let Peter go back? I thought it was because he and Lens were friends."

"Who knows... But Peter is back under Lens' beady eye now. Are you still in love with him?"

That was one hell of a question. Yes, some days I was. Others I hated him for leaving. Mostly I just found his ability to keep me hanging on to be infuriating.

"Yes, but I've at least got to the stage where I wish I wasn't," I said, wandering over to the window and fiddling with the handle. "That's a big stride for me." I searched for a change of subject. "So, if we're not going to pack, what do you want to do?"

I heard him get off the bed and approach me. I vaguely saw his reflection in the glass of the window as he came up behind me and put his hands softly on my hips.

"Well, let's see," he said lightly. "We could make out."

I turned in the circle of his arms and laughed up at him.

"Really? That's your suggestion? We should have random casual sex because you've decided that packing is boring."

"Well, why not? And it wouldn't be random casual sex. It would be very specific casual sex—you and me, repeatedly, until you've lost your voice from calling out my name..." I poked him in the ribs, and he laughed. "Well, I'm a vampire! Your satisfaction is guaranteed."

I giggled.

"Thank you very much, Nicky, but no. I'm impulsive enough, but that's not my style."

He firmed up his grip on my hips very slightly and pulled me in to close the distance between us. There was nothing predatory about him, and he looked amused rather than rejected, the white curtain of hair falling over one side of his face just a touch.

"Then you should change your style, angel, because you might be the only person I know whose love life is in worse shape than mine."

I smiled up at him, not coquettishly but genuinely. I suddenly felt the tiniest pang that he was leaving town. We might have been friends.

"Thanks, but no thanks," I said. "But I don't mind that you asked."

He grinned and I put up a hand on impulse and brushed the hair out of his face. I stopped in sheer surprise. It was the softest thing I'd ever touched. It was softer than silk, softer than mink, softer than my cat. Without thinking, I put up my other hand and ran my fingers through it. I found myself doing it again, reaching up both hands to slide my fingertips in at the hairline above his temples and down through to the nape of his neck. Moonlight-coloured hair slipped through my touch in a frictionless, shimmering waterfall. I wound my fingers into it and rested my face against his chest to feel the cool silkiness against my cheek. His grip on my hips hardened.

"Toni, are you sure that was a no, because it feels very much like a yes?"

His voice was careful, studied, a little more gravelly than usual.

I leaned back and looked up into his eyes, that polar blue that I'd noticed the first time we met. He was beautiful and he wanted me. Hell, that would do.

"It's a yes," I said. "I deserve a good time."

"I'll make you very happy you said that," he promised.

And then he cupped my face in his fine-boned hands and bent down to kiss me.

Chapter Twenty-Six

His lips were cool and smooth on mine, soft at first but quickly more demanding, more devouring. I slid my hands onto his slim waist, letting my thumbs slide down to rest on the bones of his hips. He made a soft, pleased noise and I realised I could feel him rising against me as passion took hold. He took his mouth off mine for a moment.

"You're enchanting," he said.

He drew me towards the bed and pushed me gently down, kneeling in front of me. He pulled us together so that I was perched on the edge of the mattress, my knees parting around him and the skirt of my sundress beginning to ruck up.

"You've enchanted me," he continued, and began to kiss me again.

I opened my mouth to him without hesitation, and for a while we explored each other with lips and tongues. He was a very agreeable person to kiss, and I let my hands slide up from his waist to the small of his back. He was more muscular than I'd anticipated, and he pressed into my touch with obvious pleasure.

His own hands crept to my waist and then up to my ribs and finally to just cup the underside of my breasts. His kisses moved from my lips to trace my face, my cheek, the sensitive skin in the curve of my jaw. Then he began to kiss his way down my neck until he came to the top button of my dress. I got a mouthful of silky hair for a moment and then his fingers followed his lips, and I felt the first button go. He very deliberately teased apart the fabric, opening it to reveal a little triangle of flesh that he kissed his way down. Another button gave way, and his kisses moved an inch or so lower, almost into cleavage territory. Then another and another and my dress was open to the waist.

"Nicky," I gasped in sudden panic because we'd gone too far too fast, and I didn't know where the off switch was.

If you meet a guy at a party, there's time. Time to flirt, to make decisions and then to slowly build up to the moment. You start with a look, then a touch, a stolen kiss or two—maybe something more intimate in the kitchen while pretending to fetch drinks. Then there is the trip home, perhaps huddling together in a dark taxi or pooling change and snuggling up on the bus. There is the build-up of desire, the pleasing acclimatisation as what is strange becomes familiar, the delectable dance of discovery…

I'd had none of that. Within seconds of saying yes, Nicky was kneeling by the bed in front of me and in three buttons' time I would be down to my knickers and my second thoughts. I wanted to run away, flee down the stairs and hide in my car. I swallowed. It was too late for that.

Not that I really had grounds for complaint. He was doing all the right things and he was doing them well. He caressed my breasts with his fingertips, his cheek, his lips and then his teeth. I found myself gasping in pleasure. My body was screaming yes; everything else was going into fight or flight mode. I gripped the edge of the mattress, and—looking down—saw my knuckles whitening.

I also saw Nicky, his eyes closed in bliss, kissing his way lower. The last button gave way without the slightest struggle, and he slipped the fabric of my dress open and away.

"Nicky," I whispered again; I wanted to ask him to stop but nothing else came out.

"I love your voice," he said, without opening his eyes. "I love you just saying my name."

Then he looked up and whatever he saw made him frown.

"Hey," he said gently. "That's not right."

He took my hand and pressed a kiss into the palm and then onto my wrist. Then he took the leather cord of his shirt and tucked it into my grip.

"Just tug," he said.

I looked down. The end of the cord was capped with a miniscule steel cylinder, just a quarter of an inch long. I kept my eyes on it as I pulled slowly, and it slipped free of the tiny little rivets up the front of his shirt, one by one, making a soft little snick as it slid out of each metal ring. Finally, the cord came free in my hand, and I dropped it on the bed and pushed open his shirt. I moved my hands inside and cautiously stroked the muscled swell of his chest...

That was all it took. All the desire and abandon that had been evading me rushed in all at once and set my world on fire. I was finally kissing him back, pressing myself into him and letting my hands roam the entirely appealing contours of his body.

He ran his fingertips from my hips to my feet, competently unbuckling my sandals and easing them off, his hands firm on my ankles for a moment. Then they slid up to my calves, my knees, stroking the outside of my thighs and then moving inside. His kisses moved lower... and then lower still and I gasped because he was tracing my most intimate landscape with his tongue through the thin silk of my thong, pressing into the wet fabric to explore.

I tried to tell him not to stop, but the sound that came out didn't have any words in it or any proper syllables. I looked down to see him take the top of the lace neatly in his teeth and drag it downwards, and managed to make another little noise that I hoped he would take as encouraging. I must have pitched it quite well because he stood up and dropped his shirt on the floor. It would have taken me twenty minutes to get out of leather trousers that tight, but it took Nicky about four seconds.

I breathed a sigh of appreciation because while Nicky fully dressed was scenic, Nicky clad in nothing but a layer of sweat was a sight everyone should see once before they die. He was one of those people who are just beautiful all over, and I was getting a good eyeful of all over. He had skin like an English peach and the slim, toned physique of an athlete or a dancer. And there were other things. They looked good, too.

He caught my eye and smiled. I didn't think it was the first time he'd had that reaction.

"See anything you like?" he asked.

I moved backwards to give myself more bed and held out both my hands to him.

"I like everything I see," I said. "Come here so that I can close my eyes and check it all out in braille."

He obliged, laying himself over me and moving against me so that I could feel his arousal, hard and eager. I reached down to stroke and discovered that things felt quite as good as they looked. He reciprocated and I found myself pressing up into his touch because he'd found the perfect middle ground between hard and soft that had all my nerve endings lining up together to do the Macarena or maybe a heady-paced tango.

"Heavenly," I said when he paused. "I think I'm in heaven."

"I thought you'd changed your mind," he said. "I thought you were going to bail on me."

He leaned over me to spread my hair out on the pillow; his own swept across my face as he pulled back to admire his work.

"I nearly did," I admitted. "But I didn't know what to say. What would you have done?"

He pressed his body over mine again. I realised we were about to make love at last, and whatever my earlier doubts, it wasn't coming a moment too soon. He moved rhythmically against me, dragging out the moment. I got another mouthful of silver-white hair and reached up to brush it aside. I stroked his face and he turned to kiss my hand again.

"I'd have coped," he said. "Been very dignified. Begged, cried, grovelled. Offered you money, maybe my first born."

"You don't have a first born."

He reached down, fitting himself perfectly to me.

"Damn, you're right. Hell, I'd have offered you Rainbow."

I laughed. I opened my mouth to tell him that would have been the clincher, but what came out was a cry of pleasure because he'd stopped playing the anticipation game and moved into the close. I had a single moment of my earlier panic, because no matter how amazing it all felt, things had moved from off to on at a breakneck pace. But then he drove all of his hardness into my softness, and it wasn't panic anymore. It was just pleasure.

Because he was a delightful lover. There was an urgency and fervour in his lovemaking that was completely infectious, and I'd caught it almost before he'd begun. And we were perfectly matched. His rhythm was ardent but never rough and I found myself rising to it without ever having to learn the tempo. He kissed my face, my eyelids, the soft skin of my neck, and by the time he moved back to my mouth again he was kissing the little cries of climax off my lips.

He paused only when they'd peaked and ebbed, and then peaked again. He eased out of me. His own arousal was undiminished; he looked poised to pounce on me at the slightest provocation—or even none at all. He lay on his side and gazed at me, and I rolled over to look back.

"You're adorable," he said. "I adore you. Do you always come that quickly?"

I blushed and shook my head.

"Actually, I don't. I think it's just you."

"I like that thesis—we'll test it out very soon. Tell me what you like."

I reached over to stroke him with both hands.

"You," I said. "I like you. Just like this."

He closed his eyes for a moment and then reached down to capture my busy fingers. He didn't move them away, just held them still around him.

"Tell me," he said. "Tell me everything you want me to do to you."

"I can't just select menu items! We're not in a sushi bar."

"I don't see why not. And if you want me to dress up as Elvis and sing to you, you need to give me some warning. I probably have enough white Lycra, but I'd need to hunt for the lyrics."

I laughed but shook my head and he didn't press the point. Instead, he lay on his back and pulled me to him.

"We'll make it up as we go along then," he said softly. "You make me feel inventive."

Inventive. Also insatiable. After an hour of his attentions, I pleaded exhaustion and hunger and crept down to the kitchen for a snack. He let me get halfway through a piece of toast and honey before he repurposed the entire two-pound jar for a recreational activity I hadn't even encountered online. After a pleasant and truly eye-opening half-hour, we both retreated to the shower, at which point he reneged on his promised to cut me some slack and shagged me up against the tiles.

"I'm done," I said, sitting on the side of the bed, towelling honey-scented water off my hair. "If you want any more sex, you have to do it on your own."

"Will you watch and mark me out of ten?"

"Nope, I'll be asleep."

"Really?"

"I might get a second wind if you're lucky." I looked over at him, lounging naked on the eiderdown and watching me hopefully. "You asked me what I like; what about you? What do you want?"

He told me. I blinked. I'd always known he was whimsical—look at the man's taste in clothes—but really.

"Fine," I said agreeably. "Knock yourself out."

I blow-dried my hair into soft waves and powdered my face. I painted on lip gloss in a wet, red shade that I would normally have left on the shelf. I added mascara and—because it was Nicky—smoky eyeliner that was half goth, half slut. I sat on the white coverlet of the bed wearing nothing but the odd goosepimple and regarded him a little shyly.

"What you wanted?" I asked.

He fitted the film carefully into the Leica.

"Everything I've ever wanted," he said. "You're every fantasy I've ever had. No, don't pose, just be yourself."

He took the first film slowly at first, and then with more confidence towards the end. When it was finished, he put the camera down. He took me in his arms and made love to me extremely thoroughly and quite fiercely until I was just a couple of seconds into paradise… and then he pulled away and left me gasping for more as he loaded up the second roll.

"Now," he said, raising the camera again. "Now tell me what you like."

So I did. I looked into the lens and opened my wish list at page one. It was the second time I'd told a man all my fantasies. The first one had been a vampire, too. When the second roll was finished, I took the camera off him and pulled him back onto the bed.

"Enough," I said. "Come and finish what you started. I've given you more than enough to go on."

Nicky kissed me until the red lipstick was worn away and pleasured me until the eyeliner ran down my face in rivulets of sweat. He let me sleep after that, the heady, post-coital slumber of drowned contentment.

He woke me an hour before dawn, pressing kisses into whatever bits of me he could peel the eiderdown off. I protested sleepily, but he persevered until I sat up and rubbed my eyes, gritty from going to sleep without taking off my makeup.

"We are not making love again," I said firmly. "You've worn me out. There is no third wind."

He finally inveigled his way into kissing my mouth. It was delightful, but it would have needed to be genuinely miraculous to make me change my mind.

"I just wanted to wake you in time to say goodbye," he said. "And because I'm not stupid, I made you some coffee."

He had, indeed; there was even a tray. I added six sugars and sipped. I realised that he had showered and dressed while I slept.

"Do you want me to go down with you?" I asked. "I'll stay with you till sunrise if you like?"

He looked disproportionately pleased with the suggestion, so I washed smears of makeup off my face and cleaned my teeth before tugging on his dressing gown and following him down the hall stairs.

"Are you sure you don't want anything from this house?" I asked as he unlocked a door that opened off the kitchen. "I can arrange storage for you through Bean and Heron."

He didn't answer immediately. He led me down black marble steps to a cellar full of rack after rack of flashing lights. When he'd said a van was coming for his IT kit, he probably meant something with eighteen wheels and climate control.

I watched as he operated a mechanism in the wall, opening a panel to reveal a space about eight-foot square and four-foot high. Soft lighting illuminated quilting, cushions and a recessed bookshelf. He helped me in, and we curled up together. It was soft and warm.

"Push it closed when you leave, and it will lock," he said. "And no, I'll build new memories. Take anything you want and get a house clearance firm to sort the rest. I'm done with it."

I thought he was wise, all things considered. There were a lot of things he probably wanted to forget about his time in Staffordshire. Dead girls—four of them now—not to mention Dylan Moss.

"You drew a lot of short straws, Nicky," I said, and I rested my head on his chest. "You deserve better."

He shook his head.

"I deserve sod all, Toni. I should be lying on my back rotting in that hospital. Better still, I should have died when the damn car hit the concrete bollard and blew up."

"That's rubbish! Why would you even say that?"

"Because I wasn't alone in that car, angel. My fifteen-year-old baby brother was in the passenger seat next to me. I didn't even check he was wearing his seatbelt before I took off like a prize wanker to show him what a hotshot his big brother Nicky was. He died before the ambulance reached us. I got a second chance I didn't deserve, and he got a nice headstone. You know how good my parents were about it? They even had it inscribed 'beloved son and brother.' I told you that you didn't know me."

"I don't care," I said. "You did a stupid thing, but people do a lot worse and don't get punished like you did. Stop blaming yourself. You made a mistake. You didn't mean to kill him."

He held me close to him and dropped his chin onto the top of my head. I got another mouthful of his long, white hair and brushed it out of my mouth.

"God, Nicky, I've never had a lover with long hair before. Is it normal to eat this much of it? I'm going to be picking it out of my teeth for weeks."

I spoke as much to change the subject as for anything else, and I could tell that he knew it. He stroked my face and I felt him smiling.

"Definitely. Welcome to a man's world. Face powder over your lapels all the time and a mouthful of mousse-flavoured hair every time you go for a kiss. Angel, you know I don't have to go. I could stay here in Staffordshire. Or you could come with me, if you prefer—I don't mean to my uncle's wine cellar, by the way. I would find somewhere lovely for you. Here, Brighton. Hell, anywhere you want."

I pulled away and stared up at him in shock. He was the wrong man in the wrong place at the wrong time—saying all the right words.

"What happened to a night of casual sex because you hate packing?"

He leaned back in and kissed me. It lasted a while and—when he finally stopped—I was sorry for the first time in my life that summer wasn't winter, because if it had been December, the sun wouldn't be up for hours.

"What can I say, Lavington Windsor? I didn't expect to feel this way about you."

I didn't reply straight away. A tiny bit of me was tempted, but one night of passion didn't mean I knew enough about him to even contemplate agreeing. I'd moved in with a vampire I barely knew once before. I nearly hadn't lived to tell the tale. Well, I could learn from my mistakes. Instead, I just said:

"I don't mind anymore that Benedict told you I am a necromancer."

He looked at me in some surprise.

"Benedict didn't tell me. He was furious when he found out I knew. It was Oscar."

"What?"

Oh, crap.

"I was at Emir's with Kirsty, and I didn't give my seat up to Oscar with sufficient alacrity. He's always hated me and so he delivered a little speech designed to tell me what a nobody I was. Classic Oscar… You know, I'm a second generation vampire, I'm Benedict's head of security, my girlfriend's a necromancer. Blah blah."

I wasn't really listening. I was mostly thinking about how much humble pie I was going to have to eat for Benedict. Again. I owed him a very substantial apology. I'd given him hell for telling Nicky about my powers, and now it turned out he never had.

"I hate the dawn," Nicky said suddenly. "Those helpless daylight hours stretching ahead. Vampires aren't meant to dream, but I do. I always dream about my little brother."

I looked up at him. I could have said a million things, but I didn't. Instead, I took Ignatius' little gold knife out from around my neck and pushed back the little wings that guarded the blade. I drew it across my wrist, cutting a line between the scabs that had nearly healed. I held it out to him and buried my face in his chest so he couldn't see how much I would hate what happened next. I felt his cool lips on my skin, the touch of his tongue, the soft suck, the pain… I screwed my eyes shut and though of summer evenings and kittens and champagne and new shoes and anything, absolutely anything, apart from what was happening right then and right there. I felt his body ripple with ecstasy against mine, heard his voice raised in pleasure. I breathed in, then out, in, out. It wasn't working. There was acid in my throat. Please stop soon, Nicky. Now is good…

When he did, I took my time before raising my face to his so that he wouldn't see what I'd felt—the fear, the pain, the nausea. I wasn't a great actress, though, and something in my expression filled his own with doubt.

"Oh, God. Did it hurt?"

I shook my head.

"No," I lied, but I could see he didn't believe me. "Not so much."

"I won't do it again," he said. "Not if it hurt you. I'll never do it again, I promise. Not ever."

"I just wanted to make you happy."

"I'm happy," he said. "I love you."

I felt my mouth drop open in surprise.

"Nicky," I began.

I stopped short; nothing else followed because I didn't have a clue what to say.

And then I felt the sun rise.

Chapter Twenty-Seven

I SHOWERED IN Nicky's en suite, standing in the jets forever until I felt flayed clean. I half-dried my hair and plaited it back, then dressed in the previous night's clothes. They weren't fancy enough to scream 'walk of shame' at passers-by, but the little suede dress wasn't my normal work attire. I decided to swing by the cottage before going into the office, knowing looks from Bernie would never improve the average working day.

But I had plenty of time and, if I was going to sell the house and its contents for Nicky, I was arguably already on the clock. So I took my time walking round, vaguely trying to put together a valuation in my head.

Lily's room was bare and stripped. I suddenly realised what had been in the holdall by Nicky's wardrobe. He was leaving clothes, jewellery and furniture—but taking her paintings. I couldn't fault his choices.

Lorraine and Caroline's room was unchanged—a riot of girly domesticity that Kirsty's jealousy had put an end to. On a whim I took a silk scarf that I knew Claire would love and tucked it into my pocket.

Kirsty's room... It made me uncomfortable just walking into it. Had she brewed her evil cantamen up here? I didn't really want to know. I opened drawers casually. Perhaps I should get that nice lady from the dress exchange over? The bathroom was awash with little wicker baskets, heaped with gel and lotion and mousse and creams. What had Nicky said about the cabinet? Oh, yes. I fiddled for a few minutes and then worked out how to unhook it from the bracket on the wall. There was a space behind, quite deep, the sort of architectural feature you end up with when you convert an old house. There was the same manky smell that my mother's chest gave off, there were dozens of little packets. There was also something worse.

Three empty glass bottles, exactly the sort that you see in old films, sitting in the windows of village pharmacies. They were made of emerald green glass with little clear stoppers, the kind you'd expect to be sealed with wax and string... The stoppers were thrust casually back into two, the lid of the third lay on its side next to the tiny flagon. They were all labelled: Lorraine, Caroline, Lily. So far, so creepy. It was the fourth I really disliked. It was full of a viscous clear fluid with a nasty glitter to it, and the stopper of this one was still sealed and tied up. The label made my blood run cold. 'Lavington' it said. Nothing more. Just my name.

I'd been next. Had Kirsty found out that Nicky had visited my house? Had she seen me in the graveyard outside the church where Lorraine's vigil had been held? Had she read the texts we'd sent to one another? I'd never know, and I didn't want to. I took the little flask and put it in my handbag. I would ask Emir how to safely dispose of it. I didn't want to stay in the rectory for a moment longer after that, so I hurried down to the car. The weather had reacted to the general pathos of my mood and the sunny streak had ended with a vengeance. It was pissing it down, a heavy summer storm, and I mourned my lack of coat as I sprinted from the porch. I drove home in the early morning light with the wipers on their fastest setting.

I'd lived with Paul for six months and we didn't exactly keep tabs on one another. To an extent we didn't need to—neither of us had the most exiting of personal lives and if I went out to raise the dead, I tended to take him with me—but since he'd come back from

Amsterdam, things had been different. There were people on the fringes of my life that I didn't want him to meet, people I wanted to protect him from. But the previous night—that was something else.

I just didn't want him to know what I'd done.

Firstly, there was the slightly awkward situation that I was meant to be dating Jay, the man everyone adored, including me in my own way. Then there was the more nuanced complication that Nicky was a vampire. I'd sworn off dating vampires for very good reasons. And then there was the confusion of not knowing how I felt about him. We had nothing in common. He owned more clothes than me—damn it, the man wore more makeup than I did. I'd met him less than half a dozen times, and he led a life that meant nothing to me, in the dark web world of hackers and their code. We weren't natural soul mates.

I didn't know my own motives and I wasn't sure of my ground. I'd never been unfaithful to a boyfriend before. Had I been now? You could argue that a vampire didn't count, and most vampires certainly would. It seemed the easier code of conduct to go with. Truth be told, I wasn't ready to tell Paul because I hadn't yet worked out what to tell myself. So, when I got home to find he wasn't yet back, my first feeling was one of relief. Then panic, of course, because for weeks people had been trying to kill me and I didn't want Paul to be hit by shrapnel.

I changed into work clothes and made a pot of lapsang and some toast. I was just wondering whether to start phoning when the sound of his moped on the road allayed my concerns. I took out another mug and cut two more slices off the loaf and began to toast them.

The front door opened and closed. I heard Paul clear his throat as he stripped off gloves and leathers and hung them up in the hall.

"I'm making you tea and toast," I called.

He didn't answer and came through hesitantly. He looked tired and disheartened. I frowned.

"I thought we won—wasn't it a good match?"

"Match was fine," he mumbled, sitting down at the table and slurping some tea.

I dumped a plate of toast in front of him and pushed the butter and jam across. I sat down and picked up my own mug.

"What went wrong? I thought you would be back yesterday, anyway."

He stared into the depths of his tea.

"I was. I got back before you came home from work. Then Bethany rang. She said would I mind very much bringing the films she lent to me over to her new flat—you know she's just got her own place in the new development where St George's used to be."

He was procrastinating. Of course I knew where Bethany's flat was. I'd written the lease myself for her landlord and helped carry the girl's dressing table up three flights of stairs. I watched as he turned the mug round and round on the table.

"She opened the door in her underwear," he said after a long pause. "Then she took it off."

Ah. The oldest trick in the book. Now wasn't the time to tell Paul I'd used it myself more than once. And he was an eighteen-year-old healthy male packed with enough hormones to bring Godzilla into heat. Bethany had played an ace. Paul hadn't stood a chance.

My silence clearly disconcerted him.

"What was I meant to do?" he asked in a plaintive voice.

I had to laugh.

"Paul, if you don't know that, I am not drawing you diagrams. Anyway, you got an A* in Biology. I only got a C."

"Here's the thing. She dumped me and I was OK with that. Then she got off with my best friend to make me jealous and I wasn't OK with that at all. Then we made up and agreed to be friends... and now this. Toni, my brain hurts. Dating should be fun. This is more like Kafka."

I was with him. I didn't like Kafka. Or Nietzsche. I was more of a Dickens girl or Jane Austen... But Paul was still talking.

"Then she asks if we're back together. What can I say? The honest answer is no, I've lost all respect for you. But by this time, we're in bed, so I can't say that. I feel manipulated. I'm going to university in a few weeks. I don't want a long distance relationship.

I was thinking with my libido, not my brain."

I felt a smile cross my lips. I'd spent all night thinking with my libido, and I couldn't fault it. I closed my eyes for a moment and pictured Nicky pushing his tongue into me through the wet silk of my thong, Nicky sliding my underwear off with his teeth, Nicky stroking me with fingers soaked in honey, Nicky hard and fast inside me... I gave myself a little shake and opened my eyes.

"...just don't know what to do," he finished.

I regarded my protégé with sympathy. There was absolutely nothing I could say that would help him to navigate the perilous field of dating breakups. I had been there, and I would doubtless be there again. No matter what he did, it would be the wrong thing. Welcome to the world of romance.

Not that I was doing any better myself. What ace had Nicky played that I hadn't been watching out for? Had Toni been stage-managed just as sweetly as Paul? I pushed the thought away.

"Honestly, Paul, you should just go to bed and sleep for a few hours," I said. "You're exhausted and miserable. It won't solve anything, but at least you'll have the energy to think. I'm going to work now, so the house will be nice and quiet. And there's half a lasagne in the fridge that Henry made, which you're welcome to scarf for lunch when you wake up."

He nodded vaguely, the weight of the world still on his shoulders, and I left him eating toast and drove to work. I also felt, reading between the lines, that he'd met someone else but wasn't ready to tell me yet. His angst seemed excessive otherwise. After all, no one wants to be left without a pint.

The morning passed far too slowly. I left a flurry of texts for Claire, asking her to meet me for lunch, and was relieved when shortly after noon she wandered into the office.

"Hurry, darling," she drawled. "In the final stages of starvation. Haven't had a bite since elevenses and I've been teetotal since just after midnight. Let's run over to the Swan and get them to pop out a cork or two."

She waited until we had two cold glasses of fizz and some olives sitting in front of us before casting an expert eye over me.

"You look sleep-deprived, smug and carpet-burned," she said. "I'd lay good money you've been taking protein shots all night. I've rarely seen a girl look more shagged out. Did you take my advice?"

Her advice? Oh yes, Claire had told me to wash Peter out of my head with a deviant no-holds-barred shagathon with someone hot and immoral.

"I spent the night with someone I hardly know who's leaving the county tomorrow," I admitted. "But I wouldn't call him immoral. He's actually very sweet."

"Well, it's a start, I have hopes for you yet. How was it?"

"He was an absolute delight. He made me laugh all the time. I can't remember enjoying sex so much." She looked startled but I carried on almost without thinking, "God, Claire, I'd forgotten that making love was meant to be fun. There was none of Oscar's macho athletics and none of Peter's bewildering technical perfection. We just had a completely lovely time."

She downed her drink and wrinkled her brow at me over her menu, signalling for the waiter to come and top us up.

"Darling, I don't want to burst your bubble, but that doesn't sound like a one-night stand. If I didn't know you better, I would say you were describing falling in love."

She popped an olive into her mouth. I was ambivalent about olives—they were the sort of healthy thing Jay kept in his salad fridge. I gave a mental sigh; it wasn't just the fridge, was it? If my men were meals, Jay would be healthy, organic and perfectly balanced in terms of protein, carbs and fat, served with silver cutlery on a china plate with the calorie count printed on the side, just visible under the mound of healthy salad hanging over the rim.

Nicky would be cake.

He'd be a frosted celebration of delectable empty calories that you ate with your hands and couldn't put down until you'd consumed every last mouthful. The fat and refined sugar would wind themselves around your arteries until your blood ground to a halt and your heart burst into a thousand pieces.

"I love cake," I heard myself say.

"What's that, sweetie?"

"Um, nothing," I said.

Of course, Benedict would be a long, tall drink of absinth laced with cocaine. I shook my head.

"Nothing at all," I added. I took a fortifying swig of fizz. "Look, I'm not in love with Nicky," I said firmly. "I don't have anything in common with him. We said goodbye and I don't expect to see him again."

"I hope you're right, Lav, I really do. Usually when people say they're in love, it's a good thing. Given your history, I would pop over to the doc and see if they have a pill for that yet. Now, do you want lamb cutlets or the pigeon?"

Claire had always been the best of friends to me. Neither of us shone when it came to romantic entanglements, but I was the more soft-hearted. As a result, while my failed relationships tended to end in tears—mine, in general—hers tended to go down in flames. I wasn't sure I preferred her path, but she certainly seemed to have a quicker recovery time than I did.

I walked back to the office in a thoroughly distracted mood. Halfway there, I realised that the bottle I had retrieved from Kirsty's little hidey-hole and tucked into my handbag was banging around against my hairbrush. I took it out, handling the thing with some disgust, and buttoned it up in the pocket of my raincoat instead. Leaving it at the cottage seemed like asking for trouble, but the last thing I wanted was to spill the damn stuff.

Jill Fletcher lived in a converted smallholding well off the beaten track a few miles east of Hilderstone. It wasn't a million miles from Emir's bar, but as that still placed it squarely in the middle of nowhere, I'd struggled to find her a new tenant for her little annex. And I wasn't sure that location was the only problem. Jill bred pedigree Nebelung cats, and the aroma of feline—not a scent that perfumeries spent a lot of time chasing down—tended to hang around the garden when the wind dropped.

The approach was a steep drive that wound through overgrown

scrappy woodland, the land too poor for agriculture and too rocky for orchards. You could probably have grazed a few sheep or even goats on it. No one had bothered for years and elder, gorse, hawthorn and briars were filling the void. The farmhouse itself wasn't large. My estate agent's eye told me that it was constructed of local baked bricks from the late seventeen hundreds. It would have been bright red for a couple of decades before fading to the current orange beige. A couple of outbuildings had been built at about the same time.

The rain was coming down in sheets again by then, so I tugged on my coat and legged it to Jill's back door. She must have seen me coming because it was opened before I had to knock. She was buttoning up her own coat as I hurried in and shook out my wet hair.

"I hope you brought your keys, because I have to zoom," she said. "You don't need me anyway, do you?"

"I'm just trying to earn my fee, Jill," I said. "I haven't done any of the proper paperwork for you and I know you've been paid for six months but I'll feel better once all the boxes are ticked. Oh, and I checked—you're meant to have done a residency check but if you sent me a photo of his passport, I can do that for you."

"Thank goodness, because he's the perfect lodger," she said. "He's so quiet, and he's hardly ever in. Listen, poppet, I'll leave you to it. I know he's out because that enormous people carrier he drives isn't in the yard, so you can be sure you won't find him in flagrante delicto or worse."

I wondered what she thought would be worse, but then the woman cleaned litter trays as a hobby, so I didn't really fancy enquiring.

"Right you are," I said cheerfully. "I'll post you anything that needs signing."

Jill's annex had once been a small milking parlour and was a little removed from the main house. Her lodger had double-locked his door, which surprised me—goodness knows who he thought would come all this way to burgle him—but was a plus as I could be certain that he was out.

I let myself in and pulled the door to behind me. It was the old-fashioned kind that doesn't lock automatically and needs a key to secure it. I took out the original inventory. I'd checked it off four months ago when Jill's previous tenant had announced that his nostrils wouldn't take another night of eau de Nebelung and left in search of fresher pastures.

The new resident was scarily neat. Everything was lined up, folded, ironed, dusted... it made my head hurt. In the kitchenette, the few bottles I could see were in immaculate rows. Three forks in the draining rack all had the tines turned the same way. Here was a man who made Peter look like a slob. Some paperwork sat on the coffee table. I glanced at it. A passport. Hang on: two passports.

I opened the first passport. Jiří Tabor, resident of Prague. The photograph was of a blond boy barely out of his teens—certainly not the Jiří I knew who worked at an undead bar in the woods. The second one bore the name Yves Toulon, resident of the village of St-Bertrand-de-Comminges, but that face I did recognise. It was indeed Emir's new assistant, the man who had stood by the market stall in Stafford town square and told me that to be parted from the one you loved was life's cruellest blow, who'd told me that I should follow the man who'd left me and force him to change his mind. He cooked with a lot of garlic and liked Richard Clayderman. The waitress had been right all along and so had I—he was French. I'd found Sophy's stalker.

I clapped my face into my hands. No wonder he'd been wearing makeup. He wasn't trying to challenge his masculine side—he was covering up the injuries inflicted on him by a recently deceased buzzard and an undead stag. There'd been plenty of clues, but I'd missed them all.

Things fell into place with a certainty that made me sure I was right. Four boys had come from Czechia with one-way tickets and driven straight up to Staffordshire. They must have been on their way to a rendezvous with the local Assemblage community, or more specifically a rendezvous with Emir the witch. And Yves had impersonated one of them, passed himself off as the real Jiří. Was Emir still wondering why the other three hadn't arrived yet? He would wait a long time.

What my brother had told me finally made sense. In the last service station, they'd bumped into a French man. It must have been Yves, the man convinced that evil forces were keeping Sophy away from him. He'd eavesdropped on their conversation, seen an opportunity, and introduced himself. What story had he told? Whatever it was, they'd agreed to travel on with him, they'd even waited so that he could pull his car onto the hard shoulder just after theirs, but then he'd wiped them off the road. He must have already decided to steal one of their identities. It had been a desperate act and had nearly been a waste of time anyway. Three of them had died, but then things hadn't gone Yves' way. Had he not been first to the scene? Were there too many people around for him to finish off Jiří and take the ID he clearly wanted?

Not one to be set back lightly, he'd followed the real Jiří to the hospital and stolen his things. Finally, he could travel to Emir's and pass himself off as a legitimate, indeed anticipated, member of the undead scene. All he had to do was frost glasses and garnish martinis until Sophy came. But she never did. Still wound up in her own confusions, she'd never yet visited Emir's bar. And he was running out of time. Emir hadn't twigged yet because he didn't read the newspapers or leave the woods much, but he must be wondering every day why the other three still hadn't arrived. And the real Jiří could regain consciousness any moment. Yves had been a crazy man before he'd set foot on English soil. Now? Desperate would probably do as a descriptor.

I put my hands to my face again. It was early afternoon. The sun wouldn't set for hours. I would text Aidan and then phone Camilla. I fumbled in my bag for my phone but, as ever in the remote hillsides of Staffordshire, there was no signal. The rain had turned to a thunderous cacophony while I'd been blundering around the flat and I saw the flash of lightning even as the sound of the wind swelled to a roar. It was only when the annex door swung open that I realised the noise of the storm must have masked the sound of Jiří's car—or Yves, as I now knew him to be called. He stood in the doorway, silhouetted against the darkening clouds.

There was no time for me to run or hide—and nowhere to have gone even if there was—so I stood, paralysed for a moment, staring at him.

He wasn't sporting a dapper paisley waistcoat and evening suit that afternoon. He was wearing dark jeans and a long raincoat, both soaked through by the rain until water ran off and pooled around him. His light blond hair had shrivelled into wet rat tails, framing a pale, rather angular face. The dark brown eyes held something I didn't like, the reckless, single-minded pureness of purpose that you see on TV evangelists and the criminally insane. Except that I didn't think he was about to sing hallelujah or exhort me to praise the Lord.

Worse, he wasn't alone. He was carrying the limp figure of a woman in his arms, and not in a nurturing way. Her hands and feet were bound, and she was gagged. It took me a moment to recognise Camilla because under the gag her face was bloodied and her eyes swollen. He didn't look much better—his face and arms were covered with scratches and bite marks. A chunk of hair was missing, leaving a bloody wound over one ear. Rain had washed the blood into his collar. She'd fought like a cornered fox before he took her down.

He did a double-take when he saw me but didn't lose his cool for a moment.

"Two of you," he said. "Très bien. I like to hedge my bets."

Chapter Twenty-Eight

I FLICKED MY eyes around the room. I didn't see anything I could bludgeon the man to death with or impale him on. More importantly, he was blocking my path to the door. And I knew I couldn't take him on in any kind of fair fight—he'd shrugged off a zombie stag with not much more than a black eye. He had to be tough as old rope.

"Yves," I said, playing for time, "you don't have to do this. We can find a better way. Sophy likes Camilla—she wouldn't want this. She's a gentle person."

The brown eyes filled with a zealot's rage. For a moment I thought I'd said the wrong thing, but then I looked into his eyes a moment longer and knew it was simpler than that. Yves was a crazy man—nothing I'd said would have been right.

"Sophy loves me," he said. "Only me. We're meant to be together. Whatever they've done to keep us apart will mean not a thing when she sees me again. It's as I told you—we'll kill any who try to keep us apart."

It wasn't quite what he'd said to me in the town square. It was slightly worse, but who was keeping tabs? I glanced round the room again, but nothing came to mind. I looked at Yves, the man I'd known as Jiří. He'd seemed perfectly normal and lucid when we'd met before. How could a man who'd lost it this badly seem so sane?

"Sophy's beautiful, I know," I said in a soothing voice. "I've seen her dance. She's so elegant. Did you dance with her?"

He looked up at me, and the rabid expression softened. A touch of radiance crept in. I was reminded of a documentary I'd watched about a preacher who held wild snakes when he spoke to his congregation. The expression on his face as he praised the Lord and spoke of the miracle of salvation was too close to Yves' for comfort. People who think they've found nirvana are people you should run away from. Or lock up.

"Yes," he said. "I held her in my arms. The candles burned low around us."

He sank onto the small sofa, still clutching Camilla in his arms. The sound of the rain turned up a notch and there was a crack of thunder. A proper summer storm was building. He dropped his face into Camilla's hair for a moment, and I knew that in his sick, broken mind, he was dancing with Sophy.

"Love is the only thing that matters," he murmured.

I'd said that myself once; had I sounded as deluded as Yves? Probably so. I looked at his dropped head, his closed eyes, and the distance to the open door, and decided I probably wasn't getting a better chance.

"Hold on to that thought," I said, and I dropped my clipboard and the two passports and bolted.

I'd never have made it if he'd had the sense to put Camilla on the floor when he sat down. As it was, he had to disentangle himself from an unconscious woman before leaping to his feet after me, and it gave me the milliseconds I needed to make it through the door ahead of him. I slammed it behind me and randomly turned left, and then left again.

My plan was only to make it out of sight before he could open the door to follow. And while it seemed to have worked, I found myself behind the annex in a typical farmyard miasma of dead tractor parts and rolls of fencing wire, with no good idea of where to go next.

"Think, Toni," I muttered. "And keep moving."

I ran past a thresher the size of a small bus, sunk up to its wheel hubs into the soft ground. It looked like the main axle had broken years before, but no one could be bothered to care. The thing squatted in the thorny scrub like a tyrannosaurus rex—huge, dead and obsolete. I ran round it and flung myself against the side to catch my breath. From here, I would be hidden even if Yves worked out where I'd gone.

I crouched down and peered through the fractured rusting metal body and discovered that he already had. He came round the edge of the annex, his eyes on the ground. I must have left tracks that the storm hadn't yet obliterated. He looked up and squinted at the thresher through the sheets of rain. I realised with a sinking feeling that my hiding place was a very temporary refuge.

I cast around me. The scrubby hillside led down through low trees and spiny looking bushes. Just a quarter of a mile away I could see the main road. If I got enough of a head start, I might make it... And then if I could flag down a car... A lot of ifs and not a lot of choices. I started running.

If I'd been wearing jeans and boots, I'd have stood a chance. I so wasn't. I was wearing flat sandals and a sundress with a flappy raincoat, and I made it about two hundred yards before I went arse over tit and rolled down the hill for a bit.

The ground had felt slippery as hell underfoot, but once I was slithering down it on my face, it turned out to be hard and stony. All the foliage that had seemed mushy and slimy against my bare legs revealed itself to be pointy and scratchy once you got up close. It was composed of fifty per cent thorns and the rest spines. After I'd slithered for what felt like about a mile and eaten a good mouthful of wet soil, I drew to an abrupt halt by the unplanned tactic of sliding headfirst into a tree. My handbag went flying, the contents soaring up into the air and hailing down around the hillside.

I spat out a mouthful of leaves, or possibly centipedes, wiped mud and raindrops out of my eyes and blinked up the hill. Not good. Yves had spotted me, and he was barrelling down towards me, wearing all the sensible footwear and trousers that I'd left on my bedroom floor that morning.

Briars hung on tenaciously to my coat and hair, and by the time I tore myself free I was minus a few lumps of coat and a few scraps of Toni, and I could tell I was almost out of time. Yves was gaining on me, and he wasn't on his hands and knees spitting out foliage. He was bounding down the hill like a hound with a scent and an empty stomach. I found I had no appetite to be taken down like a bunny, so I sat in the wet grass, the rain soaking me to the skin, and watched as he drew to an awkward halt in front of me.

I couldn't have made an impressive opponent—I'd lost one coat sleeve and my skirt was shredded. My hands and wrists were torn open and bleeding, and I rather thought I'd split open my scalp where I'd banged my head into the tree earlier. Something warm and salty was running down my face and into my mouth and it sure as hell wasn't béarnaise sauce.

"You stopped running," Yves said in his soft French accent.

He eyed me warily as though I might be packing a Kalashnikov in my knickers. Sadly, I wasn't, so I didn't answer him immediately, conscious that anything I said would probably be taken badly. I blinked rainwater out of my eyes and tried to think of something noncontroversial.

"Yup," I said eventually. "How did you meet Sophy? Are you from the Assemblage she went to in France?"

He stopped, the mention of Sophy too powerful to brush aside. Again, the feverish light in his eyes softened.

"I joined two years ago with my vampire, Genevieve. But when I met Sophy, I knew. The past, it was nothing, you understand? Will you stop running and come with me now?"

He'd beaten Camilla unconscious and tied her up; God alone knew what he had planned. He was a lunatic who wanted to slay the world to make his imaginary romance real. I decided to play for time.

"Yes, but I can't walk," I said. "I hurt my ankle going down. You'll need to help me."

He rolled his eyes and knelt down next to me.

"I think…" he began.

He didn't finish. I'd whacked into enough rocks sliding down the hill. The one I had in my hand was smooth and heavy, and when it smashed into his temple he went down like a ninepin. Sticks and stones really do break bones, or at least make an excellent start.

I scrabbled to my feet for what felt like the hundredth time and looked down at Yves. His face was white, blood trickling sideways into his hair from where the rock had broken open the skin. I didn't think he'd be out for long—he was already whimpering—but I had nothing to tie him up with, nothing that I could think to slow him down. And so help me God, with the best will in the world, I couldn't club an unconscious man to death with a rock. I didn't have it in me. In a spirit of desperation, I tugged off one of his shoes and hurled it down the hill as far as I could manage. I gathered up the contents of my handbag that I could find and then hared back up the slippery slope. I'd already proved I wasn't going to make it to the road without breaking my neck. Maybe I would do better back at the farmhouse.

I took the pace a little more cautiously than on the way down. I didn't want to make my lies about hurting my ankle into a reality. And in truth I couldn't have made it much quicker. The rain had made the grass into a perilously slippery slope and the ground around the thresher, when I reached it again, was a veritable quagmire. I squelched my way back to the annex, where I found the door ajar. I flung myself through it and slammed it behind me. Perhaps the easiest solution would be to barricade myself in with Camilla until I could summon help?

Or not. I swore with frustration when I remembered that the annex had no landline. And I would struggle to barricade myself anywhere. When my handbag had gone AWOL, I'd lost the annex keys...

"Bugger," I muttered, looking around wildly for inspiration. "Bugger bugger bugger."

I could make another run for it and hope he didn't catch me, but I hadn't made it far the last time. People in films jump-start cars, but I had enough trouble figuring out the machinations of a new hairdryer, so that wouldn't happen. In the end, it turned out my options were a lot more limited than I hoped, because even as I was playing them in my mind I saw the figure of Yves Toulon through the window, staggering past the dead threshing machine. I cursed at his lightning recovery time—he was clearly even tougher than I'd realised—but then he'd moved out of my line of sight, presumably towards the front door. The door I couldn't even lock.

I put both hands on the top of the little sofa and jerked. I tugged it frantically across the floor, avoiding Camilla's pale, quiet form, and rammed it up against the door handle. Seconds later, it turned, and I heard Yves curse. He said something in French and shoved, but by sheer luck the sofa had jammed against the wall and steadfastly resisted him.

I sank down next to Camilla—he'd gagged and bound her with what looked like tent rope, and I flailed with the knots quite futilely for a few moments before abandoning them. I scurried to the kitchenette and opened drawers until I found something small and sharp. Yves was still banging and cursing, the door opened just two or three inches. I could see his fingers around the edge. I started on Camilla's feet first, sawing as fast as I dared, terrified I would cut her if I got it wrong.

The ropes parted and I shuffled up to her hands, thwarted by how tightly he'd knotted the cord and how deeply it pressed into her skin. I couldn't avoid inflicting small cuts on the both of us, and my fingers became slippery with blood before I'd finished.

I didn't get to the gag.

The window by the door exploded in a hail of glass behind me. I leaned over Camilla to try and shield her, but we were both showered in razor sharp shards. Turning my head, I saw Yves clambering through the aperture he'd made. He'd had the sense to throw a tarpaulin over the upper edge to avoid shredding himself as he forced his way through, but blood was pouring down his face where I'd struck him. He didn't look happy.

I stuffed the little blade I'd been using into my coat pocket and hurtled towards the kitchenette again, grabbing the biggest and shiniest thing I could see from the knife rack. I waved it at Yves as menacingly as I could.

"Stay back," I said, my voice sounding far too quiet in my own ears and not nearly fierce enough.

He ignored my words and walked towards me. After two paces he was leaving bloody footprints on the glass-strewn floor. I backed up until I was pressed against the kitchen counter.

"Why didn't you finish me off when you had the chance?" he asked. "You could have killed me out there."

There were many reasons. Firstly, because I'd never killed anyone before—not anyone who wasn't dead already, and even then, never soiling my own hands. Oh, I'd set it in motion. I'd made Sister Mary Markus take down Spiky Mikey in the school gym, but never touched him myself. I'd stood aside as Aidan ripped Grahame Martin's sorry throat out and hadn't felt my conscience stir. I'd vomited up champagne in Nicky's kitchen while I knew that upstairs he was taking care of his own personnel problems, but I hadn't tried to stop him.

And there was something else. Even Sophy hadn't wanted to punish Yves. She'd had her own reasons, I was sure of that, but whatever they were, she'd decided he deserved to live. I thought she'd had a hard time and I hadn't wanted to make it worse. I'd hoped for a better way.

And also because he'd stood with me in the town square and told me to fight for my love. There was good in the man, buried deeply to be sure, but still in there. I'd hoped for his redemption.

All these things… But mostly, it was because I just hadn't had the nerve. I hadn't finished Yves off because I'm soft-hearted. It really boiled down to that.

"Because I'm a fool," I snapped. "Next time I'll lay into you like a baby seal."

And I flew at him with the knife.

I could have saved myself the effort. He stepped far too neatly to one side and the next thing I knew he had twisted easily out of my grasp.

"There won't be a next time," he said.

And he punched me in the face. I went out like a lamp. It was almost a relief.

I WOKE IN a world of pain. I had a mouthful of congealing blood and a headache that made even my post-birthday-party hangover pale in comparison. I felt as though I'd consumed an entire bottleful of tequila shots and then tried a boxercise class. Against the barman. Who I hadn't tipped.

I let my brain settle awkwardly into my skull and tried opening my eyes. The brightness was agonising, but I blinked through it. Not bright summer sun but late evening—the sun would set soon. I was in a car, crumpled up on the back seat. My legs were tied but not my hands—maybe there was a limit to how much rope even Yves kept around the house for trussing up random visitors. I had enough trouble keeping enough milk in the fridge. Or teabags for that matter.

I twisted my head around. Yves was in the driving seat. We must be in the enormous people carrier that Jill Fletcher had mentioned. I wondered where Camilla was and turned my head the other way. I caught a glimpse of a foot on the second row of seats. Yves had talked about hedging his bets. What did he want with us?

"You're awake," I heard him say; I swivelled back and saw him watching me through the mirror. "That's good. The blonde won't come round."

I was clearly destined to end up in cars with homicidal maniacs. I would have preferred a different destiny, but no one had given me a menu. I glared at him through what felt like two black eyes. I rather thought I'd broken my nose again.

"That sometimes happens when you beat someone up and knock them out," I said acidly, my voice sounding muddy in my own ears. "She probably doesn't mean to be uncooperative."

"It's no matter," he said. "When we get to the Stone House, you can show me Sophy's rooms. When the sun sets, we'll be together forever."

He'd given up waiting for Sophy to come wandering out to Emir's bar and was going to seek her out at the source. I thought he was going to get precisely nowhere. Did he think that the Stone House was empty and unguarded in the day? I wasn't sure how the vampires secured their home in the sunlight hours, but I was damn sure that they didn't stick to crossing their fingers and wishing very hard. If I was a super-rich, old vampire, I would pay whatever it took to make sure that, in the hours when I was helpless, all the forces I could muster would be watching my back.

There was another slight flaw in his plan. The Stone House was a damn labyrinth, and I didn't have the faintest idea where on earth Sophy's chambers might be. I looked around me and didn't like my options—tied up in a moving car wasn't a good starting point, especially when the weapons at my disposal appeared to be Yves' wet coat and an elderly road atlas. If he'd used handcuffs, I'd have stood a chance. Locks I could pick. Knots I was less of a Houdini with.

"Humour me here," I said, spitting out a mouthful of blood onto the seat. "If Sophy loves you, why did she leave you to come back here and why hasn't she responded to your attempts to get in touch with her?"

"Benedict and his people must have forced her," he said, with unwavering certainty. "I've sent her messages in code, telling her how to meet with me, but she never shows. They must be holding her prisoner."

I'd seen Sophy a few times. She loved the Assemblage. She'd hated France. The only negative thing in her life now she was back seemed to be the unwelcome arrival of my current chauffeur. Still...

"Are you sure she knows the code?" I asked brightly. "Maybe she's not a natural cryptographer?"

"She knows, it's certain," he said. "I used the letters in the poem I wrote for her as the key."

Oh Lord. Poor Sophy. I'd been there—a lovelorn creep at school had fallen for me. He'd written me poems, too. In Klingon.

I knew why Sophy hadn't been able to meet up with her biggest fan. Some time or other he'd inscribed a bloody verse to her, almost certainly an impassioned tome of undying love. She'd stored it in the proper place—a bin bag—but he probably thought she slept with it under her pillow. And now his missives telling her where to find him were untranslatable.

I thought about whether to break the sad news to him, and decided no. The truth hurts when you are as batty as a box of frogs.

"I see," I said kindly. "Unless they've stolen your poem and burned it, of course…"

He laughed at my foolish suggestion.

"I gave it to her a year ago," he said firmly. "She will know it off by heart by now."

Of course that had happened. I felt the car turn and saw trees overhead through the rain. I rather thought we were by the river, and the bridge by the little antique shops. The car drew to a halt. I watched in confusion as he manhandled Camilla into the front of the car. He removed her gag and then climbed back in next to her. He looked at me and raised a hand so that I could see the knife he was holding. It was sharp, it was shiny, and it was far, far too close to Camilla.

"Listen very carefully," he said. "I'm going to tell any guards that we were attacked; we're here to be healed when the sun goes down. If you make a scene, I will kill her. If you tip them off, I will kill her. If anything else goes wrong, I will do it anyway—so don't even think about it. Are we clear?"

His plan was so stupid that whatever I did, it was going to go wrong. He thought he could bluff his way past anyone who tried to stop us and wander to Sophy's door with a comatose Camilla in his arms and an obedient Toni trotting alongside giving him directions. It would go wrong before he got out of the damn car. I looked at the rain pouring down outside and his coat sitting next to me on the back seat, then I looked at the knife in his hand and reviewed my options. Not many, and not good. I'd worked out what to do but I didn't like it. I should just have screwed my courage to the sticking point and laid into him with a rock when I'd had the chance. Next time I'd try to be less squeamish. Scratch that—there wouldn't be a next time. I was giving up vampires for good this time. No more exceptions.

"We're clear," I said. "I'll be good as gold."

The little knife I'd secreted in my coat pocket was digging into my hip. So was the bottle that I'd taken from Kirsty's nasty hidden cache. I waited until we were moving again, and Yves had his eyes on the road before I cut off the string and chipped away the sealing wax from the stopper. There was no scent or vapour when I opened it, but the uncanny glitter of the liquid set my teeth on edge. I wasn't doing something I was proud of—I just couldn't see a better way.

I poured the contents onto Yves' still-wet coat. It sank in with uncanny haste and left not a trace of its passing. Was that all there was to it? I'd vaguely read Paul's translations and couldn't remember anything else.

"Yves Toulon, I'm sorry," I whispered.

"What was that?"

"Nothing," I said a touch louder, hauling myself upright and leaning my aching skull against the headrest. "Just talking to myself."

"Well, shut up for now," he said. "Speak when I tell you and not before."

And he turned the car into the drive of the Stone House. We got about ten yards before his plan began to collapse in on itself.

I'd always felt that the place had guardians—just that I had a free pass. Emir had told me I had status in the vampire community, but it was clear before we'd got to the first row of trees that Jiří Tabor didn't have any. Not one, but three figures stepped in front of the car, and I saw in the mirrors that a fourth had closed in behind us. They looked big, wet and bloody dangerous, and all of them were wearing camouflage and wide belts packed with macho-looking accessories that had nothing to do with couture.

I saw Yves' hand tighten on his knife. I had to get him away from Camilla.

"Just bluff them and get past," I said hastily. "It'll be OK."

"It had better be," he hissed.

He pressed a button and wound down the window, letting in gusts of rain to soak us all. Through the film of raindrops, I could see that the nearest guard was a woman I vaguely recognised from evenings at the bar. We'd not spoken, and I wasn't clear if she was a member of a particular coterie or less formally tied to the Assemblage. Wet, black hair was tied back from her face to reveal large, dark eyes and pale, freckled skin.

"It's Jiří, isn't it?" she said. "Christ, you look a mess. Oh my God, is that Camilla? And Toni! What the hell happened to you all?"

"We were attacked," said Yves in a rush. "Camilla, she is badly hurt. I brought her here to be healed."

"Hurry up to the main house," she said, stepping back. "I'll radio ahead."

He wound up the window and glared at me. He looked shaken—perhaps now that he thought he was about to finally be reunited with his true love he was nervous? I spoke soothingly.

"It will be fine," I said. "Get Camilla out of the car before they can respond to the guard's call. You have time."

He drew up by the familiar wooden door, the puddles spraying left and right around us.

"You'd better be right," he said, turning off the engine.

He leaned over to the back seat and jerked out his coat. Then he stepped out into the torrential rain and pulled it on.

Chapter Twenty-Nine

WHAT'S ENVY? IF someone had a prettier pencil case than me at school, it was certainly annoying, but I didn't want to take it off them and make it mine—and then maybe throw their bike in the river just to make the point. That's envy and it's not pretty. I might briefly feel jealous of Jay's wealth, but goodness knows he'd earned it, and it hadn't protected him from life's travails. And I sometimes wished for Claire's divine good looks, but she was worse at relationships than I was. And while I'd been bitterly envious of the love my parents gave to my brother but not to me, Wills himself had always been devoted and kind to his little sister. I could never have resented him for being loved. I guess I'm not the jealous kind.

But other people? Some of them are just batshit crazy.

Kirsty had envied Lorraine, Caroline and Lily so much for having Nicky's affections that she'd been prepared to kill all three of them to get it back. Poor Irene Polkerris had been jealous enough of Derowen giving his attention to his many casual loves instead of her that she'd slaughtered him and left herself bereft and alone. Gin Martin had felt so thwarted when his mother had left her estate to me that he'd decided to kill me for the offence—even though there was sod all in it for him except the satisfaction.

But what of Yves?

We had Sophy and he didn't. We all could die on the altar of

303

his unrequited love for taking what he felt was his. Me. Jenny. Dear, gentle Camilla. Whoever. It turned my stomach just thinking about it. So I watched without too much self-recrimination as the cantamen took hold. It didn't take long.

He got halfway around the front bumper towards the passenger door, his mouth in a line, his chin up and his chest out, clutching the knife in his hand… and then his world dissolved.

He dropped the knife and looked around him. His expression was one of wonder. I'd thought him beatific when he spoke about Sophy but that had been nothing by comparison. He'd left the driver side door open, and I could hear him over the sound of the rain.

"It's so beautiful," he said to no one in particular. "Do you hear the song?"

I didn't answer. I was concentrating on sawing the cord that bound my feet together. It took a while to cut through and pull it free of my ankles, and by the time I succeeded, the woman who'd stopped our car had caught up and was staring at Yves. I fumbled with the door and clambered out inelegantly to join her, leaning against the side for support. Yves was spinning slowly, his gaze raised to the heavens. Rain splashed into his face, but he didn't seem to notice.

"Camilla's badly hurt," I said, ignoring him. "Can we take her somewhere comfortable until the sun sets?"

"Of course, but sunset's just minutes away," she said. "We might hurt her less if we leave her where she is. What's wrong with him?"

I glared at Yves; he was humming and warbling, a smile of joy showing off his white teeth.

"He's been cursed," I said evasively. "And he's not the real Jiří. He's called Yves Toulon and he's the man from France who's been stalking Sophy."

"You're joking—we've been looking for that knobhead for weeks. Is he dangerous?"

"Not anymore. If you let him, he'll probably climb up to the roof and fling himself off."

She watched him with distaste. I wondered if some of his letters had come to her.

"Hmm, I probably shouldn't let that happen," she said. "Though it's tempting."

She removed a pair of standard police issue handcuffs from her well-stocked belt and idly shackled him to the bull bars of his own car by a wrist. He looked confused and tugged vaguely at them.

"But I have to go," he said, his voice more French than usual. "C'est urgent…"

He broke off, yanking at the bars, and his captor turned back to me.

"I'm Stephanie, by the way. Can you tell me what the bloody hell is going on?"

"I doubt it, but I think he just meant to force his way in to see Sophy. He has this lovely idea that once she sees him, all the world will fall into place."

"If you'd read his letters, you wouldn't credit him with anything lovely," she said abruptly. "How do you remove the curse?"

I shrugged. He could keep it as far as I was concerned. I was soaked through and starting to shiver and there were an infinite number of ways I would rather have been spending my evening, starting with my tax return and working all the way up to champagne and strawberries.

"I think you just remove the coat—and for God's sake, burn it."

I walked round to the passenger door and opened it, kneeling down on the wet ground by Camilla's seat to take her pulse. It seemed strong and steady, and I thought that, once one of the vampires was with her, they would be able to undo Yves' nasty work. I stroked her limp hand with my own cold, wet one.

And then I felt the sun set.

I could hear Stephanie speaking on her radio—I should have guessed that the same Benedict who was building his own team of computer hackers wouldn't shun technology when it came in useful—but I'd lost interest. I wanted to go home and sleep. If I was lucky, I'd get a lift, but I'd got to the stage where I was prepared to hitch. Then I heard Grace's voice, urgent behind me.

"Let me see, Toni," she said.

I'd never seen her without her trademark little black dress and heels, but that evening she was wearing a light, silk dressing gown, already soaked through, and her feet were bare. Her skin was bone white in the early evening light, and she was biting her lip. She knelt next to me and took Camilla into her arms as though the girl was made of crystal. Even as I watched, Camilla's bruising began to fade, the broken skin to smooth and her colour to improve. But she didn't wake.

Grace swore.

"This isn't my forte," she said, her voice breaking slightly. "I'm more of a fighter than a healer. I can't bring her round."

"Where's Benedict?"

"Probably taking a fucking shower."

I managed not to laugh. Just.

"I'll get him," I said soothingly. "Don't worry."

I got as far as the entrance door before I realised I'd made an empty promise. I was too dizzy and weak to make it any further. I was freezing cold and starting to shake. I stepped into the shelter of the dark hallway, lit by a single burning torch, and slumped against the wall. I was considering my next move when I heard footsteps. A tall, familiar figure emerged out of the darkness, the elusive Benedict Akil himself.

He looked immaculate as usual and had guarded himself against the elements with an elegant wool coat. Not many things disconcerted him, and clearly none of them had happened that evening. He regarded me impassively.

"How very wet you are," he said after a moment in his deep, even voice. "Can you never stay out of trouble?"

I didn't have the energy for much repartee, so I just glared at him while I caught my breath. To my surprise, he took off his lovely coat and wrapped it round me. It was toasty warm and smelt of Benedict. I tried to step back out of temptation's way, but he pulled me to him and dropped his face into my wet hair.

"A soggy and dispirited little tiger," he said. "You always turn up on my doorstep bleeding and covered in mud. If you're looking for my weak spot, I'm not that complicated. Warm and naked is all it takes."

I would have protested but he was healing me, the flood of shimmering warmth soothing the many pains in my head and face. I meant to thrust him away, but the relief took away all my resolutions and I relaxed into his arms.

"You wish," I said. "I've already told you that will never happen."

"Ah, but I have a naturally optimistic personality."

"You mean you're used to getting your own way all the time!"

I heard him laugh.

"That, too, of course. Don't go anywhere. The children of the night apparently need their playground monitor."

He had a point. Outside, above the noise of the rain, I could hear raised voices. Mostly I could hear Grace. She sounded furious and hysterical in equal parts. Benedict let me go and walked out into the storm. I pulled his coat around me and followed.

"This is all your fault," I heard Grace say in furious tones. "You of all people should have taken more care."

Sophy's voice was soft and apologetic.

"I never thought he'd follow me," she said. "I hoped the situation would just go away when I left. I've said I'm sorry."

"He nearly killed my consort. And you're sorry?"

Benedict was watching in silence. I moved to stand at his elbow and winced at the unfolding scene. While we'd been inside, a crowd had gathered around the car. Someone had indeed removed Yves' coat, presumably with a knife or scissors, and instead of pleading to be allowed to follow his golden guide to paradise, he knelt awkwardly in the rain, still cuffed to the bonnet by one wrist. He gaped up at Sophy in a mixture of horror and despair. She barely glanced at him.

"You should never have let him near you," Grace spat. "He belonged to Genevieve. Why would you risk it all? You'd spent a century working your way out of trouble."

"I was lonely, Grace. A hundred years of being alone!"

Benedict interrupted them abruptly.

"Enough of this charming banter," he said. "There are rules, dear Sophy. And even if Grace was willing to let them slide, I'm not."

He glanced at me as he spoke. Was he claiming on my behalf the vengeance that Grace wanted for Camilla? I tried to step out of the circle of focus, but he caught my arm and held me next to him. Sophy held up her hands in supplication.

"I thought you sent me away to learn not to be like this," she pleaded. "Wasn't that what you wanted?"

If Leonardo had caught sight of her at that moment, he would have spent the next decade trying to immortalise her pathos in marble. Benedict, no surprises, was unmoved.

"Oh no," he said. "Don't throw this back on me. I told you to learn self-control, not cowardice, and you can damn well step up to the mark or bugger off back across the channel. Your choice—and make it now. I've never been renowned for my patience."

Sophy dropped her hands.

"Yes, then," she said. "I'll do it. I'm not going back."

A vampire I'd never spoken to stepped out of the circle that had formed and handed her a knife. The blade glittered in the torchlight. It looked both old and ceremonial—and wickedly sharp.

"What's happening?" I said to Benedict, urgently tugging at his sleeve.

"Her mistake, her task to remedy," he said briefly. "Though why they all make such a song and dance of it is a mystery to me. I would just tear the man's throat out and call it brunch. But the Children of Diometes love their rituals."

"Oh God. I'm not staying to watch this."

"We need to talk."

"Not here and not now! I want to go home."

He shrugged and dug in his pocket.

"Take my car, then. I'll come to you tomorrow after sunset—we'll speak then. Be there."

I didn't wait to be told twice. I fled before Yves' sorry end could remind me once again why you should never get involved with vampires. I'd always thought of myself as a quick learner, but this was a lesson I seemed to need to learn over and over again.

BENEDICT HAD UPGRADED his car since I'd last borrowed it. The same marque, but even sleeker and shinier. The seats had warmed up before I'd even left the Stone House drive, and by the time I reached the main road, I'd almost warmed through. I didn't go straight home; I needed to calm down before heading back to my cosy little home, vampire-free and hopefully harbouring gin, lemons and tonic somewhere in the kitchen. Instead, I headed down to the river and parked, letting the moonlight on the water and the sound of water passing calm me down. Vampires aren't people; you get lulled, but you shouldn't. They aren't like us. Not Benedict, not Sophy and not even Nicky. I closed my eyes and thought of other things. And slept.

The sun woke me. I'd napped straight through to dawn, curled up in the driver's seat in a warm coat. My neck ached and I was still covered in mud. I texted Paul to let him know that I was fine... and that he should cook breakfast. Lots of breakfast.

I drove back to find Kirsty's silver car parked at my kerb. Inside, Paul had taken me at my word. He was in the kitchen frying sausages, carefully turning them on the griddle. A rack of toast was half full.

"I hope you fried dozens of those or there won't be any left for you," I said, ridiculously pleased to see him. I didn't know how I would manage living alone again when he headed off to university in a few weeks. "Ditto the toast."

"There's plenty," he said easily. "I was worried about you last night."

Then he turned round and saw me—muddy and bedraggled, my torn clothes clearly visible under my borrowed coat.

"Jesus," he said. "What the hell happened? Are you alright?"

"I fell down a hill," I said shortly. "Twice. Is there brown sauce?"

I laid the table for us. There was a fat A4 envelope on it with my name on in loopy writing.

'For Toni,' it read. 'I kept one. All my love, Nicky.'

I turned it over in my hands.

"Where did this come from?"

"Oh, that. Your friend Nicky dropped it round late last night sometime after midnight. I thought he was a musician at first, what with all the hair and the clothes, but I see what you mean about him. He only stayed half an hour, but he finally got my overlay software to talk to the drum kit. I think he hoped you'd come back but he apparently wanted to be in Brighton before dawn."

I fiddled with the envelope. It was firmly sealed, and I attacked it with the kitchen scissors.

"Was he driving himself?"

"Yeah, that shiny silver sports car he's left outside. He said something about you selling it for him. Anyway, he left in a huge black van driven by a guy who looked like a ninja. Why?"

"Nothing," I said, finally managing to open the envelope.

I was about to tip the contents on to the kitchen table when I realised what was inside and hastily closed the envelope again. It held the photographs Nicky had taken the night before. He must have developed them before coming over.

"Um, just stuff," I said vaguely, my heart pounding; another two seconds and I'd have spilled forty-eight naked pictures of myself out next to the toast. "I'm selling Nicky's house for him, too."

There. No outright lies. Paul began ladling sausages onto plates.

"I liked him," he said. "I didn't expect to, but he was OK. You can have him as a friend."

"Thanks. Anyone I should cross off the list?"

"Yeah, that jerk Peter."

"Paul!"

"Just my advice," he said, putting the griddle by the sink. "Sean says I don't appreciate you, but I do. Pass the salt."

Chapter Thirty

I CALLED BERNIE and told him to hold the fort until Monday. He seemed unbothered, just mentioning in passing that Jill Fletcher had rung to say her perfect lodger had trashed the place and done a runner. I made sympathetic noises and went back to bed.

I napped until the afternoon. I woke to find that the forces of darkness had somehow removed Benedict's car and left mine in its place, and that the summer storm had passed to leave a steamy hot day in its wake. I soaked in the bath for an hour until all the mud that had congealed on my person had sloughed away. In a spirit of conscientiousness, I dropped Benedict's coat off at the dry cleaners. I then visited the antique jewellers by Wolsey Bridge and squandered an enormous proportion of the cheque that I'd cashed from John Jones and Karen. Finally, I spent exactly three hours getting ready for my unwelcome date. I settled on an emerald-green tea dress and lots of diamonds.

I also fielded a few texts on my phone. My official boyfriend Jay would be back from New York at the weekend and had celebratory domestic plans that involved his family. And mine. I frowned. He might be un-datable, but he was also proving very hard to dump. If I wasn't careful, I'd be fending off an engagement ring. I pushed the thought to the back of my mind and read the next message.

Ah. My daily dose of sweetness from Peter: the new MRI scanner was amazing; a boy whose parents had given up hope a year ago would now have their son home in time for his birthday; he loved me and hoped all was well. There was a video with a kitten. My frown deepened. I really needed to sort out my personal life.

There was a much more welcome message from Crispin. Irene seemed miraculously improved. They loved Dartmouth as much as he'd hoped. The hotel would do for now, but she was sincerely happy with the house I'd chosen, and they were eager to proceed. My frown lessened very slightly.

Most welcome of all was a message from Camilla. She was entirely recovered and thanked me for my help. Sophy and Grace were sort of on speaking terms again. Yves Toulon was no more; no one would mourn his passing.

I threw Paul out after dinner. I didn't want him running into Benedict where it could possibly be avoided. I was dreamily leafing through Nicky's photographs at the kitchen table when I heard the understated roar of the Spyker drawing in at the kerb.

I touched up my lipstick and opened the door before he had to knock. I wasn't out to seduce the man, but—as he'd pointed out—we generally coincided when I was looking far from my best. It wouldn't do me any harm to make an effort.

"Hi," I said, a little awkwardly. "Please come in."

Benedict didn't say anything, just ducked his head and walked through the hall and into the kitchen. He'd managed to find another coat, possibly even lovelier than the one I'd soaked in mud the previous night. He deposited himself in one of the chairs by the table. To my embarrassment, the cat came and prostrated itself at his feet, purring like an outboard motor and rubbing orange fur onto the man's black jeans. Fortunately, he seemed unbothered.

"I've always liked this room," he said disconcertingly.

I blinked.

"Everyone likes this room," I said, on autopilot. "I'm not sure I can take the credit. I haven't done a lot to it."

He didn't reply immediately, and I nervously made myself a drink, pouring gin and tonic into a glass and adding ice and lemon, before sitting opposite him.

"I won't offer you anything," I said to break the silence.

"Hmmm. I wish you would."

"That was a one off—an act of madness," I said. "Don't hold your breath for a repeat."

"I can hold my breath for a long time, my dear," he said, in the silky voice that told me to watch out... or make a run for it.

He showed his teeth slightly; I wished the effect was more repellent, but it wasn't, so I concentrated on looking at the bubbles rising in my glass. That didn't work either, so I hastily changed the subject.

"I need to apologise to you," I said, looking up at him. "I accused you of a lot of things when you called me over to the Stone House the other day. They weren't true and I'm sorry. This is for you."

And I put the little box I'd selected from the antique shop in front of him. I hadn't wrapped it. The only wrapping paper in my house turned out to have Christmas trees on it, interspersed with reindeer wearing festive paper hats. I hadn't thought they would send the right message.

"Good God," he said. "You must have hit your head harder than I realised. Are you sure I healed you properly?"

I gave a choke of laughter.

"Who knows? Maybe."

He picked up the box. It looked ridiculously small in his enormous hands. I'd not planned to spend nearly so much, or even a fraction of what they'd cost. But when I'd seen the little gold cufflinks, enamelled tiger heads with tiny emerald eyes and diamond collars, I'd known they were perfect. They were about a hundred and fifty years old— not as old as Benedict, but a lot older than me. And they'd cost more than my car. Grand gestures have their place.

He tipped them into one palm.

"Thank you," he said quietly. "That's very sweet. You still surprise me. I suppose I should take you out somewhere. Where would you like to go?"

The question was so totally unexpected that I just stared at him in surprise for a moment.

"I don't know, I haven't a clue. Maybe Emir's?"

"As you wish."

I blinked.

"Give me a minute then," I said. "There's something else I want you to take with you."

I walked up to my room and picked up the two contracts my grandfather had made with Azazel. I didn't want those dodgy cantamen in my house, and I didn't want anyone else to get their hands on them... but destroying them? I wasn't clear on that either.

I had a vague idea of what had happened but not why. My grandfather had been determined to purge necromancy from his family, hence the first contract. He'd failed. He must have realised his mistake when I began raising the dead. Had my parents found out, too? I had a feeling that two generations' worth of power, everything that should have gone to my father and brother, had instead passed to me. And my mother was a witch. When had my grandfather discovered that? Had my mother been delighted? Announced her intention of teaching me to be the best necromancer that I could possibly be?

Robert had given up trying to devise his own cantamen, given how the first one had backfired. This time he'd bargained for another named ancient recipe, Tabula Rasa. I had a horrid feeling I knew now what it did. It had been a stupid and desperate attempt to stop my parents teaching me to embrace my skills. I really wanted to be wrong.

I got back to the kitchen and narrowed my eyes. The envelope of Nicky's photographs had moved. I was absolutely certain.

"Did you..." I tailed off in embarrassment. "Oh no."

"They're very flattering," Benedict said sweetly. "And if you didn't want me to look, you shouldn't have left them in an open envelope on the table."

I put my face into my hands. I wanted the earth to swallow me whole. When I looked up, he raised an eyebrow.

"I must admit to some surprise," he said impassively. "My little Nicky has hidden talents."

"He has a kind heart and a civil tongue," I snapped back.

"My dear, I've seen the second roll—he clearly has a lot more than that."

"Oh, shut up."

"You're angry with me already, and we haven't even made it to the car. Normality is restored."

I swallowed any further retorts. He had a point.

"I'm determined not to squabble with you tonight," I said. "But you could look after Nicky better."

"He'll manage very well, you know. He has more charm than the rest of my Assemblage put together. The boy just needs to learn to make better choices."

As did I...

"Whatever," I said noncommittally, handing him the contracts. "I'd like you to take these back. I don't want them hanging around."

He tucked the papers into the recesses of his coat. They were written in the blood of a dead man. I'd loved my Grandfather Robert with all my heart when he was alive—now I wondered just how much of my childhood he'd ruined. We walked to the car in silence.

"What does Tabula Rasa do?"

"You must have worked that out."

"Maybe."

His voice when he responded was oddly cadenced, as though he was reading from a book. He was telling me a tale from long ago; had he only read it or had he watched the events unfold? He talked about the deities and demi-gods as though they were impetuous teenagers, walking the earth in a haze of hormones, lust and anger...

The goddess Mnemosyne, or Memory, had been the daughter of Gaia. I vaguely remembered that Rossetti had painted a picture of her, all in shimmering green with dark red hair and perfect lips. She looked like trouble. The woman had nine daughters, the Muses, of which she was excessively proud, and she thought they were lovelier than any other minxes in the world. Welcome to parenthood.

All mothers think that.

This turned out to be very bad for the famous and beloved poet Thamyris. His own mortal daughter was the inspiration for his fabulous verses, and Mnemosyne took this as a slight to her precious offspring. With the sweetness and generosity of spirit that characterised the actions of the ancient gods, she punished Thamyris with Tabula Rasa, the clean slate. Whenever he encountered his daughter, he forgot everything about her. Robbed of his earthly muse, he wrote no more poems. He died destitute and alone, his daughter having abandoned the father who had become unable to notice or love her.

It sounded horribly familiar. Now I really knew. Grandfather Robert had bribed Keira to cast it on my parents. Unable to remember me, they wouldn't be able to teach me how to use my powers. He'd robbed me of my parents' love and affection for his own agenda, and it had all been for nothing. My chest hurt. I blew my nose, grateful for the darkness of the car.

"When did you realise?" I asked.

"Not until you turned up on my doorstep with Oscar and I discovered you were a necromancer after all," he said. "Nothing made a lot of sense until then."

I didn't say anything for the rest of the drive. He drove to Emir's in about a third of the time that it would have taken me. I wasn't sure that the car had been designed for high-speed off-road excursions, but the suspension somehow coped, and we parked under the trees without anything bursting into flames.

"I've never seen you here," I said, as he opened the passenger door for me. "Not your kind of place?"

"It's my place entirely," he said. "Emir works for me."

Ah. I should have guessed. Nothing much happened in the county that Benedict wasn't up to speed on, and he hadn't set that trend in motion by luck or wishing very hard. He cast his nets carefully. And very, very thoroughly.

I walked with him through the archway and down the steps into the bar. He didn't take my hand as Nicky had done. Instead, just as we reached the foot of the stairs, he turned round and took my fingertips for an instant as though to help me down the very last step. It was a nice touch. I was quite sure he knew it.

To my surprise, Emir had a new assistant behind the bar. I recognised him—I'd seen his passport in Yves' flat. He was a slight blond boy, barely older than Paul. He was pale but otherwise in fine fettle. I assumed the undead had liberated him from the hospital and healed him after I'd driven off the previous night.

"The real Jiří?" I said to Emir.

"Indeed," he said, handing me a champagne coupe full of sparkles. "I feel such a fool."

I tried to protest but he shook his head.

"No, it's true. And the poor boy... I mean to look after him. He's lost his brother and his two best friends. They were looking for a new coterie after their vampire died in a territory dispute. I kept pressing Yves for when the other three would join him..."

"No one else suspected," I insisted. "If I hadn't seen the names at the morgue, I wouldn't have guessed either."

He trimmed a couple of candlewicks and passed me a small bowl of olives.

"You're very forgiving, considering what happened to you," he said. "I owe you and Camilla the humblest of apologies. I'm very happy to see you here tonight."

Everyone seemed happy to see us. It's amazing how welcoming people can be when you've turned up with the boss. But even Benedict seemed a little removed from his usual autocratic, arrogant self. At any rate, he hadn't slaughtered anyone by the time I'd drunk two glasses of champagne. I found myself having a much more pleasant evening than I'd envisioned.

Of course, all good things come to an end. At around midnight, he came up to where I sat talking with Jiří. Benedict put a warm hand on my shoulder.

"I do need to speak with you," he said.

Those simple words were enough to send the young Czech scurrying behind the bar, and Benedict took his place.

"Is it bad news?"

"A little. My dear, I need to bring Oscar back. I am battling on more fronts that I would like. You asked me to spare him, and I can't look that gift horse in the mouth now."

My stomach dropped. Oscar. Back in Staffordshire. Beautiful. Irresistible. Deadly. I shook my head in panic.

"I only asked for Peter's sake. If I'd realised what was going on, I'd have told you to stake him out for the sunrise."

"And if I'd guessed your motives, I'd have done that anyway. But that's in the past. He's alive, and I need the help."

I wilted. Maybe I should have hitched a lift to Brighton while the offer was going.

"Fine. Do what you must. Was that it?"

"Not quite. I've persuaded your mother's old tutor to come out of retirement. She wasn't keen but she's in my debt. She'll start in a month and come to the Stone House once a week to teach you. I'll have your rooms ready by then."

"What!"

"I told you I'd find someone to teach you," he said airily. "And I promised you somewhere nicer to crash when you were here. Anyway, you look tired. I'll take you home shortly."

Autocratic, arrogant... nothing had really changed. But a teacher! I couldn't deny that the idea filled me with excitement. Could I stop fumbling around in the darkness with my powers and maybe find out what I could really achieve with them? Might I find out why Bredon was the only zombie I'd ever raised who retained his memory? I watched Benedict work the room with his easy charm and tried to avoid feeling grateful to the man; it wouldn't do me any good.

Half an hour later I trailed him to the car, and he drove me back to the village. Between other people, the silence could have been companionable. Between the two of us, it merely seemed tense. I struggled for something to say when he pulled up to the kerb.

"Thank you," I said, somewhat formally. "That wasn't what I'd expected."

He gave a bark of laughter.

"It wasn't in my plans either, but I've almost never met you in a good mood." He leaned over the seat towards me and brushed his hot lips across mine for just an instant. "Good night, my dear."

I fled the car before he could work out what mood he'd just tipped me into. There was no need for him to know the flashback of the two of us that had jumped into my head when I felt his mouth on mine. No need at all for him to know what image had flooded my mind when Nicky had told me to picture the hottest, most arousing thing that I could think of... I ran into the house and slammed the door. I leaned against it and caught my breath, listening to the sound of Benedict's car as it pulled away from the kerb, reversed in the road and then varoomed away down the hill.

I knew Paul was home—he'd left every light in the cottage on, and that was always a giveaway. I sat in the kitchen brooding for a few minutes before realising that however tired I'd felt an hour ago, the feeling had passed. I was awake, tetchy, restless... I knew what that meant.

I idly filled a rucksack with anything in the fridge that wasn't covered in mould and then went upstairs to Paul's room. I kicked the bed until the cocoon that was my lodger rolled over and grunted.

"Hmmph," it mumbled. "S'up?"

"Come on," I said. "Get your lazy arse out of bed. It's a whole four hours until dawn."

Acknowledgments

MY SISTER AND I created so many worlds when we were little. They were populated by elves, dragons, spaceships and many other, much stranger, entities. Our tales were whimsical, luscious, sometimes oddly brutal. One took place on a ship that floated down a river or great canal, just too far from the banks for the protagonist to dare to swim ashore. Robbed of her memory she gradually explored this derelict but wondrous craft, discovering its many decks—each one harbouring its own dangers, treasures and adventures in their miniature realms—and made a new life for herself amongst its magical residents.

We replayed this story over and over again, each time giving it a different ending. Sometimes she regained her memory, and returned to her old life as a princess or warrior maiden. Other times she never did recall the past, but lived a happy enchanted life in her floating kingdom. And occasionally she remembered her old life, but was content to leave it behind and live on in this new and better reality.

But she never, ever dared to jump into the water.

We called it The Game. I don't know where the idea came from; my sister and I, from landlocked Staffordshire, had never been on a boat of any kind, let alone a great enchanted barge. A canal ran past our school; perhaps the little floating homes that passed us by intrigued us, their tiny windows concealing their secrets with crocheted curtains? I don't know. My subconscious has not deigned to inform me.

My mother called it Making Up Stories. I didn't like that at first; the worlds seemed too real to be 'made up.' My sister and I always felt we were exploring them, not inventing them. Nonetheless, they continued to make themselves available to me, even as my sister and I moved to different cities and I was forced to explore them on my own. They became darker, sometimes more violent and more sensual; at other times ridiculous, farcical delights. But they never went away.

I tried to draw them, but my mother was the artist in our family and she didn't pass that talent on to me. Eventually I decided to try something else.

I decided to write them down.

So here we are, playing in the worlds of my unconscious mind. There are vampires, and zombies, murders and mayhem, love and death. I hope one day there will indeed be elves, dragons, spaceships and many other, much stranger, entities. Maybe there will even be a great ship with shrouded decks waiting to reveal their secrets.

Thank you for joining me in The Game.

About the Author

ALICE JAMES WAS born in Staffordshire, where she grew up reading novels and spending a lot of time with sheep. She was lucky enough to have a mother who was addicted to science fiction and a father who was fond of long country walks, so she grew up with her head in the stars and her feet on the ground. After studying maths at university and training to be a Cobol programmer(!), she began writing novels to get the weird people in her head to go somewhere else. She now lives in Oxfordshire with a fine selection of cats, fulfilling her teenage gothic fantasies by moving into a converted chapel with an ancient spiral staircase—and gravestones in the garden. Her go-to comfort dish is a big plate of dumplings, her number one cocktail is a Manhattan and her favourite polygon is a triangle, though she has a soft spot for concave rhomboids.

**Find out more at http://www.alicejames.co.uk
and on Twitter @ToniWindsor**

OTHER BOOKS IN
～ THE ～
LAVINGTON WINDSOR
～ MYSTERIES ～

BOOK 1   BOOK 2

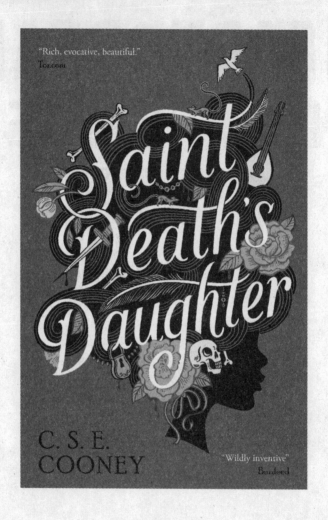

THE DARK ACADEMIA
ROMANCE TAKING TIKTOK
BY STORM!

FIND US ONLINE!

www.rebellionpublishing.com

/solarisbooks   /solarisbks   /solarisbooks

SIGN UP TO OUR NEWSLETTER!

rebellionpublishing.com/newsletter

YOUR REVIEWS MATTER!

Enjoy this book? Got something to say?

Leave a review on Amazon, GoodReads or with your
favourite bookseller and let the world know!